CRIMEUCOPIA
Hey! Don't Read That! Read This!
A Murderous Ink Press Anthology

✯✯✯✯✯✯✯✯✯✯✯✯✯✯✯✯✯✯✯✯✯✯✯✯✯✯✯✯✯✯✯

Murderous Ink Press

CRIMEUCOPIA
Hey! Don't Read That! Read This!

First published by Murderous Ink Press
Crowland, LINCOLNSHIRE, England
www.murderousinkpress.co.uk

Editorial Copyright © Murderous Ink Press 2024
Base cover artwork © James Fletcher 2024
Cover treatment and lettering © Willie Chob-Chob 2024
All rights are retained by the respective authors & artists on publication
Paperback Edition ISBN: 9781909498648
eBook Edition ISBN: 9781909498655

The rights of the named individuals to be identified as the authors of these works has been asserted in accordance with section 77 and 78 of the Copyright, Designs and Patents Act, 1988

All rights reserved. No part of this publication may be reproduced, stored in or introduced into a retrieval system, or transmitted in any form, or by any means (electronic, mechanical, photocopying or otherwise) without the prior written permission of both the author(s) and the publisher. Any person who does any unauthorised act in relation to this publication may be liable to criminal prosecution and civil claims for damages.

Every effort has been made to obtain the necessary permissions with reference to copyright material, both illustrative and quoted. We apologise for any omissions in this respect and will be pleased to make the appropriate acknowledgements in further editions.

No generative artificial intelligence (AI) was used in any aspect of the creation of this work. Without in any way limiting the author's [and publisher's] exclusive rights under copyright, any use of this publication to "train" generative artificial intelligence (AI) technologies to generate text is expressly prohibited. The author (and publisher) reserves all rights to license uses of this work for generative AI training and development of machine learning language models.

This book and its contents are works of fiction. Names, characters, places and incidents are either a products of the authors' imagination or are used fictitiously. Any resemblance to actual people living or dead, events, locations and/or their contents, is entirely coincidental.

Acknowledgements

To those writers and artists who helped make this anthology what it is, I can only say a heartfelt Thank You!

And to Den, as always.

Contents

Don't You Never Look Inside the Mojo Bag…	vii
Ms. Vermillion — Anthony Kane Evans	1
Persistence of Vision — Carlos Ramet	21
Belfast by Train — Tristan J. Deehan	35
The Mystery of the Scavenging Crabs — Christopher Deliso	45
Made in the Shade — Tucker Struyk	67
Room Five at Motel Two — Ed Teja	83
Previous Times — Gene Kendall	99
Snowballs — Hal Dygert	115
Served — Ian Blackwell	145
Larry and Me — L.C. Adams	179
Marked — Patrick Ambrose	187
A Man of His Word — Kamal Mouhoune	207
Blueberry Fields — Rand Gaynor	235
Broken Clocks — Rob Loughran	243
My Own Private Roach Motel — Edward St. Boniface	255
The Usual Unusual Suspects	293

Bart Lasiter, ex-Berkeley California street cop and new Private Eye, sees his dream when a beautiful blonde dressed in black enters his Sacramento Old Town live-in office and offers him more cash than he had ever imagined earning.

She begs Bart to free her kidnapped husband by just delivering the ransom ... alone... in a small boat... out in the deep center of Lake Tahoe... at night ...to pirates...and please, ...no police.

On his drive from Sacramento up I-80 East through the Sierras to Nevada and his client's Tahoe waterfront home, Bart encounters and follows three aging, outlaw bikers who fancy themselves as pirates, and who might lead him to the kidnappers.

At Lake Tahoe, Bart plunges into an exotic, unfamiliar world of yacht clubs, classic boat shows, casinos, and walled-in waterfront mansions. And romance?

Is this case Bart's big chance for PI success? Can dreams come true? Or will this be Bart's last case? What would Bogie do?

Paperback ISBN 9799989333714
Hardback 9798989333721

Don't You Never Look Inside the Mojo Bag...
(An Editorial of Sorts)

...Because it got the juju! An' that is hot stuff...

However, it's true to say that all 15 wordsmiths contained within the covers of this Crimeucopia, have been looking inside all sorts of Mojo bags, and are more than willing to recount what they saw.

And no less than 10 of those are new Crimeucopians, bringing new ideas, plots and styles to this Free-4-All anthology, which adds even more weight to the Murderous Ink Press declaration—You never know what you like, until you read it.

Opening the show this time is *Anthony Kane Evans*, who tells us about a Chicago meeting with *Ms. Vermillion*, before *Carlos Ramet* takes us out to the California coastline, where 20-20 is definitely needed for any *Persistence of Vision*.

Tristan J. Deehan then shouts for us to get onboard, as he transports us to *Belfast by Train*. And once ready to depart again, *Christopher Deliso* moves us off to Greece, to recount *The Mystery of the Scavenging Crabs*.

Not to be outdone, *Tucker Struyk* hustles us off to the US once more, and helps us get down and perhaps a little seedy, though he assures us that's just because it's all *Made in the Shade*.

Ed Teja then picks us up, and takes us along Highway 12, and beyond, until we stop for more than a night in *Room Five at Motel Two*. Departing before 10am, *Gene Kendall* escorts us back to 'civilisation' all the while reminiscing about some of those *Previous Times*...

Bringing us to the relative present—and Kamiakin County—*Hal Dygert* talks about Detective Sergeant Brill, and his *Snowballs*.

Ian Blackwell then lightly carries us off to good old Blighty, as he cooks up a tale, that is then *Served* for your delectation. And *L.C. Adams* keeps us in the UK, and lets us know what the situation is with *Larry and Me*.

Meanwhile, back across the Big Spit, *Patrick Ambrose* explains how Ewell Underwood got *Marked*.

Kamal Mouhoune, when not looking for Moz, once again flies us over to Algiers, and introduces us to *A Man of His Word*, before *Rand Gaynor* invites us to wander through *Blueberry Fields*—rather than the Strawberry ones.

And after *Rob Loughran* gets all Horologistical, talking about his *Broken Clocks*, *Edward St. Boniface* brings this collection to a close by taking us back into the 1970s, recounting *My Own Private Roach Motel*.

All of which, we hope, shows that whenever and wherever these authors take us, we hope you'll find something that you immediately like, as well as something that takes you out of your GPS and Timezone monitored comfort zones—and puts you into a completely new one.

Because, in the Random Shuffle sprit of our *Murderous Ink Press* motto:

You never know what you like until you read it.

Ms. Vermillion
Anthony Kane Evans

I

At the Chicago Crypto Currency Conference (CCCC), there was quite a queue for the Gents. What to do! I looked over at the Ladies. No queue. What the hell! I went and knocked on their door. Nothing. I tentatively pushed it open, went in. Nobody. I even went so far as to ask aloud if the room was vacant. No reply. I went into a cubicle, locked the door, and sat down on a toilet seat. Better be on my best behaviour, I told myself. Women and upraised toilet seats, well, they can raise hell!

Of course, somebody came in. Another guy who'd spotted the queue outside the Gents? But no, as I came out of my cubicle, there was a redhead, distinctly female (or at least feminine), looking in the mirror at herself, applying lipstick to a pair of rather thin lips. I'd put her in her late twenties, two or three years older than me, in any case.

"Sorry, there was this queue a mile long outside the Gents," I said.

"Welcome to *our* world," she said. "Well, *normally*. At crypto events and heavy metal concerts, we get a break."

"Is that orange?" I said, peering at her lips.

"Vermillion," she said. "I'm with Vermillion Valuta. Rachel's the name."

"Mark," I said. "Is that an exchange?"

"No, a coin. Brand new. In fact, it's being unveiled at this conference. You haven't seen our press release: *Vermillion Valuta Unveiled*. I wrote that." She rooted around in her tote bag. "Here, take a flyer! Come over and see us. Stand E47."

"I might just do that."

"Next to the cafeteria," she said. "You might do me a favour and bring me over a black coffee and a croissant or some Danish pastry."

"Will do," I said.

I opened the door and strode out into the hall.

*****

They'd just turned on some kind of computer-generated image—or maybe it was something as old-fashioned as a hologram—of a giant sink hole. People were crowded around the perimeter as though you could really fall into it! At the bottom of the hole was a gravestone. *Here Lies FTX*. The exchange was supposed to have been at the conference, but had gone bankrupt late last year. That fall-out was still reverberating throughout the crypto market and beyond, even pulling in film stars and pop idols. The image was in the exact place where the FTX stand should have been. It was kind of impressive. I got a slight feeling of vertigo just standing there looking down. Like when you're up on a balcony, peering over and you get a sudden urge to jump. There should have been a content warning: *Those who suffer from vertigo keep well back*. But content warnings are taboo in the wonderful and frightening world of crypto. Just as negative attitudes are forbidden. Bears – teddy bears, brown bears, polar bears, whatever-you-got-bears. Bulls, they were allowed, and, of course, that which always follows bulls: bullshit.

*****

She came out of the Ladies, the woman with the vermillion lipstick. Rachel, that was her name. I followed her with my eyes. She had good legs; I hadn't noticed them. I'd been too close up. Black stay-up stockings. An artful rip here, a ladder there. Sexy as hell. I headed over to the cafeteria. Got the coffees and the croissants in.

II

She was standing next to a green sports car. I looked at the stand. E47. *Make a Quick Million with Vermillion Valuta!* The car looked a bit like an E-type jag but wasn't. I went over. She took the tray from me and put it down on the bonnet. Then she went around to the passenger door, opened it, and told me to hop in. I *squeezed* in. She passed me the tray which I balanced—somewhat precariously—on my knees. Then she climbed in via the driver's seat.

"Cosy," I said.

"Hi!" I said.

"First break?" I said.

"Been on my feet since eight this morning," she said.

She kicked off a stiletto and started to massage the arch of her foot with one hand, while she grabbed hold of a croissant with the other. Took a bite, then washed it down with a mouthful of coffee. The tray was still balanced on my knees. I pointed over at the VV sign.

"You write that slogan as well?" I said.

"Yes!"

She smiled.

"This valuta," I said, "is it what they call a shit coin?"

She twisted her lips.

"Let's just say that we employees could choose to get paid in US dollars, Euros or in Vermillion Valuta. If you chose the crypto, you got paid double the usual wage."

"And you chose?"

"The almighty US dollar, of course."

"If I buy any Vermillion Valuta …"

"Call it VV for short, shall we?"

"Do you make any money on the deal?"

"Five per cent."

"And the guys?"

I pointed at the windscreen. There were five guys out there—all very nerdy looking in thick-rimmed spectacles—running up and down hassling people.

"Ten per cent."

"How come?"

"I sell twice as much as them and I don't even have to run around. The clientele come to me. It's fair enough, I suppose."

"It is *not*!" I said.

"Whatever. Anyway, if I was you, I wouldn't buy any."

"Sign me up for a hundred dollars worth. No, make that two hundred."

"It's just throwing money away."

"So, what! At the casino, I only play roulette and, you know what, I only ever bet on zero."

"Can you win on zero?"

"No."

"You're nuts!"

"I just like to be sure, if you know what I mean."

"No, no I don't. *Shit!*"

She slipped her stiletto back on.

"What is it?"

"Mr. Carmichael."

*****

She leapt out of the car, gazelle-like. A very sexy gazelle. She made a bee-line for a short, stocky fellow with thinning hair and thick, jam-jar-like, glasses. She linked his arm and brought him over to the sports car. She jerked her thumb at me.

"You, *out!*" she said.

I opened the passenger door and, clutching the tray, managed to get out without spilling too much of the coffee. She winked at me. Flashed ten digits, while simultaneously giving Mr. Carmichael a large smile and settling him in the driver's seat.

*****

I went next door to the cafeteria, finished *my* croissant, then looked at the orange markings on *hers*. Was that really vermillion? I mean, isn't vermillion supposed to be red? But what did I know about colours! I took out my notebook and wrote down a Cocteau quote that had come to mind. *Notes written by a poet who is awake are not worth much!* Then I started making crypto notes, based on what I'd seen and heard at the conference so far. I wasn't very motivated as every single crypto currency I'd invested in last year had gone down in value. The only bright spot was my Chilliz (CHZ), which had gone up eleven per cent.

*****

Suddenly, she was there before me. Smiling. One of her premolars a little crooked. She sat down. Took a bite of her croissant.

"No rest for the wicked," she said.

"And Mr. Carmichael?" I said.

"Fifty thousand," she said.

"US dollars?"

"You think he looked like an Australian, maybe? Do I look like someone who'd accept Australian dollars?"

She laughed. A somewhat harsh laugh.

"Do you have a cruel streak?" I said.

"Not really. Oh, he can afford it. But can you afford two hundred? I haven't put it through yet."

"Yes, otherwise, I wouldn't have done it. You did warn me, remember?"

"I suppose I did."

"What now?" I said.

"What do you mean?"

"What do you do for dinner?"

"They ring the bell at ten to eight. A ten minute warning. Closing time. At eight we leg it around the corner to Enzo's Pizza Palace. You know it? Here, let me draw you a map."

She turned my notebook to face her, picked up my pen and drew a very clear map. Even writing down all the names of the roads.

"You live around here?" I said.

"No, it's all I remember from reading Machiavelli's *The Prince*. You know, that bit about always checking out your neighbourhood."

"You've read Machiavelli?" I said.

She jerked a thumb over in the direction of the five guys, still running up and down, still hassling people, still, no doubt, a long way off Julie's fifty thousand dollar deal with Mr. Carmichael.

"It's their bible. One of them, in any case. The other is *The Art of War*. Sun Tzu. You've read it, of course?"

"No, I only read the Machiavelli as part of my Shakespeare studies."

"You should. It's a hell of a lot shorter than Machiavelli, in any case. I'll save you a place. Five past eight, sharp!"

*****

III

Rachel introduced me to the boys. Even close up they all looked the same, as though minted from the same coin.

"So, you bought into our valuta," they said.

"Just don't pull that rug, not right away anyway, give me some time to believe," I said.

They laughed, then tried to reassure me that they were not going to pull any rug, that the project was actually complete, that they were trustworthy, that their blockchain was built by some whizz-kid (they actually used that expression) who'd give Vulcan, the God of the Forge, a run for his money. I thought the phrase 'a run for his money' might not have been the best one to use under the circumstances.

*****

The conference centre was also a hotel. Rachel had a single room up on the top floor.

"How many stories up are we?" I said.

I was beginning to have that slight feeling of vertigo again.

"The eleventh. You like it?" she said.

Eleven. My third lucky number. Nine, seven, eleven. I touched that red hair of hers.

"Sure," I said.

"I mean the room."

"It's softer than it looks, your hair."

"And the room?"

"And the boys?"

"They share a suite."

"I can't help feeling that you're getting a raw deal," I said.

"I have a key, we use it as a sort of living room, or, we would if we had a spare moment! Anyway, I get to retreat up here. Believe me, after a day with them, I need a break."

"I suppose they're a special breed, nerds?"

"Oh, they're not nerds. Not at all. Those glasses, the look, all manufactured. They're supposed to *look* like nerds, but, really, they're salesmen recruited from The Hire a Top Salesman Agency, THATSA for short, you know. You must have heard their slogan: Now *thatsa* salesman! Guy who came up with that made a hundred thousand dollars just for that one slogan!"

But, no, I hadn't. Adverts came on or popped up or whatever they did and I turned the sound down or blocked them or performed whatever task was necessary to cut them out. At the cinema, I'd put my fingers in my ears and sing nursery rhymes like *Ba Ba Black Sheep* and *Humpty Dumpy*. This behaviour rarely impressed my dates.

"And your slogan—*Make a Quick Million with Vermillion Valuta!*—what did you get for that?"

"A hundred thousand."

"Dollars?"

She bit at her upper lip.

"No, Vermillion Valuta."

*****

Her bathroom, small though it was, contained a cast-iron tub; she turned both taps on full and it began to fill.

"Pass me the salts," she said. "There, on top of the cupboard. Not in it, on top of it!"

She poured some of the salts in and then used her arm, like an oar, to stir the water around, creating something of a maelstrom; I looked down into it, there was that vertigo feeling again. I thought of Edgar Allan Poe's *Descent*, of the brink of eternity as the Hantsholm-Bergen ferry started to go down.

"Don't you just love a tub full of bubbles?" she said.

I pulled myself back up. Out of Sexagesima, that second Sunday before Ash Wednesday, the day of the disaster, the ferry going down with all hands, except for the narrator, of course, he always manages to survive. *Smiled.*

"Nice," I said.

She turned off the cold tap, leaving the hot running, then started to strip. Looked at me looking down at her stockings.

"Aren't you getting in? What's wrong?"

"Nothing, I just wanted you to keep your stockings on."

"In the bath!"

"No, later, you know …"

"In bed?"

"Yes."

"So, I'll put them on again, don't worry. And what about you, will you keep your socks on for me?"

I must have looked a little startled. I was still half down there in that maelstrom. Why, I hadn't read that story since I was in my teens!

"I'm only joking," she said. "Now, let's get in before the water gets cold."

She put a foot in while undoing her bra.

"Ouch!" she said. "I hope you like it hot."

*****

Of course, swans don't have red hair, but there was something swan-like about Rachel as she half disappeared amongst the foam, stretching her neck upwards, rubbing the back of it. The ivory whiteness of her shoulders.

"Come on! Off with the socks!"

I pulled them off. I felt suddenly clumsy—my head somewhat awhirl—and rather stumbled into the tub. She caught one of my wrists and steadied me.

"You're not embarrassed, are you?"

"Well, I hardly know you," I said.

"You're willing to jump into the sack with me, but you have second thoughts about joining me for a bath, is that it?"

"The dark is something else," I said.

I raised an arm, taking in the whole of the bathroom. The overbright light, the white tiles, the white cast iron tub, the white foam, the ivory-white girl …

IV

Next morning, at breakfast, a dapper young man, came over to our table. He looked to be about my age. A small scar bisected his left eyebrow. He kissed Rachel on both cheeks then shook me by the hand.

"Julian," he said.

He had a coffee in his hand, Rachel asked him to join us.

"Our CEO," she said. "The brains behind the operation."

He laughed.

"It's not exactly axiomatic thermodynamics, you know!"

"Then how come so much in the wonderful and frightening world of crypto goes belly up?" I said. "Celsius, Babel, CoinFlex, Voyager Digital, Zipmex, Hodlnaut, FTX …"

He held up a hand.

"And that's only last year," I said.

"It's the same reason that non-crypto businesses go bankrupt. America Savings and Loan, Texaco, Pacific Gas, Chrysler, MF Global, Enron …"

It was time for me to put up *my* hand.

"Hey, you've got to let me mention the biggest," he said. "Lehman Brothers, the oh-so-traditional bank. Bad management, crooked—though lawful—practices, you name it."

"And what about *your* crypto?"

"You've invested?"

"Two hundred?"

"Two hundred *thousand*?"

"No, just a plain, old fashioned two hundred dollars."

Rachel laughed, but Julien didn't. He looked at her, as though he was disappointed.

"And this two hundred dollars, does it mean much to you?"

"You mean can I afford to lose it?"

"You a day trader or a long term investor?"

"What do you recommend?"

"Day trading. You should cash in on the twenty-first *before midnight.*"

"Then you pull the rug?"

"No, but a whale will leave the Vermillion Valuta waterways, seeking other pastures. There'll be a—shall we say—small dip. It's all about controlling the emotion of the game."

"Game?" I said.

Julian laughed easily.

"I guess you can tell I'm an old-in-the-tooth gamer, when I say something like that."

He smiled, picked up his cup and saucer, then sauntered off. He was all charm.

"So," I said to Rachel. "You're just a bunch of crooks, after all?"

"There's no law against whales."

"There might just be a law against insider whales."

She took a green napkin up to those vermillion lips of hers, then smiled at me.

"Look, it was kind of him to warn you," she said. "I also tried to warn you, remember?"

*****

V

I went for a walk, pacing the sidewalks of Chicago, trying to get some of the anger out of me and into the concrete city. Complaining about the lack of wind. How can you travel to Chicago and not experience the wind! Why, it was like going to France and not catching sight of the Eiffel Tower, like taking up to Copenhagen without paying one's respects to the Little Mermaid! Along East Ida B. Wells Drive and West Ida B. Drive, turning right onto South Clark Street just before the LaSalle Metro. Of course, I was just angry at Rachel. But why? Hadn't I had one-night stands before? Wasn't that just what she was? Right again onto East Van Buren Street, another right onto South Michigan Avenue where I bumped into a bookstore and picked up a slim volume of Verlaine.

"Excellent choice!" the bookseller said. "The setting suns, the melancholy. Yes, you've got to love Verlaine."

*****

I couldn't keep away from her. I found myself, clutching my Verlaine as though it was a lifebelt, in the CCCC cafeteria getting in the coffees and croissants, then strolling over to Stand E47. She opened the passenger door, held the tray, I got in, then she passed me the tray and went around and got into the driver's seat.

"I thought you'd run off," she said.

"Maybe I have!" I said.

"Don't look so angry, it doesn't suit you."

*****

We got into something of a routine. Dining at Enzo's with the boys. A bath. Cocktails, sometimes in the hotel bar, the boys playing pool, sometimes at the Underground Cocktail Club, if Julian was buying. Then back to her room – never mine, in fact, I moved into her room three days later. A night of pleasure and conversation. Sometimes we slept late, but it didn't seem to matter. She always outsold the boys.

*****

My investment, those paltry two hundred dollars, had already doubled.

"And the whale hasn't entered the waters yet," Julian said. "But remember, withdraw by the twentyfirst!"

He went to dance with one of the nineteen-twenties-looking girls. Rather large boned for that particular apparel, but sassy with it. The lilac décor of the Cocktail Club was beginning to pall, yet we seemed to end up more often out there than back at the hotel bar which was darker, more low key. I preferred the hotel bar as the boys were busy with pool, so didn't flock so much around Rachel. She was something of a magnet. But I wouldn't say she was a great beauty. Elegance, style, sexy-as-hell, *character*, yes.

*****

The twenties girl joined our group. Every now and again she'd stare at Rachel blankly. Julian drank Mezcal Negroni, his girl a Manhattan, the rest of us were on Raspberry Smash.

"And what happens on the twentyfirst?" I said. "A collapse?"

Julian laughed.

"No, as I think we have already intimated, a slow decline with some small recoveries along the way, you've seen the pattern if you follow crypto."

"Don't go all candlesticks on me," I said.

He laughed. Rachel wanted to dance. A long track. *Pain.* Boy Harsher. She pulled me up and dragged me over to the small dancefloor. I think it was during that track that I *really* fell for her. Certainly, it was that night she told me I'd stopped simply having sex with her and started making love to her.

*****

The twenties girl started to appear at the CCCC. She was always looking for Julian. And when Julian appeared, if she wasn't on his arm, he was always looking for her.

"He goes for the meaty types," Rachel said. "And you, you always go for twigs?"

We were in the car eating Danish pastries with custard. Very good. They call them *spandauer* up there in Copenhagen. And drinking coffee, of course. *Twig?* Yes, I guess you could call her a twig.

"Listen," I said. "Why don't you invest all your money while it is going up, pull out before the twentyfirst and then get out of this sordid business?"

"Because, Mr. Smarty-Pants, I only have a few thousand to invest, that's all I've got. And for your information, of course I'm investing it!"

*****

One evening, the whole group of us up at the bar, in the Underground Cocktail Club, the barman was giving us a rundown on the different champagnes.

"This one, pear, peach, *vivacious*. This, pear, lemon, *toasty*. This one here, you've got strawberry, ginger, *zesty*. Over there, raspberry, peach, *lively*. And, our best," here he pulled up a bottle of Dom Perignon from below the counter, "I'd say, mango, melon, *scintillating*."

We took that. After all, Julian was paying and it was only a measly six hundred dollars per bottle.

*****

They played Boy Harsher again. A different track. *Autonomy*. File under Joy Division. Not as manic as *Pain*. Of course, she pulled me up to dance, and what, that electronic music, well, the dance is always like a trance. And if it is low key like this track, then it lulls you. You could almost dance to it in your sleep.

"What if *I* put in some money for you?" I said.

"And suppose the whale sails off *before* the twentyfirst?" she said. "You can't trust Julian."

"Well, we'd just have to watch the stock all the time. First sign of a dip, we pull out," I said.

"It'd mean no sleeping," she said.

"We hardly sleep as it is," I said.

"I don't know. I don't like the idea of it. And just *what is* the idea of it?"

"After the twentyfirst, we take off somewhere. The French Riviera. Three months. See if we fit together or don't."

I looked at her there, under the disco lights, shining unremittingly. Those lips now ruby under the red and green lights. They twitched. She bit at them. She scratched a cheek. She looked at me as though she was sizing me up. This was no blank stare.

"You're not the worst guy, I ever met," she said. "Not absolutely."

*****

The DJ abruptly shifted over to an old Virgin Prunes number, *Theme for Thought*, we danced a few steps, but the change in tempo took us both aback and we retreated to our table. That track certainly cleared the dancefloor, probably deliberate. Get the punters drinking.

"You don't have the look of a day-trader," she said.

"Oh, and just how does a day-trader look?"

"Coked up to the eyeballs. Mad staring eyes. Usually bright blue. Too blue, if you know what I mean. And what if I don't want to be saved? What if I like this ... what did you call it ... *sordid* life style?"

"If you like it, well, then you could still take part in it, only you'd have some money to play with," I said.

"So, you'd invest your money and what, we split the profits fifty-fifty, is that the idea?"

"No, it was to give you *all* the profit."

"No strings after the three months?"

"Look, if we don't fit together, we don't fit together. Of course, no strings."

"I'll think it over."

"We don't have time to think it over, do we? I mean, VV is going up vertically day by day."

Of course, I didn't intend to put my life's savings into it. A third should do it.

*****

The conference came to an end. On the last day, Julian and the twenties girl announced their engagement. She showed us her ring. Diamond, of course. White gold. Simple, elegant.

"Five hundred dollars!" she said.

Big smile. I looked at Julian. So, he'd put practically all *his* money into the valuta. Otherwise, surely, he'd have bought her a more expensive ring. Made sense, of course, the investment in his own crypto. I wondered how much he'd made already on this deal. The party was at the Underground Cocktail Club, of course. The champagne, though, was now the Veuve Clicquot (Yellow label). *Toasty.* Only two hundred dollars a bottle. Not six hundred.

VI

Next day, the hotel was pretty quiet, though the day after another conference started. Something to do with security. A Canadian got talking to me up at the bar. He'd just arrived for the conference but was already stressing about all the presents he had to buy. For the wife, the kids, for his mistress. They got angry, the wife or the mistress, if he picked up something at the airport. He had to put some thought into it. I was not really able to help him. I never could understand the concept of souvenirs for people who had never been to the place. You go to Hamburg, you buy a miniature replica of Das Bunker, for yourself. To remember your trip to that place. *I get it.* But to buy a miniature of Das Bunker, of the Eiffel Tower, of the Little Mermaid for somebody who wasn't there. No, I simply *don't* understand it.

*****

Rachel, of course, had nowhere to go now. The room was cramped. You couldn't spend too much time in it, unless you were taking a bath or having sex. Even in the bathroom, even during the sex act, the laptop was on. We followed the share price of the VV on the Coinbase Exchange, though on my phone I followed it on Kraken. Not that it made the slightest bit of difference. That arrow was still flying practically vertically. Well, of course it would, or should, until the twentyfirst.

"Though maybe we should pull out before that," Rachel said. "On the nineteenth, maybe?"

*****

I kept one eye on the crypto, the other eye on the Verlaine. I was trying to translate one of his *Poèms saturniens*.

"An affable dawn," I said.

"You what?"

We were in the bath. She'd just stood up, above the foam.

"Pouring over the fields, or does *meadows* sound better?"

"What are you going on about?"

"It's just this poem, in my head."

"That's your problem, right there. I bet you believe in ghosts in fireplaces as well, don't you?"

*****

We played pool down in the hotel bar. We couldn't really afford the Underground without Julian, so we hit Stereo Bar instead. That place had four bars. We'd take a drink, then Rachel would go and ask the DJ to play some Boy Harsher. He always played *Machina*, a very poppy track. A four minute track. The large dance floor, heaved. You could take your eye off the valuta for four minutes. Nothing much could happen in four minutes, not unless you were very unlucky.

*****

Up in her room, she burnt incense. We looked at the stars. We looked for the moon, but could never find it. The laptop between us. We took turns to sleep. Three hour cycles. Waiting, just waiting for that whale to leave the vermillion waters.

"I love your room," I said.

"I'm beginning to feel hemmed in," she said. "Just how big is this flat of yours in Nice?"

"It's a pied-à-terre, a studio flat. But don't worry, with the money we are making," I nodded at the laptop, "we can rent a villa. Hell, sell the flat and *buy* a villa!"

"It sounds nice," she said. "Tell me more about that poem."

"What poem?"

"The one you were translating, the one in your soul."

VII

It was the eighteenth. Three days to go. I woke up hungover. We'd drank more than usual. She'd been on the vodka gimlets, while I'd settled for gin & tonics.

"Rachel?"

I couldn't see her. I was in a bit of a haze. I staggered into the bathroom.

"Rachel?"

I actually looked down into the bath tub. Felt a little sick. That vertigo. Vomited in the sink. Behind me, reflected in the mirror, was the cupboard with the bath salts still perched above it. I opened the cupboard, looking for painkillers. Nothing. No toothpaste, tooth brushes, odd perfume bottles, mascara, lipstick, nothing. Certainly, no painkillers. I staggered back into the bedroom. She *must* have gone down for coffee and croissants. She'd be back up. I opened the wardrobe. Her clothes were gone. *My* clothes were gone. I looked under the bed.

"Rachel?"

Nothing. I looked on the bedside cabinet for my phone. Gone.

"Not my phone!"

I looked under my pillow. There lay my Verlaine. I shook it, expecting a note to fall out. *Back in a moment, don't panic, all my love, Rachel X.* No note.

*****

I sat down, heavily, on the bed. There must be some logical conclusion to be drawn from all this. She hadn't gone. Of course, she hadn't gone. Coffee, croissants. But the clothes, the missing clothes. The laptop, my phone. The vertical line of the Vermillion Valuta. Forever upwards. It took me an awful long time to sketch the whole thing out. She had not left me one item of clothing, not even my socks. I went into the bathroom, wrapped a towel around me and took the elevator down to reception.

*****

The receptionist, a middle aged man, smiled when he saw me coming.

"Ah, Mr. Lewis, she *is* a card, sir, that Ms. Vermillion. A regular card!"

He bent down behind the counter, hauled my holdall up onto it. I unzipped it. Clothes, phone, wallet. She liked me at least *that* much.

"She was in a terrible, hurry, sir. Said she'd brought your holdall down by mistake. Of course, I suspected some kind of joke."

"I suppose she took a taxi to the airport?" I said.

He looked at his fingernails. Seemed to study them, as though he'd only just now observed a speck of dust and was contemplating how best to remove it. I took my wallet out of the holdall, extracted two ten dollar notes and put them up on the counter.

"A couple of sawbucks," I said.

He looked off into the middle distance as he brushed the notes into a drawer behind the counter.

"The airport, sir?" he said. "Oh, no. *A taxi?* Not on your life. Why the head of Vermillion Valuta himself picked her up."

"Julian? My age? A well-dressed young man?"

"Oh, no, sir. Mr. Carmichael. A rather portly gentleman. More my age than yours. The Chief Executive Officer. Staying at this very hotel, he was. Like most of the attendees of the CCCC. I mean, why go around the corner to the Metropole, which, if I may be perfectly frank with you, sir, doesn't deserve its five star rating. No, sir! Not at all. Why, their level of service is very poor. You should read the reviews on Trip Adviser!"

He laughed.

"And tell me, those reviews, did you write them?" I said.

He laughed again.

"Well, I can see why you and Ms. Vermillion get on so well, sir. You have one thing in common, a wicked sense of humour, yes, sir, just plain wicked!"

*****

I'd plucked out a shirt and had it half on by this time.

"You didn't," I said, "by any chance invest your life savings in their little enterprise, did you?"

"Oh, no, sir! What on my wages? However, Ms. Vermillion was kind enough to give me a coin for free."

He put his hand into his pocket and pulled out a coin which he spun on the counter. It caught the light and glittered.

"You do know that crypto currencies are *virtual* currencies, right?" I said.

"She said it'd go up and up. She told me where to watch it. I did, I watched it every day, whenever I got a spare moment. In the back room there." He nodded behind him. "But then, this morning, when I looked, well, it only seems to be worth zero point zero-zero-zero-zero ..."

I put up a hand, stopped him in his tracks and then slammed my hand down on the spinning coin. From my wallet, I extracted another couple of sawbucks and put them up on the counter, then scooped the coin into my holdall. He raised his eyebrows.

"You think it'll go up again?" he said.

"What goes down, must go up, right?"

"I suppose so, sir! But, you know, I'm simply too old for cybercurrency. Shall I call you a cab, Mr. Lewis?"

"No, I need a bath. How much if I keep the room until midday?"

"No extra charge, sir. We're not the Metropole, you know!"

*****

I picked up my holdall and headed for the elevator. In the bedroom, I took off my shirt and threw it onto the bed, then went into the bathroom and turned the taps on thinking to drown Rachel out of my thoughts, but the scent of her perfume lingered there. Or maybe it was the incense. Musk, plum, patchouli, jasmine, vanilla. Half in the tub, I panicked. *My passport!* I ran back into the bedroom, searched the holdall. Nothing. Zipped open a side pocket. There it was. And inside it, a fancy envelope. Embossed with the initials VV. I took it through to the bathroom with me. Threw some bath salts into the tub, made like my arm was an oar and stirred, but did not look down into the maelstrom. The water was too hot, but I climbed in anyway, then took some deep breaths until I got myself under control. Got settled. I forced myself to soak for full five minutes before tearing the envelope open with my teeth. Half ripping the letter in the process.

> *Dear Mark,*
>
> *You can't blame me. I did warn you. Again, and again. How many times I warned you. How stubborn you were.*
>
> *You hoped for a longer relationship, I know. You hoped to save me from a sordid life, I know. You believed you had penetrated to the secret poem of my soul, but you had not. I will file you away (one of your phrases which I have now adopted) amongst my top five holiday romances, though it was not, of course, exactly a holiday romance, only if I think of it as a working holiday.*
>
> *I'm sorry about the money, but a girl's got to live.*
>   *Much love,*
>   *Rachel Vermillion*
>   *XX*

Persistence of Vision
Carlos Ramet

The Chumash tell the story of a woman who was saved from rape by the waters of a mountain lake. According to that legend, to save herself she killed herself and the waters, in sympathy, kept her body intact for two hundred years.

I suppose it could happen. I've been told that in some of the surrounding mountains the lakes reach a depth of 1,000 feet and the bottom temperature never rises above thirty-five degrees. I've been told the water is as pure to drink as distilled water and a year later a coin will come out as shiny as when it was dropped in. But when, in a simple dredging operation in May 1990, a body came to the surface, I doubted it was two hundred years old. The corpse was dressed in cut-off jeans and a tee-shirt that read "Lake Takahe." A camera strap was still wrapped around her neck.

The funny part was, I knew immediately who the victim was and who had killed her. Missy Hayden drifted out to the "High Desert" and to Harborville the same year I did, 1978, and what made her case particularly disturbing was the way our lives intersected and what it said about all of us in the police force, in the town, in her generation.

She was twenty-four when she disappeared; her immaculate corpse was a dozen years old when it resurfaced.

Like a lot of people, I'd assumed she came from a big city with a lot of crime and a lot of overcrowding, but sometimes the quietest people come from the quietest places and they're seeking more of the same. She'd grown up on a farm in Wisconsin, loved horses and snow-shoeing in the woods and cross-country skiing. In college, she'd excelled in photography and in writing classes but had dropped out, like so many of us in those days, "to find herself." I guess, more than anything else, Missy Hayden had moved to California to be on her own and had thought a desert town with goat ranches was the same as where she was from.

But even in those days Harborville was a mix of vagrants, vice, and virtue—a place where drifters washed ashore onto the beige sands of the Mojave. What with the sandstorms, the stunted vegetation, the heat that split boulders, I sometimes wondered why anyone would want to live in the High Desert, especially in Harborville, where there was no harbor, only moguls and rocks and the fantasy name given to the former "Last Luck Gulch" by optimistic real estate developers. I'd had my own restless streak; Harborville seemed a long way from San Pedro, California, where I'd grown up in a Filipino community near the Army fort and not far from the turning basin of a genuine harbor.

With a Tagalog mother and an American father who'd been a military cop at Subic Bay, I'd spent my sophomore year of high school in Manila and even thought of entering the seminary. But by age eighteen, I'd had enough Jesuit education to choke a horse. I wanted the open road or some adventures. It didn't quite work out that way. After high school, I worked at a Terminal Island cannery while taking college classes at Long Beach State. I was close to earning a degree, then entered the police academy, which took me as far as Harborville.

And yet, both of us must have found it appealing, because both of us stayed a lot longer than we should have. Maybe Missy Hayden fell for the Harborville pitch that it was the "Center of the Southland." The ski slopes were about two hours to the north and west; it took about as long to get to Lake Takahe or to the nightlife in L.A. To me, that meant it was a long way from anywhere you'd want to be. But if you wanted to live cheap and didn't mind driving, Harborville in the late 1970s was a haven hidden in the dunes.

I met Missy Hayden once, then saw her often. In January 1978, I was a rookie patrolman on the force and she was a stringer for the local paper. She stood me in front of a patrol car and smiled and told me not to be nervous because this was her first real job too. I wasn't really self-conscious. At five-foot ten and one hundred seventy-five pounds I was solid, worked out and played a lot of racquetball in those days. I kept my head shaved, perhaps because it made me look more Asian. I gave her my most winning smile and stood up straight. She took my picture and asked me a few questions about where I was from and what had brought me to Harborville.

I remember a very pretty woman with large probing eyes full of curiosity and insight. Her features were very even and her lips thin. I doubt she wore any make-up. Her dark hair was cut short in a Buster Brown and she was dressed in some sort of cotton print dress, very light and practical, and she wore white sport shoes. She seemed both athletic and shy, and that appealed to me. She hid behind that fat Hasselblad camera and kept her eyes down while taking notes, and it struck me that if I hadn't been attracted to a different kind of woman in those days—women closer to my own ethnic background—I would have been sure to ask her out.

Besides, first week on the job, I needed to get settled in and take care of routine details. I was assigned to an older patrolman named MacArthur Williams. "Mac" was a sergeant who would show me the ropes. He'd moved from Oakland years ago to make it as a singer and when he had a couple of nights off still did warm-ups and in-betweens at the Parisian Room down below. But that was the only time he went to L.A., he told me. "You can keep it, man. Brothers killing brothers; it ain't worth it. I'd rather take my chances out here in the 'Big Sky' country."

We were in his office. Even though it was January and close to nightfall, an air conditioning unit rattled from the window and water dripped onto the floor. Mac had a stack of folders crisscrossed on his desk. He opened the top one, spread a half dozen forms in front of me. I signed the forms and he placed them in a folder marked "Gomecindo Harrison."

"What kind of name is that?"

I told him about my background.

"That's too much for me, man. I'll just call you 'Go-Mee'— okay?"

So it was "Go-Mee" from then on, though it sounded like an Asian noodle soup, with a little bit of everything thrown in. Filipinos were already very mixed, and I'd added "half American" to the stew. I asked Mac how long he'd been on the Harborville force.

"Nine years, man," he muttered. "I was a patrolman in L.A. But my partner got smoked in his own bed."

He was a large man, and in those days very fit. He crossed his thick arms and scratched at a scaly spot, then smiled at me.

"You want us to hire that good-looker?"

I wasn't sure what he was talking about. Mac hoisted his large frame from the swivel chair and moved over to his office window. Our beat started soon and a sunset glow pressed against the metal blinds.

"That shutterbug-chick with the camera," he added. "The one you liked talking to. She's looking for a job."

I was starting to feel uncomfortable. It was warm in Mac's office and the air conditioner seemed mostly to emit noise. He stood very close to it, flicked open the window blinds. Two patrol cars sat outside, glinting in the evening sun.

"We're looking for a crime photographer," he went on. "She applied."

I was new on the job and had just met Mac. I wasn't sure why he was asking my opinion. I could hear an ambulance go by, its siren shrieking over the whirr of the air conditioner.

"Are you with me, man?" Mac let the metal blinds click shut and turned to me. "Do you want her here?"

That might have changed everything. I could see myself with her, wandering along San Francisco's Embarcadero or maybe along San Diego's Navy Pier. I could see her hesitant smile and clear eyes. My own eyes stung as sweat ran into them. Mac must have seen me perspiring because he twisted the air conditioner dial to high. The papers on the desk fluttered from the sudden hiss of air.

I tried to recall what Flordeliza looked like. I was arranging for her to join me from Cabuyao. She was in nursing school and would finish soon; I didn't want any disruption to my plans, any shift in trajectory.

"She's not experienced enough for police work—for crime work," I suggested. "That woman with the camera, I mean." There was nothing wrong in being attracted to her, I thought, but I had a fiancée.

"Okay, man." Mac led me to the patrol car. "I can only lay it out for you to play it out. But it's up to you, man. Can't change nothing once it's gone."

*****

Mac pulled out of the parking lot onto National Trails. I could see the orange light hard against the hills, turn the folds of the mountains into black furrows. Our first stop was the bus station. Those early experiences are carved into my memory by the vividness of youth and fear. I wonder now in retrospect if Missy Hayden hadn't experienced something similar her first few nights in Harborville—the oddness of the names (Scissors Crossing, Jumbo Rocks), the pungent smells of the night desert (a scent of burning orange peel or tea), the strangeness of the sights: the aerodrome windmills flapping like immobilized birds, the lighted Greyhound station staggering out of the dark and embracing us. For that, surely, is where she would have arrived after two or three days riding across country. I wonder what she would have thought seeing California for the first time, with its transients and violent hobos, its men living out of lockers in the Greyhound station.

We were on a routine public nuisance call. Mac parked in front of the glass doors. I swung out of the patrol car more nervously than I'd intended. The ticket clerk stepped from behind his counter and pointed to the washroom.

Inside, a crowd gathered near a sink where a wino, bare-chested and yellow, bent his head beneath a gushing tap. Something dark and slick ran down his ribs and splattered a sickening red against the white polished porcelain.

"Get him a doctor," someone called out.

"I don't want none." The voice came from under the tap. The wino's back straightened. He stood up from the sink.

"I don't want no doctor." He put up his fists menacingly. "Ain't nobody taking me to no doctor," and as he spoke the dark blue puncture in his throat opened and closed like a tiny mouth.

*****

Her case collided with my life in another way too. Years later, assigned to review old files, I wondered if a man could fall in love with someone he'd never really known. By then, I had already been married to Flordeliza for nine years; she lived in San Bernardino with our two children, a boy and a girl. She was a nurse at the County Hospital and the children attended Catholic school. But I couldn't forget Missy Hayden; the police department may have tried, but the more we tried the more we remembered.

An Assistant Investigator by then, I sat at my desk and read through the thick green folder, with its clippings from a time that no longer existed, its letters from a person who had ceased to speak. I was afraid, somehow, to open that folder but when I did her picture stared out at me: her same kind eyes and pursed lips, her same look of inquisitiveness and intelligence. I suppose that's the way we like to think of ourselves when young: ready to face the future. But I was the future she could never know—a thirty-three year-old police investigator who had let her down. Her clear eyes seemed not so much endearing as reproachful: they said, why did you let him go?

I read one of her letters and felt that much more involved.

"Life just seems to soar by," she'd lamented to a college friend, someone she'd apparently traveled with in Europe. "Being back now in the U.S., I don't know, it's more than just culture shock after all the time we spent visiting castles and museums. I feel almost like I'm on a treadmill these days, running faster all the time: the computer revolution, software and designer social mixing, credit cards and asteroid games, and nothing for me to hang onto."

A lot of us felt that way in the seventies. It seemed strange reading through the file because the changes continued to come at me.

In another letter, she complained about the singles scene.

"Why do I even bother going?" she had written to an older sister in Milwaukee, "and get pored over like I'm a picture in a magazine. The men here at Lake Takahe are so full of themselves, all they want to do is talk about their vacation in the Bahamas or how much property they own on the shore. And yet I know I don't want to play the drifter all my life, Margot, despite what I might tell myself at times. I guess a time will come when buying furniture with some guy who's halfway decent will seem better than just jumping from place to place, but it's not now. I appreciate your worry, Margot, but I'm not ready to fade into the great masses of suburbia—not yet. There's still too much living ahead of me."

Ourselves as we liked to think of ourselves—full of rebelliousness and hope. Missy didn't stay long on the *Daily Standard*, from what I could tell from the file. She'd quit within a month and moved up to Lake Takahe, waitressing at night and skiing all morning. She'd stayed on that summer, hiking and trying to sell some of her photographs to outdoor magazines. There was a photograph of her lounging near a hotel swimming pool. It was a snapshot, really, and she seemed to stretch comfortably the length of the deck chair, her long legs crossed, her flat stomach tanned and slightly oiled, her hands knitted behind her neck so that her elbows fanned out invitingly, like wings. She was wearing a dark bikini and, although the quality of the snapshot wasn't good, I could tell her face held that same slightly quizzical, slightly dubious expression, the one that said: "I can be your friend, but you can never really know me."

The blue eyeball of the swimming pool glared at me. I felt grubby looking at the photograph, dirty, like some college kid who falls in love with the dead smile of the Playmate of the Month and keeps the creased image pinned to his closet door for years. I buried the photo quickly. How can a man become infatuated with spots of silver nitrate and colored ink? I read on through the interviews and letters, the original police report, the follow-up, the queries from her relatives. The newspaper account describing her disappearance near the Chumash Trail and the questioning of a suspect brought back memories. I was involved back then, when she was still alive, involved more than I'd ever wanted to admit, and now it seemed I was involved in a grossly different way, in some sort of bizarre courtship, with me talking to her friends, her parents, discussing things with them. The only difference was whenever I showed up to meet with Missy Hayden, she wasn't there.

*****

It rained that autumn night in 1978 when we stopped the suspect on a simple violation of the vehicle code. I was riding with Mac and the rain hammered so hard on the roof of the patrol car that we could barely hear each other speak. "You just gotta take it slow tonight," he half-yelled, "and not worry about making no book. You make book, it don't matter if you break your neck out here in this Navy bean soup."

It was true: the desert rain was so heavy it was almost black. We were inching our way down Seventh, past the storefronts used in a Gene Autry movie, toward the railroad station and the old water tower. I couldn't see any of this, but I knew our approximate location. I couldn't see any of this because when the headlights fired into the rain, the rain haloed the light right back at us.

A pick-up truck swerved, its one taillight bouncing dizzily in front of our windshield. "Slow and easy," Mac Williams called out loud. He leaned forward, stared through the rain. His hands choked the steering wheel. "If he goes straight, we'll nail him. If he turns right, he can go on down the line."

The truck went straight through the intersection and Mac flicked on the red and blue light. The driver pulled over. "Slow and easy," Mac cautioned. He opened the car door like a shield, eased his legs out behind it and then, dressed in his yellow slicker and with a yellow covering over his cap, stood to his full height. The rain cascaded down him; he moved into the glare of our headlights and then toward the pick-up truck.

As per procedure, I stayed in the patrol car, watched and waited, radioed-in our position and the license plate number of the truck. I could see Mac, his yellow form bent, the rain bouncing off his back, leaning into the window. The license plate check came back: the truck belonged to a Ray Earl Owens, an ex-con with a record that ran to several pages: burglary, assault and battery, attempted rape, breaking and entering, violation of parole—but the truck was free and clear, duly registered and the yearly fees paid.

I learned a lot from Mac Williams, mostly about taking it slow and easy. He walked back from the truck, his face grim and sallow in the rain. He sat next to me and flipped open his citation ledger to reveal two crisp twenty dollar bills pressed into the binding. "Can't hold an honest citizen who just wants to pay his taxes." Mac Williams smiled. "Police tax." He started up the car.

*****

A week later, the news broke in the local paper. A young woman had disappeared in the Cortez Mountains and had last been seen accepting a ride from a man driving a tan pick-up truck with a broken taillight. I told what I knew to the Investigating Sergeant, and so Ray Earl Owens, who lived in a hardscrabble trailer park along the Arroyo Seco, was brought in for questioning.

"Lived here all my life," Owens announced, which was lie number one. We knew he was originally from the Texas Panhandle but had been in and out of so many foster homes he'd really been raised all over the Southwest.

"What's your present employment?" the Investigating Sergeant asked while I took notes.

"Ex-military. Retired," he told us, and that was lie number two. His one year in the Army had ended with a disorderly conduct charge. When he worked, according to his neighbors, he did odd jobs on some of the local ranches.

"How old are you, Owens?"

"How old do you think I am?"

The rap sheet stated he was forty-six. I thought he looked a dozen years older. His face was pinched and coppery and only a few strands of red hair covered a sun-spotted scalp. But his heavy shoulders and compact physique made me think of a much younger man. He'd rolled up his sleeves to reveal sinewy forearms and a tattoo of a tiger's head.

"Ever done time?"

"What do *you* think?"

"I think you'd better start answering my questions. When was the last time you saw Melissa Hayden?"

"Like I told you, she was hitchhiking and I gave her a ride. I dropped her off near the Chumash Trail. Never saw her again."

"So how'd you end up with her camera and her handbag?"

"She was in a hurry to get out of the truck. She forgot 'em."

"Was there any money in the handbag?"

"I wouldn't know."

"'Cause there's none now. Why was she in such a hurry to get out of your truck, Ray? What did you do to her?" And on and on in that elaborate ritual of parry and thrust, in which we accused Owens of everything and he admitted to nothing. We couldn't hold him without more evidence, without the body which was not to be found. Toward the end of the questioning, the I.S. pointed to a fleshy mound in Owens' upper arm and what appeared to be several old burn marks.

"How'd you get those scars, Chester? Those 'distinguishing marks'?"

Owens stood up. Dressed in faded jeans and a blue work shirt, he looked lean and muscular. He wore a tooled leather belt stamped "Earl" and several turquoise and silver rings on his fingers. "None of your damn business. You charging me with something?"

"I said how'd you get those scars?"

He fingered the lump gently. "My foster dad shot me with a BB gun once. Put me in a dryer once and turned it on. Any other questions? Or am I free to go?"

*****

I turned left at Scissors Crossing and thought about lives that seemed connected. When I became a detective lieutenant some eleven years after she had disappeared, new information was presented to us in that slow, steady accumulation of facts that would one day result in "justice." By 1989, Ray Earl Owens was serving time again, for armed robbery, and confided to a cell mate that he had once raped and murdered a hitchhiker and hidden her body "where even the vultures wouldn't get to her."

I drove past gullies created by flash floods, past *piñon* trees and *llorosa* bushes that turned the desert floor a drab grey. More than anything, I wanted to reopen the case. It nagged at me like the secret sins of a Catholic childhood and I wanted desperately to see some sort of justice restored. I hadn't yet realized that a compromised and artificial justice is perhaps all we can ever have, something more akin to revenge.

I was on my way to see Mac Williams. He'd already retired from the force and lived at the top of Red Rock Canyon in a modernist spread with a view of the valley. I turned left on Sandstone Road and snaked along the side of the hill, past houses suspended from the cliff side. A red-tailed hawk rose up from a spider bush, soared on outspread, mottled wings. Near the top of the hill, I could see Mac's home. It looked like layers of glass and cut stone stacked at sharp angles. I parked in front of his solid oak garage door, got out and pressed the doorbell.

"My old walking partner!" Mac grinned and pumped my hand. He was dressed in a red bathrobe with a padded collar. His hair had turned completely white. I asked him how he'd been.

"Doctor said no more three-egg breakfasts for this old troublemaker. Otherwise, I'm fine. Come in, man."

We sat on his patio on two lawn chairs. Across the valley, I could see the shadow of clouds moving across the rock hills, like hands caressing them, and the outline of the old stagecoach trail. I told Mac I thought he could help me with some information, that I was considering reopening the case we'd been involved with so many years before.

"You won't ever get a conviction without the body." Mac tugged at the sleeve of his robe. "Maybe it'll turn up one day, maybe it won't.

Without the body, there's no proof she's even dead."

I don't know why I said as much as I did. Maybe because the burden of the past turned around in my mind like the hands of a clock. When I started speaking, it was in a voice I didn't recognize, one that sounded shaky and thin.

"What I really want to know is why we stopped Ray Earl Owens that night in the rain, and let him go. Can you tell me that, Mac? We're responsible, do you see?" and the idea at last took shape, formed in front of me as I spoke. "If you change one small action, everything else changes too." The idea took on the clarity of a dream—and its elusiveness and craziness too. I knew it, but insisted that if we'd just questioned Owens longer, issued him the traffic citation he deserved, he might have appeared in court. "That would have delayed him. Do you see? Then he never would have been at Point A when Missy Hayden was. Their paths never would have intersected. He wouldn't have been driving on that road at the same hour she was hitchhiking."

Mac drew in a deep breath, held it as if it were cigarette smoke. When he exhaled, his white mane shook from side to side.

"Listen, man. Feeling guilty ain't gonna change a thing—not in this life or the one to come. You just gotta look out for number one, and right now you ain't looking out for your own peace of mind."

He propped himself up on one arm, pulled the bathrobe tight around his waist.

"I don't feel sorry about nothing—not about no Missy whatever her name was, not about no Ray Earl Guitarstrummer, not about what I had to do to get me a good retirement and this house. I'm telling you," Mac said, "You can't spend your whole life feeling sorry for what went wrong. If I did that about all that's gone on in my life, I never would stop crying."

*****

In places where the water ran as cold and clear as ice water, her body had remained pristine. When the dredging barge, assigned to dig a channel for a new marina, dumped its load of shale and sand and scrapings into the deepest section of the lake, the dead were disturbed and the lake loosened its lover's grip on the body of Melissa Hayden.

Her body blue and puckered, her white eyes gazing as they gazed on her last day on earth, wearing a haircut that was more than a decade out of date, she floated up from the bottom of the crater lake as all things do—gently, waveringly, unrecognizably, spiraling larger and larger until at last it broke surface and the bargemen saw what it was and choked back their fear and denial.

I felt differently about things when I found out. In a case that had begun with a clear answer, what mattered was how we solved the question of our own souls, balanced our own guilt against the culpability of others. Mac had denied any responsibility for what went wrong, but the two of us had rowed out on a moonless night in 1980 to the middle of a black lake that looked like opal, searching for her two years after she had disappeared. We must have known where she was; we must have sensed that she was in a place that was as suffocating as abandoned dreams remembered, a great pocket of blue ice that would hold its secret for so long that Mac and I could both believe we had never been involved. I thought of the Chumash and their legends and knew they were right: sometimes the things you value most have to be killed in order to be preserved.

Belfast by Train
Tristan J. Deehan

Thing about it was, I was needin' to get outta Dublin. Didn't really matter where. I just needed to. Before everything happened, I was already a long, long ways past me breakin' point. I had just turned 47 years of age, and both myself and everyone else I'd known knew that 47's far too old an age to be involved in the shite I was involved in at the time. You start movin' slow, you start forgettin' simple things…you just can't sustain that kind of lifestyle anymore. And of course, my less-than-glorious return to shootin' up didn't help matters, either. I needed somethin' to numb myself to the world, and the business I was in put me face to face with skag all hours of the fuckin' day. It was easy access. A catch-22, that was.

From the second you're in it—in the business, I mean—you're already livin' on borrowed time. That's just somethin' you needed to fuckin' accept, like. At the age I was at, I may as well been beggin' the reaper fer a death certificate, hat in hand. The sad reality—the depressin', soul-destroyin' reality of the fuckin' thing—is that I somehow managed to dodge everything death could throw at me year after year, and I don't think I was deservin' of any of it. But Jamesy, who really was me best mate, and, if I'm bein' honest, was the only person I could put my absolute trust into…he was cut short. Those depraved cunts just fuckin' well left him there bleedin' out onto the cobblestones. Took a knife to him right in the middle of the fuckin' day. The poor bastard didn't deserve any of that shite. He was a good man, Jamesy.

The boys that got him, they were up-n'-comers, they were bold— they were thinkin' that they had what it takes, like. But I wasn't fuckin' scared of the lot of 'em. I'd dealt with their type many times before. Still, even then, Jamesy's slayin' was the proverbial straw that broke the camel's back fer me. I needed time to think—to reflect on my past and my present. The present involvin' havin' to deal with school-age rivals who thought they were big men, and the past involvin' everything I'd done and everything I left behind. The people I hurt. The people I killed. Me mother, me father, me two brothers, me only daughter…my whole life in Belfast, I deserted. So that's where I felt I needed to be. Belfast.

Before leavin' fer the station, I decided to cook up. I just couldn't resist the allure of the needle. Not with all the pressure—not with all the fuckin' grief. The feelin' flowed through my body like honey. Sweet, slow, and nurturin'. It was half past 8 and I was already thoroughly fucked on skag and two glasses of Scotch…so, needless to say, the day didn't start off grand. Nevertheless, I put my pistol into my back pocket—I always had to have it—forced the rest of my shite into my carry-on, and made my way to the front door. I could just sleep it off on the train, I remember thinkin'.

I managed to inspire enough motivation inside myself to stumble outta me flat and over to Connolly Station. I recall the weather bein' bloody rotten that day. Couldn't place my fuckin' umbrella, so I was forced to sit on the train, soaked and freezin' like I'd just jumped headfirst into the Irish Sea. The train was set to leave at quarter past 9, and all the seats had these wee little digital signs over 'em that showed peoples' names. Seated across from me was a fat old couple—the man was glarin' at a newspaper and the wife was tappin' away at her phone with an index finger like a fisherman's hook. I really shouldn't speak so harshly of the two of 'em, though…they both were as quiet and as inoffensive as I needed 'em to be. Like I just got through sayin', I wanted to use the two and a half hours of my trip to gather all my thoughts into neat little piles. But with my state, that proved to be easier said than fuckin' done.

As the train went along, I felt a profound sense of calm sweep over me. The naggin' shivers I had started to wane as well, thank Christ. Lookin' out the window, I was reminded of a beauty that I either forgot a long time ago or just chose to ignore. It's hard fer people who've been livin' in one place all their lives to appreciate what's around 'em. You just sorta get used to it all, like. It was particularly hard fer me, with how devoted I was to the urban sprawl. But just then—right at that moment—I felt it stronger than ever. The beauty, I mean. The coast, the sea, the cliffs…it really is something special when you look at it with a different perspective. An older set of eyes, like. The rain had lessened to a drizzle, so I could get a good glance at the stirrin' waves slammin' against the coastline. It was fuckin' gorgeous, but I couldn't exactly tell you why. It was just gorgeous.

Starin' at the passin' shores led me to the ruminations I expected I'd have given how little focus I had left in me at the time. I needed to ground myself and think about how to correct the insult that was Jamesy's death, to find a way to kick this reinvigorated fuckin' drug habit, and to figure out what the fuck I was actually gonna be doin' in the north fer five or so days—but instead I started thinkin' on me and Jamesy's history as mates and all the shite that led us down the paths we took.

Jamesy and me, we met in primary school in east Belfast. I suppose I can say that we bounded over a kind of background that wasn't all that uncommon back then, and probably still isn't to this very day. Workin' class family, a drunken bastard fer a father, and, as sad as it is to admit, a hopelessly effete mum. Our parents could be brutal in their ways, but we were given much more freedom than we had any right to have. It was somethin' of a paradox, like. We did everything in our power to avoid goin' into school, and the shite we got into wasn't ever what could be viewed as constructive to the community. I've debated with myself about this many times throughout my life, but as of right now, I'm thinkin' that I've come to the conclusion that nature is king in our cases. We were born criminals. Simple as.

Once we got into our adult years—I was 20 maybe, Jamesy 19 or 18—the both of us had come to the consensus that Belfast had fuck all to offer. We had spent our childhoods fuckin' about, stealin' worthless shite from the shops down the road, smoking fag after fag, drinkin' drink after drink…it didn't take much lookin' in the mirror to see that we were complete and utter wankers. Also, me bird at the time, Cam, she had gotten pregnant, and I was about 70% sure it was mine. I was fuckin' terrified at the thought of fatherhood. Couldn't conceive it, couldn't imagine it…certainly couldn't appreciate it the way I should've. We came to the name Aoife together, and fer a brief time, I could feel a sense of love between us. That feelin' died soon after she was born, though. Fuckin' shame, that was.

Jamesy, he didn't have the same weight hangin' over him. He just resented his fuckin' life, and much like myself, he could plainly see that the grass was greener in the south. In Dublin we'd still be wankers, but at least we wouldn't be bored off our arses 24/7. We struck gold in that regard, sure, but realistically speakin', bein' bored would've been the better thing in the long run. Livin' the "normal life" isn't as bad as it seems. I often find myself wonderin' about how my trajectory would've gone if I'd stayed and became a family man with Cam and Aoife. There's no point speculatin' now, though. No fuckin' point at all.

So, once our minds were made up, we migrated to Dublin without much plannin' outside of Jamesy makin' mention of some cousin he had who worked in the city. Michael was his name. We ended up stayin' with him in his place fer a couple months…he was a decent bloke, all things considered. He'd go out with his wee guitar and busk by day, and at night, he'd set up in the pub across the street. He was near mad and essentially a junkie, but again, he was easy to get along with if you could handle the random fits of rage and squalor he kept. Always wondered how he ended up, Michael.

It was through Michael that we had our first taste of true drugs. The man wouldn't have anything to eat fer what seemed like days on end, but you could always count on him to have something to smoke, snort, or shoot up. He was always keen on sharin' as well, which is a rarity fer an addict who could barely afford a pint. You could tell that he hated bein' lonely, the poor bastard. From that point, it all but consumed our lives—every part of it, like. It was the first and last thought we'd have each and every day. Drugs, drugs, the occasional shag, and more fuckin' drugs. I'd reckon that our passion fer it as consumers made migratin' to the mercantile sector an inevitability. In fact, the two of us made that our goal. A goal we'd mention only in passin' remarks, but a goal nonetheless. We wanted to be more than what Michael was. We wanted to deal.

It didn't take long fer us to get into the Dublin nightlife, which I can properly say reached its absolute peak back in the 90s. After that, there was nothin' but decline. It was a dangerous fuckin' cesspool—no fuckin' arguments to be had there—but those nights, they were truly special. Life-affirmin'. Jamesy had managed to build some skills as a DJ, so he was always lookin' out fer gigs. That was his dream beneath the dream. Myself, I had sought work as a bartender at the club Michael turned us onto. New World, it was called. Everything about the place was cuttin'-edge—the look, the people, the quality of the product, the music…fuckin' everything, like. It was *the* place to spend your nights at, and fer our purposes, it was the perfect place fer makin' connections.

This was the beginnin' of the end. The true end of innocence fer us, if you can even call it that to begin with. It was in New World that we met Z, the manager of the club. Never did get to know his real name, which you'd think odd given our long history as business partners. He's since past now. Cardiac arrest, they said. But I can't say I was at all saddened by the news. He had a certain kind of charisma to him that you just couldn't ignore. Many—myself included, at least fer a time—just saw him fer what he presented on the surface. A jolly Croatian bloke who just wanted everyone to have a good time. That wasn't the real him, though. The bastard was ruthless in how he operated…I'd go as far as to call him fuckin' evil. The Beast of Dublin.

The crime business is one of simple truths. Pimpin' and pushin', they're merely a service—a commodity. And the money, just a motivator. Power…that's the real score. Thrills, as well. Z understood those truths and decided to embody them. If he liked you—if you did what he was wantin' you to do quick and without question—he'd show his respect with the appropriate pay and praise. But if you didn't live up to expectations, he wouldn't just want you removed from the equation…he wanted you to suffer. To feel pain.

With time, Jamesy had managed to solidify a regular gig at New World, and he really did do great work. Relentless beats, fuckin' enormous sound…Jamesy was magic on the buttons. I recall people bangin' on about him with zeal—with enthusiasm. He was somethin' unique. An innovator. Far better than me, even at his worst.

Jamesy and me created a reputation fer ourselves at the club. People knew us as good blokes—people you'd want around. People who knew people, if that makes any sense. Naturally, Z had taken notice of this. He approached us with the prospect of doin' more than what we were doin' as club staff. We were taken aback by it, in spite of it bein' exactly what we were questin' fer. This was our chance to elevate. To attain the same kind of money and respect that Z and his men exuded. Z controlled the flow of drugs in the club, so bein' with him was the key. We started out dealin' E and hashish before movin' on to harder material. In those days—at those points in our lives—the money we made wasn't like anything we'd ever seen before. We felt like we were fuckin' rockstars. But as it always goes, more money equated to more responsibility, more headache, and more pain.

Eventually, Z came to me with a job I knew I'd be given someday but halfway hoped I'd never have to deal with. Jamesy and me weren't strangers to violence—at least the juvenile kind, like. We'd grown up usin' it on our peers only to receive it double at home. But Z didn't work on that kind of level. He was a man of extremes, and he expected the same out of his people. The job I'm referrin' to was one focused on a kraut by the name of Fredericksen. I never really got to know the bloke, but that's probably fer the best.

To put it in simple terms, Fredericksen…he was the first. It makes me ill even sayin' it, but that's the way it is. He was the first person I'd ever killed. He was one of Z's men, but from what he'd said to me,

Fredericksen fell behind on his earnin's one too many times. They'd went and given him a beatin' as a punishment, but it didn't change much of anything, apparently. He was unreliable in Z's eyes. Useless. Even worse, a liability. It was easier to operate in the 90s, but even then you couldn't afford to lose your grip, like. So, Z wanted him done. He didn't want Jamesy in it yet. "He will haff chance himself after," the sadistic bastard said to me. He wanted it to be just me this time. Just fuckin' me.

Z gave me a pistol to use fer the job. Gave me a shitey run-through on how to use the bloody thing and sent me on my way. He truly gave fuck all about the methods—he just wanted results. He told me to feign like I was collectin' money from him, which was two-thirds true. That way, Fredericksen would let me into his flat unopposed. And that he did. I was shakin' like a fuckin' leaf that night...I went and snorted some coke before the big event, but that only made it worse, I reckon. So, I knocked on the door and he let me in quick. The place was bare, sparse with the lights, and not much in the way of furnishings. The typical abode of an upstart who's tryin' to work his way up the ladder. He seemed in good spirits...almost jovial, like. He did a good job this time. Met his quota with money to spare. Fuckin' hell...now I'm really startin' to remember just how wrong it all felt. I should've just turned around and gone home.

I begun puttin' the stacks of money into the bag I brought with me. He had offered me a cup of tea as a sort of expression of bonhomie between colleagues. I nodded yes. He then turned to the sink to fill the pot. That was the moment. The opportunity. It needed to happen right fuckin' now. So, y'know, I went and did it. Took the fuckin' gun out, aimed at the back of his head, and pulled the trigger. The noise and force of the thing almost sent me to the floor. Halfway killed me ears, as well. I think he died on the spot, but I can't be sure of it. A lot of it is just a blur. I do remember that he'd fallen forward against the sink and landed on his back, though. Fuckin' horrible, the blood. I didn't hang about to examine the scene, of course...I took the money and fucked off back to the warehouse Z told me to go to after it was all done. I'd had other people done since then, but Fredericksen haunts me still. Well, all of 'em do, but him especially.

I snapped myself back into reality after starin' listlessly into space fer what had felt like hours. It wasn't hours, though. It was thirty minutes at best. I was startin' to fiend again. I needed to get the image of Fredericksen outta me head. Jamesy too, fer that matter. Thinkin' about 'em made my chest tighten up. I wasn't wantin' to give into the temptation yet again, but I just couldn't help myself. I brought the gear with the intent of fuckin' well usin' it, so there was nothin' to stop me, like. I really was a sad case.

I got up from the seat, passed by the old couple, and went fer the toilets. Lucky fer me, it wasn't occupied. It was small—like an airplane's—and reeked of shite and stale piss. I put that aside, though…gettin' high was worth whatever it needed to take.

I got the needle primed and my left arm tied. I was about to do it the same way I had always done, but my eyes got fixed on a tattoo I had on my arm. It was Aoife. Her name, I mean. I got it before I left Belfast…it may as well have been there all my life. But this time, seein' it…it just broke me. I burst into tears…cried fer the first time since I didn't fuckin' know when. I didn't even know why I was there—why I was in the train. I hadn't seen or spoken to Aoife or her mum in over twenty years, so I had no idea where they were livin' or what they were doin'. They might not've even been in Ireland at all. There's no way of mendin' that. No fuckin' way. And to make it worse, after Jamesy was killed, I had no one else left. No friends, no real family…nothin' at all. Just whores, associates, and people who wanted me dead or jailed. I always tried to justify it or block it all out with excuses, but that was the point where I felt like I'd finally reached the end of the road. I was lyin' earlier when I was said I wasn't scared. The new gangs that were startin' up in Dublin were beyond my capacity. I was too weak and too tired.

Y'know, it's funny, really. The pistol I had, I brought it with me purely out of routine—out of second nature. It was my lifeline…me ol' sword and shield. A truly terrible thing, guns are. They result in nothin' good. But yet, I chose to keep 'em close to me heart. I chose to go down this path. As did Z, Fredericksen, Jamesy…the whole lot. The problem, though…the problem's that there's no redemption at the end of the tunnel. All you do is pretend to be hard only to get done by the next man in line.

I put the needle down. Tossed it, more like. Then I got up from the toilet seat and faced the mirror. As I stood, I could feel the pistol run up against my upper thigh. I took it in hand. It was cold to the touch…almost like ice. I stared myself right in the eyes. I thought about everything. Considered fer a second that I could still turn myself around. I'd been doin' this fer all these years, so why stop now? But no. I just couldn't accept it. Either I become like Jamesy, or I leave the game fer good. Those were the only two options. But you can't *really* leave it, like. It's what I was, what I am, and what I always fuckin' will be.

I pressed the pistol's muzzle to the bottom of me chin. Prayers were mumbled. Then came the apologies. I said sorry to all of 'em—even the dead ones. Jamesy, me parents, me brothers, Cam…everyone. I lightly placed my finger against the trigger. Thought about all the mess and noise it would make. I'm sure it scared the shite out of the whole train, but there's no way fer me to say fer certain. I clenched me teeth, drew in a deep breath, and…I did it. I actually pulled the fuckin' thing.

And y'know what?

I've never felt better.

The Mystery of the Scavenging Crabs
Christopher Deliso

1

Bougainvillea shaded the terrace where Commodore Stathis held court; an ascending eruption of purple, this flowery network snatched at the late morning sunlight, protecting his guests from July's torrid heat. Active even in retirement at his Halkidiki holiday home in Greece's northeast, the navy veteran enjoyed keeping things ship-shape; and so the car he'd sent early that morning, to fetch these special guests from the airport in Thessaloniki, an hour's drive west along the Aegean littoral.

The commodore's guests were Grigoris Kardamylios, Greece's most famously obscure private detective, and his new Turkish girlfriend Ayşe, a visiting professor of English literature at Athens University. They'd flown from Athens at the invitation of Stathis and his wife, Irini, to pass some idle days by the sea. With their son Kostas being away, the older couple considered the pair as almost their own children. While Irini set down Greek coffee and sparkling water, Grigoris was recounting his latest success.

"Stathis, your tech support was invaluable in the case of the Black Cat," he said. "A beautiful thing."

"I still don't believe that happened!" laughed Ayşe, her big eyes lighting up a soft moonlike face.

"I read about it in our friend Areti's newspaper column," said Stathis, sipping his coffee. His face suddenly soured. "What am I thinking—the season for these things has passed!"

He flipped a half-gnawed date over the terrace into the dust. Grigoris laughed and gazed at the misshapen fruit, noting the small army of ants that soon besieged it.

"Too bad you didn't learn English," he said, showing Stathis an elegant paperback. "You'd enjoy this maritime intelligence memoir, by a First World War Irish sea captain in the British Navy. I'm right now near Gallipoli, on the Bay of Moudros on Limnos. On the last page I finished, the sailors went ashore for food. They started to collect crabs, and became excited—until they discovered that the whole horde of crabs had been scavenging on a decaying horse. The poor sailors—they then started vomiting! Yes indeed, quite lost their appetites. True story!"

"My God!" said Irini, blanching. "Grigoris, you always mention the most macabre things."

"I… I mention what's there," the detective said simply.

From out of nowhere, a strange argument broke out behind him, on the other side of the narrow street overlooking the commodore's flowering terrace. Being a touristic village on Halkidiki, the argument's being in English was unsurprising; but the tone and accent of the male speaker was both disconcerting and intriguing to the detective. Grigoris and Ayşe could understand the argument, but not see it, their backs being turned to the speakers, whereas their hosts could see it but not understand what was being said. After two minutes, the loud male voice had ceased; only the soft sobs of a woman emanated from behind the bougainvillea.

"What was that about?" said Irini in a low tone. "And why was that tourist so nervous with Popi? She's just the receptionist at the pension."

Grigoris said that the man was an angry pension guest, who claimed his car had just been stolen. He had apparently come down for breakfast, and afterwards noticed the car was missing. Grigoris asked if his hosts knew the pension's owner.

"Of course!" replied Irini. "Aspasia is a good woman, but since her husband—anyway. A tourist's car was… stolen? From our village? Impossible!"

"If the man has really gone now to the beach, as he stated, please call the receptionist here," Grigoris said. "Something's suspicious, but time is against us."

Invigorated by the scent of adventure on the breeze, Commodore Stathis pulled together his bulky frame and walked off the step, returning with the receptionist. Her face was sharp and seemed to Grigoris inclined to sorrow, though she was glowing with youth. He learned that she'd known Stathis and Irini since starting her job that June, when her sport management faculty in Thessaloniki had adjourned for summer. Speaking in a matter-of-fact tone, Grigoris introduced himself as a detective, promising all would be well.

"A detective?" repeated Popi with misgivings. "My boss has no money for—"

"Don't worry, you and her are like neighbors to my old friends, Stathis and Irini," cut in Grigoris magnanimously. "It'll be a complementary case."

"Tsk! Never a simple holiday with you, Grigoris!" said the detective's girlfriend, clicking her tongue, as Stathis looked on keenly.

"If I understood, that man is lodged at your place and awaiting his wife to join him from Skopje," said Grigoris. "And he complains his BMW was stolen while he ate breakfast… but how can he know that? It could've been stolen in early morning, or last night, no?"

"Yes, you're right!" Popi replied excitably. "And he threatens to tell my boss I am to blame! I was on the shift, yes, but no one entered the pension this morning! Anyway I couldn't have seen his car, if it was parked as he said, on the street behind."

"The *Skopiani*!" scowled Commodore Stathis. "Always complaining that we Greeks break their cars or steal them when they come here for their holidays! As if we have time to waste caring about them! Ha—they call themselves Macedonians, but this is the real Macedonia! They are really Bulgarians—why they don't try the sea in Bulgaria instead? It's because Greece is the greatest country on earth! Am I wrong?"

Ayşe's lips moved but Grigoris lightly tapped her foot under the table, encouraging her to bear with the commodore's crabby outburst. Irini, who had promised Grigoris that her nationalistic husband would be on best behavior, considering that Grigoris was bringing a Turkish guest, just seemed perplexed by this unexpected enigma. Silence fell, until the detective waved his coffee, almost spilling it in his excitement.

"Two questions," he said. "First, why do you serve a breakfast, when most pensions have their own kitchenettes?"

"We do too," said Popi. "But there's so much competition this year, from Air B&B plus the generally high prices—Aspasia wanted to do everything to satisfy the guests, even breakfast."

"Which also adds to her costs," reflected Grigoris. "So theoretically, someone could have taken your guest's car keys from his room—except you saw no one go out. Is there another exit?"

Popi replied that there wasn't, adding that the guest's room was above the breakfast hall, on the first floor, and that its balcony was also being repaired, meaning its window only opened vertically. The only staircase passed the reception desk, and no one had gone in or out. Grigoris listened intently and rubbed his forehead, looking at his watch.

"My second question: he told you he won't report the theft to the police."

"What?" blustered Commodore Stathis. "Why wouldn't he tell the police? A fine car like a BMW—"

"He was saying things like, 'what will the police do, laugh? Just another Macedonian tourist who deserved it,' and things of that nature," replied Grigoris.

"Now, who does this fellow think he is!" thundered Stathis. "A Slav talking like that to a decent Greek girl—and to think here, in the real Macedonia!"

"Relax," laughed Grigoris. "I'll solve this. Now Popi… I expect he will return, and check out within an hour. It is most urgent that I enter his room for a few moments while he's still at the beach."

Nervously, the receptionist agreed. The pension was of the typical, three-story structure that exist everywhere in Greece: boxy, whitewashed, familial, pillars intermingled with vines and boasting only a few rooms. Popi said the man had been given a double room wedged in between a family room and a single room. The former, further one, hosted a family, also from Skopje, whereas the single had quartered, until the previous evening, a quiet young Greek man.

"I didn't ask his name," murmured the receptionist, in reply to Grigoris' persistent questioning. "He seemed like a student. He stayed only one night, though he paid for last night too, and then suddenly left—he asked when the bus to Thessaloniki would come. I told him, and he left."

"Really?" said Grigoris excitedly. "How did he pay? Did you record his ID?"

"He paid in cash, upon arrival," said Popi. "But the season being so difficult already, my boss said not even to record such local tourists in the guestbook."

"Hmm," said the detective, rethinking the whole strange case. "What about the man from Skopje? Did you record him in the guestbook?"

The receptionist confirmed that she had, but had forgotten to scan his passport. "He also arrived the day before yesterday—he said his wife will come tomorrow. And his car was very nice, a new-looking black BMW. He parked on the upper side-street. I should have—"

Grigoris interrupted, announcing that he and Ayşe would pay to stay in the room vacated by the young Greek man that adjoined the suspect's room, though they had planned to stay at Stathis' home. Popi seemed surprised, but said they could check in right away, as the young Greek man had left the room in immaculate shape: in fact, he hadn't even opened the sheets, the soap, or removed the paper strip from the toilet.

"It was like he was never there," the receptionist said, her sharp lips pursed. "But I saw him go in myself!"

When asked whether the pension had a security camera on the guest floor, Popi explained that the owner had complained such luxuries were too expensive, and anyway unnecessary in such a safe village. She ushered Grigoris into the guest's locked room before returning to Stathis' terrace, where she told a surprised Ayşe of Grigoris' new plan; the professor took their suitcase and waited nervously in the vacant room adjoining the absent guest's one, listening as Grigoris paced around on the other side of the thin white wall. Aware that he was in a precarious position, and fearing the tourist would return, Ayşe felt her senses unusually heightened; the wail of a baby from the family room beyond sounded to her like a police car's siren. Soon a mother's voice came consoling it in an unknown Slavic language. At last, the detective quietly entered, a confident smile on his face and his notebook in hand.

"It's solved," he whispered.

"What?" Ayşe replied, looking dubiously at his scrawled notebook as they sat on the bedside. "I don't understand why you don't just get a Smartphone."

Grigoris shot his girlfriend the piercing look reserved for only one thing, that symbol of the 21st century which he most despised. The moment of irritation having passed, he spoke.

"The least likely scenario is that the BMW was stolen by the pension owners. The less likely, is that it was randomly stolen. The most likely, however, is that it was given away—that is, the Greek man who previously occupied the room we're now in took it last night, and the two guests were secretly working together."

"Really?" Ayşe said, her pastel blue-green eyes widening. "How do you figure that?"

Grigoris recounted his newest discoveries. While the guest from Skopje indeed had a North Macedonia passport, the name on it, a 'Sabir Jakuposki,' indicated that far from being the angry nationalist Stathis had presumed, he was from the country's obscure Slavic Muslim minority, the Torbeshi. Further, he had an ID card from a German hospital, indicating he worked as an expatriate doctor, and a second passport, Bulgarian, which however showed no stamps or signs of use.

"Why would someone working in Germany, with an EU passport from Bulgaria, visiting an EU member like Greece, *not* use his Bulgarian passport?" said Grigoris. "It's clear that this Jakuposki wanted to act just now, to create a public scene so that anyone overhearing would think he was the victim of just another theft or attack against cars with so-called 'North Macedonia' license plates, which unfortunately, does happen every summer in Northern Greece because of our own nationalists, regardless of what Stathis wants to admit," Grigoris continued. "But the question of why he complains, but doesn't want to inform the police—we must wait."

They sat in the stuffy room in the midday heat, with only the balcony window cracked vertically. After some tense minutes had passed, Ayşe whispered of a sound in the hall. Indeed, the mysterious Mr. Jakuposki had returned; they heard him turn the key and loudly enter his room. The couple looked at each other in excitement, craning their necks toward the white wall. They heard the man shower then mutter angrily to himself while pacing his room. Then, Ayşe sat up straight; the man was talking out loud to someone who was not there. Grigoris understood enough to know what he didn't understand.

"He's speaking Turkish!" the detective whispered. "He must be talking on the phone—and avoiding the Slavic language, so those people in the other room won't understand! What's he saying?"

"Hush, you," said Ayşe. "Let me listen!"

As Grigoris watched impatiently, he noted her look of amusement. Brushing her long, curling blond-brown hair back from her ear, she went up to the wall, leaning her head closer to it.

"He asked about a football match," Ayşe reported after the man had ceased talking and she was back by the bed.

"What?"

"Yes," she whispered. "He was asking, 'do you think Real Madrid will win tonight?' And so on. Nothing important, sorry."

The detective exhaled in frustration, but then froze; he could hear the man, whistling beyond the thin wall, hastily moving about. Soon after, the sound of the key in the adjoining door registered, followed by the unmistakable sound of suitcase rolling past them down the hall outside.

"As I suspected!" whispered Grigoris, staring into space. "I wonder if the man he was speaking to in Turkish was also the one at this number."

Ayşe gaped at the detective's notebook, opened to another page. "Where did you get that?"

"It was the only sent call on his phone," replied Grigoris with a laugh.

"Just because I won't buy a Smartphone doesn't mean I can't operate one! So this Jakuposki, here for only two days, has a Greek SIM card and number in his phone. The number he rang up here, last night at 11:01PM, is a *stathero*, a landline… and somewhere in Thrace, judging from the prefix. Can you check it for me? This is easily done online, you know."

Ayşe input the number into a website. It came up as a lumber warehouse in the tiny village of Thermes, north of Xanthi in Thrace. The discovery excited Grigoris tremendously. From its name alone, he said, the village must have a thermal bath; he added that the mountainous area, where the Rhodopi Mountains spilled over from Bulgaria into Greece, was also the traditional home of a part of Greece's Muslim minority, the Pomaks, a holdover from Ottoman times. He marveled at the strange symmetry of encountering two Slavic-speaking Muslim minorities from neighboring countries in the very same morning.

"Nowadays, that whole area is mostly empty. The men, of working age at least, are in Germany or some other EU country," observed Grigoris. "Not much economy in Thrace, unless you enjoy picking tobacco."

"I know of these people," said Ayşe. "The Greek state calls them 'Greek Muslims,' while the Turkish government calls them part of Greece's Turkish minority. I remember now, one of my students in Istanbul was hired as a tutor by the Turkish consulate in Komotini near Xanthi, to educate the villagers in Turkish."

Grigoris jotted notes, as if he might forget his girlfriend's words, and said that every detail, however seemingly irrelevant, might in time become useful.

"So what now?" she said. "Follow Mr. Jakuposki?"

"I doubt we'd recover his car that way," Grigoris said. "I suspect he left in such a hurry just now because I also… relieved his wallet of 100 Euros. Therefore, he now knows that someone entered his room, since his argument with Popi. The final test will be whether he blames her again for a theft, or chooses a different option."

"Grigoris, you're terrible!" exclaimed Ayşe. "Stealing from some tourist!"

The detective just shrugged impishly, making no apology. Suddenly, his face changed, struck with some flash of insight.

"Ayşe, please search on your phone! Type in, 'corporate sponsors of Real Madrid' for me."

She complied and scanned the search page, showing it to the detective.

"Aha," he said, with a beatific smile. "BMW's a sponsor! The man was talking in code about his car! Quickly, we must go down and see what has happened—it may not be too late!"

2

It was past 1pm, and Grigoris and Ayşe, having discussed their own options, found Popi downstairs with the pension's owner, Aspasia, a dour woman in her sixties. They learned that the guest, Mr. Jakuposki, had left a few minutes before; through sideways inquiry, Grigoris carefully ascertained that the tourist had made no further complaints about either the alleged theft of his BMW, or the actual theft Grigoris had himself just perpetrated against his wallet. Jakuposki had simply paid for his room, including the coming night, announcing that his wife was ill and he must return to Skopje. He'd asked only for a taxi to Thessaloniki.

"I hope we don't see him again," continued Aspasia, nervily. "We don't need any more trouble. I hope better tourists will come—it's already the last week of July."

Grigoris assured her that better tourists would certainly come and, as a sort of prescient sacrifice, offered Ayşe up to the pension's greater good, as part of the plan he'd privately formulated with her upstairs. While negotiating this plan, Grigoris had also phoned Stathis, who complained vociferously but was secretly delighted to learn he would be going on an adventure that required packing a swimsuit, toothbrush, snacks and his favorite vehicle.

When Grigoris crossed the street to Stathis' house and publicly announced that both Stathis and his green 1984 Land Rover Defender 110 were needed at once, the retired navy man thus feigned irritation at the detective's having ruined their plans for a grand welcome lunch. As his wife of many years, Irini suspected that Stathis was protesting too much, and so she pretended to be annoyed as she packed the homemade spinach-and-cheese pies, prosciutto, sausages and water in a bag, along with pajamas and the swimming trunks Grigoris had strangely insisted upon.

After Stathis had bid farewell to his bemused wife, Grigoris followed him to the beautiful machine in the garage. When its driver revved the engine, the off-roader rattled, then roared to life, and they were on their way to fill up the tank. In the bright sunlight, the vehicle appeared to Grigoris as a most formidable olive instrument of off-road war, a sort of irritable terrapin on ridged tires, its smash-mouth grill standing high between headlights dead set on conquering the open road ahead, and a detachable canopy roof letting in limitless possibilities for conjecture and conversation. In short, it was the perfect vehicle for an investigator's road trip.

"I love that you've never customized this car," said Grigoris with a laugh, wind flowing through his wavy brown hair. Neither man liked air conditioning, and the hot breeze of the afternoon motorway made Stathis feel as if he was, indeed, back on active duty.

"Why would I?" he scoffed. "After all, I'm a Greek! We didn't change our religion despite 500 years of Turkish enslavement—unlike these Pomaks you're taking me to! But the mountain roads north of Xanthi aren't so bad—I don't know why you insisted we take the Land Rover. Still, I'm glad you did. I never get to drive it anymore."

Grigoris replied brightly that Stathis shouldn't worry about damaging his vintage British vehicle, or the moral failings of the Pomaks' ancestors, for that matter, because on this day the retired commodore would have bigger fish to fry. If Grigoris' suspicions were confirmed, the seaman would actually be frying himself in a pool of hot water in just a few hours. As the detective scrawled notes, comparing his ever-emerging thoughts to his previous citations, he commented rapidly on how the commodore would have to pretend to be his uncle with a knee problem. No one would suspect anything, if they were disguised as spa tourists.

"I'll believe it when I see it!" scoffed the old military man, perspiration and sun gleaming from the balding crest of his head. "It's always so theatrical with you, Grigoris—we could've simply phoned the Xanthi police chief to—"

"No!" the detective cut in. "The locals only ever screw things up! If this mystery is as I suspect, a large international network's involved. All we can do is gather intelligence."

"You mean, we won't recover the BMW?" said the commodore, annoyed. "I don't see why—"

"We'll be lucky if we do," Grigoris said. "But we'll be safe, at least. Just have faith—if not in me, in God—and remember this car is our protector and defender."

He adjusted the radio to a traditional station that he knew Stathis would appreciate. It was blasting the doleful laments of *rembetika* music, the Greek blues genre that once had sung of the tragedies of the Greek immigrants from Turkey, following the 1923 population exchanges. Some of Stathis' ancestors came from the Turkish mainland. The fierce nationalism that had inspired a long naval career had come to him from the memories gathered by those ancestors and the waves that had borne them from the former Ottoman Empire a century before.

After an hour of scrub forests and arid, rocky scenery, the motorway veered towards Kavala, affording views of the sea. As they snacked and talked, leaving the pretty port town behind them for Xanthi and the Thracian interior, Grigoris' phone rang.

"What's up, my dear?" he shouted into the roaring wind, and hastily turned down the radio as he scrambled for his pen and notebook. Amused, Stathis looked on while driving and chewing his spinach-and-cheese pie.

After a brief conversation, Grigoris reported that Ayşe had gone to the trouble of 'clearing' Aspasia and Popi of any involvement in the BMW's disappearance. In fact, after interviewing the worker at a souvenir shop opposite where the BMW had been parked the evening before, she had learned that the worker had admired the car so much that he'd even inspected it, after its owner had left. He had noted the car indeed had North Macedonia license plates, but didn't think to record them. He had told her only that it was a black BMW i7.

"One of those fancy electric cars!" scoffed Stathis. "Over 100,000 Euros! What a con!"

"Electric?" said Grigoris, lost in thought. "That's… thank you, commodore. I think we made the right decision, after all."

As they ascended towards Xanthi, and then passed it, the sun dropped on their left-hand side, coming and going in dazzling patches between the increasingly forested and cooler air of twisting mountain roads. They'd left all traffic, and signs of life, behind them. Now they were on the Greek B-roads of old, the rubble-strewn and precipitous paths that led to a forgotten and barely-visited bit of the southern Balkans. After 40 kilometers of climbing, Grigoris noted the road signs as he had anticipated. They led to the small village of Thermes, a ramshackle place lacking any of the welcoming appeal of a classic Greek village. He was elated to see, on the right, a simple public thermal bath, and a sign for some sort of communal hostel on the left.

"It's perfect!" he said. "Now, let's get you in the water, my dear 'uncle,' so I can find where that lumber warehouse was that our Mr. Jakuposki rang up last night at 11:01—ha! The sort of work ethic they must have, to operate at such an hour on a Sunday night, too!"

Reconciling himself to his infernal allotted fate, and for the first time putting the pieces together, Commodore Stathis said only that he feared leaving his Land Rover alone in such a place.

"No!" replied the detective with a grin. "As I said, it is precisely that car which will protect and defend us here."

They parked and entered the drowsy hostel, which seemed

completely unvisited. A local of about Grigoris' age, but reed-thin and with a flat skull only partly rounded by a few tufts of hair, led them to a large room with many beds. The room reminded Grigoris of his military service in the 1990s, and seemed to appeal to Stathis too for its barracks-like austerity. There were no other tourists, and the fee was modest. Grigoris recited his charade about bringing his ailing uncle to the thermal bath to help his injured knee. The hostel-keeper seemed satisfied, and gave instructions on accessing the spa. They were lucky they'd come in time, he said, as it would close in an hour. Grigoris thanked the man and ensured that Stathis, swimming trunks on and towel in hand, crossed the street and entered the unremarkable pool and its gurgling, mineral waters.

"Now remember what the nice man said, dear uncle," mocked Grigoris. "Don't overdo it in these hot waters! I'll have a coffee and check on you in an hour."

Stathis grumbled a goodbye as the detective began searching for the mysterious lumber warehouse. According to his calculations, it should be up the road, beyond the village center, on the road leading towards other Pomak villages and the forested mountain border with Bulgaria. He passed a run-down café where several local men smoked and drank from diminutive Turkish tea cups. The detective could feel the eyes of the locals upon his unfamiliar ambling form as he passed uphill, and was glad to be past them when then, further up the road, he finally saw a large aluminum-framed building with a small sign reading, 'Hasan Export.' While the name matched that of the lumber storage facility that had come up with Jakuposki's dialed phone number, its door was locked with a heavy chain. Neither people nor parked cars were about.

Hiding his excitement, Grigoris trudged back to the café and ordered a Greek coffee from the sleepy-looking young man working there. The detective tried to begin a friendly chat, but the waiter was disinterested in Grigoris or his story; and when the detective asked about the closed lumber storage facility, the man simply said it had gone out of business, due to the bad economy. Then Grigoris asked whether the café had a television; he said he was hoping to watch the Real Madrid club friendly match versus Milan that evening, and asked the waiter who he thought would win. The man looked at Grigoris strangely.

"I'm sorry, we're closed in evening," he said. "And no television. You are staying in our village tonight?"

Grigoris nodded, mentioning his recuperating uncle, and gestured towards Stathis' Land Rover Defender, parked seductively in the distance by the hostel. He watched sideways as the waiter went to chat in Turkish with a pot-bellied old man in a striped shirt. Grigoris presumed he was the café owner, and noted that both were looking at him with interest, as if they couldn't come to a conclusion about the outsider. This suited the detective perfectly, and he sipped his coffee in the cool of the mountain evening. Then, he realized their work was not done; for the customs of a Pomak village precluded any sort of nightlife. When it came, darkness would bring a new challenge entirely.

He checked his watch. *Poor 'Uncle' Stathis must be properly roasted in that sulphurous cauldron by now*, mused Grigoris. *Tough old soldier.*

Paying for his coffee, the detective slipped away.

3

After Grigoris and the now red-faced and relaxed commodore had returned to the hostel, finding themselves still alone, they revised their battle plan. Stathis had thoroughly enjoyed the inexpensive mineral bath and found that, while dehydrating, it had opened his thoughts in a way very complementary to Grigoris' own peripatetic reconnaissance. For one thing, Stathis spoke of a new-enough, Turkish-built mosque on the mountain border with Bulgaria, which had greatly excited the Greek intelligence service about 15 years before.

"I knew I remembered this place from somewhere," Stathis concluded. "Also, last year, they opened a new border crossing northeast of Thermes, accessing Zlatograd in Bulgaria. In the middle of nowhere! The Athens government said it was all for building better bilateral relations, but I recall the Bulgarian leadership talking about their state interest, to buy up shares of Alexandroupoli port in Thrace."

"Very interesting," murmured Grigoris, scrawling notes.

"The Bulgarians won't be satisfied until they steal Greek territory to the Aegean!' grumbled Stathis. "They've been that way since forever. They never learn, despite losing the war in 1913, and 1918, and 1945… Now they just use Brussels to play off the Turkish threat, and push their interest. But I'm retired—not even my wife listens to me!'

Grigoris laughed and recounted his experience at the closed lumber warehouse and café, leaving out the locals' interest in their activities but explaining the problem that nightfall presented. As there was nowhere to go in this conservative village, there was no reason to be outside after dark. But, if Grigoris' hunch was right, they needed to get back to the warehouse unseen, or any intelligence-gathering would fail. Stathis scratched his bald head and brooded. It was a simple enough challenge, he said, but the hostel could have a night watchman. Further, other locals could see them from their homes, and the wind could blow their foreign scents into the waiting nostrils of vigilant village sheepdogs.

"Just a logistical issue," replied Grigoris. "The important thing is the café people, if they're in on it too, think I'm crazy. I asked them about tonight's Real Madrid game. Of course, the summer club friendlies are being played in America. So the match won't start until 5AM Greek time. But I'm certain the real 'action' will begin as soon as it gets dark here. Let's get dinner while we can. We must take a risk."

Leaving the room, they found the same receptionist who'd greeted them earlier. After asking about places to eat, Grigoris asked casually if there was a television in the hostel, so that they could watch the Real Madrid match. The man, who seemed startled, said that one restaurant operated, but apologized that the hostel lacked a television. Clearing his throat, he said that he would go home soon, so they'd best take the key to the hostel entrance. Elated, Grigoris thanked the man. Commodore Stathis, looking with a sad nostalgia at his classic Land Rover, followed Grigoris to the eatery.

"I hope you know what you're doing!" he scowled. "I fear we'll have to walk back to Halkidiki—that is, if we even get out of here."

"Don't worry," soothed Grigoris. "As I said, your car will protect and defend us. That man just told me everything I need to know, and I promise I'll tell you too."

"Yeah, great," grumbled Stathis, and commented bitterly about the lack of alcohol on the menu.

They ate salad and roast goat, the day's only offerings, and some stale *loukoumi* that the waiter brought on his own initiative. They were the only guests, and the only sound was the unnerving tension generated by the silent employees of a public serving house anxious to go home. They ate in silence, and Grigoris looked at his watch. The hour was approaching.

"Let's go for it," he whispered. "It'll be dark, but I think I memorized the route there."

The commodore nodded and after paying, followed Grigoris out. The darkness had fallen decisively and the only sounds came from the mountain forest at night, of owls and insects and the gurgling of the mineral waters; if they had any secret ally in this mad quest, Grigoris thought, perhaps it was the sound of the percolating underworld waters, drowning out their footsteps…

They were alone, the village having gone to bed, the café Grigoris had previously visited now shuttered. Gingerly, the hairs raised on their necks from the excitement of a nocturnal quest into the unknown, the two men slowly clambered up the village's central street. Just enough moonlight seeped out of the heavens to guide them, while the mountain constellations seemed unusually low and tangled in the sky. Scanning the horizon, Grigoris suddenly swung his arm, warning Stathis to take cover.

Retreating behind clustered pines and kneeling, the two watched in astonishment as a small army of men, some carrying flashlights, appeared from the village's upper part. They assembled before the allegedly closed lumber warehouse, 'Hasan Export,' and one fellow was loudly unlocking the door, while giving orders to another in the Slavic language that Grigoris could not understand but recognized as the Greek, Bulgarian and Turkish fusion known as Pomak, spoken by perhaps 40,000 people in Greece.

"I was right!" whispered the detective excitedly. "Thank you, God!"

Stathis hushed him and pointed at the street below them; up it were coming several cars, stealthily and without headlights, quickly disappearing inside the warehouse.

"There was a Toyota, a Mercedes, an Audi, and I could not see, because of the dark, but probably a black BMW!" whispered Stathis in excitement. Suddenly, his expression changed to one of dismay. "Grigoris! What if my car is next? We must go back!"

"No!" insisted the detective fiercely. "Trust what I said. We must get closer. Come on!"

The small army of villagers quickly disappeared inside the warehouse, leaving only one man outside to keep watch. Grigoris scanned rapidly at all possible angles of approach, assessing contingencies and variables, and then spoke.

"We must get that guard away from his post, and see what's going on inside. There's no other entrance. If I can creep around from the far side, and you can distract him somehow for a few minutes—"

"But what about my Land Rover?" pleaded Stathis in despair.

"Look, if someone steals it, we know they're going right here, nowhere else, so…"

"So why don't I… bring it to them?" Stathis said, in a sudden reverie. Both men fought their compulsion to burst out laughing.

"A pincer move! Yes! It's so mad, it just might work," said Grigoris, handing him the hostel key. "Get all our stuff out of there and into your car. Then drive up here, very slowly, in about five minutes. We'll figure this out!"

Jubilant and recommitted fully to the mission, the former navy man nodded and slipped back toward the hostel, leaving Grigoris alone to deal with the guard. Picking up a good-sized rock from the ground, he crept slowly past the far side of the windowless building. He could hear the sounds of heavy machinery from within. The sound of electric sparks, of soldering and hammering told him, even without visual proof, all he needed to know.

Rounding the other side, Grigoris realized he was now exposed against the building's moonlit side; if the guard, or anyone loitering nearby, happened to be looking in his direction, he'd have no place to hide. Action was imperative; making a full circle and standing behind the guard's close side, he flung the rock with all his might at the café's distant window.

It was a direct hit. Hearing the sound of breaking glass, the guard trotted off to investigate. Grigoris used the moment to slightly open the warehouse door. Exactly as he'd suspected, the 'lumber warehouse' was really an illicit chop shop. Inside, all of the cars that had just been driven inside and more were mounted on ramps. Swarms of workers were scuttling them for their valuable parts. Luckily, the noise of their combined labor had kept them oblivious to the sound of a window breaking outside. The welders and solderers wore protective goggles and suits, while others jabbered to each other in Pomak and Turkish and occasionally, Greek, carefully removing and stacking parts. The efficiency and industriousness of these workers, who so rapidly were reducing once-proud thoroughbreds of the automotive world to not even skeletal remains, fascinated and distracted Grigoris so much that he forgot about the guard.

"Hey! What are you doing?" the latter called out, mixing his languages in his panic at seeing an intruder at his vacated post. Getting no response, the guard pulled a knife from his belt and waved it threateningly at the detective's neck.

Grigoris just smiled and apologized in Greek. For, as he stood trapped against the chop shop's door by the threatening guard, he could see rising up the hill the pale, heroic lights of a Land Rover Defender 110.

As Stathis honked the horn, the confused guard turned to see this new complication. Parking and stepping out in front of the headlights' glare, the robust retired commodore stood, hands ono hips, and shouted at the guard in the official Greek of the military academy.

"What in Hell's the meaning of this, boy? Put that thing down! Let my colleague go."

Slowly, the guard lowered the knife, the moonlight capturing a new gleam of opportunity in his eye as he reassessed the strange scene before him.

"That's right," said Grigoris in the comforting tone of the hostage negotiator. "We're just trying to do business, if you'd let us bring the car in."

The guard nodded and flashed his light at the Land Rover. Grigoris walked towards Stathis and eyed him knowingly as he walked to the passenger's door. Stathis turned on the engine, the guard still fixing his light on them and clutching his knife. Stathis slowly moved the vehicle forward, and then suddenly accelerated, forcing the guard to dive for cover, before quickly turning the Land Rover and driving out of the village at top speed.

4

Detective Grigoris did not see Commodore Stathis again until October, when they made yet another pilgrimage to the Orthodox monasteries of Mt. Athos, on Halkidiki's third peninsula. By that time, the October weather in Greece was much better than it was in Germany, where Sabir Jakuposki had been arrested a few weeks before for involvement with a previously unknown European car theft and smuggling ring. Several other arrests had been made in Greece and elsewhere. In keeping with his practice, Detective Grigoris used his media contacts to make sure that others got the credit for the Thermes investigation, leaving him comfortably uninvolved.

"But how did a Polish king come into it?" asked Stathis, as they reclined in the cool of the afternoon in a serene flat-stoned monastery courtyard, sipping gritty, and sadly weak coffee, while eating halva.

"From your comment about how we Greeks never changed our religion under the Ottoman occupation," said Grigoris. "While we were driving to Thermes. Then, I dismissed it as a typical comment I'd hear from you over these last 23 years. But my mind drifted later to John Sobieski, the Polish king who defended Vienna from the Turks in 1683, the Hapsburg leaders having been too cowardly to defend their own realm. And that reminded me of a detail from last fall, from a colleague of mine, Klaus–ironically, an Austrian–working at the EU's border management agency, FRONTEX, which is based in Warsaw, as you know."

"Of course!" laughed Stathis. "We have their cooperation since even before the migrant crisis, I know them well. What was this detail?"

"Klaus reported a large-scale police operation involving FRONTEX, to crack down on illegal chop shops in both EU and Balkan states," said Grigoris. "So I began to think that really, the BMW could be headed to such a place… after all, expensive electric-car parts are in demand on the black market. And your statement in the village, about a new border crossing to Bulgaria at Thermes—well, this sealed the suspicion I had had since hearing the strange complaint of Mr. Jakuposki! Of course, it was because Jakuposki was only a hired driver to get the car out of Skopje and into Greece. It had been stolen, as we now know, by a Montenegrin in Croatia and brought to Skopje via Kosovo."

Stathis laughed and a curious monk, who was a friend of theirs for years, sat down to listen to Grigoris' tale while weaving a black prayer bracelet.

"What an odd thing," the monk said. "We will pray for the salvation of his soul, and hope he turns away from sin."

"Father, you may try, but the man in question is a Muslim Slav," cracked Stathis.

"He's not a career criminal," said Grigoris. "His lawyer's arguing that he only accepted the job of moving the car to help pay his son's medical school expenses. Also he was unaware that the car was actually stolen."

"Really?" said the monk, weaving away. "I am just a poor wretch before God. I will pray for him anyhow."

Grigoris laughed. "Stathis, the new border crossing detail was also significant, and I must thank you. It added importance to that very remote, but also strategic and thus, vulnerable village for criminals."

"Really?" shuddered the monk, rubbing his white beard. "I'd not like to go there."

"It's perfectly peaceful, Father—too peaceful," said Grigoris. "Greeks avoid the Pomakochoria, and tourists rarely visit either, though a few do for the mineral baths. And the locals who work in other European countries might come in expensive cars with foreign plates. So no one would suspect a thing, when cars arrive there and leave invisibly, in little pieces… From Thermes, it's a short drive to that remote Bulgarian border crossing, as well as the sea at Kavala—not to mention the motorway that runs from Greece's land border with Turkey to the Ionian Sea, and Italy thereafter."

"Indeed," said Stathis. "A cleverly strategic location. But, we could've gone in my regular car—though I did enjoy getting to drive my Land Rover Defender again!"

"Actually, it was a key part of my plan," corrected Grigoris, "and one I could not share with you, as I knew you would not agree if I told you. I'm glad the Father is here, as I should ask him for forgiveness for misleading you for our greater good."

"Huh? What do you mean?"

"You must remember to listen carefully!" chuckled Grigoris. "I told you that your most valuable car would be our 'protector and defender.' I realized we had no protection in a a Pomak village; only by making the locals believe we were perhaps, just perhaps, secretly 'businessmen' disguised as spa tourists. Only then could we move safely in the village at night. It was a high risk, high reward scenario. I knew that if I told you beforehand, you would never agree, and that if we took your regular, beat-up old car, the locals would never believe we could be secretly complicit in international smuggling. I hope you forgive me."

"Of course not!" retorted the embarrassed commodore. "When did you have time to think of that whole scenario?"

"Before I called you from the pension's room, where I was forced to wait with Ayşe, when Jakuposki was checking out."

"What're you saying?" replied Stathis, rubbing his head. "That's a load of—"

"Think whatever you like, but I am at peace with my decision and I entrust it to God to judge. I hope you will forgive me for deceiving our friend Stathis, Father."

The monk simply waved his hand and crossed himself, leading Grigoris to smile and continue.

"Of course, I must credit Ayşe, who translated Jakuposki's phone comments from Turkish, about Real Madrid, which tipped me off to the possible existence of the chop shop in Thermes. She also discovered that the listed 'Hasan Export' lumber company was actually owned by a ship repair firm in Alexandroupoli, near the Turkish border on the sea, and run by some colorful characters from Greece and Eastern Europe."

"Ha!" cheered Stathis. "And to think that your Turkish girlfriend was the one to discover a criminal smuggling company based in Alexandroupoli, when that town's been crawling with FRONTEX officers for years! Well, the Europeans can work on their suntans while pretending to work on protecting our borders, I guess!"

"What's this—a Turkish girlfriend, Grigoris?" said the old monk, eyes fixed on his bracelet-in-progress. "Is she a Christian yet? It wouldn't do for you to marry a Muslim, you know. Isn't there some nice Greek woman for you, my boy?"

"My grandparents would agree with you, Father. Sorry, I can't convert her. But anyway, her main religion is literature… she's a professor of English literature, of all things."

"English literature?" said the monk, eyes wide. "I know very little about the world. Pray for me, the both of you, will you? And how is your son, Stathis? Still unmarried?"

The former military man looked down with profound sorrow. "I think we have lost him, Father."

"I understand," said the monk, glancing up from his weaving and flashing a brief patient smile. "I will pray for his soul, and for yours too, Sthis. And even for Grigoris—and for the car smuggler, of course."

Made in the Shade
Tucker Struyk

"Man is least himself when he talks in his own person. Give him a mask, and he will tell you the truth."

— Oscar Wilde

Guided by the dull lucency of a lighted mirror's LED strips, Doris Logan managed to blend and buff the gray-brown contouring of Virgo du Cul's face. Her eyes squinted at the young drag queen's malar. "For cheekbones as high as yours, you've got to find the bottom edge of that bone and curve the line down towards your jaw," she said. "See?"

She stepped back, to let Virgo look at herself in the mirror.

"That gives your cheeks some definition." She raised her false fingernail at Virgo's mien. "And use a shade lighter than your skin tone to accentuate your cheekbones. But," she half paused for dramatic effect, "For the hollows of your cheeks, swipe with a darker shade."

Virgo turned from side-to-side, pouting her lips as she primped and preened the wig atop her head. Suddenly, her face fell.

Perplexed, Doris followed her gaze toward an intruder found in the mirror's reflection. A man—brown suede jacket, cashmere scarf, nice hair and nails—slouched in the dressing room's doorway with a drink in his hand. His dodgy gawk turned into a crafty smirk.

Doris groaned. Her eyelids tapered to an even squint.

"Renard Boivin," she said, in a mock Québécois accent. "I thought this bar had bouncers to keep reprobates like you out."

Renard raised his hands in the air, his grin widening. "Huh, and here I thought reprobates were always welcomed at the Doll House? Besides,

I come bearing gifts." He set the drink down on the dressing table. "Whiskey sour. Your favorite."

Virgo got up from the makeup chair, pointedly refusing to look directly at Renard. "Speaking of," she said, "I'm going to get a drink myself."

Doris huffed. "Don't bother, you can have mine." She slid the glass toward Virgo. Her adamantine eyes circled back to Renard. "Matter of fact, you can have him too, but I'll be the first to tell you that you can do better than some common clown fucker."

Virgo tittered.

Renard's anger flared. "Oh, yeah? If I'm the clown fucker, then who's the fucking clown?"

Doris shoved passed him, and by the time he strung together his crude words into a sentence, she was already down the hall and out the back entrance. The brick walls along the alley behind The Doll House were graffiti covered and gang tag marked—the pavement slick from an off-and-on downpour of rain. She took a couple of steps then, behind the overflowing dumpster, she spotted her customer, Cole Slate.

Scrolling through social media sites on his phone—the pale, blue light that shone in his eye reflected what he watched back out into the world. As she sauntered over to him, her amaranthine bouffant dress hit his peripheral vision and caught his eye. In one fluid motion, she handed him a plastic baggy and he slipped her the cash in exchange.

He slid the bag into his pants pocket. "You know," he said, "I've been waiting out here in the open for over an hour. What am I supposed to do if a cop comes by?"

She shrugged. "Sweetie, it's a dime bag," she said. "If you want the five-star treatment, buy a pound next time. I'm busy."

He admired her form in that gown. His eyes lingered on the shape of her hips. "Does the five-star treatment come with a date?"

She batted her false lashes. Beneath an hour's worth of makeup, her face flushed. "Honey, these days, all you need is a pulse and a retirement plan to get me in your car."

With a hint of a smile, he gently swayed his shoulders back and forth. His hands placed in his pockets. "You don't say. What about your friend, Echidna Extraña? What's it take to float her boat?"

Doris rolled her eyes, her face going vinegar sour.

"Echidna? You shitting me? Shoot. She's a cheaper date than I am." She waved a half-dismissive finger at him. "Honey, with the grass you've got there, you're already as good as gold."

His smile spread. "Thanks." He tried to sound casual, but failed. "Hey, is there any chance you could take me backstage to meet her?"

Her lips tightened, as she sized him up. After a thorough inspection, she shrugged. He seemed like a nice enough kid. "Sure, follow me."

She took him by the hand, through the back entrance, and brought him into the main dressing room. Inside, Virgo was applying setting powder, while Echidna was dabbing rubbing alcohol on various strategic spots on her face where she planned to tape back the skin.

As Doris entered she threw her arms up in the air and kicked her hip to the left. "Well, sweetie, welcome to the fabulous, the one and only, Doll House!"

Cole rubbernecked, in a far-off gape. He was like a kid in a candy shop.

The two drag queens viewed him with a look of open repugnance.

Doris turned to face the dolls. "Now ladies, play nice. This is my friend, Cole. He's a really big fan."

That was greeted with a "Yutz" from Virgo, who shrugged her shoulders in the mirror. Unperturbed, Doris continued, "He wants to know if he can smoke you out before the show."

Echidna and Virgo's 'ice twins' demeanor softened to a tepid warmth. They turned to one another, then looking over her shoulder, Echidna said:

"Sure, why not. After all, it's always nice to hear from a fan."

With a quiet snicker, Doris left them to their devices.

She walked out of the dressing room, and along the back of the Doll House stage. Plain and simple, a rectangle with a 3ft runway platform.

Overhead, several multi-colored LED lights, and a remote spotlight. The stage wasn't high, but tall enough to give a girl a nasty ankle injury if they didn't keep their eye on the edges when performing.

Either side of the runway were several rows of old ex-cinema flip seats. They had been rescued from a skip when the city had pulled down the Roxy a block or two down from the Doll House. They looked more than a little tired and worn out.

Down the opposite side stage steps, her eyes wandered, taking in the main club room as she made a beeline toward the bar. She liked to think of herself as the Doll House's unofficial hostess and chanteuse, and on her brief stroll, she clocked Renard glowering at her from across the room.

He sat alone in the semi-darkness of a booth, nursing his drink and grinding his teeth as he took in Doris' soufflé sleeves and the tea length cut of her dress. She gave him the cold shoulder, then settled herself down onto a barstool in front of the Doll House's distinguished bartender, Dick Van Damme.

Behind the counter top he was washing and polishing a highball glass. He was a broad shouldered 6-4, clad in a single-breasted, classic black evening suit with narrow lapels and a tailored waist. The open shirt collar didn't reveal any expensive chains, but his gold, fixed back cufflinks were a sight to behold.

"Hey," she greeted him, "Be a sweetheart—I need a whiskey sour, like you wouldn't believe."

He pulled a face, his forehead creasing in emphasis. "I thought lover boy over in the corner booth," he tipped his head towards Renard, "got you your drink."

She grumbled. "Don't even mention him. I don't know how I'm going to get through the night with him leering like that."

He put the highball glass back on the shelf, saying, "We're not all as flawless as you, Doris." He turned to face her, leaning his back against chiller units, hands raised. "What can I say? The guy's obviously enamored with you and, well, who can blame him? You're a catch."

Doris waved her hand as if swatting away a fly. Dick said: "Just let him lurk for a week or two and he'll forget all about you; he'll have moved on to the next mademoiselle."

In a flash, the bar owner, Robbin Farley, stormed out from his office and stomped his stumpy legs over to the counter. Robbin wore a spread collar shirt and a pair of chinos. His arms crossed, while his choleric eyes zeroed in on Doris' perturbed countenance. "Who's the loafer smoking weed in the changeroom with Virgo and Echidna?" he asked.

Doris fluttered a dismissive hand through the air. "Relax. He's a paying customer and it's a dead night. Be grateful he's here at all."

Robbin brindled like a junkyard dog. "Hey! I've yet to see a dime from that schmuck!"

Doris removed some cash from her handbag and held it out in front of his face like a lure. With a greasy smile he snatched the bills from her hand.

"Happy?" she asked. Her eyelids fluttered, as she brought her index finger in front of her lips. "Now, hush. The show's about to start."

The house lights dimmed. Throughout the room all chatter ceased. Dick cleared his throat, then reached for the microphone holstered at the side of the bar.

In his Greatest Showman voice, he announced: "Ladies, gentleman, and non-binary friends! Introducing to the stage for your delicious delectation: the mother of monsters, the mistress of mayhem, the she-viper of Puebla…Echidna Extraña."

A fanfare from the sound system, Echidna hit the spotlight right on cue, and took the stage, in a half-woman and half-snake costume. Under the stage lights, the viridescent sequins of her scales radiated with brilliance, while her self-possessed strut had the cold-blooded bearing of Tomyris, as she stood upon the severed head of Cyrus II. Dramatically she tugged the rope in her hand and dragged on stage a reluctant Cole. He anxiously shuffled towards her, before she put a hand on his chest and stopped him—a big, stupid grin plastered upon his face. She danced circles around him. Her legs and hips gyrated to the beat of *The Rocky Horror Picture Show*'s "I Can Make You a Man," lip-syncing along with the lyrics. Her stomach expanding and contracting as if she really were singing it herself—the veins of her neck visible and pulsing. In that moment, despite the sparse crowd, the Doll House was galvanized. Eventually, even Cole became caught up in the rhythm and broke out in dance.

Doris was feeling a rush, and while her feet tapped against the barstool she saw Dick's hands and fingers beat time on the bartop.

Even Virgo burst forth from the dressing room to join in on the atmosphere, losing her balance on her knock-off Jimmy Choo spike heels so she collided with Doris in a rush of high spirits.

Robbin watched on with his usual stone ambivalence, while Renard kept his eyes on Doris rather than Echidna. He shook his head at her merriment, his nose upturned by the whole affair.

Just then, Echidna's mercurial movements slowed to a constant sway. She grew stagy and stilted, staggering on her platform shoes. Her eyes glazed over and she froze. While the music continued, her lips went static. Her cheeks seemed to flush—so much so it was obvious even under her blusher. She planted herself at the edge of the short runway, looking like a deer puzzled by oncoming headlights. Behind her, Cole stopped dead in his tracks. His smile faded to an overstrung wince.

Doris and Virgo exchanged a sideways glance. This was definitely not part of Echidna's act—even though the audience was eager with anticipation to see what would happen next.

All of a sudden, the lights went out—blackness engulfed the main barroom.

In the darkness, a loud thud followed by murmured voices. What patrons there were, shifted uneasily—now unsure if this was part of the act, or not.

Then, just as quickly as they had gone off, the lighting came back on again. As eyes adjusted to the burst of illumination, people were confronted with something more than just an ad-lib.

There, splayed out in front of the stage, laid Echidna in a serpentine pose. No obvious signs of life, she was motionless—her face and neck turning a bright cherry red, and around her made up lips there was an obvious cyan hue.

Initial shock over, Doris sprang into action. She pushed her way through the people now surrounding the body, muttering "Sick bastards" when she saw several punters filming with their cell phones. "Give me some room here!"

Kneeling down as best she could, she checked Echidna's wrist and neck for any signs of a pulse, but found none. The skin was already becoming cool to the touch.

Standing, she turned to the group that had amassed around her and declared, "She's dead."

Virgo gasped. "Echidna's dead?"

There were sounds of shock and surprise from what had become Echidna's final audience.

Doris started to size up who she felt were the obvious suspects that surrounded her.

Before the blackout: Cole was on the stage. One look at his eyes told her he was still buzzing from the weed. Still didn't rule him out though.

Dick stood watching from behind the bar. He always seemed like a nice guy—but didn't they say that about serial killers as well?

And Robbin—a poisoned apple if ever there was one—had been sat on the barstool right next to Doris–his Shirley Temple seemingly forever untouched.

After the blackout: Cole had jumped off the stage and stumbled through the theater's stalls. Dick had kept a close eye on the situation from the area of the bar, and Robbin had been halfway across the room when the house lights came back on.

Just as Doris took note of everyone's whereabouts, she caught Cole at the edge of her vision, inching toward the main entrance. She tilted her head up, her voice loud enough for everyone to hear.

"Everybody stay put!" Then, she gestured to the front and back of the building. "Virgo, lock the doors. And Dick, call the cops."

Virgo beat Cole to the doorknob and stood nose-to-nose with him, before he finally backed down and rejoined the group in the middle of the room.

Dick nodded, then scrambled to dig his phone from his jacket pocket. He had 911 on speed dial—and a Louisville slugger under the bar top—just for 'emergencies.'

Robbin looked down at Echidna's body, then turned to the crowd. "Everybody remain calm. There's been an accident."

Doris' bottom-heavy lips pouted, in a dubious moue—her index finger propped upon her pointed chin. "No, I don't think so." She leant forward so she was level with Robbin's face: "I believe someone here has committed murder."

Robbin glared back at her. "Whoa! "Let's not jump to any conclusions here." He shook his head, his hands gesturing from the stage, to the place where Echidna's body had landed. "It looks like she fell off the stage during the power cut."

The patrons mumbled to one another in agreement.

Doris tried to hold back her obvious frustration. "Okay," pause, deep breath in, "then how do you account for Echidna's performance?" She paused for several relaxing breaths, but she knew Robbin didn't have an answer. She bent forwards again, eye to eye. "Echidna never chokes like that. She looked worn out, unwell even." She pointed towards Echidna's lifeless face. "Also, take a peek at the color of her lips." The patrons leaned in for a better view. "That's not lip liner or lipstick, baby. They're edges are as blue as a bluebonnet in May. Believe me, honey, that is nowhere near normal."

Her audience muttered in concord as she continued. "If you ask me, Echidna was poisoned before she ever took the stage."

In unison, the crowd set their sights on the bartender.

Dick adopted a truculent stance, standing on the balls of his feet, hands raised as if he were surrendering.

"Hey, now, everyone, let's take it easy here. I've no qualms with Echidna. Hell, I often covered her bar tab, so why would I do a thing like this?"

Robbin glared at the bartender, but remained silent as the patrons muttered and mumbled amongst themselves until Doris had finally had enough.

"All right! Enough, fellas. I mean, who died and made you lot judge, jury, and executioner?"

Among the crowd the dissenters fell silent, while over at the bar Dick's hands were now placed over his heart. "I didn't even serve Echidna a drink." He pointed an accusing finger in Cole's direction. "What about the weed you plied her with before the show? Who's to say you didn't lace it with something?"

Once all eyes came back on Cole, his movements became restless. He bit at the chewed end of his thumbnail, eyes staring wide with unease.

"If the pot was laced," said Robbin, "then why isn't Virgo experiencing any of the same symptoms as Echidna?"

Virgo tilted her head downward, her eyes closed and her arms waving about in front of her, until she had everyone's attention. "I didn't smoke with them," she chimed in. "I was too busy putting on my face."

The patrons redirected their animosity back towards Cole.

He crossed his arms, pointedly looking toward the backstage area, thinking about the exit that led out into alleyway—pressure mounting as each passing second slipped through his fingers. Then without warning he erupted into a dead sprint, trying to get to the backstage area.

Renard broke into hot pursuit, and Cole failed to keep ahead of the French Canadian's pace. Renard tackled Cole to the ground, mere feet from the backdoor. Using a wrestler's grappling hold—his mesomorphic form pressed against Cole's, holding the man down by a tumult of knees and interlocked arms—he had Cole pinned to the floor. "Stay down, buddy!"

Doris raised an eyebrow. Her lips parted in a coy simper. In the midst of mayhem, she now saw Renard in a totally new light—

fascination and allure rekindled within her. The sight of his muscles alone, was enough to make a woman swoon.

Cole retaliated as best he could, his limbs trying to push against the full weight of Renard, in a desperate bid for freedom. "I didn't do anything! I swear! "Let me go."

Renard sneered. His upper lip curled to a crooked, almost theatrical smirk. "Oh, yeah? Why'd you run then?"

Cole banged his forehead against the floor. "I can't be here when the cops come," he said, "but I didn't kill Echidna." His face scrunched to an aggrieved pucker. "I have a warrant out for my arrest; not for murder, for petty theft charges." He crowed. "I may be a lot of things, but I'm not a killer."

"Yeah, right," said Renard. "Save it for the cops."

At the Doll House front entrance, the doorknob rattled. Then, the person on the other side pounded on the door. "Police! Open up!"

Robbin dashed to unlock the door and let them in. Two patrolmen entered cautiously, not quite sure what to expect, holsters unclipped but guns not drawn. Some of the clientele gave them a predatory eye over, and pronounced them "Nice…"

Still with his hand close to the butt of his gun, one said, "We got a call about a potential homicide. Is that's what's happened here?" He looked over at the body of Echidna on the floor.

Behind the pair the main door was pushed wide and Doris caught a glimpse of a plainclothes detective. He stood in the entrance and flashed his badge as the two uniforms nodded acknowledgements.

"Detective Barrett, Fifteenth Precinct." He looked in his early 50s, salt'n'pepper black hair, stubble starting to show through—given the time of night it was understandable.

Doris approached him. "That's your man." She pointed towards Cole—ensnared underneath Renard. "Right there."

The detective gave the signal and the cops took it from there. They relieved Renard of his seizure duties, grabbing Cole by the collar of his suede jacket, hands immediately behind his back, handcuffs clicking loudly in the silence.

On his feet, Cole shouted, "This is a mistake! I didn't do anything! Why would I?"

Regardless, the two uniformed patrolmen frog marched him out and into their patrol car, heading back to the Fifteenth.

*****

Several hours passed as Detective Barrett took down names, addresses and statements—the patrons leaving one by one, no doubt to recount every 'sordid detail' on social media, before finally returning to the banal tediums of everyday life.

Doris turned to Renard. He met her gaze with interest. His skepticism now faded to enchantment.

"Hey," she said. "How are you holding up?"

"To be honest with you, I've had better days."

Doris chuckled softly. "Haven't we all, honey."

A pained expression crossed his face as he sighed heavily. "And, to be really honest with you, all my best days were spent with you." He reached out and took her hand. "I miss you, ma chérie."

She blushed. Her free hand fidgeted with the wig atop her head. "Well, lucky for you, you look like you have plenty of good days left in you."

Renard smiled. He moved in closer to her. "You wouldn't be interested in going back to my place, would you?" he asked. "Maybe catch up on lost time?"

She shrugged. "If you're offering me a drink, I won't refuse."

"I think a cocktail might do us both some good."

On their way out, Doris was stopped by a tired-looking Detective Barrett. He did his best to smile pleasantly as he wagged an assertive finger at her.

"What can I do you for, Detective?"

"Please, don't go planning a weekend getaway anytime soon," he said. "The case isn't quite closed just yet."

He took out his wallet and passed her his card.

"Look, I know it's been a hell of a night, but…. If you feel something might have slipped your mind, let me know." He winked. "In my line of work, every single detail counts."

Doris inserted the card into her handbag. "Thank you, Detective Barrett. I'll be sure to give you a call."

*****

Renard lived in a neo-Tudor home in the Old Town district, on the outskirts of the city. A tidy configuration of high-pitched roofs and pseudo half-timbered and whitewashed exteriors.

Renard paid the taxi (as befitted a gentleman) and once through the front door, Doris headed for the open plan living room, sinking into the seat cushion of a high-backed carved armchair. Meanwhile, in the kitchen, Renard poured a couple of glasses of red wine. Doris knew the wine would be like Renard himself—cheap, but palatable. And at that moment in time it suited her just fine.

While waiting for her drink, her eyes wandered the living room: soft side lighting complimented the various dark woods, family photographs, ornate reproduction tapestries, casement windows… All glimpses into Renard's character, conscious or subconscious.

Then something—some anomaly—made her stop. Her gaze halted by an old picture. "You still have this photo?" she asked. "The one of us at the Doll House."

Renard called out from the kitchen, "I couldn't bring myself to take it down." He paused. "Call me sentimental, but I wanted something to remember you by."

Doris smiled to herself. Pleasant perceptions tunneled their way into the framework of her brain. Suddenly, all of Renard's chary attributes were reconsidered; his ogling became pining and his transgressive actions became nothing more than timid courting.

While she pondered what was taking him so long, her mind revisited how the night had unfolded. The performance, the death, the chaos. Cole's self-justifying words had rattled her to her core—why would he kill Echidna? A question Doris could not answer satisfactorily.

She shook her head. That was going to be a matter better left to Detective Barrett and his analytical processes.

Yet the mental question still poked at her brain.

For a person who smoked the same supposedly laced weed as Echidna, Cole did not exhibit any of the same symptoms as her. A chill ran slithered along curves of her spine. Perhaps, Cole was innocent after all? Perhaps it wasn't the weed that had killed her. Doris hesitated.

Then another thought struck her. The specter of a whiskey sour in a Delmonico glass placed upon the makeup vanity.... The same drink Renard had ordered for her back at the bar....

Just then, Renard came into the living room with two wine glasses in his hands. As he sat down on the sofa beside her, she desperately tried to make the muscles in her face relaxed to a vacant expression.

But it didn't help, and it felt like the capacious room had somehow compressed down to the size of an inset cabinet. Her lips pursed and her mouth felt dry—leaving her feeling that she was backed into a corner with a psychopath.

He offered her a glass of boxed cabernet. "It's not exactly Château Lafite Rothschild," he said, "but it gets the job done. That's for sure."

Doris set the glass aside. She rose to her feet. Her knees barely supporting her weight. "Excuse me. I...I need to use the powder room."

He scratched at the stubble on his chin. The smile faded from his face. "Okay," he said. "I'll be here when you get back."

She hurried off to the downstairs bathroom

With the door shut behind her, she caught her breath, then removed Detective Barrett's business card from her handbag and dialed the number. Each second seemed to drag as the phone trilled, until....

"Hello, Detective Barrett, Homicide.

In a hushed tone, Doris said, "I'm in trouble. I'm at 357 Connaught Drive, over in the Old Town district. Please, send help."

She was suddenly jolted by Renard knocking at the bathroom door.

"Hey, Doris," he said. "Are you okay in there?" A fearsome reticence accrued in the absence of acknowledgement. He stomped his foot. "Did

I do something to offend you?"

She remained silent, her phone still pressed to her ear.

"Don't worry," said Detective Barrett. "I'm on my way."

She hung up, put the phone back in her bag, ran some water as if washing her hands. "I'll be out in a minute or two, honey." She wasn't sure if she'd managed to keep her fear out of her voice.

The knocking grew to pounding, as Renard increased the intensity of his punches. "Open up!" She remained silent. He tried to sound calm. "Look, it doesn't have to be like this." The door lock rattled and it looked like the hinges would give from the doorframe.

"Open up, damn you!"

The door juddered and the paneling started to crack and split from the force of his fists. "I'm going to take great pleasure in wringing your pretty little neck, and dumping your body over the Jackson Reservoir road bridge."

Doris panicked. As the barrier between the two of them started to break, her hand fumbled through her handbag for a can of pepper spray. Seriously, she knew she had put a fresh can in her bag two days ago… There, in one of the damn side pockets….

Putting that to one side, she ripped the toilet seat off of the commode—she needed a physical weapon, and that was as good as anything else available.

Moments later he burst through the splintered wood, hinges barely hanging onto the doorframe. She could see the state of his knuckles, battered and bloodied, along with the metal figurine he'd used to smash the door lock.

It was down to a basic Fight or Flight reflex—she had been a fighter, ever since her childhood—and attack was her only way forward.

She immediately dowsed his face and head with pepper spray, sending him staggering sideways into the bathroom wall, the back of his head cracking the vanity mirror. Then, she swung her other arm and struck him with the toilet seat. The hard plastic collided with the side of his face, the bright chrome fittings leaving jagged scratches down the side of his face. Dazed by her assault, he slid down the wall and ended up collapsed. That bought her enough time to veer around him and get out of the confines of the wrecked bathroom.

Now all she had to do was successfully get away from the house without Renard coming after her. Yes, he knew where she lived, but she didn't think he would be stupid enough to try to kill her again.

As she flung open the front door she practically ran into the arms of Detective Barrett, accompanied by the two patrol cops that had attended the Doll House murder.

"Oh. Thank. God," she said. "He's in there—in the bathroom." She indicated to the two patrol officers to go into the house.

To Detective Barrett she said, "It's Renard. He's the killer. He poisoned Echidna when he tried to poison me." She turned and pointed towards the living room. "Check the wine on the table."

They found Renard, still sprawled against the bathroom wall, dazed and moaning, "I'm going to kill the bitch. This time I'll make sure I get the right one…." One of the officers applied handcuffs while the other radioed for medical support to attend.

As they waited for the ambulance to arrive, Detective Barrett asked: "What happened here?"

Doris tried to smile, but the feeling of tiredness was catching up with her. "Renard tried to poison my whiskey sour back at the Doll House. When he killed Echidna by mistake, he told me he wanted to make up, then brought me back here to finish the job."

As the patrolmen escorted Renard outside past Doris and the Detective, Renard made to have the final word:

"You're nothing but a has-been busted queen, you know that? You're going to get what's coming to you, one of these days."

Doris scoffed. "You're really going to call me busted when you're the one in a pair of cuffs? You poor thing. Don't you know? Your best days really are behind you."

Detective Barrett shot the cops an authoritative look. "Make sure you read this killer his rights. Don't want him getting off on a technicality," he said. "He'll have plenty of time to talk to his lawyer—though I doubt very much if the DA will consider cutting him a deal."

He turned to Doris, with a slightly sheepish smile on his face. "I apologize for the outburst." He cleared his throat, and a touch of concern sounded in his voice. "Are you okay?"

Doris twirled a finger through the bangs of her bouffant wig. "I am now," she paused a little, possibly for effect, then said, "Thank you. I owe you my life. How could I possibly repay you?"

He shook his head. "No thanks are necessary. If anything I should be the one thanking you. You just saved me a lot of time and effort."

She tossed her head back, letting her voice drop a little in tone and volume. "Well, there has to be something I can do. For a start, how does a free show at the Doll House sound?"

"You know what?" Detective Barrett smiled, "I just might have to take you up on that offer."

Room Five at Motel Two
Ed Teja

The intermittent squeak coming from the right rear wheel grew more shrill about the time she left what the sign claimed were the city limits of Magdalena, New Mexico.

Not a city. And she doubted that was just her opinion.

The lonely road went to another blip on the road called Datil. It only mattered because that's where she intended to turn left onto Highway 12 and head south toward the town of Reserve.

Back roads out here were open and felt free.

If it weren't for that annoying noise, the squeal from the rear, Helen would have been optimistic about her chances. Who'd look for her out here?

But in those wide open spaces, the sudden shift the rear wheel made from annoying squeak to a shrill whine had her cringing and gripping the steering wheel tighter—as if that made a difference. She couldn't help tightening her grip. The damn sound struck a chord. Whatever car part was protesting, calling out for attention, it sounded like some goddamn banshee screaming, warning her that things were about to go south.

It was banshees that did that, wasn't it?

She couldn't remember, but she recalled something about banshees and premonitions of the apocalypse or a financial collapse, or some cataclysmic shit.

Not at all reassuring.

That screaming didn't help her state of mind. Taking these empty highways had seemed the safest option, but if her car died out here, seeing as she'd thought it the better part of valor to ditch her cell phone, she had no way to summon help.

Nothing was close out here. In fact, the closest place to her was what they called the Very Large Array which was coming into sight on her left. It spread out all over hell and gone. Miles of antennas. Or antennae. Whatever you called them.

The installation must have cost a bundle, and she thought the name was pretty dull—Very Large Array. Not particularly creative, that name. But, hey, government.

She'd read that the scientists had put up all those dish antennae and pointed every single one out into deep space so they could convince the Martians not to invade us.

The conversation had been going on a long time now... as long as she could remember. By now, they had to be negotiating terms.

The array place wouldn't do her any good if her car crapped out, if that damn wheel stopped turning. Heck, even if the array was working fine, in tip-top shape, and the Martians were home, it wasn't likely she could convince alien life forms to call Triple-A for her. Even if she could interrupt whoever was chatting with them and ask them for help, even if there was cell service out here, who would she call?

She'd let her road service expire long ago. When was it, something like five years back now? Yeah, back when she lost the job at the bank.

You wouldn't think counting money accurately and not accidentally pocketing some wouldn't be so hard to do, but there you were. Here she was.

Anyway, now that she remembered that, she gripped the damn wheel and willed Belle to make it another thirteen miles to Datil.

Belle was the name she'd given her 2000 Impala.

Not that she'd be safe in Datil. But she'd been there once and remembered seeing a gas station.

Of course, if she stayed in Datil, the creeps after her could find her even easier. The town maybe had 100 people in it. She would have been less visible in metropolitan Magdalena (pop. 938 according to the sign).

Besides, gas station or not, getting her car fixed, well, that took money.

Towing charges would add a bunch to it.

It wasn't like she had ignored the problem.

Back before she scampered or scarpered, or whatever they called getting your ass out of town, she'd taken the car to the garage twice. Naturally, it wouldn't squeak for them.

You can't fix what ain't squeaking.

Well, the whole damn car was on her last legs. The old girl was almost as old as Helen, but she hadn't kept itself in good shape. Belle didn't do a thing to help keep herself in shape. Not a single thing.

She didn't know if twenty-three was old for a car. Seemed like that was old. It seemed reasonable that some smart person probably had created a conversion from car to human years, like they had for a dog's age. She remembered that as being seven to one. If it was the same, and then that made Belle around one-hundred and fifty or sixty something.

Multiplying twenty-three by seven while she drove, she couldn't keep the last digits in her head. She wasn't a multitasker, but that sounded right. Then he remembered the conversion depended on the breed. Of dog. The conversion thing for dogs depended on the breed. So, for a car, the model and the maintenance a person did probably factored into it, if you wanted to be picky.

And, while Helen had never actually changed Belle's oil, she had been religiously putting in a quart of brand new oil every time she stopped for gas, which was a lot more often that she would have liked.

What was Chevy thinking about when they put those big motors in these cars? It wasn't like you were gonna race them, so maybe the oil companies paid them something to promote people buying those big engines.

Who knew?

The good news of the moment was that Belle didn't seem particularly flustered by the whine from her right rear. Of course, ears weren't standard equipment on cars, not American cars, anyway, as far as Helen knew, so Belle wouldn't hear it. But if it got much louder, she risked getting pulled over for impersonating a police car... the siren, see?

Except sirens didn't sound like that anymore and the real concern wasn't cops. Not at all. But attracting attention meant the creeps might notice her faster. Finding a place to hide seemed the logical course of action. Ironically, after making the biggest score of her life, Helen was cash strapped. To hide, she'd have to find a job. Of course, she wasn't likely to find something as exciting as her last job as a customer service rep in a call center (joke, ha ha!) and she couldn't exactly produce references.

Maybe she could work as a waitress, or in a mom and pop store. It couldn't be anything big. Not a place that filed computerized records and sent them off to computerized offices that did whatever they did with what she'd heard called big data.

Interesting term, big data.

Someone like her, who tried to stay off the grid, probably had smaller data than most people. Less of it, for sure. Like, she'd never filed her income tax return, so they wouldn't have any of that. But she had several social security numbers. That made her feel good. When she worked using someone else's social security number, they'd get credit for her income and that meant they'd have more money when they retired.

When she made the turn at Datil, right there at the gas station/convenience store, Belle seemed a little reluctant to accelerate back up to speed. It pleased her that she'd remembered the place correctly. It pleased her even more that the shrill whine had suddenly faded.

Southward ho, the wagons.

Hey, she was on an adventure. She and Belle were out on the open road, and there wasn't a cop car in sight and, more important, no sign of that silver SUV she'd spotted two days back. The silver SUV that she was sure belonged to the rather humorless guys she'd worked for in Albuquerque.

She wondered what kind of gas mileage they were getting.

Fortunately, they didn't know Belle. Not on sight, anyway. If they did... well, she wasn't entirely sure what would have happened. They would definitely want to express their displeasure at her abrupt departure, especially since she'd left with some of their... call it their product line.

Served them right for being self-centered bastards who weren't supportive at Helen's attempts at self-improvement. Well, she wasn't trying to improve herself, to be fair. Just her circumstances. But she needed to improve them far away from the people who provided the inventory she would sell to finance a better life.

Unfortunately, like most start-ups, she was starting out cash poor and Belle, her right rear, was starting to complain loudly again.

The car began slowing.

She pushed the throttle down.

Belle accelerated, but sluggishly. And then slowed.

Not good.

Taking her foot off the gas, she let the car come to a stop at her own pace, guiding her safely off to the side of the road.

Getting out to stand beside her old friend, Helen inhaled the air. Tinged with sage, it smelled fresh. Then she took a tentative look around at the beautiful scenery. At the lovely, completely empty, two-lane road. Reluctantly, she turned her gaze to the car, taking in the dent in the right front fender left by a shopping cart, the sunbaked and peeling paint on the roof over the windshield, and then stopping to linger, staring at the flat tire.

The totally shredded flat tire.

The bent rim.

"I guess the wheel bearing stopped bearing the wheel," she said, channeling her inner mechanic.

This was known in automotive circles as Not Good. Even Helen knew this was something that changing the tire would not solve, even if she had a spare tire to put on. Which, for the record, she didn't. The damn things were expensive.

She'd come too far from Datil to go back there and anyway, it seemed visible, vulnerable to passing Silver SUVs. There had to be some place south, further down the road where she could find help. It wouldn't do to worry about how far "down the road" help might be. She had no options. Happily, she was wearing jeans and trainers.

The idea of leaving Belle sitting there alone bothered her. Of course, this was New Mexico, not New York, but she'd risked her life for the stuff in that trunk. She wouldn't rest comfortably with it out of her sight, and being comfortable was the entire reason she'd taken the risk.

Not that the boys from Albuquerque knew the car or would likely drive along and pop the trunk on every abandoned car they came across.

They wouldn't want to attract attention.

No, they would want to find her—live and in person. They'd want to take her to a quiet place where they could convince her to tell them where she had their shit stashed. They'd want her to hand over the airline carry-on bag. A bag she'd never carried on.

The original plan, their plan, involved her catching a flight to Phoenix—hence the bag. She'd made the trip twice before, with Nick. He introduced her to the people at the other end and showed her how and where to make the exchange.

This trip was her first solo run and as much fun as it was, she decided to make it her last trip. There was no future in doing these runs for this crew. It didn't pay enough that she could completely stop doing the escort work for them, so what was the point? Retirement at twenty-three on their money was more appealing.

She considered getting the money and disappearing in Phoenix, but she didn't like Phoenix that much. But starting off right away gave her a head start. The day before the trip, she drove to the airport, left Belle in the parking lot, and took a taxi home. The next day, when Nick dropped her off with the carry-on and her ticket, she waited until he drove off from the "loading and unloading zone only" before walking out. She put the bag in Belle's trunk and drove away.

As luck would have it, that carry-on, with its extendable handle and little wheels for whizzing through the airport, was going to have to earn its keep.

Life is filled with lessons, and Helen quickly learned that tiny wheels and rough asphalt do not coexist well. Alternatively, the soft sand and intermittent verge along the road made walking (and rolling) down the highway the better option.

Traveling toward her unknown destination with her cargo bouncing erratically behind her, Helen was given multiple reasons to regret that her employer had shopped for travel luggage at a box store.

For one thing, the labeling was incorrect. This particular bag had been marked "traveler's friend," when, clearly, "cheap shit" would have been more appropriate.

After one wheel fell off, Helen discovered that the "quickly converts to a backpack" feature involved painful cheap plastic straps. Still, it worked. As a result, she was only suffering from minor dehydration and leg cramps when she came around a bend in the road and discovered Valhalla, Nirvana... one of those paradise places.

When salvation came into view, it consisted of four rather dilapidated buildings.

The closest building was a gas station. Not a very prosperous gas station with a service bay where a person could perhaps make a wheel bearing once more bear a wheel.

Next door to it sat a house. A faded, wooden-frame that might have looked all bright and cheerful back in the Depression era.

A hand-painted sign over the door of the next building, a squat adobe building that had to date from the days when Spain ruled the land, announced Lizzy's Diner. A sign on the door said it was open, although peeking in the window, she didn't see anyone inside.

Clearly, she'd missed the lunch rush.

Just beyond the diner were the low-lying, paint-peeling, grubby walls of a motel.

"MOTEL TWO," a large sign said. Well, it actually said, "_OTEL TW_," but Helen cleverly filled in the blanks.

Best of all, it didn't look totally dysfunctional. A sign clearly marked the "_FF_CE" where she could check in. A red neon sign in the window actually worked and advertised vacancies. Better yet, unlike the gas station, she saw someone inside.

Not entirely a ghost town, then.

The filthy door squeaked when she opened it. A little bell over the door that rang when it opened wasn't nearly as loud as the squeak.

The office was rather well-kept. Clean and neat. A homemade banner on the wall, needlepoint, she guessed, said, "New Mexico, Land of Enchantment."

The man behind the desk looked up. An old guy. Not as old as her car (converted to people years) but maybe forty. He wore ugly metal-frame glasses, had a short haircut that looked like his barber hated him, and a short-sleeve shirt and tan slacks. And there was the tag on his shirt that said MOTEL TWO: CHEERFUL GEORGE.

"Hey, there," he said. "Welcome to Stopping Place, New Mexico."

Strange name for a town.

"Is that where I am?"

"It sure is. And I am Cheerful George. Can I help you?"

"My car broke down," she said, jerking her thumb in the direction, vaguely, of Datil.

Cheerful George nodded. "According to the visitor's bureau, sixty percent of our visitors are here for that reason."

"You have a visitor's bureau?"

"My wife, Patty Anne. She also runs the diner."

"Not Lizzy, then."

He shook his head. "Lizzy disappeared a while back. Patty Anne took it over."

That made the place sound better. Someone else had disappeared here. Maybe she could, too.

"What about the other forty percent?"

The question spread a thoughtful wrinkle across his forehead. "Hunters, mostly. It ain't hunting season right now, though, so we got rooms."

"I'll take one," she said.

"Cash or credit?"

"Credit card." She had one that she'd slipped out of her last boyfriend's wallet. It was one he kept for dire emergencies. This situation definitely qualified as dire.

"Need a photo ID," he said.

She smiled. Fortunately, Harry Arnold only used his first initial and last name. So she'd convinced a computer graphics guy she dated to make a copy of her driver's license that gave her name as Helen Arnold. Laminated, it looked perfect.

"How long you intend to stay with us here at Motel Two, Miss Arnold?" he asked.

A reasonable question.

"Until I can get my car fixed."

He nodded. "You got a good mechanic?"

"I got no mechanic," she said.

"I could recommend one."

"Great. Who is that?"

"My brother, Bill."

"How do I get my car to him?"

"I'll have him fetch it with his tow truck. All for one low price. I'll put it on your credit card if you like."

She liked and gave him the car keys, the model, make, and license plate number.

"That's a classic," Cheerful said.

"It's a beater."

"Still... fixed up, I bet she could be worth a bit."

"I guess. Will he get it soon? I hate the thought of her sitting there, maybe getting vandalized." Or having the goons catch up to her.

Cheerful nodded. "Right away. Don't you worry."

His wink suggested he suspected there was more to her need for urgency than vandals.

"And don't worry about your privacy," Cheerful said. "We know folks don't come out here to socialize."

Puzzled, but pleased, she shifted the carry-on/backpack into a less uncomfortable position, then scooped up her room key, and wandered down the row of doors to Room Five.

The air in the room was musty, as if the room had been closed up for a while, but the air con came on with a roar and soon was blasting cold air.

She latched the door and put on the useless little chain.

The blessings of her refuge continued as she found the shower had hot water and the towels were thin, but serviceable and clean.

Overall, the room would serve as a substitute for heaven long enough for her to shower and pass out on the bed.

*****

Hours later, she woke, cold and disoriented. The air con was still blasting away and it took her a few moments to get… her bearings.

Yup, even fuzzy headed, she remembered she was there because of Belle's non-bearing bearing. She got up.

"Damn, but I'm hungry," she said.

Her thoughts turned to her bag. She didn't see it. Even though the door was still latched, her heart pounded as she jumped up, and searched the room, only to find it lying untouched under the bed where she vaguely remembered stuffing it.

She dressed in her dirty clothes. There were fresh ones in the car and if the tow truck had brought it, she could get them. She pushed the bag back under the bed and headed out. Couldn't drag the damn thing around forever.

The warm, dark air outside the room smelled fresh and invigorating, infused with the smell of sage and a perfume that had to come from a flower.

A light from the diner reached out to her and hooked itself to the hunger pangs in her belly. The place still looked empty, but jiggling the door handle opened it and she wandered inside.

"Anyone home?" she called.

"Menus are on the tables, honey," a woman called out. "Seat yourself and take a look. I'll be out in a bit."

She slid into a booth by the window where she could look out at the road in the dimming light.

"Expecting someone?"

Helen glanced up and saw an older woman in an apron, carrying an order book. "Are you Mrs. Cheerful?" she asked.

"I'm Patty Anne. Cheerful is my husband," she said. "Ain't he just got the strangest name?"

"I'm not expecting anyone," she said.

Just watching her back.

"Good," Patty Anne said.

That seemed odd. "Good?"

"Few enough know Stopping Place is here. Even folks who intend to come here can have a tough time finding it."

Helen thought about the drive and then her walk here. What she remembered about it was that it pretty much followed a straight shot down a flat road all the way from Datil.

"Why do they have trouble finding it?"

She smiled. "They usually go right by without seeing us. Even if they see us, the place looks deserted."

It did that. Then she laughed. "Few people stop at Stopping Place."

"I didn't see a sign," she said.

The woman gave her a tight-lipped smile and shook her head. "Whenever the fool road department puts one up, we take her back down."

"Why?"

She sighed. "A body gets tired of having too many folks traipsing all over the place. Having a few, like you and Al, well, that's fine. But more'n that and… well, just plain whew!"

"Whew," sure summed things up for Helen, all right. "Who is Al?"

"That's your neighbor. Fine young man in Room Six."

Stomach pains refocused her attention. "Can I get a big burger and fries and a chocolate shake?"

"You sure can, darling." She wrote it down, like she might forget it. "Best in town, too."

"Where else is there to eat?"

Patty Anne laughed. "No place at all. Nary a one."

Then she disappeared into the kitchen, leaving Helen alone with her thoughts. Unfortunately, that wasn't a particularly comfortable place at that moment.

It got her wondering who they'd send after her. Nick was the most likely person. He had a way of finding people. Of course, that was in the city. Out here, he couldn't just threaten enough people until he found someone who knew where she was.

With luck, they'd expect that she'd run to Santa Fe or over to Oklahoma, maybe. Hell, if she had made good time, she could be in Seattle by now. Well, Las Vegas, anyway.

Which wasn't a bad idea. Vegas, that is. She didn't know anyone there anymore, and that was a plus in terms of staying hidden. They wouldn't have any leads. And how hard could it be to find a buyer for a backpack full of top-grade junk in Las Vegas?

Better yet, she'd stick to her plan and get to Jessie, over in Flagstaff. Why sell the stuff wholesale when, for a small cut, Jessie would handle the repackaging, dilution, and distribution?

Retail was a slower path to riches, but she wasn't in a rush. She didn't see getting rich as a momentary thing, like winning the lottery. No, it was a process, a journey to be savored.

She just had to live long enough to savor it.

But Vegas was a sweet thought too. She smacked her lips at the prospect of cashing in those particular chips. And she wouldn't blow it all gambling this time, the way she did with the money she'd taken from Jerry when she worked for him running that scam on old folks.

That hadn't been a big haul, but having that much in her hands all at once got her a little dizzy and she'd been stupid.

"Never double down on tens," she told Patty Anne when she came out. She carried an enormous platter of food and a tall, thick shake that was the creamiest brown Helen could imagine. Helen's mouth watered.

"I never would do that in a million years," Patty Anne said. "Eat hearty."

The food tasted wonderful.

Patty Anne told her she'd put the meal on the tab that Cheerful was running. Perfect. Her con was still working.

With a full belly, she headed over to get clothes from the car and see what Cheerful's brother might tell her.

"Wheel bearing went," the big man said. "Fucked up the axle bearings."

None of that mattered now. Only one thing did.

"Can you fix it?" she asked.

"Got to order some parts out of Socorro, but yeah. The work is a day or two once I got the parts."

She retrieved her clothes and cosmetics and headed back to her new home—Room Five of Motel Two. The motel room wasn't bad. No worse than sharing a crappy apartment with two other girls who worked for the escort service. Here she had some privacy.

But there was a downside. When she got to the room, the door stood open.

*****

Helen wished she had a gun. Not that she'd ever fired a gun, or ever wanted to shoot someone, but, stepping into the room, she was certain having one would make her feel better.

Or not.

Stepping through the door, she froze. The bed had been moved, and the bag was gone.

Her future was gone. "Idiot!" she said.

The fight went out of her and she sank down on the floor. Things had gone from bad to hopeless in a minute. Now what? If she stayed here, the goons might find her. More likely, before that, the credit card company would alert Harold and he'd cancel it. Then George would call the cops.

"Helen."

She turned and saw George peeking in the door. "What?"

He wiggled a finger. "You best come with me."

So, sooner than she expected, she was busted. She didn't have the heart to run or fight. Instead, she meekly followed George to the office.

A young man, about her age, with long hair and scruffy jeans, and Patty Anne were there. So was her bag.

The bag sat open on a coffee table and two of the many packets of white powder were open.

"This is Al," Patty Anne said. "Your neighbor."

"Hi," she said.

"You know what this stuff is?" Al asked.

"Not for sure," she lied.

"Me either," Al said. "I guess it's supposed to be junk, but it ain't."

"What then?"

He smiled. "Some substitute. You know what heroin is supposed to taste like?"

"I'm no junky," she said.

"But you thought you were carrying junk."

She made a face. "Yeah."

"So, taste it."

When she'd traveled with Nick, he had made her taste the product. "If you are going to be handling it, you need to know what it tastes and smells like," he told her.

Curious, she sniffed at the white powder. It didn't smell right. She wet a finger and poked it in the powder, then tasted it.

"Ugh!"

This wasn't anything like the stuff he'd had in her sample. It was acrid, bitter. No, more sour.

"Try the other one," George said.

She wet a finger and put it in and tasted it. "Same awful shit," she said.

"Seems you been hauling around a mix of baking soda and maybe rat poison," Patty Anne said. "Not a good recipe for anything."

"Fuck," she said. "I don't get it. Nick had to have swapped it."

"What was the deal?" George asked.

Dazed, she spilled it out, explaining about the flight to Phoenix and her plan. "Why would they give me bad stuff?" she asked. "I was taking it to regular customers."

George smiled. "They could have been testing you, seeing if you'd deliver the product or do what you did. It might be the cops got wise, and they wanted you busted with whatever crap is in that bag. It could be they hoped you'd pull it off and get paid for nothing."

She groaned.

"Ultimately, who knows?" Al asked. "It ain't like you can call them and ask for clarification."

And it didn't matter.

"And you can't go back," Helen said.

George went to the coffeepot and poured some into a Styrofoam cup. "There is good news," he said.

She laughed. "Really?"

He pointed. "Given this is shit, there probably ain't no one after you at all. Why spend a lot of time and money chasing someone who has nothing of value?"

There was that.

"We could've kept your bag and left you thinking you had their stuff and we ripped you off," Al said.

That had dawned on her. "Why didn't you?" she asked.

Patty Anne smiled. "We decided you are one of us, dearie. Motel Two at Stopping Place is where some of us come to rest for the rest of our lives."

"We have no other place to go," Al said.

"Stay here? And do what?" she asked.

"We need a night clerk for the motel," George said.

"At least once a week," Al teased.

"Al works for Bill," Patty Anne said. "When he has any work."

Al grinned. "Well, seems that right now, we are restoring a 2000 Impala. Should bring a decent price when he's done."

Her car.

"Since you can't leave, you won't be needing it," Patty Anne said.

"And the proceeds will help settle your bill, squaring you up," George said.

"So I work for you?"

"You get your room and board and we can work out a salary," he said.

"Plus, if anyone comes around looking for a gal on the run, none of us knows a soul like that," Al said. "That means you can rest."

She sighed. "So I'm the night clerk at Motel Two at Stopping Place," she said.

"Ten miles from Datil and two miles from nowhere," Al grinned.

Nowhere, she thought. The place they were all going.

"Don't take no out-of-state checks," George said.

Previous Times
Gene Kendall

Detective John Lane certainly didn't resemble any detective from those prime-time cop shows. An unassuming man of medium height with a rapidly balding scalp and at least one chin too many, he was past forty, usually adorned with a measured, inscrutable expression. A crumpled suit hung on him this morning like it didn't want to be there.

Those shows on the television, they were something. Car chases, shootouts, zany street informants. And they'd gotten so stylish, lately. Attractive young actors with feathered hair or ridiculous sideburns. There weren't a lot of hunks strutting around the station where he'd been assigned, and not a single boss who would've tolerated those chic fashions.

Detective Lane's normally sphinxlike demeanor wasn't so cryptic today. News on the radio during his ride over had outright dampened his spirits. A riot in Miami, the kind not seen since the '60s, following horrific allegations against the local PD. Reports of yet another new cult forming, this one targeting teenagers. And, of all things, Mount St. Helens had just erupted in Washington state, thanks to a sudden earthquake. It'd be days before the death count could be accurately totaled.

He'd tried turning the dial, hoping Burt Bacharach or Seals and Crofts would be there to soothe his nerves. All he got were commercials.

Were he given to pessimism, he might muse that the world had gotten knocked off its axis one evening while all her lowly citizens slept in their cozy beds. Or maybe humanity had poisoned it with something more toxic than air pollution. Inspired the poor, sick planet to go off into some insane suicide spiral, and most of society was eager to join in.

How long he'd carried this sense of unease, Lane didn't know. Maybe for over a decade now. But it got worse, each year. Was possibly deteriorating by the week. Last Tuesday, Lane's barber suggested he stop trimming his sideburns. Told Lane he was the last customer keeping those things short and stubbly. Madness had poisoned society, no doubt.

But Detective Lane had less ponderous concerns this morning, the arising day lit by a sun that seemed indifferent to the springtime. Approaching the front steps of Clarence Phieffer's sprawling lakeside home, Lane did his best to straighten out his creased suit and fix his lips back into a horizontal line.

Meeting the famed painter—the man behind countless lush, lurid, and alluring *Flint O'Connor* paperback covers—was something Detective Lane would've considered an amusing novelty, a cute party story, in a different context. In his younger days, when he still wore glasses and hadn't yet licked his asthma, he would've killed for the opportunity.

No longer a kid, today a man wrestling against middle age and still bruising over two uncleared cases from earlier this year, John Lane had to squelch any adolescent hero worship. Clarence Phieffer could make claim to being the finest commercial illustrator of his generation, but he was also now a person of interest in a grizzly crime. One that involved a faulty brake line and two victims. One still in the hospital, the other due for a graveside burial tomorrow afternoon.

Phieffer's doorbell sang a chipper ditty. Lane had to buzz it twice before Phieffer appeared at the door, offering both a pleasant smile and his palm for a shake.

"I take it you're the detective I spoke to on the phone?" asked Phieffer in a voice as amiable as it was whiskey-burned.

"That'd be me," Lane answered, squeezing the hand tight and straightening his posture. "Got this shiny badge to prove it."

Phieffer motioned for Lane to follow him inside. "I have some chilled Cokes if you'd like to join me," he said over his shoulder.

Lane indicated with a murmur that he did, as he took in the sight of Phieffer's living room. Coffered ceiling, natural lighting, Victorian armchairs, mahogany bookshelves, marble flooring, and French doors providing a view of a vibrant nearby garden. Those paperbacks had treated Clarence Phieffer quite nicely.

Above the fireplace was an oversized recreation of a classic *Flint O'Connor* cover. One of Lane's favorites, one he remembered from the window display at the bookstore across the street from his father's bakery. The painting depicted a professional thief, rugged yet princely, dressed in a tattered single-breasted suit and clutching a silver Beretta 950 that gleamed under the silvery moonlight.

And clutching Flint was an olive-skinned beauty with flirtatious eyes. The lady was clad in an evening dress far more tattered than Flint's suit, meager scraps offering only a hint of modesty. Lane's sainted mother did not possess a tolerant and broad-minded opinion of this piece, that afternoon she'd discovered the paperback in Lane's room while folding laundry.

Other kids at school were forced to endure similarly uncomfortable conversations with their mothers, regarding that debonair thief and the watercolor renditions of his lady friends. It was a nationwide controversy, but a mild one. One that passed; seemed perhaps quaint in the light of the counter-culture's assault on traditional mores.

As Detective Lane took a seat on an ornate piece of antique furniture, Phieffer entered with two icy cans of Coke and two straws. Many years ago, Lane had watched a documentary on the O'Connor phenomenon. A much younger Clarence Phieffer was interviewed, an obvious model for the hero he'd grown wealthy depicting on book covers and promotional posters. A robust, darkly handsome lad with sleek raven-black hair, mile-wide shoulders, bronzed skin, and impeccable teeth.

The man joining Lane on the couch today was barely recognizable. Still tall, yes, but his face was bloated, his nose had blossomed, and that golden skin had lightened into a sickly pallor. He wore a white silk shantung suit with an open-necked shirt. Something he paid a stylist for, Lane had to figure, something Phieffer still wore with confidence, despite his deteriorating looks.

Lane cracked open his soda and inserted the straw. "Just the two of us, Mr. Phieffer?"

Phieffer gave a slight bob of his head. "I wanted you to know, Detective, I intend to cooperate fully with your investigation. Dee was someone I still care deeply about, and Gabriel…well, despite everything, I'd like to think he was my friend."

No lawyer. Not even a mention of one. Detective Lane allowed himself a moment of optimism. Taking a pull on his straw, Lane enjoyed the sugary taste and uniquely thick texture of his chilled soda.

"I appreciate that, Mr. Phieffer. We're still early in the investigation. You need to realize, speaking to you, that doesn't mean we've made up our mind about anything. If you just answer the questions honestly, tell me what you can remember about all this unpleasantness, I think it'll help us a lot."

"Sure. Absolutely. I want to be…helpful."

"If I didn't tell you earlier, Mr. Phieffer, I am a fan of your work. Had a pile of *Flint O'Connor* paperbacks next to my bed, growing up."

"That's nice to hear, Detective. Regardless of the, ah, circumstances, it's a pleasure meeting a fan."

Lane released a gentle cough, indicating a change of topic. "Well, regarding your wife—I apologize, ex-wife…"

Phieffer lifted both hands. "Okay, now, you should know Dee and I, we were talking about starting over. Together, that is."

This young lady, Dee, Lane had spoken to her mother only an hour earlier over the phone. Sweet, midwestern lady. One who'd tried to warn her cornfed daughter about traveling to California, about the dangers she'd find there.

"That's interesting. Because based on what we've learned so far, it seemed she had moved on with Mr. Graham."

"Affairs of the heart, Detective. They're often so complicated, aren't they?" Phieffer took a lengthy sip of his soda, then readjusted himself.

"I promise you, though Dee hadn't fully cut things off with Gabriel, she had indicated that what she wanted, more than anything, was reconciliation. With me, that is."

"And is there a note or telephone message that you have indicating this?"

Phieffer muttered "no." Said it like a boy caught with a broken vase on the floor and a baseball bat hidden behind his back.

"Anyone in Dee's life that could corroborate this?"

After a pause, another muttered "no."

"Well, we're hoping she'll be able to speak again soon. I'm assuming she'll be able to verify what you've told me. Correct, Mr. Phieffer?"

Phieffer's eyes flashed. "I couldn't speak to that. Her memory, it could be…that accident, it was so awful."

"Indeed it was. And, God willing, we'll soon have some answers and you'll be able to put the awful thing behind you. Now, you hadn't been married to Dee for long before Gabriel Graham entered the picture, correct?"

His thick restless fingers tap-tap-tapped against the Coke can. "Yes. I needed a model for my work. He…well, I think it's obvious why he was hired."

Phieffer was referring to young Gabriel Graham's striking resemblance to the fictional Flint O'Connor, hero to pulp connoisseurs the world over. And any dead-ringer for the hero could also pass as the twin of Clarence Phieffer—several pounds and several years ago. How Phieffer worked that out in his head, spending how many hours a day studying this young bohunk's face and impeccable form, was a topic Detective Lane found intriguing.

"Having to hire a model for the 'role,' so to speak," Phieffer said, his face turning grave, "after all those years merely using a mirror…I don't mind telling you it was something of an adjustment. But Mr. Graham was pleasant enough. We grew close; enjoyed conversations about wine and song. Of course, had I known about his relationship with Dee, how quickly he'd placed moves on her…"

Gabriel Graham might've been as much of a womanizer as Flint O'Connor, might have lacked any of the redeeming qualities that made the thief so roguishly charming, but he didn't deserve to go out the way he did. Didn't deserve to have his body mangled up with the innards of a '78 Datsun 280Z.

"And seeing your pretty young wife run off with a handsome new beau, I'll guess this was a heavy thing to deal with."

"It's possible I overindulged in strawberry wine to soothe my sorrows. Not the healthiest way to ease the pain, but I made my way through it. As I mentioned earlier, Dee and I came through the other end of this. Came through it healthier and happier, I promise you." Phieffer relaxed on the couch and steepled his fingers. The earlier restlessness was replaced with quiet serenity. He looked at Lane with eyes that almost read as sincere. "Once she recovers, once all of the turmoil regarding the crash is resolved, I'm looking forward to starting a new chapter."

Lane said nothing, studying Phieffer's newly blissful expression. He sucked a long drag out of his straw, then said something provocative. Said it flat and level, in classic cop cadence, though. Said it in a way that could've inspired any number of responses. "This new chapter, it might be difficult, though. You're now competing with a ghost, you realize. Someone Dee might not be so eager to leave in the past."

"True love, Detective, it always finds its way," Phieffer answered, sunshine and spring flowers in his voice.

"And if Gabriel Graham was someone standing between you and this true love; if he was sending you threats, or mistreating your ex-wife in some way, doing something that might've driven you more than a little nuts…you'd tell me about anything like that, wouldn't you?"

Slight irritation showed in Phieffer's eyes. Only slight. "There was nothing that dramatic, Detective."

"If things weren't as peachy-keen as you're saying, if you did something you felt pressured into doing, that's something we'd need to know, Mr. Phieffer. For your sake, we'd need to know that as soon as possible."

"What happened was a tragedy, Detective," Phieffer said, standing. "One I had no involvement with, I promise you." He again offered the detective his hand.

In less than five minutes, Lane was back on the road. Back listening to bad news on the radio. He'd have to wash his hands when he got back to the station. It always made him uneasy, made his skin clammy, shaking hands with a murderer.

*****

"I wish to speak to Detective Lane," Clarence Phieffer told the desk sergeant, after the man with bee-stung cheeks and stripes on his shoulders managed to pull himself away from the phone.

"Well," the sergeant answered with a smirk, "I wish to help you do that. Have a seat and he'll be with you shortly."

Phieffer, with a cylindrical cardboard container tucked under his arm, moved to the indicated bench and took a seat. Drumming fingers against the tube, he took stock of his surroundings. To his right, two young cops in uniform were dragging along a woman he assumed to be a prostitute. To his left, a handcuffed teenager with a mohawk and spike-studded jacket was getting prepped for his mugshot. As the officer rattled off the instructions, the woozy teen suddenly keeled, spewing vomit across the cop's shoes.

He didn't have to be here. Phieffer had survived his interview with that obnoxiously bland Detective Lane without ending up in handcuffs. For all he knew, the investigation would determine the brake line malfunctioned on its own. Or some figure from Gabriel or Dee's life might emerge as a more probable suspect.

Neither were angels. Both had pasts, people holding grudges, he could safely assume.

More than once, he eyed the door. Contemplated leaving before the detective caught sight of him. Phieffer knew this was a risky play. But, he'd been rerunning his conversation with Detective Lane for two days now. Reliving every awkward response, every expression he'd failed to mask.

This was Phieffer's chance to do better. To show he was cooperating, had nothing to hide.

Detective Lane emerged from a closed door further down the hallway. Approached Phieffer with more verve in his step, a breezier hint of confidence. His suit still didn't fit properly, still looked as if he'd done something to offend his dry cleaner, but Lane wasn't swallowed up by the thing today.

"Mr. Phieffer. Wasn't expecting to see you again so soon," the detective said as his greeting, hand extended.

Phieffer rose, fumbled with the tube as it fell to the floor. With slight crimson in his cheeks, he recovered and pressed flesh with Detective Lane. "I was curious, Detective, about the investigation. If there's been any developments."

The thin line that defined Lane's mouth suddenly curved, formed something resembling a smile. "We could have a conversation about that, sure. Why don't you join me in here?" he asked, jerking his thumb toward a room down the hall.

Phieffer followed Lane into a cold, gray room, mostly barren except for a wooden table and a half-dozen filing cabinets positioned against the wall. And there was that wide, expansive mirror on the left wall. Phieffer wasn't an idiot, he knew what could be on the other side.

And he knew Detective Lane was not his friend. But this was something necessary, something he'd been psyching himself up to do over the course of two sleepless nights. He wouldn't be screwing this up.

"I wanted you to have this, Detective," Phieffer said, handing over the cardboard tube.

Lane dug inside and removed a glossy print. Garish colors, bold compositions. A suave-yet-savage male locked in an embrace with a raven-haired, wasp-waisted female with demonic eyes. "That's a limited-edition poster," Phieffer said with pride. "Flint O'Connor facing off against the Jade Lady. It's, well, I signed it for you, Detective."

Lane observed the print in silence. His lips again formed that almost-smile.

"You, ah, said earlier you were a fan."

"Thank you, sir," Lane said warmly, returning the print to the tube and placing it by the door. He motioned towards the table, inviting Phieffer to take a seat. "Yeah, Flint O'Connor was a hero of mine, growing up. It's cute, how he only steals from other thieves in those books. I ended up working on the other side of the law, but I still think he might've had some influence over me."

"At one point, I believe half the nation's youth wanted to follow in his footsteps. I once saw the enrollment numbers on the fan club, Detective. Quite impressive."

"I guess Flint was the last of an era," Lane said, joining Phieffer at the table. "Don't really see too many books like that anymore."

"The times do move on, something I've been forced to accept. We're on our fifth author now—oh, don't tell anyone I said that. The creator's contract has him credited as writer until one year after he dies."

Lane released a quick whistle. "Sounds like a sweet deal."

"He's done rather well for himself. As have I." Phieffer fiddled with his cufflinks, then relaxed in his chair. "The others in my field, they didn't have the foresight to demand things like royalties and profit participation."

"I see it's been good to you. Got you that nice house." From his suit jacket, Lane produced a pack of Marlboros. "Cigarette?"

Phieffer nodded in the affirmative. Leaning over, Lane flicked a brass Zippo and sparked the cig.

"The publisher stammered and squealed, naturally," Phieffer continued after a lengthy and refreshing exhale. "But they knew I had them over a barrel. No one else could capture those features that so uniquely say *Flint O'Connor*. The author even had to edit his prose in the second novel; had to make his descriptions of Flint more closely match the cover."

"Yeah, huh?" asked Lane, propping his elbow on the table and resting his head against his fist. "Never knew that. And you've been doing this for over thirty years now?"

"Indeed I have. Although I fear an era is at its end. Like you said, the men's adventure market isn't connecting with the readers of today."

"Gotta be television, right? Easier, cheaper thrills. Why settle for one babe on a paperback cover when you have three of 'em in live-action…three of 'em in tiny outfits, doing their karate chops and whatnot?"

"Yes, heaven forbid the youth pick up a book. Engage those feeble imaginations."

"It's like all of society's gotten lazier. Sloppier. Look at how people dress now. Those awful, shaggy hairstyles." Lane's eyes closed. He spoke with unmistakable disgust. "Like they can't be bothered to take care of themselves, show an ounce of self-respect. How people treat each other, the way they talk now. Disgraceful."

"I couldn't agree more, Detective."

Lane stood, rearranged some items atop one of the filing cabinets, then returned with a glass ashtray. "Regarding the investigation," he said, sliding the ashtray towards Phieffer, "I have to say things are advancing slower than we would've liked."

"If it helps, I could provide a list of Dee's associates. Previous paramours, ex-friends, that sort of thing."

Lane returned to his seat, again with that almost-smile. "Wow. Sounds like the girl's led a full life in those…twenty-one years, was it?"

"Experienced beyond her years. Must be why she was drawn to a fossil such as myself."

"And you've been to the hospital to visit the poor thing, I assume?"

"Not as yet," Phieffer said as he ashed the cigarette, then swiftly returned it to his lips. Another taste joined the tobacco. Salty. Like it might've been sweat. Which was absurd, because wasn't this room too chilly only a minute ago? "The thought of seeing Dee in that way, it…well, as I understand the situation, she isn't fully awake yet. Wouldn't even know I was there, correct?"

"And when she's able," Lane said casually, "she's going to say the same things you were telling me the other day?"

She would be doing no such thing, but Phieffer couldn't tell him that. "I'm certain she will."

"She isn't going to be blaming you for anything? Not going to be telling me about how much you hated Gabriel Graham, right?"

"In the spirit of honesty, Detective, I'll tell you that I did indeed hate Gabriel Graham. At one point." Smoke blew out of Phieffer's nostrils. Curled like octopus tentacles then disappeared. "Before our reconciliation."

"Hey, he took your lady. Who wouldn't hate that kind of SOB?"

"Even before that, I regret to say. He was the right man for the role, the perfect embodiment of Flint O'Connor, yet…the sight of him. As if reality had split thirty years back, and I was now encountering my younger self."

"It bother you that bad?"

Phieffer's mind involuntarily turned to Graham. To his imposing physique, the sharp angle of his chin, the tautness of his marshmallow-brown skin.

There might've been a bead of sweat forming on Phieffer's forehead at that moment. Something moist, something slowly crawling down. It was possible, maybe likely, it would be rolling between his eyebrows any second now. He fought against the urge to swipe it away.

Lane's eyes, which still held more sympathy than judgment, didn't leave Phieffer's. He repeated his question.

"Oh, *bother* me? No, no. Did I imply that? I apologize. No, I merely found the similarities…unnerving. His secret affair with my new bride—yes, that was more than enough to stir fits of choleric anger. But that fire managed to die down eventually. We made our peace, found a way to move forward."

"Hm. Well, about that, we have reason to believe Mr. Graham wasn't so willing to move on." Lane folded his hands, removed any trace of a smile from his face. "You see, his parents gave us permission to search his home. Only got back half an hour ago. It's something we have to do, you understand, to learn what we can about a victim. And what we discovered about Mr. Graham and your ex-wife, about their home life...well, as we were saying earlier, about times changing..."

Lane's voice trailed off. He shot Phieffer a look, indicating that Phieffer was obligated to finish this thought.

Phieffer—an arctic chill now crawling in his bones, his skin dampened with sweat—only stared.

Lane pressed his hands tighter together. "I know there's this saying that every generation thinks they invented, um, *relations*. And I can still remember, how people reacted to your paperback covers, how...racy they once seemed. But, previous times, it's hard to imagine couples having, ah, setups like we found in Mr. Graham's home. In his, ah, bedroom, that is."

"What are you...?" Phieffer attempted to ask, his voice a raspy whisper.

"We found the camera, Mr. Phieffer. And on their nightstand, found a fresh envelope with your address printed on it. No stamp on it yet. Maybe they were out."

"I'm not sure...you're implying that..."

Lane reached to Phieffer's still hand and removed the cigarette. As he stamped it out into the ashtray, he asked in a somber voice, "How many of those photos did they send you, Mr. Phieffer? How long had they been doing that? Long enough to get your blood boiling?"

"No..."

"Long enough to get you contemplating something you wouldn't have considered otherwise?" Lane didn't say it like an accusation. Didn't say it like a stern patriarchal figure, passing judgment. He said it like an arbiter of truth, like he was the only person on this earth who should be privileged to hear these words.

Phieffer's reality, for one interminable moment, wasn't this room. It was the past. The days when he could've passed for Gabriel Graham's twin.

No. Flint O'Connor's twin.

The thief's love interests were there. Rendered in stunning color, all modeled after Phieffer's real-life conquests. Every pouting lip, every heaving bosom, every pair of never-ending legs.

Dee was there. Was joined with Phieffer in concupiscent ecstasy. But not the Phieffer of today, with the disappearing chin and sagging pectorals that caused him to flinch every time he passed the bathroom mirror.

No, Dee was with the Clarence Phieffer of yesteryear. The one she hadn't known the pleasure of enjoying. The one that could've kept her satisfied, could've fulfilled every desire and not left her tempted for one moment to stray.

But he had to question if that was truly what he was seeing. Was it young Clarence Phieffer, or Gabriel Graham in nude embrace with Dee? Was this a fantasy, or the memory of a photograph? One sent to mock an aging idol, to pour salt into a nasty wound?

"They were goading you, Mr. Phieffer," spoke a stoic voice, penetrating the ether. Phieffer blinked, finally wiped the sweat away, and faced again the gunmetal gray reality of this room.

"It was a sick, mean-spirited thing for those kids to do to a man," Lane continued. "Something previous generations wouldn't even consider, not in their darkest, most shameful moments. But people today, these sick kids, they lack even basic dignity, don't they? Don't even think about how their depravity can affect others, do they?"

Something moist, even saltier than sweat, was reaching Phieffer's lips. Something that would never touch Flint O'Connor's face. Tears.

"I think there's a reason why you came here to talk to me, Mr. Phieffer. A reason why, both times we've spoken, it's been one-on-one. You didn't have to do this. Could've kept your mouth shut."

Something warm now on Phieffer's shoulder. It clutched tightly, but it didn't feel oppressive or menacing.

"But you had to tell someone, didn't you? Had to explain why you did what you did, and why it doesn't make you some kind of monster."

Phieffer opened his mouth to speak, but didn't feel his mouth move. Wasn't even sure if he was still in his body. He heard his voice, though. Stumbling, tripping over words, but speaking the truth. Speaking something that inspired that warm presence on his shoulder to squeeze even tighter.

*****

Phieffer had been told—months back, over drinks with his publisher's newly promoted CEO—that one segment of their audience remained strong. Men's adventure, *Flint O'Connor* in particular, maintained its popularity amongst America's growing prison population. Was their only expanding market, in fact.

It was a small bit of trivia, not relevant to Phieffer at the time. Something he'd nearly forgotten.

Outside these walls, the world was indeed changing. But inside, there was a predictable, daily rhythm.

His first week in prison, one of the guards made a crack about Phieffer's previous career. Did it in front of a pack of inmates. Later, Phieffer considered the man might've done it as an act of kindness.

After all, Phieffer was decades older than the average inmate. Not an ideal candidate to join one of their gangs. Too snooty to adjust to the culture. An easy choice for a discreet shiv between his ribs, were a gang prospect in need of a fast, defenseless target.

But the Aryan Brotherhood, Nuestra Familia, and Mexican Mafia— each of them counted *Flint O'Connor* fans amongst their number. And art class was three days a week.

The gangs provided him skin mags for reference. Wanted to see their latest masturbatory fantasies dressed in mars violet, cerulean blue, and raw sienna bikinis. Wanted cotton candy blush on their cheeks, golden caramel highlights on their skin, and they wanted these fantasy women paired with that rugged thief. As much as they loved their ladies, they didn't want Flint O'Connor to receive short shrift.

He had to be featured prominently in the painting. Had to be the classic image, never updated to conform to the latest fashions. A swimmer's build, a mechanic's arms. And that granite chin, never wavering. Never drooping, never turning to putty.

A mirror wouldn't serve as reference. Not these days. Phieffer kept a collection of the paperbacks by his side. Had to spend hours at a time, studying those chiseled features, that pristine body that no longer existed.

It was subpar work. Derivative of what he'd created in the past, copies of a copy. It saved him from beatings, or maybe worse. But it was its own form of punishment. The cruelest Clarence Phieffer could've ever dreamed.

Miles away, Det. Lane was adjusting the rabbit ears on his television and preparing himself for another hour of mindless "cop" action. Detectives with designer shades and handlebar mustaches. Muscle cars and skin-tight trousers. Not one beer-belly amongst the crew.

There was the single clink of an ice cube hitting his glass of room-temperature soda. A commercial for the evening news followed by the station ID. He'd sworn these ridiculous shows off, but the previous episode had ended in quite the cliffhanger.

Two months ago, Lane had rescued his old paperbacks from his parents' garage. A stack of them sat on his coffee table. That signed print remained in its tube. He was still debating, whether or not to hang the thing up.

Snowballs
Hal Dygert

2005
Part I: Detective Brill

Terry Brill arrived at his aunt and uncles' Kamiakin County ranch under a bit of a cloud. One of five siblings who'd grown up in Portland, he was the only one who'd taken a shine to the ranch and ranch-life. He'd worked there during his high school and college summers. He still came to visit, to hunt and fish, and just to knock around the backcountry east of the Cascade Mountains in Washington State. His Aunt Wanda could be trying at times, but he dearly loved his Uncle Stan.

Now forty-two years old, Brill had worked the last fourteen years for the Portland Police Bureau. He was currently a detective sergeant assigned to the Bureau's burglary/pawnshop detail. Actually, at the moment, his connection to the Bureau was problematic.

A week before Thanksgiving, a snitch he'd been leaning on fairly hard shot and killed her abusive boyfriend and accidently electrocuted herself when a clock-radio fell from a windowsill into the tub of water in which she'd been bathing. For this the Bureau had summarily suspended Brill—as if he were somehow responsible for the demise of these two fuckups—for the administrative equivalent of negligent homicide. No criminal action had been filed.

The internal affairs investigation into the matter Brill had guessed would take no more than a couple of weeks after which he'd be cleared and reinstated. As far he was concerned, his suspension was political: the Bureau's newly installed chief, a so-called reformer intent on dialing back what "the community" called aggressive policing, was flexing his muscles.

Rather than wait out the suspension in his Portland apartment, Brill called his uncle Stan and asked if he and Wanda would mind if he camped out in their bunkhouse. He provided Stan with a summary of the allegations that had resulted in his suspension and assured him that they lacked merit. Stan said he'd have to check with the boss but one way or the other, he'd call him right back.

Stan, Brill was confident, would have no trouble letting him stay; he was less sure of Wanda who, as she frequently noted, "had her scruples." But when Stan called back it was to say by all means to come ahead. "Wanda says, you be sure to be here in time to sit down with us for Thanksgiving dinner."

The original ranch, consisting of a two-story house, a barn, a shop, corrals, and the bunkhouse sat together on one side of a graveled and graded county road. Two years before, after fifty years growing wheat and alfalfa and running a small herd of beef cattle, Stan and Wanda had retired. They still owned the land, some 3,000 acres, but were leasing it to a neighboring farmer. Their new home, situated directly across the road from the old one was a spacious double-wide trailer.

Brill arrived the day before Thanksgiving, spot-cleaned the bunkhouse, and arranged his things. Early the following morning, after stuffing himself with Wanda's ranch breakfast, he drove the fifteen miles into Glenview, the county seat, population 3,500, to pick up a few things that Wanda still needed to round out her dinner menu. It was there, in the parking lot of the Fair and Square Market that he learned of the murder of Vannoy Tellman, a prominent rancher. Brill had never met the man but knew the name from his time working at Stan's ranch.

Tellman was old family, big money. His murder would no doubt shock the citizens of Glenview and of larger Kamiakin County. It wouldn't help that the suspected perpetrator was a burly, unkempt, bad-tempered drug dealer named Enrique Valdez who remained at large.

And who, even three days later on the Sunday after Thanksgiving and despite the best efforts of the Kamiakin County Sheriff's Department, remained at large still.

Part II: Church

Stan and Wanda's church sat in the northeast corner of a country crossroads. It was high-spired and painted all in white except for two green doors that met in the middle and opened outward. One of the doors was propped open with a brick

Stan found a space among the vehicles parked in a field adjacent to the church. Twittering greetings as she went, Wanda led the way into the church, through the narthex, and along the central aisle. She found seats on a pew to the left, back four rows from the altar. No sooner had they settled into those seats than Wanda reached a bony arm across Stan's paunch and twisted a thumb in Brill's ribs.

"Look there," she whispered, nodding toward a pew on the front right. "Look what just pranced in on hind legs. Sheriff Carmody. Had to make his grand entrance."

Wearing a green-trimmed, khaki police uniform, a slim six-footer slipped into the second pew. He had a pale moon face, pink cheeks, and colorless baby-fine hair. He looked comfortable enough until he caught sight of Wanda's fierce glare. Then the pink spread from his cheeks up into his hairline and down his neck. He turned away.

"Frank Henning's puppy dog," Wanda whispered. "Bought and paid for. Frank and his slutty new wife. That's them, the high and mighty Hennings, sitting in front of our so-called sheriff."

"Now, sweetheart," Stan said.

Wanda harumphed and settled back in her seat.

Near the fire door in the church's left front corner an easel displayed an enlarged photograph, a head-and-shoulders shot two feet square, of a bull-necked man with short gray hair and dark eyes. Strung between the easel's front legs a banner read, "Called Home."

Brill bent toward his relatives. He pointed at the photograph through the back of the pew. "Tellman?"

Wanda whipped around and glared across Stan's paunch, looking to see if Brill's question was meant as a joke.

"The name's familiar," Brill said. "It's just that I never set eyes on the man, at least so far as I recall."

Apparently reading Brill as sincere, Wanda dialed down the glare. She opened her purse and extracted a lace-trimmed handkerchief. She touched the handkerchief to her lips.

"That's Van." Wanda held her watch up to her ear and then used the dampened handkerchief to polish the watch-face crystal. "Vannoy Tellman. May the Lord bless him and keep him."

Brill nodded and straightened and leaned back in his seat. He looked again at the photograph, a washed-out image in black-and-white. Not that the subject looked washed out. More like a country hard-ass whose smile didn't so much engage as challenge the viewer.

The service commenced. According to a sign out front, Pastor Vernon Considine was the head honcho here at the Poplar Grove Church of the Redeemer. He was a compact middle-aged man whose sloping wrestler's forehead, fleshy and deeply creased, sheltered restless gray eyes.

The pastor's voice was less than compelling. Sitting down after the first hymn, Brill almost nodded off but—courageously, he thought—fought the urge and managed to stay awake for the rest or the service.

After intoning a benediction Pastor Considine marched up the central aisle into the narthex where he awaited his congregants for handshakes and post-service chit-chat. Before joining the line Wanda hurried off to use the restroom. Brill and his uncle found an out-of-the-way corner to await her return.

The pastor had exchanged civilities with no more than half a dozen members of the congregation when Frank Henning burst into the narthex leading a small posse that included his wife and the pink-cheeked sheriff. Henning's wispy gray-white hair, thin on top, long on the sides, was pushed back of both ears. He wore a sheared fleece coat over a gray pearl-buttoned shirt.

Frank Henning, the high and mighty, a personality worthy of notice. But not half so much as Mrs. Frank Henning, a big-haired ice blonde with vacant eyes and a rack it appeared she had taken pains to conceal, as if big jugs were a no-no in church. She looked fifteen or twenty years her husband's junior. The slutty new wife. Yes, indeed-y.

Skirting the line, the heels of his Western boots canting him forward, Henning made a dash for the church's front door. He spoke to no one. He walked on his toes, his gait a mincing quickstep. He looked like a man running downhill, struggling to keep his feet.

"Brother Henning?" Pastor Considine struggled to make eye contact. "I thank you and your wife for attending this morning. Sheriff, God bless."

Without any reply Henning led his troops out the door.

Pastor Considine heaved a great sigh. He resumed greeting those in line, firmly shaking hands but now wearing a downcast expression as if saddened by his failure to engage with Henning.

Brill turned to Stan and spoke in a low voice. "What's the big deal?"

"This fella Considine is our new pastor. The old pastor, Frank's man, had preached here, what, going on ten years. Didn't keep up with the times. The congregation voted in a new board of elders, and they showed his pastor the door."

"Different styles?"

"Night and day. Frank's man was Old Testament. Every week, a new postcard from hell."

Wanda returned from the restroom. She grabbed Brill's left bicep and tugged him toward Pastor Considine.

"Pastor?" Wanda said. "I want you to meet my nephew, Terry Brill."

Brill felt embarrassed of her barging in, cutting in front of the others. He looked back to see if those waiting resented the intrusion. To the contrary, they broke ranks and gathered up front, seemingly eager to take in the anticipated conversation.

"I'm so glad you were able to join us." Considine clung to Brill's hand.

"Well, Aunt Wanda was keen on my coming. And as I expect you know, she can be quite persuasive."

"Surely a force to be reckoned with," Considine said. "I understand you're a police officer."

Brill withdrew his hand from the pastor's. Not really, not at the moment.

"More than a police officer," the pastor continued, "a detective, city trained and tested in fire." The preacher didn't wait for affirmation but ploughed ahead. "I'm sure you're aware of our tragic murder Thanksgiving morning. We buried the victim yesterday. Van Tellman was a member and a good, good friend to this church."

The parishioners in Brill's immediate vicinity were nodding and wringing their hands.

"Yes, sir," Brill said, "I understand Mr. Tellman was shot and killed."

"And his killer is out there." The preacher turned his gaze to the yard beyond the church's front door. "Somewhere." Considine turned back to Brill.

"We are a rural community," he continued. "Most of us live with our families on farms and ranches. It's fair to say, I think, that under the circumstances, with a good man cut down in broad daylight for no apparent reason and with the killer at large, people are frightened." A couple of "Amens" underscored Considine's observation. "What we are wondering, hoping, asking, even praying is that you would be willing to help find Van's killer, Detective Brill."

"I'm flattered you'd ask," Brill said. Thinking, don't be a chump. Keep clear of this mess. "But, as I expect you're aware, I don't have any authority outside Portland." No need to mention that at the moment, he didn't have police authority anywhere on God's green earth. "You have a sheriff," Brill continued, "a member of your congregation, I gather. I'm sure he's an able man."

Brill heard grumbling.

"They already figured out who done it," cried a voice in the crowd, "and even with a name Sheriff still can't find him."

"With Tellman, they have a suspect?" Brill turned to the man who'd spoken. A thickness of red membrane rimmed each of his tiny eyes. Coarse white bristles sprouted randomly from his ears, nose, and chin. He looked like a Billy-goat.

"Yessir," the man replied. "They found a gun, found the murder weapon with fingerprints on it. My sister works in the courthouse and that's the true story."

"I don't mean to judge," Considine said. He cleared his throat and considered his words. "You're right, Sheriff Carmody is a member of this congregation. I know he means well and he does the best he can. But he's an elected official and it's my sense—my sense, and that's all it is or can be—that professional skills were not necessarily what elevated him to public office."

"Bare-naked in Alaska, that man couldn't catch cold," Wanda exclaimed, "let alone catch a crook." The crowd tittered.

"I tell you what," Brill said. "I don't know if there's much I can do, but I'll at least do this. Tomorrow morning, first thing…I'll stop by the courthouse and talk to the sheriff. We'll see what he has to say."

Part III: Sheriff Carmody

Brill guessed that a man who'd been elected sheriff not for his investigative skills or experience but for his political connections wouldn't be at all keen on Brill's joining the search for Enrique Valdez. He wouldn't want to be shown up. Brill understood those feelings and likely would have stood clear of the matter if during the course of their discussion Carmody hadn't been such a turd. But turd he was, and Brill left his office determined to pull the Valdez rug out from under his feet.

First thing upon leaving, Brill called a buddy of his, a former Portland Police Bureau colleague named Jess McCarry, who now worked for the Tri-State Narcotics Task Force—TNTF, pronounced "tintif"—and asked if he had any intel on Enrique Valdez. "I don't need the full Monty," Brill added. Task force files were highly confidential and he was asking a lot of his buddy. "All I need to know is whether or not he's got a finger in the Kamiakin County drug trade. That and a last known address."

"When do you need it?"

"Sooner the better. The guy's wanted for a murder up here. He's been in the wind since Thanksgiving."

McCarry called back that afternoon. "You're in luck, amigo, TNTF has a file on Enrique. No starring role, but he's a player. Looks like he mostly moves wholesale lots from points east to points west. Also, some retail dealing to customers in between, tweekers the big fish don't consider worth the time or the risk."

"You got an address?"

"What we have on Enrique is a couple months old. I think it's still good. This is on the Washington side of the river. 15654 Cobbs Hill Road, off the Borden Highway."

"I think I know where you're talking about. I take that Borden route sometimes. It's a back way to my uncle's."

"Where Valdez lives is a trailer. Blue tarp over the roof at one end and one of those flying saucer sized satellite dishes in a field out back."

"How about a vehicle?"

"What's registered to him is a 1989 Mercury Montego four-door sedan. White top, maroon body." McCarry recited the plate number, and Brill wrote it down.

"Physical description," Brill said. "Let me guess: black hair, brown eyes, 6' 1", 220. DOB 7-29-85"

"Bingo. What's that, your generic Mexican outlaw?"

"A blowup of this dude's driver's license photo is taped up in every storefront in Kamiakan County. So, tell me about Enrique."

"A farmworker when he was a kid, but then he grew up and changed jobs. There's his size to consider and the vigor of youth. On top of that the snitches say he can get mean, agreeable one minute, in your shit the next."

"Probably sampling product."

"It's been known to happen."

"I wonder if he's packing. They found his .45 in a ditch down the road from the murder scene."

"Be that as it may, I don't know many in his line of work who don't pack. Anyway, T, I got to sign off. Good luck. And this conversation?"

"Never happened," Brill said.

"Heigh-ho, Silver," McCarry said, and hung up.

*****

Brill delivered Valdez to the Kamiakin County sheriff's office at 10:30 on the night of Thursday, December 1st. At gunpoint he prodded the wet and shivering prisoner up the deserted courthouse steps and back to the sheriff's office. Two deputies sat at desks in the half-lit interior, doing paperwork, awaiting calls for assistance.

While one deputy looked on, the other sauntered up to the front railing, a puzzled look on his face. "Whatta we got here?" The deputy's failure to recognize the outlaw was, perhaps, excusable. Valdez's hair, shorn in his driver's license photograph, had grown out and he'd put on at least thirty pounds.

"Enrique Valdez," Brill said. I suggest you get some iron on him right quick and get him into a cell.

"Whoa!" The deputy fumbled a pair of handcuffs from the case on his belt, pushed through the gate, and secured Valdez's hands behind his back. The second deputy, gun drawn and held in the ready position, came forward. Together the two men searched Valdez, relieved him of belt and shoes, and locked him in a holding cell.

Brill looked on until they had completed these tasks, then turned to go.

"No, no. Wait," the first deputy said. "Let me call the sheriff. He'll be wanting to talk."

Brill waved goodbye, jogged back to his car, and raced away. He'd played the scene just the way he wanted to, like the Lone Ranger—deliver the villain and disappear in a cloud of dust.

Who was that masked man? People would find out sooner or later.

By the time of Monday morning's arraignment, some had.

Part IV: Eva Ruiz

Before climbing the courthouse steps for the arraignment, Brill put on a ballcap and adjusted it so that the bill mostly concealed his face. He stood on the curb, opened his flip-phone, and punched in his aunt and uncle's number. He was surprised when Stan answered. Stan and Wanda had yet to adopt cellular service. Stan was answering their landline, meaning they were still at home. Brill notified him of the crowd size. "I'm guessing you might have trouble finding seats."

"We're not going to make it," Stan said. "Your aunt has a doozy of a nosebleed. We still haven't got it stopped. She's too weak to travel."

"That's a pity. I know she was eager."

"She says you're gonna have to come over to dinner tonight and tell us what happened."

"What time?"

"6:30 she says."

"See you then. Give her my best."

"Detective Brill?" The man asking the question stood at the top of the courthouse steps watching Brill's ascent. He wore a gray herringbone carcoat, rimless glasses, and a fleecy gray Russian-style hat. He looked ready for the weather. Snowflakes, the first of the season, were falling around him.

"Who's asking?"

"Rich Clausen, *Glenview Record*."

A reporter, which explained the flip-front notebook. Who'd tipped him off? Probably Wanda, nosebleed and all, the minute she'd realized she wasn't getting in on the action.

"Was it my aunt that called you? Wanda Brill?"

"Confidential source." Clausen's grin confirmed Brill's suspicions. "Do you have a minute?" Clausen asked. He stood a step above Brill, blocking his way.

"Don't you want to see the show?"

"You know the drill. The prosecutor reads the charges. The

defendant pleads not guilty. The deputies take him back to his cell. Anyway, I have a reporter inside. Look, I own *The Record*. Van Tellman was a prominent man in this county. I'm going to run his story and keep it running. People are full of questions and you have the answers. How did you know where to find Valdez? Why didn't you involve the sheriff? What happened out there? This story deserves more than a couple of thirty second clips on TV."

"TV?"

"CBS and Fox, the Portland affiliates." The poor guy sounded discouraged, as if the media battle for Brill's time and attention was already lost. "They park their vans behind the courthouse. The feed is better from there."

"They ran the garbage wagons all the way up here from Portland? I'll be damned." After feeling a moment's elation, Brill considered how a TV news story on his freelance police work might play into the bureau's disciplinary action against him. Not so well, he supposed. Not that what he'd done was precluded so far as he knew, more the idea of the thing. Local newspaper coverage, though, he couldn't see making much of a stink.

"I tell you what, I'm gonna take a peek in the courtroom, then I'm going to take off. I'll talk to you in your office first thing in the morning. You say when."

Disappointment clouded Clausen's face.

"I'll give you an exclusive, swear to God. I have no desire to talk to TV."

The arraignment was over by the time Brill managed a peek into the crowded courtroom. The judge had already left the bench. Valdez stood behind defense counsel's table. He wore an orange jumpsuit that was at least two sizes too small. He was shackled and it appeared that his hands were chained in front to a locked waist-belt.

A burly, balding man stood to Valdez's left, a Hispanic woman to his right. The balding man was at least as heavy as Valdez, though an inch or two shorter. The woman's dark hair was short, thick, and more wavy than curly. The woman and the balding man whispered across the front of the outlaw, who watched as if at a tennis match. Two deputies stood nearby, attentive though out of earshot, or at least pretending to be.

Hat pulled down over his face, Brill found Clausen off to one side of the courthouse lobby, standing with a bright-eyed, clear-complected young woman.

"Detective Brill," Clausen said, "may I introduce Jill Stoddard, *The Record's* ace reporter?"

Stoddard looked wide-eyed at Brill. "Really?"

"I confess. And you're a reporter?"

"*The Record's* one and only. Also, photographer, bookkeeper, file clerk, and part time janitor. I work cheap." She nodded at Clausen. "I'm his daughter."

"Were you in there for the arraignment?" Brill asked. "Did they allege aggravating circumstances?"

"Still under review. A death penalty case will bankrupt this county. Given the victim, though, I don't see that the prosecutor has much choice. No bail by the way, at least for now."

"Who's the defense attorney?" Brill asked.

"Ronnie Sepper," the girl said.

"Any good?"

"Hard-working," Clausen interjected, "too much on his plate."

"Appointed or private?"

"Public defender," the girl said.

"Who's the other one, the woman?"

"Sepper's girl-Friday," Jill Stoddard said. "Also, serves as his Spanish-language interpreter, Eva Ruiz."

After reconfirming arrangements to meet in the morning, Clausen told Brill how to escape the courthouse through a basement door. Good idea. The more he thought about it, the more he wanted to avoid the TV people. They could definitely complicate his situation back in the city.

Leaving footprints in what had become an inch or two's

accumulation of snow, Brill was angling off the courthouse square when Eva Ruiz, hurrying along the same sidewalk, brushed by him without an apology. She carried files under one arm and walked with her head down, preoccupied, cutting right along. Nice shape, nice swing to her walk, trailing a scent that it wouldn't take a bloodhound to follow.

Interesting thought. As a cop, if he wanted to talk to anyone on the defense counsel's team, he'd first have to get defense counsel's permission. But in these circumstances, suspended from the city force and neither formally nor informally deputized to local law enforcement, he wasn't a cop. He was an ordinary citizen, operating independently of the criminal justice system, free to pump or sweet-talk information from any susceptible source.

Brill quickened his pace. He followed the interpreter across the courthouse square, then north two blocks on First Street, and left on West Main. Valdez was in custody, yes, but why should he quit the case? He'd be a while yet in Kamiakin County. He needed to find a diversion.

Eva Ruiz entered the Frontier Restaurant and Lounge through a recessed street door. Brill followed soon after and found himself standing on a mushy square of shag rug in a dank vestibule.

A central wall divided the dining room from the lounge. A doorway to the right connected the vestibule to the vast, low-ceilinged dining room where maybe half the scattered tables were occupied. Eva Ruiz had taken a seat in the rear right corner. She gave the waitress a peremptory order without consulting a menu.

Brill pushed into the lounge, left through a saloon-style set of swinging doors. He marched straight to the bar and ordered black coffee and a shot of Canadian Club. May as well give the woman a few minutes to eat her lunch.

Alternating, he sipped from the shot-glass and from the mug. After a while, he turned, leaned back against the bar, and surveyed the booths set back-to-back against the opposite wall. Only one was occupied: a middle booth where a couple with faces like day old apple crullers were picking at their lunch platters. Beyond the last booth an open doorway connected to the dining room.

Brill washed down the last of his whiskey, laid a ten on the bar, and sauntered through the back doorway into the dining room. Eva Ruiz had a file open and what looked like a half-eaten club sandwich pushed off to one side. She gave Brill a quick glance and looked back at her file. When he drew closer she closed the file and watched him neutrally through eyes that were large, dark, and long-lashed.

"I hope you'll pardon the intrusion, miss" Brill said. "I'm here this morning from out of town. Leaving some papers at the auditor's office. I saw all the commotion, heard about this murder case, and looked into the courtroom. I sure admire what you're doing. That has to be hard duty, representing a person accused of murder." Listening to himself, Brill wished he'd pitched his come-on in a lower key. But flattery usually did the trick no matter how hokey it sounded.

Eva Ruiz touched a napkin to each side of her mouth. "Mr. Sepper is the attorney. I help him with interpreting and such."

"I must've misunderstood. Interpreting. Huh. So, you're still right there in the thick of things." Eva Ruiz looked straight at him, unblinking, no expression on her face.

"Sounds like this Mr. Tellman was a pretty important fella hereabouts. A real loss." Brill observed a moment of silence, intending to convey his appreciation of the gravity of the situation. From here the trick was to get the woman to reveal any potentially damning admissions Valdez might have confided. "Does he seem contrite at all, Mr. Valdez? Does he say anything along those lines?"

A fly had landed on one of the points of Eva Ruiz's sandwich. Still looking directly into Brill's eyes she waved it away. Her gaze then shifted to a point beyond his right shoulder. Brill looked around. Without his having heard, the apple cruller couple had sneaked up behind him.

"You're the one that caught him, ain't you?" the cruller woman said. Her companion leaned close to the woman's ear and whispered that yes, this was Stan and Wanda's nephew, Detective Brill.

"We just wanted to thank you," the cruller woman said, "for all you done."

The old man doubled up his arthritic right hand and struck himself twice on the breastbone. "I tell you what." There were tears in his eyes. "We been livin' under a terrible strain."

Brill could see that the conversation was drawing the attention of the rest of the lunchroom crowd.

"This here's Detective Brill," the old man announced to the room. "That captured the Mexican."

"You answered our prayers," the old woman said.

Brill drew a deep breath and looked back at Eva Ruiz. She was pulling on her coat.

"Worth a try." Brill shrugged. "No offense."

"I'm not from around here." Eva Ruiz mimicked Brill's gee-whiz delivery. "No, you're not from around here. You crawled out from under a rock." Eyes front, she brushed past him and quickly made her exit.

At the same time, restaurant patrons were converging on Brill, faces beaming, applause building.

The celebration went on at embarrassing length. At last, the cruller woman, who'd made herself mistress of ceremonies, took Brill's hand and pulled him around behind the table at which Eva Ruiz had lately been seated. "Mexicans," she said. And then as if to blow out candles on a birthday cake, she leaned over the table and pretended to spit on the remains of Eva Ruiz's half-eaten sandwich.

Part V: Gary Oakes

Intent on escape, Brill maneuvered his way into the restaurant's vestibule. Admirers still surrounded him. He felt increasingly claustrophobic. The comingled odors lifting off the floor mat and off the crowd's old winter clothes smelled like a wet retriever. He hoped for arriving customers and a chance to slip away in the scrum. None came.

Snowballs

The top half of the restaurant's front door incorporated three staggered windowpanes that were narrow, butterscotch-colored, and semi-opaque. A man's indistinct silhouette whirled and dipped and cut back and forth across the windowpanes as if cast by a flamenco dancer. The man appeared to be smoking a cigarette. It sounded as if he might be singing.

The door opened outward. Brill managed to get hold of the handle and open the door just a crack. He heard singing, yes. Then, no singing. Then the singer yanked the door all the way open, pulled Brill out onto the sidewalk, and shoved the door closed except for a crack through which he addressed the crowd.

"Sorry folks, that's all for today. Detective Brill has work to do."

Given his antics the man's voice sounded surprisingly authoritative. He pushed the door closed the rest of the way. No one came out.

"Thanks," Brill told his savior, a big raw-boned man, age anywhere between thirty and fifty. He held an inch of unfiltered cigarette between nicotine-stained fingers of his left hand and bounced on the balls of his feet.

"No pro-blame-o," the singer said. He tilted his head back and blew a stream of smoke at the sky. "She ain't a bad gal."

"Who?"

"Eva, man. Eva Ruiz."

"You were inside?" It seemed as though Brill would have noticed. In addition to his size and agitated demeanor, the man's pale skin gave off an eerie foxfire glow.

"Yeah, yeah, yeah," the man said, shimmying backward along the snow-covered sidewalk, arms outstretched. One front tooth was made of silver and as big as a logger's thumbnail. "Caught your act from the wings, man. Was chillin' in the kitchen, chewin' the fat with chef Bobby Ray. I come out the rear door and around through the alley."

"I'm not exactly proud of that trick I tried to pull on Ms. Ruiz. She did exactly what she was supposed to do. Told me to fuck off."

"Best lookin' gal in the county," the man said. "Course a lot of folks around here can't admit it on account of she's Mexican.

"Anyway, Detective Brill," the man continued. He danced from foot to foot. He flicked the fingers of both hands at Brill's chest as if he were casting a spell. "Welcome to Kamiakan County. Pleased to introduce myself. Gary Oakes. Native son. Pleased to make your acquaintance. Totally, totally at your service."

"Service?"

"The Tellman murder, man!"

Brill looked into the man's dry, staring, bloodshot brown eyes. Crazy? Possibly. "Tellman? I don't know, Gary. I think we pretty much have that case put to bed."

"Do you now." Oakes flicked his cigarette stub to the pavement and ground it to mush under the toe of his boot.

Brill genuinely appreciated Oakes's rescue effort. But now the man was annoying him, annoying him more than a little by insinuating that he'd arrested the wrong man. Of course, in a way Oakes was right. Especially this early in a case, a good cop kept an open mind with respect to the perpetrator. Brill had to acknowledge that he was more invested in the Valdez solution than he had any right to be.

"So, Gary," Brill said, "all the jitters and jumping around. You a drug addict, or what's your issue?"

"That's harsh, man." Oakes made a show of dropping his hands and gaping open-mouthed at Brill. "That's like objection, irrelevant."

Brill shrugged.

"Oh, I get it," Oakes said. "You got you a warm body. You got a beaner to take the fall. Don't matter if he done it or not. Man, that's so Kamiakan County."

"See you around." Brill headed back toward the courthouse where his Bronco was still parked.

"Hey, I'll drive you," Oakes called after him, eager again.

Brill shook his head without turning around. Oakes ran up ahead of Brill and turned to face him. As if panhandling, he backpedaled and delivered his pitch. "Means, motive, and opportunity. Am I right?

"Means," he continued. "Okay, so Tellman is shot with the heavy artillery. Hey, I ain't about to deny that Ricky Valdez gots a cannon or two in his arsenal. But shit, so do ninety per cent of the friends and neighbors."

"Here," Oakes called out. He'd stopped back-pedaling and stood at the curb, slapping the snow-covered hood of a Chevrolet pickup, maybe a '74 or '75. Brill walked past him. "Here's my rig," Oakes continued. "Wherever you're going, we can get you there, no pro-blame-o."

Brill had noticed several pro-blame-os in passing the truck: cracked glass, bald tires, fenders and lower door panels patched with body putty. He imagined the disintegrating exhaust pipes and undercarriage, holes in the floorboards, carbon monoxide seeping into the cab. No, he wasn't about to get into Oakes's truck, though out of habit he did note the license number. Meanwhile, he thought back to church and the man who resembled a Billy goat, his assurances that the gun with which Van Tellman had been shot belonged to Enrique Valdez.

"Means," Brill said, stopping and turning to address his would-be assistant. "Not that I'm in a position to tell you why, but let's take it as a given that means is established. Opportunity. Valdez will swear he was somewhere else or with somebody else. That's also a given. What'll you bet his alibi doesn't shake out. And wherever he was on Thanksgiving morning—his trailer, some migrant camp, hell, anywhere in the damn county—he'll have been close enough to do the deed. That's opportunity."

"Motive, man." Undeterred, Oakes pressed his argument. He looked right, then left, then leaned in conspiratorially.

Before Oakes could spill his secrets Brill bid him farewell and resumed his trek.

"No motive," Oakes called after Brill. "Ricky Valdez and Tellman was best buds, man, amigos. I'll swear under oath. And I'll be one of many, man, one of many."

Not my business Brill told himself, lengthening the distance.

"And them with motive? Question is," Oakes persisted in a fading voice, "when it comes to motive who ain't on the list?"

A door slammed back where Gary Oakes had parked his truck. A large, low-torque engine revved. Brill glanced over his shoulder. Its engine alternately roaring and sputtering, Oakes's pickup pulled away from the curb, executed a U-turn, and lurched along the street.

Motive. Brill decided he'd better hear what Oakes had to say on the subject. He slipped between parked cars into the street. The pickup slowed to a stop. Brill opened the passenger door and climbed in. Silent at last, silver tooth prominent in the middle of a shit-eating grin, Gary Oakes shifted into gear and eased out the clutch.

"Okay, Brill said. "I'm listening"

Part VI: Ramsey Station

After completing his breakdown of the Tellman case Oakes dropped Brill off in front of the courthouse where only his Bronco remained. He brushed snow off the windshield and mirrors. He had intended initially to return to his aunt and uncle's. The snow was already four inches deep and showed no sign of letting up.

But Brill was still mulling over what Oakes had told him about Tellman. His enemies—again according to Oakes—were many and their complaints legion. Even so, everybody in the county—almost—seemed to like Valdez for the Tellman murder. Ronnie Sepper and Eva Ruiz were paid to raise doubts which, Brill supposed, was not quite the same as differing with public opinion. The one person who had differed, differed expressly, openly, and earnestly was Gary Oakes.

The fight for control of the Poplar Grove church created a long list of potential enemies, the Frank Henning faction, some of whom, Frank especially, were more than a little worked up over the matter. In Wanda's opinion Tellman was one hundred percent on the righteous side of this dispute. How would she react to the list of charges Oakes had leveled at her hero: sleeping around, bullying and threatening parties involved in his business transactions, a skyrocketing drug habit fueled by product purchased from Enrique Valdez, trading looted

Indian artifacts on the underground market. There were whispered allegations of spousal abuse.

To the extent a picture is worth any words at all, the picture of Tellman propped up on the easel at his celebration of life sure as hell squared with the picture painted by Gary Oakes. Brill remained ashamed of himself for being so ready to join the Valdez-did-it crowd without exploring the alternatives. He remained ashamed of the trick he'd tried to pull on Eva Ruiz. Would he feel the same sense of shame if Eva Ruiz wasn't a knockout? Maybe not. But he wanted to see her again, to explain himself and seek a pardon. What better way than to finger one or two people with grudges enough against Tellman that the defense team could create reasonable doubt in the minds of a jury.

Still undecided on which way to go, Brill absently reached down and scooped up a handful of snow. Soon, he was shaping it into a snowball. Ideal texture. He reared back and threw at a lamppost across the street. He threw another and another until, after his shoulder had loosened up some, he hit the target.

Brill looked at his watch. Three-fifteen. Dinner at Wanda's wasn't till six-thirty. Might as well put the time to good use.

Oakes lived in Ramsay Station, named for the engineer-poet who'd helped railroad magnate James J. Hill push the Great Northern's roadbed through the Columbia River gorge. The sun-bleached, sand-scoured town sat twenty road-miles south of Glenview on the Columbia River's north bank. The last ten miles of the trip traversed a series of long switchbacks, dropping more than fifteen hundred feet from the rolling plain on which Glenview was situated to the flats along the river.

Brill set off for Ramsey Station through driving snow which he thought might turn to rain in the course of his descent. If anything, it only came down faster and harder. He was as happy as not to join a slow-moving caravan of vehicles which a county sanding truck led to the bottom of the grade.

There, all vehicles except Brill's turned either east or west onto the state highway. His was the only vehicle headed for Ramsey Station.

The town's permanent population was at most five hundred. But the houses were spread out all over the place as if people had built wherever they felt like, not according to some larger plan or county rule.

It was several years since Brill had visited. What would be open this time of day—four o'clock? The tavern certainly—and maybe the mercantile if it was still in business. At one or the other he could likely get directions to Oakes's house.

Rolling slowly toward the town center, Brill noticed snow-forts facing each other on either side of the road. Each was chest high, semicircular, crenellated on top.

Brill braked to a stop, watching snowballs arc over the road. Kids wearing gloves and coats that seemed too light for the weather were running, skidding, and winging the snowballs at one another. Others crouched behind the forts, popping up to throw. Brill guessed they ranged in age from eight to fifteen. Any girls? Given the clothes it was hard to tell.

Resuming progress, Brill took hits on both flanks of his car. He stopped and rolled his window down a couple of inches and the opening quickly became a target. No big deal. At that age he'd enjoyed the snow in just the same way.

"Hey," Brill called out. "Question for one of you. Easy question. Answer gets you five bucks."

Two of the larger boys broke away from the now co-mingled group. Each wore a knit brown baklava with round cut-outs over the eyes and mouth, giving them the appearance of Ice Age woodchucks.

Brill said he was looking for a guy named Gary Oakes and hoped to get directions to his house. He pulled a five-dollar bill from his wallet. The boys exchanged glances that cemented a conspiratorial silence.

"I knew him in the Army." Brill tapped his nose and snorted a mock line of wacky-dust from the last joint of his index finger. He mimed the recoil of a punch in the face.

The boys snickered. One reached in for the five while the other gave Brill directions.

Snowballs

It was nearing the 4:30 sunset, soon to be dark. Brill soon lost his way among the unlit, unmarked, snow-covered streets. Or maybe it was just that the kid had given him bogus directions. Good thing he knew Oakes's pickup, the tail end of which his headlights picked up in the mouth of a detached one-vehicle garage. He parked the Bronco directly behind the pickup.

Oakes's house was the basic box, at best one-thousand square feet. Likely mindful of flooding, the builder had perched the house on a waist-high foundation.

Four unrailed steps led up to a porch, also unrailed, and to the front door. There were no tracks in the snow-covered approach. Maybe Oakes was elsewhere. But lights were on in the house, his rig was in the garage. Brill had noticed tracks angling from the garage's entrance toward the back of the house and, he guessed, a back door.

At Brill's knock, Gary Oakes opened the door a crack and peered across a six-inch span of heavy chain. His face expressed first a narrow-eyed guardedness, next the pleasure attending the unanticipated visit of an old friend, and finally an anxiety that seemed to find focus in the semi-darkness beyond Brill's shoulder.

"Where's your rig?" Oakes wanted to know. He wore bib overalls over a flannel shirt and a thigh-length corduroy-trimmed denim jacket.

"Parked right behind yours."

"You drive by here a few minutes ago?" Oakes stood with his left flank pushed close to the gap separating door and doorframe, his right arm shielded from view. He talked over his left shoulder and continued to gaze uneasily beyond Brill into the snow-speckled dimness.

"Not before now. Why?"

Oakes gnawed his lip and didn't answer.

Brill grinned. "How 'bout I come in for a minute?"

Oakes looked back over his right shoulder and then looked down the length of his right arm. Brill understood that his prospective host was easing back the hammer of a cocked handgun.

"Dust yourself off," Oakes said. "You can come in and sit a minute, but then you got to go."

The door closed and opened again, just enough to let Brill slip inside. Oakes's gun hand hung loose. Now obviously placed in the right-hand pocket of his denim jacket, the gun pulled it off-kilter.

Brill found himself in a combination living room-kitchen tidier than Oakes's appearance and demeanor had led him to expect. Fixtures fashioned from vintage brakeman's lanterns hung from the ceiling and bathed the room in a warm reddish light. Antique clocks and frames with the glass pressed over artistic arrangements of Indian arrowheads hung on walls that had been paneled with plastic-over-plywood laminate.

Oakes retreated to a sofa pushed back against the left wall and lowered himself onto the far end. "I can't talk to you no more."

"Why's that? Two hours ago, up on top, you couldn't stop talking."

"I since been warned."

"About what?"

Magazines catering to rock hounds and treasure hunters lay on a low table in front of the sofa. Brill dropped onto the sofa's near end and crossed one knee over the other.

"Warned that the Tellman case is sheriff's business. Not mine. Not yours. 'Specially not yours. Up in Glenview when I split for home, a deputy followed me out of town and pulled me over. Interfering in police business, he says, is a crime that could put me in jail."

Brill picked up a magazine. The cover showed the seamed face of a desert rat displaying a hunk of turquoise in either gnarled hand

"And that's not all he said," Oakes continued. "He said if I didn't butt out they'd spread word I been selling drugs. Let the Mexicans fix my hash."

"Well, in fairness, you have been, haven't you? Selling drugs?" Brill returned the magazine to the table.

"No, I never."

"Come on, Gary, don't try to bullshit an old street narc. I lean on any kid in this town, he's gonna point a finger at you. How do you think I found my way here? But hey, I'm not askin' for admissions. I understand your predicament."

"You got to go." Oakes popped up from his chair. He hurried to the front door, undid the chain, and eased the door open a foot. "Matter of life and death."

"In a minute. Don't worry. I've gotta be up the hill and out to my aunt and uncles for 6:30 dinner." Brill stood and turned to look at the wall. Reaching across the back of the sofa, he tapped the glass covering several of the more shapelier and colorful arrowheads displayed in the frames. "You got some beauties here. Lot of hard work, am I right?"

Oakes shrugged guardedly, but Brill could detect a collector's pride. "How old are you, Gary?"

"Thirty-nine," Oakes muttered, easing the door closed though not latched.

"No kidding," Brill said. "Well, hey, you're looking good for your age. The reason I'm asking, I'm remembering that since the early seventies looting an Indian burial site, even a village site, is a federal felony. So, unless you dug these arrowheads—'points' is what we used to call 'em back in my grave-robbing days—as a toddler, then what you got here is multiple felony counts. These days they're actually putting people in prison for looting, and the fines, man, you'd never get out from under."

"I didn't dig 'em," Oakes protested. "I bought 'em and traded 'em off different people."

"Sure, you did. And I bet you got the paperwork squared away on all those transactions. Now I'm not saying I feel a particular inclination to mention any of this. I'm just saying that if the subject came up the conversation could go one way and it could go another."

Brill smiled at Oakes and shook a finger at him.

"I know what you're thinking," Brill went on. "You're thinking God willing, in a minute Detective Brill be out of my house and presto, this stuff be gone. But let's take it the next step. Think of all the work you put into this, the satisfaction you get from these frames. What are you gonna do? Bury 'em? Sell 'em? Never see any of it again?

"I hope you appreciate what I'm doing here. I'm appealing to your better nature. I'm talking about Tellman and I'm talking to the Gary who wants to put the right man in jail for his murder. You've already helped me a bunch, discussing various motives including the church dust-up. Problem is, if church is the motive, I've got myself a big bunch of suspects. I got to start somewhere. So that's all I'm asking. If you were me, where would you start? With Henning? With Henning's pastor who lost his sweet job in the pulpit? Should I be working a different angle altogether? See the respect I'm showing you? You're local knowledge, just like you said when we first met. I'm sincerely asking, what would you do?"

Oakes shifted from foot to foot and gnawed his lower lip. "One name," he said. "One name and one name only and you didn't get it from me."

"Couldn't have," Brill said. "Never was here, never in touch."

Oakes was perspiring and breathing heavily, as if he'd run a long way. "Butch," he said, "Frank Henning's stepson, Butch LaMott. Headed to rehab a couple days ago. Just up and disappeared."

"Where in rehab?"

"Some place in California. That's all I know."

Brill felt pretty cocky, stepping out Gary Oakes's front door. The feeling didn't last. The kids from the snow forts—at least he assumed it was them—swarmed from behind the house, each cradling an armful of snowballs.

The kids formed a semi-circle in front of the porch, pelting Brill unrelentingly—bam-bam-bam—like a phalanx of pitching machines. Why? Was this a town where ill-will was attributed to every stranger? Was it because they'd read Brill for a cop and didn't like his leaning on their pal Gary Oakes? Had they crawled under the house and eavesdropped on the conversation?

Above Oakes's front door was a massive light fixture fitted with a searingly bright bulb. From a barge? A tugboat? He didn't remember it from when he went in. Had Oakes switched it on?

Brill shuffled backward into the cone of light. He neared the door feeling like a would-be escapee in a prison movie. Not the star, one of the expendable characters. First in the searchlight, then riddled with bullets.

The gang yipped and growled, advanced and retreated.

Brill pressed himself to Oakes's door and turned the handle. Locked. He banged the door with the flat of his hand. No response.

What first appeared to be a young kid ran out of the darkness lugging a bucket made for the beach: cartoon starfish, seahorses and shrimp cavorted on the pail's hot pink sides. The kid was short, yes, but maybe not so young as Brill initially thought given the acne and feathery mustache. Whatever he was carrying was a heavy load. He transferred the bucket from hand to hand, listing from side to side with each transfer.

Once within the semi-circle formed by his mates, he plunked the bucket into the snow. Eyes continually fixed on Brill, kid after kid reached into the bucket for a handful or whatever was in there. Gravel, it turned out. They studded their snowballs, then packed and repacked them till they were hard as ice.

Snowballs which at first had merely splatted against Oakes's door now tattooed it. They hit every part of Brill's body. His head and crotch were favorite targets. He managed to duck or dodge away from most of those thrown at his head. Sort of comical…if you weren't on the receiving end.

But then an ice-ball, fist-sized, thrown with conviction, caught Brill square on the left side of his face. Next thing he knew he was lying in the snow beside Gary Oakes's porch, slowly regaining consciousness. Knocked off? Slipped off? How long ago? There was no one around to enlighten him. His assailants had disappeared.

Can't have been out too long, Brill thought. He was cold, yes, but not like he'd been locked in a deepfreeze. He looked for his car. It sat right where he'd left it, in Oakes's driveway. His keys, wallet, and phone were in his pockets, his watch still strapped to his wrist. It didn't seem as if they'd robbed him.

His watch had a glow-in-the-dark dial. He had to squint to make out the numerals and the positioning of the hands. They kept moving around on him, skittering over the watch face. A little after five? Plenty of time to get up the hill, if conditions allowed, and make it to Stan and Wanda's in time for dinner. Not that he felt like eating. He felt sick to his stomach and he had one hell of a headache.

Brill struggled to his feet where he teetered dizzily. He took a step towards his car and the pain in his left hip stopped him…cold. He imagined himself tipping off the porch in deadfall, too numb-minded from the ice-ball's impact to stick out a hand, manage a shoulder roll, or otherwise mitigate contact. For sure, slamming his head on the ground. And, if he hadn't broken his hip, he'd sure bruised the hell out of it.

Brill collapsed in pain. Next thing he knew, Gary Oakes was kneeling at his side. The porch light was out.

"What's wrong with you, man?"

"Concussion? Maybe a broken hip? Gonna need a crutch or a cane to get to my car."

"And your face, man, it's all messed up."

"Got hit with an ice-ball. Had a bunch of gravel in it."

"Yeah, that's something they'll do around here. They can be mean little bastards. You got scratches all down the side of your face." Oakes craned his neck up and searched the perimeter. "I got to get you the fuck out of here before the neighbors come to gawk. Tell you what I'm gonna do. First, I'm gonna stick you in my truck. Then I'm gonna go park your car somewhere near the tavern. Then I'm gonna drive you up to the hospital in Glenview. You got insurance?"

"Yeah."

"Probably the first cash customer they've had in two weeks. Fuck, for you they'll roll out the golden wheelchair."

"I appreciate your taking the trouble," Brill said.

"It's my own ass I'm saving from trouble." Oakes pulled Brill to his feet, ducked under his left arm, and more or less dragged him to the garage.

Brill woke up inside Oakes's truck, leaning against the passenger door. Oakes was getting in the driver's side. "Here's your keys," he said.

"Keys?" Brill didn't remember giving Oakes his keys or noticing that he'd been gone. He took the keys and shoved them in his pocket. He looked over his shoulder. Indeed, the Bronco had disappeared. "It's in front of the tavern?"

"Actually, it's off to the far side, so's you can't see it from the main drag. Okay, we're outta here. Lay down on the seat, at least till we're clear of town."

"I might throw up."

"I'd rather risk that than risk somebody seeing us together."

Brill lay down. Was it better to close his eyes or keep 'em open and look up through the windshield?

The road up the hill had been ploughed and sanded and Oakes had no problem getting to the top. He had the truck's heater working. Brill was sitting up. The warmer the truck's interior, however, the more he felt his injuries. The left side of his face ached. It felt wet. He patted it with the palm of his hand and it came away showing blood.

"Okay," Oakes said. "At the hospital they're gonna ask what happened. They might call in the sheriff. In fact, I'm guessing they will. What're you gonna tell 'em"

"Let's see...."

"You're gonna tell 'em you got rolled. You don't remember exactly when or even where. They'll believe it. You got a concussion. Yeah, you woke up and your car was gone."

"But I've got my keys."

"Shit. Yeah, you do. Tell yah what, give 'em back to me and I'll put 'em on top of your front driver's side tire. And where is your car?"

"At the tavern."

"Which tavern?"

Brill took a moment trying to remember. "Ramsey?"

"That's the one. And where are your keys?"

Brill knew the answer to this one. "Driver's side front."

"And are you gonna mention my name or any part I played in this business?"

"Nope."

Oakes pulled his truck to the curb on a dark street and turned it off. "We're right around the corner from the hospital." He and Brill both lowered their heads as a car drove past. "And we are sure as shit sitting ducks for anyone who knows my rig.

"But wait a minute," Oakes continued. "Didn't you tell me you had to be at your aunt and uncles for dinner?"

"Oh, shit. Yeah. At six-thirty."

Oakes grabbed Brill's left wrist and looked at his watch. "This is Stan Brill you're talking about, right? Your uncle? They live out the Glenview Highway?"

"That's them."

"Forget the hospital. I'm taking you there. Way safer."

"I don't know," Brill said. He was having a hard time working out the consequences.

Oakes was already pulling away from the curb. "That's where we're going. And here's one more thing," Oakes said. He handed Brill a slip of paper. On it he'd written, "Butch LaMott. St Luke's Rehabilitation. Dixon, California."

"This is it?"

"At least it's where he was headed when he left here. Sometimes people veer off on the way… been known to do that myself. But it's a place to start."

"I appreciate the contribution," Brill said, sticking the slip of paper in his shirt pocket.

"It's like I been tellin' you, man, since the first time I saw you. Enrique Valdez may be a bad hombre but he didn't kill Tellman. Even if every fool in this county wants him to be the one. Screw them. Let justice be served."

"Was it Butch LaMott?"

"Coulda been, but I don't think so. I just think he knows who did."

After a long pause during which Oakes sat high in the driver's seat nodding to himself, he turned to Brill. "Okay, this oughta work. The story you tell your aunt and uncle? Gonna be the same story you were gonna tell at the hospital. In fact, they'll probably take you to the hospital. So, everything will jibe."

"And, come to think of it, assuming you're going to the hospital you better give me back that slip of paper. The wrong person might find it while they're fussing over you."

"And notify Frank Henning."

"Or some of his bunch. Or the sheriff."

Brill pulled the slip of paper from his pocket and returned it to Oakes.

"You got sunglasses in your car?"

Brill said he did.

"Are they in a case?"

Brill said they were.

Oakes waved the slip of paper. "I'll put this inside the case. Then even if you don't remember where it is you'll find it come the first sunny day."

"Then I'll find Butch," Brill said, "swear to God. And then I'll find whoever it was that killed Tellman." He brushed under his nose with the back of his index finger as if to stop a sneeze, then asked: "Hey, am I right that the snow has stopped?"

Leaning forward, Oakes squinted through the pickup's smeared windshield.

"Sure enough," he replied. "At least for now."

Served
Ian Blackwell

1

The meat cleaver chopped through the bone. Jill threw the meatless end away; Tom watched her through the hatch.

"There we go. Means a bit more space in the oven. Have you ever worked in a restaurant before?" Jill said, placing the leg of lamb into the casserole dish.

"Never," Tom said.

"I see. Ever worked in any kind of customer service?"

"I've worked in a bar."

"That's a start. Although we're a small restaurant, it gets busy. Once upon a time we ran this place ourselves but it soon became impossible so we were forced to get outside help. You'll have to think quickly because our customers don't like waiting. Most of them will have already been queuing for a while."

"I'll do my best."

"Yes you will."

Tom watched Eleanor set the tables on his side of the hatch in the empty dining area. Jill started grating cheese; her brother Aaron towered in the kitchen corner, chopping carrots.

"Our parents opened here in 2002. Dad passed away a few years ago," Jill said.

"Sorry to hear," Tom said.

"It was hard for Mum but she persevered and made it happen. Aaron and I always helped out and we started working here full-time when we finished school."

Tom watched the siblings prepare more food. Then he pointed at the closed door to the left of the two huge fridges and looked at Jill who had her back to him. "Hey Jill, what's through that door?"

The grating and chopping sounds dropped dead. Jill's head raised, facing the wall in front of her. She turned her head and peered over her shoulder at him. "That's where we marinade pork. Only Mum, Aaron, and I can go in there. Mum will tell you that very soon, I'm sure."

"Hey, am I going to get any help here or what?" Eleanor said.

"Coming now," Tom said, springing to life. He lifted a load of napkins and walked over to Eleanor.

"Thought I'd save you," Eleanor whispered. "They get prickly when you go anywhere near that door. Sam gave me and Ollie the secret marinade speech and she'll definitely be giving it to you too. This restaurant is their lives. As far as I can tell they've no partners or friends or anything outside these walls."

"Oh, okay. Thanks. It went very tense there suddenly," Tom said.

2

Sam's wide frame filled the dining area's doorway soon after the tables were set. "Hello everybody. Ready for another busy evening?" she said.

"I am," Eleanor said.

"Yeah," Tom said.

Sam looked at him. "Tom, are you happy you know what you're doing? Any questions?"

"No. I'll be okay."

"Be sure to write orders as neatly as possible. If you're unsure of anything, please ask. Eleanor will keep you right. She's good," Sam said.

Eleanor smiled, playing with the silver, heart-shaped pendant around her neck. "Thanks."

"Be ready, Tom. The queues are nearly always out the door because they can't get enough of the best pork in town," Sam said.

"Yeah, I noticed there's a lot of pork dishes on the menu. I suppose it makes sense, seeing the restaurant's called *The Fat Pig*," Tom said.

"It's down to the marinade. It's a family secret. Other restaurants would love to get their greasy hands on it, I know it. That's why we don't let anyone outside our family prepare it. Richard and I put in all of our time for many, many months to perfect the recipe. It's our finest achievement and now Richard is gone. It's now a tribute to him, like this whole business. I will never let anyone have our recipe. Never." Sam pointed through the hatch at that door. "Which is why we prepare and marinade pork in the back, out of sight. You're not allowed in there." Sam's face softened. "We can't be too careful, unfortunately. It would ruin our restaurant's success. We've worked too hard to let that happen. We put everything into this."

"Understood," Tom said.

"Good. Now I'm going to go upstairs and make a few calls. I'll be back in a while," Sam said, leaving the dining area.

3

Tom locked the door behind the last customers and sighed. He turned and skipped along the short corridor back to the dining area and saw Sam standing there, smiling at him.

"You weren't messing. They never stopped coming," Tom said.

"And you did really well. I'm so glad I gave you the job. You were both great," Sam said, looking at Eleanor.

"Thanks, Sam. I'm used to it now," Eleanor said.

"There's some ribs leftover so get them down your gullets," Jill said, setting a large plate of them onto the hatch ledge. Sam carried them to the nearest table. Tom and Eleanor walked over and lifted a rib each. The barbeque aroma smothered Tom's tiredness.

"I must admit I've been looking forward to trying these. They smell beautiful," Tom said.

"And taste beautiful as well. That's why we charge top prices," Sam said.

Tom took a bite; the soft meat dissolved in his mouth. He cupped his hand and caught the sticky meat sliding off the bone. He grinned at Sam and Jill's expectant faces. "These are the best ribs I've ever tasted," he said.

"I know," Sam said.

"A lot of love went into those ribs," Jill said.

"You can tell. They're so good," Eleanor said, taking a bite. Sam and Jill watched them eat, feeding off their enjoyment.

"You're on the early start tomorrow, Tom?" Jill said.

"Yeah. Midday?" Tom said.

"That's right, you'll be helping me put away the deliveries. Which means you're staying behind tonight to help clean, Eleanor?"

"Yes. I'll be ready in a minute."

"No rush. You enjoy the ribs and I'll tidy in here," Jill said, disappearing from the hatch back into the kitchen.

The ribs had been reduced to a pile of bones within minutes. Tom wiped most of the sauce off his hands and face with a napkin, and he washed the rest off in the kitchen sink. He said his goodbyes and grabbed his coat from the little cloakroom under the stairs beside the front door. Sam opened the front door for him. "See you tomorrow at twelve," she said.

"Yeah, see you then. Have a nice eve," he said, heading along the street. Sam watched him all the way to the bus stop.

4

Tom arrived back at work just before midday; Jill opened the door and let him in. "Hi, Tom," she said, yawning. "Another day of madness ahead. Delivery should be here soon."

"Okay. Were you guys late getting away last night?"

"Yes it took longer than expected."

"I'll be through in a minute, I'm just going to the loo," Tom said, taking off his coat.

"Sure."

Jill watched Tom skip up the stairs. A faint smell offended Tom's nostrils, and it grew stronger along the corridor.

Like rotten eggs.

The bathroom window was wide open and the heavy, invisible cloud in the air clawed at his nostrils. He was in the kitchen a few minutes later.

"Jill, what's that stink upstairs?"

Jill's face froze. "Oh...we cleaned the sink and toilet. Don't worry about it. It'll be gone soon."

"It's foul. What did you use?"

"Chemicals...Excellent for killing germs. Don't worry about it."

Soon there was someone pounding on the back door.

"There's a delivery," Jill said. She pulled a set of keys from a drawer, stuck one into the lock, and turned it with a loud clank. A miserable-looking man was standing there holding a cardboard box with a clipboard on top. Behind him was a van with its back doors lying open.

"And here's the pork," Jill said. "Hi, Jim. Many deliveries today?"

"Loads as usual," he said, coming in and dumping the box on the counter.

"Hiya," Tom said. The man grunted in reply, lifted the clipboard, and handed it to Jill which she checked and signed. Tom started pulling on the flaps on the box.

"Leave that alone. Go and set tables until the other deliveries arrive and then you can help put them away," Jill said.

"Right," the delivery man said, leaving. Jill moved towards that door beside the fridges. Then she stopped and stared at Tom.

"Okay," Tom said, "I'll go start on the tables."

"Yes."

Tom started towards the dining area. Something glinted under the table beside the door. He bent down and closed his fingers around the cold item. He held it up. Its broken chain slid onto the floor.

Eleanor's heart-shaped pendant.

"This is Eleanor's," he said.

"Is it? Give it to me and I'll look after it for her." Jill said. Tom dropped it into her hand and watched her lift the chain off the floor. "Now hurry on. The other deliveries will be here any minute." Tom obeyed. He heard a key rattling in a lock and turning, a door opening and closing, and the door locking again. He tiptoed to the hatch and peeped into the kitchen; Jill and the box of pork were gone.

Gone marinating.

Tom heard the front door unlocking and opening; he grabbed handfuls of knives and forks and started setting the nearest table. Sam appeared at the doorway.

"Hello, Tom."

"Hiya, Sam."

"Is everything alright?"

"Yeah just setting tables, waiting for the deliveries."

"Where's Jill?"

"Erm...I think she's marinating the pork."

"Did you get up to much last night?"

"No just watched some episodes of *Armageddon Now*. You?"

"Nothing really."

"It's Ollie who'll be waiting the tables with me tonight, isn't it?"

"It is. A good worker."

"Great."

Sam nodded and disappeared upstairs. Five minutes later the phone started ringing. Tom set down the cutlery in his hands and walked over. He lifted a pen, opened the diary, and picked up the phone.

"*The Fat Pig*, Tom speaking, how may I help you?"

"Hello? My name is Amanda and I'm Eleanor's mother."

"Oh, hiya, her pend..."

"Have you seen her? She didn't come home last night and we thought she might've stayed at her boyfriend's but he hasn't seen her so we're very concerned."

"Last time I saw her was last night before I left here. Hang on and I'll get Sam the manager."

"Thanks very much."

Tom skipped through the corridor to the hallway and up the stairs. He knocked on the office door.

"Yes?" Sam said.

Tom opened the door; Sam was sat behind a desk piled with

paperwork. "I've got Eleanor's mum on the phone. She said Eleanor didn't come home last night. Can you speak to her?"

"Well of course," she said, reaching out. Tom handed her the phone. "Get yourself back downstairs and keep yourself busy, Tom. Thank you."

5

Tom carried on setting tables. Soon he heard Jill return to the kitchen, open the oven door, and slide in something heavy. Then he heard the front door being opened and closed; Aaron had to duck his head under the upper door frame to the dining area. He looked at Tom and grinned.

"Hiya, Aaron," Tom said, smiling into his vague eyes. Aaron nodded. "Eleanor's mum called. Eleanor didn't go home last night."

Aaron's grin fell.

"What was that?" Jill called.

"Eleanor. She's missing," Tom said.

Jill appeared at the hatch. "Oh my. I'm sure she's alright. Maybe she went to her boyfriend's?"

"Apparently not," Tom said.

"Didn't notice anything different last night. She left here at 2 a.m.," she said.

"I gave the call to Sam. I think she's still on the phone to her now."

The fruit and veg delivery arrived in numerous boxes. Jill taught Tom to check over the fruit and veg already in one of the two fridges and to throw out anything unfit for consumption, then she talked him through how they like that fridge arranged. Tom looked at the other fridge beside it. "What's in there?"

"That's where we keep meat," Jill said. She pulled the fridge open, showing clean, empty shelves. "We get fresh meat deliveries every day. We manage our stock pretty good so most of what comes gets used the same day. This shelf is for beef, this one is for lamb, then chicken, and fish," she said, pointing at each shelf.

"Okay. So pork isn't kept in there at all?"

Aaron stopped unpacking the vegetables onto the counter, then carried on at a slower pace. Tom felt the kitchen air pushing down on him.

"No," Jill said.

A sound at the doorway caused them to turn: Sam was standing there with the phone in her hand and her mind miles away.

"How did it go?" Tom said.

"She's obviously very upset. All I could tell her was she left here around 3 a.m. last night."

"I thought she left at two?" Tom said, looking at Jill.

"Did I say 2 a.m.? I don't think I did but if I did I was mistaken because it was 3 a.m. because we left just after then," Jill said.

"Ah, okay," Tom said.

Someone's fist hammered the back door.

"Another delivery," Sam said.

6

The coldness slapped Tom's face when he hopped off the bus onto Argyle Street a few days later on a grey afternoon. He walked along the street to *The Fat Pig*, noticing a police car parked outside. He knocked the door and tucked his hands into his armpits, looking up and down the street; a few people were walking along and a car with steamed windows rolled by. A tall, thin policeman emerged from Kelly's Newsagent next door carrying a notepad, spotting Tom and smiling.

"Hello there," he said.

"Hiya."

"Do you work there?"

"Yeah."

"Great. I'm PC Earl. I tried knocking the door but no answer so I've been busying myself asking around the other businesses. I'm very interested in talking to you and your colleagues."

"Is it about Eleanor?"

"Eleanor Kirkby, yes. How'd you know?"

"Her mum phoned a few days ago saying she was missing."

"Yes. Sorry, what's your name?"

"Thomas Smith, Tom."

PC Earl pulled out a pen and started writing. "And when did you last see Eleanor, Tom?"

"Three days ago when I left here."

"What day?"

"Monday eve."

"What time?"

"Erm...Around midnight."

"And did you notice anything unusual about her? Anything at all?"

"No, she seemed fine to me."

"Didn't say anything about where she was going after, what she was going to do, anything?"

"No."

"Did she ever talk about her future plans?"

"Well she's been planning a holiday to Italy with her boyfriend Matthew for ages. She said they've booked the flights and the hotel so they just have to decide what all they're going to do when they get there. Can't think of anything else."

"Thank you for your time. I would like to speak to your colleagues as well. It would be better to do that before you open. When will they get here?"

"Sam and Jill should be here already so I'm surprised they didn't hear you knock."

Tom rapped the door with his knuckles a few times. Sam opened the door. "Hello, Tom. Looks like you've brought a friend," she said. "How can I help you, officer?"

"Hello there. I'm PC Earl. I'd like to speak to you and your colleagues about Eleanor Kirkby."

"Of course, officer. Please come in." She stepped back and pulled the door open; Tom allowed PC Earl to enter first. Sam and PC Earl disappeared to the office upstairs. Tom hung his coat in the cloakroom and went through to the dining area where Ollie was setting tables.

"Hiya, Ollie," he said.

"Good day, Tom. Who's the fella I heard?"

"A policeman asking about Eleanor. He's upstairs with Sam now."

"Ah, there you are now. I hope Eleanor is well but it doesn't look good if I'm being honest. Hopefully they find her though."

"What was that?" Jill appeared at the hatch.

"There's a policeman upstairs with Sam, asking about Eleanor."

"Good. I'm glad they're on the case. Her family must be worried sick."

PC Earl soon came down the stairs, spoke to Jill and Ollie, and left after scribbling down their answers.

7

Tom was leafing through his newspaper in the tearoom upstairs during his break. He was scanning the job section when one advert caught his eye:

> Waiter / Waitress required—Immediate Start
> Full-time / Part-time
> The Fat Pig
> Gladstown
> Tel: 0848 2534591

Sam said nothing about getting another waiter. Nobody has said anything.

Tom looked at the date on the front page: Tuesday 14 April 2022.

That's two days ago.

A little box in the page corner stated: Deadline Monday 12 pm for complete ad requests for next issue.

That ad would've had to have been placed three days ago—the last day I saw Eleanor. It almost looks like someone knew Eleanor would disappear.

Tom tried to engross himself in the sports section, but it didn't work: he kept thinking about that advert.

There's no 'almost' about it. It does look like someone knew Eleanor would no longer be working here.

The door's hinges squealed, making Tom jump in his chair. Sam entered, walking behind him towards the kettle. "Hello, Tom. Just making a cup of tea. Would you like one?"

"No thanks Sam, my break's nearly over."

"You sure?"

"Yeah."

Tom watched her lift the kettle and move to the sink. She turned the tap; the rushing water noise burst through the silence. He stared at her back as she filled the kettle. He breathed in.

"Just reading the paper here," he said.

"Hmm..."

"I see we've an ad for another waiter."

Sam turned off the tap and closed the kettle's lid. She placed the kettle back on its base, turned it on, lifted a mug, and dropped a teabag into it. Her head turned to him and her smile was big. "Yes, that's right. Did I not mention it? I had Jill organise it. It gets busy here so I thought another pair of hands would be helpful."

"No, that's the first I've heard of it. Is the new waiter to replace Eleanor?"

"It seems that's the way it's going to be now."

"What I mean is, did you put that ad in the paper to replace Eleanor?"

Sam's smile lowered.

"No...I was going to get someone regardless," she said.

"So in terms of waiters there would've been me, Eleanor, Ollie, and then another one. Don't you think that would've been a bit much?"

Sam's face hardened. Tom saw her fist tighten on the counter beside a big, sharp kitchen knife. "Do not tell me how to run my business, thank you very much Tom. And what is it with all these questions? What's on your mind?"

"N...Nothing I...I just thought...it was strange."

"Yes, I see what you mean. We were aiming to expand our team, yet now we're replacing. The advert is lucky timing, if that's what you can call it, and that's all it is. What else could it possibly be?" she leaned back and laughed, bringing both hands to her chest. "I shouldn't laugh, really. It's a very sad situation. I hope they find Eleanor and find her soon."

The boiling kettle clicked; Sam poured it into her mug. Tom stood up, folding his newspaper. "I better get back," he said, pulling the creaky door open and exiting.

"Yes you should."

8

"Hurry up, Tom. You're taking too long," Jill said.

"I'm going no slower than normal."

"Just shut up and get on with it."

"Where's the bin keys?" Tom was clawing through the many things in the kitchen drawer.

"They should be in there as always."

"They're not."

"They better not be."

Jill sighed, stopped wiping the bench, and marched over, glaring into the drawer. She grabbed and tore out a bundle of envelopes, tossing them onto the worktop. Her hand dived back into the drawer and searched. Then Tom heard the jingling of keys and watched her hand come back out and dump the bin keys on the counter.

"There. How could you not find them?"

"Sorry," Tom said.

"Honestly. Sometimes I wonder about you, Tom. Now get a move on."

Tom lowered his head. He lifted the keys and the plastic bin of discarded bones and fat, exited out the back door, placed the bin beside the bigger bins, held the keys up to the light, and picked out the right key from the bunch.

Sam, Jill, and Aaron have been proper cold towards me the last few days since I asked Sam about that ad. They're still being nice to Ollie.

He stuck the key into the red meat bin and turned it. The lid pushed back; a waft of rotting meat attacked his nose. He peered in. The weak floodlight above the door wasn't enough so he pulled his phone out and turned its torch on. There were bones, stringy meat, and lumps of fat. But a large, pink pile towards the back caught his eye. He pointed the light at it; racks of pork ribs were piled high.

Why are they throwing all that out?

He leaned forward, grabbed one of the ribs, pulled it to his nose, and sniffed.

It hasn't gone off. But there's no way they've made a mistake, surely. Better not ask about it though or they might get even more snappy with me.

He closed the lid which clicked locked. Feet shuffled behind him; a tall figure was coming through the darkness towards him carrying large, white things. Aaron emerged into the weak light with his head lowered. He raised his head and saw Tom. His huge frame froze.

"Hiya, Aaron," Tom said, looking down at the four sealed, white buckets Aaron was carrying. "Whatcha up to?" Aaron lowered his head again, shrugged, and carried on. He knocked the door open wider with his big shoulder and entered the kitchen. Tom lifted the container and followed him. Jill had a key with a round, yellow keyring out and turning in that door which must not be mentioned. She stopped when she saw Tom and stared at him. Tom looked down at the buckets.

"Sometimes we marinade at home. So get out of this kitchen and find something to do," she said.

Tom placed the bin back and fled to the dining area. He heard that door opening.

Marinating at home? Why not just do it here? Strange.

9

Tom and Ollie were spraying and wiping down the tables after they had closed for the night; Jill and Aaron were cleaning the kitchen in silence.

"I'm kinda glad I've got you here to talk to," Tom whispered to Ollie, eyeing the hatch.

"Why's that?"

"You're the only one I can have a chat with. Everyone else is on the verge of biting my head off."

"Yep, I've noticed that...Maybe they've had a dispute between themselves and are cranky about it."

"They've been okay with you."

"True. What did you do? Sneak in through that door in the kitchen no-one talks about?" Ollie laughed.

"No."

"I'm sure it'll be grand."

"Hopefully. Do you know there's an ad in the paper for another waiter?"

"Really?"

"Don't mention it to them, but there is."

"To replace Eleanor, obviously."

"No. The ad was submitted before she disappeared. Sam said she had already decided to get someone before she knew Eleanor was missing."

"Fair enough."

"Don't you think it's strange they didn't say they were going to advertise for someone?"

"Maybe they forgot to say."

"Not strange at all?"

"Doesn't bother me. I just want to get home and the sooner we finish, the better, so speed up."

Tom squeezed the trigger of his cleaning spray: the nozzle croaked and sputtered, dribbling some cleaning solution down his hand. "Looks like I'm out," he said, "but I don't want to ask for more because they're so snappy. Can you do it?"

"Just go and get it yourself. The storeroom is upstairs, the door at the very end."

"Will it be alright to go in there?"

"Yep, I go in there to get stuff all the time."

"Right. I'll be back in a second."

Tom left his cloth on the table and exited to the hallway, realising he now treads around work rather than walks.

We'll see how things go. If they keep being horrible to me then I'm out of here. They can put two ads in the paper.

He skipped up the stairs and tiptoed past the office, tearoom, and bathroom. A floorboard beneath the carpet groaned. His ears listened for any sounds behind him all the way to the door at the end of the corridor. The door handle was stiff but turned. The rusty hinges clawed through the silence, tightening Tom's shoulders. His hand found the light switch, turning it on. There were white walls with shelves covered in dusty, brown boxes and a mop and bucket on the floor. He stepped into the room. There were boxes in the far corner stacked taller than him. Something big and blue was peeking out from behind them. He crept over for a quick look.

It was a large, blue barrel. It had a red 'Corrosive' sticker on it and was labelled 'SULFURIC ACID'. He could see the top of another blue barrel behind it.

For cleaning? It's a lot to have just for cleaning toilets and whatever...

A look in some of the boxes on the shelves revealed cleaning products like washing-up liquid, dish cloths, and disinfectant cleaning sprays. He pulled out a spray bottle and left, swinging the door closed behind him to hasten the creak of the hinges.

When Tom arrived home later that night, he searched online for what sulfuric acid is used for. His whole body softened when most of the results said it's an excellent toilet bowl and drain cleaner. He moved his cursor onto the X at the screen's corner. But then one search result title at the bottom caught his eye:

Can acid dissolve a body? | Opinion

Words like 'crime', 'gruesome', and 'notorious killer' were in the snippet text. He gripped the mouse, bringing the cursor to the link, and clicked on it. The page took ages to load.

The headline read: 'The acid test: the killers who used chemistry to cover their tracks'.

It was written by a chemistry professor called Emma Stockley. He scanned down the article: 'Sulfuric acid causes destruction via hydrolysis of large biomolecules (such as carbohydrates, lipids and proteins)...can destroy bone and teeth within a day…Marvin Laing, also known as the 'acid killer', used sulfuric acid to dispose of at least three victims' corpses…was only caught after neighbours complained about the pungent smell…the egg-like smell is caused by the liberation of hydrogen sulfide…'

The bathroom was stinking of rotten egg the day after Eleanor went missing.

Tom leaned back in his chair and closed his eyes.

I'm thinking too much. Eleanor will turn up soon and then I'll know I was stupid for even having such thoughts. I've a wild imagination…

10

Tom hopped down the bus steps onto Argyle Street the next day. It was a cold mid-morning; he took small, careful steps on the ice-dusted pavement. He kept his eyes on the pavement in front of him, glancing up now and again. He saw a police car outside Kelly's Newsagent next door to *The Fat Pig*. PC Earl emerged from the newsagent's carrying a CD case.

"Hiya, officer," Tom said, smiling.

PC Earl looked at him. "Hello there…it's Tom, isn't it?"

"Yeah. Any luck finding Eleanor?"

"No, sadly. But I've finally been able to get a copy of the CCTV for the night in question." PC Earl pointed up at the space between the newsagent's door and the shop sign. "You see that little black cube there?"

"Yeah."

"That's a security camera, and an expensive one at that. You wouldn't know it was there, would you?" PC Earl said.

"It doesn't even look like a camera. Did you only see it today? Is that why you're only getting the footage now?"

"No, I knew it was there. But the owner was away, and he is the only one who knows how to operate his system. The son couldn't work it, neither could I, and no-one at the station has used this particular one before either." He shrugged. "Couldn't see Eleanor on the footage I got from other stores. It's a funny one. She's disappeared without a trace, just like many homeless around here."

"Homeless?"

"Yes. Many homeless have gone missing over the years, so much so there's not many around anymore. We've no idea how many have gone missing because most of them aren't reported. All I know is it's me that ends up being sent to investigate the ones that are. Never turns anything up though. It's sad, really, how people can go missing without much fanfare."

"Yeah."

"It's funny how so many have disappeared though. It's also funny how two people who worked in the same place have gone missing."

Tom's face fell flat. "What was that?"

"Eric Chambers. He used to work at *The Fat Pig* about three years ago. One night he didn't come home from work, just like Eleanor. Was never seen again. To happen twice really is something, don't you agree?" PC Earl stared, waiting.

Tom realised he forgot to exhale; he let the air escape him. "Really?"

"Yes, really. I find it unusual you're only hearing about Eric now. I would have thought someone would've said something, especially because another employee of theirs has gone missing."

PC Earl watched Tom place his hand on the lamppost beside him and stare at the ground. Tom took another breath. "How long have you worked there?" PC Earl asked.

"A week."

"And is it going well?" PC Earl asked.

"Fine, fine," Tom said.

"Have you seen or heard anything unusual?"

"No."

"I'm going to give you my card. If you do notice anything unusual, anything at all, call me." PC Earl pulled out a business card; Tom took it. "Anything you tell me is confidential."

"Thanks," Tom said.

"Take care of yourself, Tom. And remember: anything at all, call me."

"Will do. See you later."

PC Earl opened his car door and climbed in. Tom watched him start the engine and pull away. He stared down at the ground again.

It's proper strange no one mentioned Eric. It looks like they've got something to hide. Two people going missing from the same business. But surely they've nothing to do with it. Surely...

He looked at the newsagent's door.

If I knew Eleanor left work that night, I'd know her disappearance has nothing to do with them.

He walked to the door and pushed it open. The electric bell rang out, alerting the man in his sixties behind the counter. He looked at Tom and smiled. "Mornin'."

"Morning. My name's Tom, I work next door." He pointed at the wall towards the restaurant. "I was just speaking to PC Earl. This is probably a strange request but do you mind if I have a quick look at your CCTV, if that's alright?" He eyed the monitor sitting on a high shelf behind the man.

"Er...Sure, don' see why not. Haddit installed a year 'go 'cos you neva know. Dat policeman was tellin' me 'bout the missin' girl." The man lifted a remote control sitting beside the monitor. "So what time period you wanna look at? Prob'ly Monday night, the same period I burned for dat cop."

"That would be great. Can you start around midnight, please? Can we fast-forward and all?"

"We can. We'll start a' midnight and fast-forward and slow down when we see somethin'. How's dat?" He pointed the remote at the screen, brought up a menu, and started selecting options.

"Yeah that's great because I start work soon so I've only got a few minutes."

"Right. Here we go."

The screen showed the dark street around the newsagent's door. The pavement in front of *The Fat Pig* was at the top of the screen. The screen's corner said 00:00:00. Then fuzzy, white lines started wriggling across the screen. The man pressed play when there was movement around *The Fat Pig*'s door at 00:03:21. A figure emerged.

"That's me," Tom said, watching himself walk out of the frame, "And that's Sam." They watched Sam watch Tom walk to the bus stop.

She watched me for quite a while there.

"Keep going, please," Tom said.

The minutes piled on to the clock. Tom noticed 2 a.m. pass and nothing. 3 a.m. came and still nothing.

At 03:39:09 there was movement; the man pressed play again.

A large, round figure emerged: Sam. She looked up and down the street as she held the door open for the two tall people who joined her: Jill and Aaron. They also glanced around as they waited for Sam to lock the door. Then they walked away together.

"Okay. Speed it up again?" Tom said. The man did so; nothing appeared on the screen until after 6 a.m. which was someone walking past.

"I better get to work," Tom said. "Thanks for letting me look at that."

"Is dat it? Did you see what you expected? Was one of those people the missin' girl?"

"Thanks again. I have to go." Tom left and knocked on *The Fat Pig*'s door. It opened to reveal Sam's sour face.

11

The venomous looks from Sam and Jill kept Tom's head down; he busied himself putting away the deliveries as they arrived whilst Jill chopped vegetables. Tom signed the pork delivery man's pad and placed the box on the counter.

"Leave that there. I'll deal with it," Jill said with her back to Tom.

"Okay. I'll work on other boxes."

Tom dropped the heavy box down amongst the other boxes on the counter. There was a sharp knife beside him. His fingers pulled the flaps open on another box. A peep back at Jill told him she still had her long back to him. The flaps on the box of pork were easy to open, revealing pink and red, packed tight with ribs. He lifted the knife, careful to make no sound. Jill's back was still turned. The knife sliced a deep groove on one side of the top rack of ribs. It did the same to another rack, and another, and more. The flaps folded back into each other and the knife was hidden between two other boxes. He moved back to the other box he had opened and looked inside: beef.

Jill dropped her knife and turned.

"Where's the pork?"

"It's this one," Tom said, pointing at it.

Jill pulled the key with the round, yellow keyring out of her pocket, walked over to that door, and unlocked it. She pressed the handle and pulled the door open a little. Her cold eyes caught Tom staring; Tom closed his eyes and turned back to the box of beef. He heard her footsteps on the tiles, coming towards him. His shoulders tensed up. Then she was beside him, lifting the box of pork. "Get on with those deliveries. And don't take all day like you usually do," she said.

"Okay."

Her footsteps moved away. Tom heard a light switch flick on and the door was closed and locked. He turned back to the closed door.

I want to know what goes on in there.

Someone was coming through the dining area; he lifted the box of beef and carried it to the fridge, dumping it down on the worktop beside it. A glance over his shoulder showed Ollie's face lighting up the doorway.

"Tom."

"Hiya, Ollie. How's it going?"

"Not too bad."

"Good job. I'm wondering: you know the way Eleanor has gone missing?"

Ollie's smile weakened. "Yep?"

"I ran into PC Earl earlier on."

"That's the cop who was asking us all about Eleanor?"

"Yeah. He told me that Eleanor isn't the first person to go missing from this restaurant."

"Is that right?"

"Yeah. A guy used to work here called Eric. He disappeared as well."

"That's a good one." Ollie studied Tom's face and leaned closer, smiling. "What's your thinking?"

"Nothing. It's just…it's strange. What do you make of it?"

"Do you think the Arthur family have been killing off their staff?" Ollie lifted his head and laughed. "Do you think they had to lay them off but didn't want to pay out? Or maybe the Arthurs are cannibals and are feeding people to the customers?" Ollie stopped laughing when he saw Tom staring at him, unsmiling. "Sorry. I shouldn't be saying stuff like that. Sorry, it's just the way you came across."

"Came across like what?"

"You know…the way you were saying…it's strange two people who worked here are missing."

"Yeah, it is strange, isn't it?"

"Ah, I think you're being way too cynical, Tom. Too many conspiracy shows."

Tom saw someone appear at the doorway behind Ollie. He leaned to one side to see who it was; Sam's face turned cold when their eyes met. "What are you two talking about?"

"Nothing, just messing around," Tom said.

Ollie turned and looked at Sam. "Yep Sam, just carrying on. You keeping well?"

"Where's Jill?" she said.

"In there," Tom said, pointing.

"Right. One of you get those orders away and the other get the dining area ready."

"With pleasure," Ollie said, stepping around Sam's round frame and out of the kitchen.

Sam stared at Tom who turned back to his box of beef and pulled the fridge open, pretending not to notice her. He could feel Sam's stare burning into the back of his skull. Then he heard her walk away and the back of his skull began to cool.

12

Another frosty evening at work was slow to pass for Tom despite it being busy as usual. Sam saw the last table of customers out and locked the door behind them. She came back into the kitchen, pulling her big coat on. Aaron followed her with his coat and scarf already on. "Right people, we're away home," Sam said, smiling at Jill and Ollie. She then gave Tom a wide smile; he stood there open-mouthed. Aaron smiled and nodded at them. Everyone returned their farewells.

"I'll lock the door behind you," Jill said. She followed Sam and Aaron to the front door, let them out, and came back. "I've got a few things to do so I'm going upstairs for half an hour. You guys hurry up because I'm tired and I won't have you guys holding me back." She disappeared out of the kitchen and through the dining area.

"I can do the kitchen," Ollie said.

"It's alright, I'll take care of the kitchen," Tom said.

"Sure?"

"Yeah. When you're done in the dining area you can help me, if that's alright."

"We'll see. I'll be going home on time," Ollie said.

"Yeah, just see how you get on. I'm going to empty the bins."

"Grand."

Ollie lifted a cloth and cleaning spray out from under the sink, left the kitchen, and started triggering the spray and slapping his cloth around table tops. Tom pulled open the messy kitchen drawer and wriggled his hand through its contents, closing his fingers around the bin keys when he saw them and pulling them out. He opened the backdoor and stepped outside with the meat bin under his arm; the container landed on the ground beside the large bin. The key unlocked the bin and the lid slid back. Tom paused and listened; he could hear the faint sounds of Ollie cleaning. His phone came out of his pocket, its torch awoke, and it pointed into the bin. Tom peered in, fighting to ignore the smell repulsing his nose's nerve endings.

Pink and red glistened; bones stuck out in all directions.

There was a pile of pork ribs close to him. He grabbed the rack at the top and examined it: there was a sharp cut at one end. The next rack had the same. His hand fished out more racks: they all had the marks he gave them earlier. Tom stared into the bin, into the abyss.

Customers who've ordered pork haven't been getting pork. So what have they been getting?

Memories took over: all of the times he'd gobbled down ribs they cooked for him, enjoying every second, savouring the taste of...

A burning mouthful of stomach contents slapped the back of his throat. He swallowed hard. Gravity's strength multiplied, pulling his weightless head downwards. His hand grabbed the rim of the bin, his mouth opened, and he inhaled; the taste of rotting meat made him retch and swallow again. Sweat flowed from every pore. His nose leaned away and sucked in as much air as it could.

It was pork, it was pork.

Eleanor, Eric, and all the homeless who disappeared.

No...Surely not. There is no way anyone could get away with something like that...

His back straightened up; his hands held on to the bin. The sulfuric acid from the bathroom upstairs swirled around his mind, the same kind of acid that can be used to dispose of bodies. He remembered the stink that tore at the inside of his nostrils the day after he last saw Eleanor.

In theory, they could've killed her, butchered her up, and left the unwanted parts in a barrel of acid overnight. Then they could've poured the barrel down the toilet and flushed it away. Then they could've fed her to customers as pork. They might even have taken some of her for themselves. There wouldn't be a trace left of her. The same could've happened to all the homeless and Eric as well. No one would ever suspect it. If anyone ever does, they could prove they've been getting pork deliveries and say that's what they've been using.

But if such a thing has happened to all the missing homeless then it would take a lot of acid. This place would be stinking all the time.

I've seen Aaron take in buckets of marinated pork from home though. They're always here every day before me so they could be taking loads more buckets in without me knowing. If they're doing most of their people-butchering at home, then that would mean not stinking the restaurant out...

But why kill Eleanor?

PC Earl did say there's less homeless around so stock could be running low. They could be desperate to meet demand and maybe slaughtering staff has worked before...

He peered into the kitchen at the closed door in the corner.

Marinating goes on in there...Marinating of human flesh.

Tom's lunch exploded out of him and into the bin, an avalanche showering half-digested food all over the ribs and Tom hoped it would also smother all of his dark thoughts so he'd forget all about them. His stomach emptied. The last chunks spat out and he wiped his mouth with the back of his hand like he did on many drunken Saturday nights before. He felt a little better, but those dark thoughts remained.

13

Tom filled a glass with water in the kitchen and took a long drink, washing away most of the foul taste.

My imagination is mental. It really can't be what it looks like. The pork in the bin must have been dropped on the floor or something, all of it...

PC Earl's card was lying at home somewhere.

I should phone him, tell him what I think. So what if it sounds mental? He's got the footage, he probably already knows Eleanor didn't leave here that night.

He emptied the other bins, locked the back door, and chucked the keys back into the drawer, pushing and flattening them among everything else in there so the drawer would close. His hand started to close the drawer but stopped: something in there caught the light, caught his eyes.

A round, yellow keyring.

His heart tried to leap out but it was trapped. His sweaty fingers closed around the keyring and lifted; the attached key slid out from under a slip of paper. It had string tangled around it but a quick shake freed it. Tom leaned his head and peeped out the hatch to check on Ollie: he was hurrying around a far table, missing large areas with his wet cloth.

Tom stared down at his hand.

Don't know why the key to that door is here, but it's here.

It lowered into his pocket.

Ollie will be away home soon. I'll try and have a quick look. It could be my only chance.

He started spraying and wiping down the kitchen surfaces, leaving the area closest to that door alone so he could pretend he was cleaning there later if required. Ollie came back into the kitchen.

"That's me done, boy," he said, hurling his dishcloth into the bin.

"So that's you away home then?"

"It is indeed. I'm getting out of here." He pulled open the cupboard door under the sink and dropped his cleaning spray in. "I'll shoot up and get my bag and you can let me out."

"No worries," Tom said. His heart climbed higher in his chest with each beat, still trying to find a way out of this. Ollie rushed out of the kitchen. Tom stopped wiping and looked down at the floor under the table, where he found Eleanor's pendant.

She was attacked. Her pendant's chain was broken in the struggle. She fought hard but was overpowered. It would've been easy to drag her limp body across this floor and through that doorway.

Tom closed his eyes and sighed.

No. That didn't happen. Eleanor wasn't in the CCTV footage because she left by the back door. Forget about the other guy Eric. The acid stink was nothing more than a powerful way of cleaning drains. Sam was telling the truth about the ad and really did want another waiter as well as Eleanor. If I can, I'll have a quick peek behind that door after I let Ollie out. That'll put my mind at ease and prove I overthink things too much. There'll be nothing in there except buckets of marinade or whatever. I'll lose my job if I get caught but I don't like this job anymore anyway and at least I'll get a life lesson in how ridiculous I am.

"Goodbye, Jill. See you tomorrow," Tom heard Ollie shout; Jill shouted something back. Tom started towards the front door, straightening up when he realised he was creeping. He forced his stiff body to relax, to pretend there's nothing to hide. He emerged from the corridor, meeting Ollie hopping off the bottom stair.

"Goodnight Ollie. See you tomorrow," Tom said, unlocking and pulling open the front door.

"Indeed you will, Tom. See you later."

Ollie stepped outside and carried on walking; Tom closed and locked the door, leaving the keys dangling in the lock. He looked up the stairs, leaning to one side to see some of the top half of the closed office door; light peered out from around its edges.

"Jill?"

Footsteps. The office door opened and Jill stuck her head out. "Yes, Tom?"

"Er…I'm just checking if you'd like me to crack on with the cleaning?"

"Yes, Tom. I'm going to be in here for say another twenty minutes. Is that okay?"

"Yeah, no problem."

"Thanks, Tom. I'm sorry. I'll definitely be no longer than twenty minutes." Jill smiled and disappeared, closing the door.

Tom shot along the hall with his hand clasped over his pocket, stopped in the dining area, and listened back towards the staircase; a few seconds of silence passed. He rushed into the kitchen towards that door.

14

Tom placed his hand on the door's cold, rough surface. His hand was shaking.

There's going to be blood everywhere. Who knows how many people have been butchered behind this door?

He pulled the key out of his pocket and stared at it.

I'm being silly. All they've got behind there is pork and their precious marinade.

He turned, leaned towards the kitchen hatch, and listened: nothing. The key slid into the lock and turned, awakening the mechanism; the clanking made Tom's palms sweat. Then the key couldn't turn any more. Tom listened out again: still silent. His fingers wrapped around the cold door handle and pressed it down, pulling the door ajar, and revealing silent darkness. He reached inside; cold air grasped his fingers as they fumbled around the wall for the light switch. They found one and pressed it on. A tired bulb flickered on, giving a dull glow, forcing the darkness to retreat to the end of a short corridor. The bottom of the rough walls had dark stains along them.

Still no sound from the restaurant behind him. His feet crept along the cement floor. Everything beyond the corridor's end was still hiding in the darkness. The smell of the marinade, once comforting, now haunted the cold air.

They didn't drag Eleanor through here.

He slowed down when he was close to the corridor end and stopped when he reached it. The marinade smell was stronger, thicker, threatening. His hand found another light switch on the edge of the unknown and turned it on.

A powerful light burst into life, killing the darkness, revealing everything. He was in a room. There was a long, steel workbench against the far wall. The left side of it had four large, white buckets on it—the same kind he saw Aaron bring in before. The right side had the largest wooden chopping board Tom had ever seen. Millions of chop marks curved its surface. There were faint red stains all over it and on the floor in front of the bench.

Blood from pork, not from people.

There was a small, steel table to his left. It had a mountain of clean knives and cleavers stacked on it. He looked at the buckets and stepped forwards, but something on the small table made him look again.

A small axe.

Don't see what place that has in meat preparation. Never mind. I'll just look in the buckets, see it's only pork and marinade, and get back to the kitchen. Can't believe I'm doing this.

His reluctant feet had to be pushed towards the plastic buckets. He stopped in front of them. They had lids clipped onto them with thick, red marinade stains around the rims. He grabbed the handle of the nearest one and tested its weight: heavy. His fingers slipped under the lid and pulled it upwards, forcing it off; a smooth, dark marinade surface rested at the halfway point.

Nothing but marinade. There's nothing out of order here. Now get out and never come in here again.

Tom clipped the lid back into place. He turned around.

Sam, Jill, and Aaron were there. Their faces were twisted with fury. They closed in around him.

"Er...I am so sorry...I...I just..." Tom said.

Sam stepped forward. Tom turned to her, raised his hands, and opened his mouth to speak. Aaron jumped forwards, swinging his arm; the crack of shattering bone exploded through the silence. Tom collapsed to the ground with his leg twitching. A pool of blood grew outwards on the floor, flowing from where the small axe was buried in Tom's temple.

15

There was a loud knock at *The Fat Pig*'s front door the next morning at 10 a.m. Sam opened the door; PC Earl's stern face. Eight police officers stood poised behind him. Sam stared open-mouthed.

"Samantha Arthur?" PC Earl said.

"Y...Yes?"

PC Earl held out an envelope. Sam looked at it, then accepted it. She opened her mouth to speak but the police officers pushed past her and swarmed out. PC Earl stepped inside and stared into Sam's eyes. "I've just handed you a warrant to search the premises. We've reason to believe Eleanor Kirkby didn't leave here on the night she disappeared. Do you have any information as to her whereabouts?"

"No I...I've already told you that."

Jill and Aaron stormed out from the dining area. "What the hell is going on?" Jill said.

PC Earl started climbing the stairs. Jill chased and overtook him, stopping at the top of the stairs, blocking the way, and towering over him.

"If you don't stand aside I'll arrest you for obstructing a police officer," he said.

"I want to know what you're doing," Jill said.

"This is outrageous. I have never seen the likes in all my years. I want you all out. Now," Sam said.

"We'll leave when we're done," PC Earl said over his shoulder. He turned his face back to Jill. "I will not ask you again. Move."

Jill dragged herself backwards onto the landing. PC Earl climbed up and looked in through the open office door; two police officers were opening cupboards and clawing out their contents.

"Anything?" he said.

"No," the nearest one said. She pointed at the wall in the direction of along the corridor. "We haven't got that far yet."

PC Earl looked along the corridor. "What's over there?" he asked. He watched Sam and Jill swap glances. Aaron looked down at the floor. Two male police officers appeared from the staircase. "Nothing downstairs," one of them said, "except there's a door in the kitchen that's locked."

"Where's the key?" PC Earl asked the Arthurs.

Shy glances. They avoided his eyes.

"Smash it in then," PC Earl said.

"Will do," the same officer said, heading back down the stairs.

PC Earl looked at the other officer. "The two of us will go this way." They strode along the corridor towards the bathroom and storeroom.

PC Earl stopped. "What is that smell?"

"Bleach or acid or something," the officer said.

"There's nothing over there," Sam said, taking a few steps towards them, "just a bathroom and a stockroom."

"So you won't mind us having a look, will you?" PC Earl said.

"I want you all out of here now. Don't have any doubt about me putting a complaint in about this. It's absolutely disgusting."

"You all stay there," PC Earl said, waving his pointed finger at the Arthurs. He carried on along the corridor and the other police officer followed.

"You should all be out there catching proper criminals and not bothering innocent people like us," Sam called after him. She looked round at Jill and Aaron's concerned faces and joined them in watching the police officers open the bathroom door and enter.

PC Earl stuck his head back around the doorway. "Why do you keep a barrel of acid in here?"

"For cleaning the toilet and drains," Sam said.

"Quite a big barrel for that, isn't it?"

"We buy in bulk."

"And I must say it's quite dangerous. What's wrong with bleach?"

"We kept getting a sewage smell when we used bleach which isn't good for business when you run a restaurant. Though I'm sure you wouldn't understand that seeing you're hassling honest taxpayers like us. Hurry up and have your look around and get out. We've nothing to hide."

"In good time." PC Earl's eyes moved from Sam to Jill to Aaron. "So the barrel contains acid. Is that right?"

"Yes," Sam said.

"Nothing else?"

"Like what? Honestly, officer, we've a restaurant to get ready for opening and you're wasting our time. What's your badge number?"

"I'll give it to you in a minute. Stay there," PC Earl said, disappearing back into the bathroom. He walked over to the barrel.

"Be very careful. See the lid? It's not been put on properly. The fumes could get ya," the other officer said.

"I see. I wonder if..." PC Earl said, looking around; there was a toilet roll on the ledge of the open window. He picked it up and stretched his arm out, keeping his face and body as far as possible from the barrel, and used the roll to flick the barrel's plastic lid off. The lid dropped onto the floor.

"Ya don't wanna be breathing that in. Cover your mouth," the other officer said, pulling his jacket up over his nose. PC Earl straightened up and did the same.

"Enough of this nonsense. I want you all out of this building now," Sam said from the doorway.

"You're hindering an investigation so go away," PC Earl said.

"But there's nothing in there."

"Then you've nothing to stress about. Now go away or I'll have you charged for obstructing a police officer."

"Everything alright over there?" an officer shouted from the top of the stairs.

"No. Bring some officers over here. This lady is hindering the investigation," PC Earl said.

"Oh, come now..." Sam said.

"Get away from the door. Go away back along where you came from," PC Earl said.

"But officer..."

"Go. Now. One more word and I will have you arrested."

Sam dragged her wide figure from the doorway, out of sight. PC Earl tiptoed to the door and swung it, slamming it shut. "Right. We're going to look in this barrel because something doesn't seem right."

"I'm sure my eyes are starting to burn," the other officer said.

The two officers stepped forward with their faces covered and peered into the barrel. The clear liquid surface was a few inches short of the brim.

There was something in there. Something big, dissolving and flattening.

"What's that?" The other officer said.

PC Earl leaned closer.

"Careful now," the other officer said.

PC Earl stared at the white thing covered in pink patches, dropped in there, resting against the side of the barrel. The round part nearest the surface had lots of light-brown, fibrous material coming out of it.

Hair. PC Earl thought it looked like that lad Tom's hair only now bleached lighter and the skeleton's shape with stringy pieces of flesh hanging onto it reminded him of Tom and even though most of the face had been burned away he could still see Tom there too and there's a hole in his head and this has blown the situation into front page news and PC Earl now knows a lot more grizzly things have happened under this roof and he better get his colleagues over here because who knows what those sick creatures in the hallway are capable of.

The door swung open; another two officers are standing there.

"Everything alright?" one of them said.

"No. There's a body in there," PC Earl said, pointing at the barrel. "This is now a murder investigation. Arrest them," he said, moving his finger to the wall the Arthurs were behind.

They all headed straight for them.

"You're all under arrest on suspicion of murder. We're taking you into custody to question you regarding this and to avoid flight from justice. You don't need to tell us anything other than your personal details," one of the officers said.

"What? Murder? What in God's name are you talking about?" Sam said.

"This is absolutely crazy," Jill said, letting one of the officers handcuff her hands behind her back; Aaron's face was stern but he let himself be handcuffed too.

"What's that in the barrel?" PC Earl said.

"What do you mean? It's just acid," Sam said.

"There's someone's remains in there."

"What? Oh my God. Are you sure?"

"Are you telling me you know nothing about the remains in that barrel of acid?"

"I don't know anything about it. There must've been a terrible accident. Oh that poor person. Who is it? How did he get in there?"

"How do you know it's a he?"

"I don't...I just...assumed."

"Get them in the van," PC Earl said. Jill was led away by one officer and Aaron had one on either side of him. Sam snatched her hand away from the officer trying to handcuff her; the officer grabbed her wrist, slapped the handcuff on, and tried to grab her other wrist.

"This is absolutely insane. We haven't done anything," she said.

"And now you're resisting arrest. Come along to the station and we'll iron this all out," the officer trying to cuff her said.

"No."

"Come on of that," a big officer said, clasping a massive hand on her shoulder and twirling her around, showing her free arm to the other officer who obliged. Sam tried barging herself free but the big officer grabbed her other shoulder and pushed her along the corridor. "Now you're going to behave yourself," he said.

"Shut up. Just shut up," she said. PC Earl and the remaining officers watched her leave, shouting, struggling to wrestle free.

"How do we handle this? The body will have to come out of there, surely?" one of the officers said.

"I imagine so. We better give Phil in forensics a shout because I've never dealt with anything like this before," PC Earl said.

"Same for all of us I'm sure."

The police carried on searching the property whilst PC Earl made the phone call, twice explaining it. The national headlines soon followed.

Larry and Me
L.C. Adams

Larry said he'd meet me on the dock at one. Half an hour later and I'm still waiting. It's exasperating and makes me think of all the times he's made me wait and how rude it is. I always forgave him, just as I'm forgiving him now. Because that's what we do when we love someone – we forgive them.

I glance at my watch. Thirty-five minutes I've been here. He's kept me waiting longer. The more I think about him, the unhappier I become...

*****

'You're late.'

'Sorry, babe.'

I pushed against his chest when he tried to hug me. 'Get off.'

'Don't be like that, darlin'. You know I didn't mean to be late.'

Looking into his bright blue eyes, I drowned a little. 'So, why are you?' It wasn't the first time and it annoyed me because he'd told me he loved me and boys that loved you were never late, so my friend Carol said.

'I stopped to get you this.' He pulled out a small box, presented it to me before opening it. A shiny dress ring sparkled. 'It's a topaz, your birth stone.' He smiled and executed a cocky roll to his shoulders.

I liked his swagger. A lot of the girls couldn't abide his overconfidence, but I adored it. 'How do you know that?' I nudged him.

'I asked your brother.'

'Johnny? He knows shit.'

'Language.' He leaned in, kissed me, his tongue gently finding mine. He stepped away just as I was beginning to enjoy the taste of him.

Fiddled clumsily before sliding the ring on my marriage finger. 'Marry me, Lizzie.'

*****

Wandering up and down like a lost pup, playing with the gold bracelet Larry gave me last week, for no particular reason. He does things like that all the time. Flowers, jewellery. Chocolates only sometimes because he says he doesn't want me getting fat. *Cheeky sod.* I slapped him for that, and he pushed me onto the kitchen table and made love to me so tenderly.

I'm thinking I should call him. It irritates Larry when I do that, but it's been forty minutes and I'm pissed off. It was his idea to meet me here: 'It's a surprise,' he'd said.

I take the mobile from my pocket. I've been checking it every five minutes or so. Larry will text sometimes, but not very often. I don't know why he has a phone. *Yes you do, Lizzie.* Even so, he still hates them. Hates the way they've taken the romance out of everything.

'Before mobile phones we used to talk to each other,' he'd say.

'We talk to each other, silly.'

'Yeah, when you're fed up with checking Facebook and Twitter and Instagram…' he stops there and smiles sadly and rolls his shoulders, but not in that cocky way he used to when we were younger.

*****

'What d'you want one of those contraptions for?'

'I want to be able to talk to you wherever you are.'

'But then I'd have to get one too.'

'Yeah, I know.' I gazed at him. 'Come on.' I took his hand and led him into town.

The eyes of so many followed us. Larry was a popular bloke, and that pleased me. He was like a king walking among his subjects, people all but bowed to him. I enjoyed being his woman. Enjoyed all the attention.

In the phone shop, the man behind the counter fell over backwards to please us. I smiled at Larry and lifted the latest model into my hands. Fondled it, ran my fingers over its slim, metallic surface. Sensually eyeing Larry, promising so much.

'What about this one? It would be perfect for you.'

'Nope, don't want it.'

'Larry,' I gave him a big-eye roll and he grinned, squeezed my arse. 'For me. I can stop worrying about you then.'

'Yeah, that's what I'm afraid of.'

Frowning, I pushed his hand away from my backside. 'Please yourself.'

He pulled me close, tightened his arm around my waist. 'Go on then.'

*****

Larry's voicemail kicks in.

'Larry, where the bloody hell are you? I've been waiting three quarters of an hour for you. Call me back, now.'

Wait another ten minutes. Nothing.

I walk to the edge of the high wall and peer down into the salty brine of the North Sea. Doubt there'd be crabs in there now. Pollution probably killed off the sea life years ago.

I'm cold.

*****

'Hey, watcha doing?'

'What does it look like I'm doing?' I stared at the lanky kid, leaning over me as if he knew me, or something. No one should get that close. Not even my brother got that close.

'Watcha got there?'

'What does it look like?' I shot a glance to the sky. I should ignore him. My dad would have my guts for garters.

Never talk to strangers, you hear me?

I looked at the kid again. He wasn't a stranger, well, he was, but not that *kind of stranger*.

'Let me see.' He nudged my arm.

'Give over.'

'Aw, c'mon, let me see.'

Sighing, I leaned sideways, and he peered downwards at the lowered bucket, his arm brushing against mine. Boys didn't hold my attention much, but there was something about the way he inclined towards me, all warm and solid. Sparks shot up my arm and gathered at the back of my neck. Tingled like you wouldn't believe.

'Cor. That's a big'un.'

I pulled the bucket from the salty water and straightened, lifting it with me. 'He's mine.' I gazed at the ten-legged creature and mentally promised I'd release it later, when I was alone. I never did what the other kids did. That was cruel.

'Your dad'll like that for his supper.'

'It's mine.' I cuddled the bucket to my chest.

'Okay, I was only saying.'

'Yeah, well, don't.' I walked away in a huff. He didn't follow.

Later, he glided through the door of our house as if he'd been there hundreds of times before. Johnny grinned at my mum.

'This is Larry, he just moved in round the corner.'

My mum smiled and asked him if he wanted to stay for tea.

'Yes, please, Mrs Mack.' He glanced at me briefly then followed Johnny to his bedroom.

'Nice young man,' my mum said, winking at me.

'If you like that kind of thing.' I pouted.

'Go wash up and help me with the tea things.'

Larry and my dad hit it off straightaway, which was a new thing for my dad. He was a difficult man to penetrate, but Larry didn't have a problem. I looked at Larry with renewed interest.

Maybe Mum was right.

*****

I cuddle myself. I didn't think to bring a cardigan with me. It's late August and the days start to get brisker around two-ish. It looks like it might rain too. That's all I need. Where the hell is he?

'Larry, will you please call me.'

I should leave. Let him turn up to find me gone. It would serve him right. Somewhere deep inside, I know something's up.

*****

'Have you seen Larry?'

My brother shook his head, but I knew he was lying.

'Okay, where is he?'

'I dunno. I'm not his fucking keeper.'

'Don't swear.'

'Don't tell me what to fucking do.' Johnny leaned towards me, and I braced myself, hands on my hips. He knew what he'd get if he so much as laid a hand on me.

'Step back, buster.' Larry slid between us and stabbed his right index finger into Johnny's chest. 'She's your sister. Show some respect.'

'Sorry, Larry.'

'Don't say sorry to me.' He stepped sideways and Johnny blushed.

'Sorry.' His eyes burned into mine and I could see he wasn't, not really.

'Sorry, Lizzie.' Larry's mouth brushed against Johnny's ear.

Johnny winced. 'Sorry, Lizzie.'

'I don't think she believes you.' He grabbed Johnny's left arm and twisted it behind his back. 'Kiss her. She might believe you then.'

'Larry, don't, it's okay. I believe him.'

'Fucking kiss her.' He pushed Johnny towards me.

Johnny's lips grazed my cheek. 'You'll pay for this, sis. One day, I swear you'll pay,' he whispers.

I moved away and wiped his touch from my skin.

Larry laughed. 'That's better.' He released Johnny's arm and came up beside me, swung me around and kissed my mouth, burying his tongue inside, his erection pressing against my crotch. He finished and turned back to Johnny. 'That's how to kiss a woman, Johnny. You should try it sometime.'

Johnny almost ran from the room.

'You shouldn't torment him.' This time he'd gone too far. I didn't forgive him like I usually did. And I spurned his advances until he apologised to Johnny.

*****

I look round at the sound of a motorbike and smile when I see the Kawasaki hurtling towards me. At last. But as it nears, I can see it's not Larry.

'Where's, Larry?' The bike stops in front of me, Castrol fumes fanning my nostrils.

Johnny smirks. 'Where he should've been a long time ago.' There's blood on his lip and he dabs at it carefully with the heel of his right hand. The knuckles are red and look swollen.

'Johnny?' I don't like it. I'm scared. 'What the hell happened? What have you done? Why are you riding his bike?'

'Get on.'

I climb behind him and settle into the groove of the familiar seat – my groove. I don the helmet and breathe in Larry's smell. Johnny sets off and ten minutes later we're pulling up outside the police station. He dismounts, turns, and grins.

'Follow me, little sister.'

He flashes his badge at the officer behind the reception and the armoured door gives way.

I hate my brother.

*****

'Where have you been, Larry?' Another late night of waiting for him to come home.

'Shush. Give us a kiss.' He pulled me to him, smothered my mouth with his. The familiar stirring between my thighs. His hands pushed up my skirt, searching fingers reached for my knickers.

I batted them away. 'Where have you been?'

'Shit ...' he stepped back. 'Where do you think?'

'I don't know, that's why I'm asking.'

'If you haven't worked it out by now, babe, then I'm not going to tell you.'

I could smell alcohol and tobacco smoke and something else I couldn't put my finger on.

*****

A week later, Larry's in prison where he's awaiting a bail hearing. I'm sitting in a cubicle separated by a glass panel over a desk. Larry's smiling his usual cocky grin and I'm finally facing my demons.

There's a telephone on both sides and he gestures for me to pick mine up. I do what he says and hold it to my ear. My hand is shaking, and I want to get out, but I have to be strong – for him, for myself.

'Hey, babe.'

'Larry?' I press my other hand against his hand against the glass. They won't even let me touch him.

'How're you doing?'

Tears well in my eyes. 'How are you doing?'

'Me? Ha! I'm okay.'

I look at the purple-blue stain above his right eye. 'No, you're not.'

'What, this?' He breaks contact with the glass and points at the bruise. 'You shoulda seen the other bloke.'

'Don't joke, Larry.'

He folds himself forwards. 'I miss you, babe.'

'Then why didn't you meet me when you said you would?'

His hand is back, pressed against mine. 'Babe …' he hangs his head a little and peeps through his fringe. Usually that would make me laugh, but not today.

'I don't know, babe, I just had this one thing to do—'

And there it is. That *one* thing which is always more important than me. Than us.

I slap the glass against his hand. 'But you know how long Johnny's been waiting for a chance to put you in here.'

He nods but doesn't say anything. Holds my gaze. Looks beaten somehow. Mentally, not just physically.

'So why didn't you come?' I stretch my fingers, imagining them raking his hair. It needs cutting, and it looks dirty. 'Don't they let you shower in here?'

He smiles.

I don't smile back. No forgiveness this time. 'Why didn't you come, Larry?'

'I don't know.'

And that's his answer to every bloody thing he's ever been late for in his entire bloody life. In our entire bloody life.

I've lied to myself for years. Made excuses for him. Told myself it isn't true. That he wouldn't do it, any of it. But there comes a time when we have to own it. Larry was never an innocent kid. He's not a good man. Larry isn't what I dreamed he would be. What I dreamed we could be.

'Larry …' the tears fall, and I want something. Something I've never wanted before. 'I wish we'd never met, Larry. I wish we'd never met.' I stand, staring at him, remembering all the times he'd never given me a reason to believe. I told myself he wasn't dealing. I told myself the presents he gave me weren't the product of drug money. That the shiny new motorbike we loved to ride together was honestly acquired.

A perfect pear-shaped drop rolls down his cheek. 'I'm sorry, babe …'

'It's too late. You're always too bloody late.' I drop the phone and turn away. Run as fast as I can.

To be anywhere but there.

*****

'Do you remember when we first met?' Larry rolled us onto our sides and looked into my eyes. 'You wouldn't give that crab up for love nor money.' He laughed and stroked my hair, ran his finger along my bottom lip.

'And you were determined to get to know me better.'

He nodded. 'Fool not to, babe. You were the best thing I'd seen since, I don't know, the sunset?'

I laughed. 'And my dad liked you, so …'

Smiling, he moved on top and stroked my left breast, glided his thumb over its raised nipple. Kissed me tenderly, just right, his tongue sliding in and around and out again. My legs apart, inviting him in.

I prayed we'd never separate.

*****

The only thing I can see as I escape through the exit door is Larry's hands pummelling the glass. He's shouting but I can't hear him and maybe that's a good thing.

Marked
Patrick Ambrose

Ewell Underwood seethed.

When the holidays ended, so did his security gig. Not that he could've gotten to work anyway. With steam billowing from beneath the hood of his pickup, he wouldn't make it out the driveway much less to the scrapyard where he bought the busted radiator. He'd have to hike fifteen miles to kick that junkman's ass.

Down to his last beer, he grabbed his Marauder knife, flattened his other hand on the table and stabbed between splayed fingers, leaving ruts in the oak surface. The weapon blurred as he ramped up speed, fusing with his grip like a natural appendage, hand and dagger morphing into a seamless tool. That's what it took to win bankrolls off boozehounds in afterhours dives. Some chumps would wager a week's pay on a pinfinger challenge.

But an empty wallet won't get you a seat at their table.

He glanced across the room at the remains of his savings—a garbage bag full of returnable bottles and cans. Until those government deadbeats processed his tax return, he was stuck at home toking Screambud, tending tomato seedlings, and listening to Reverend Bullard remind his radio audience that the Good Lord looked out for true believers. A fifty-dollar check could even fast-track that spiritual guidance.

The daily stroll to the mailbox resulted in the usual disappointment—no tax refund, just a campaign leaflet plugging Boone Dobbins for Spoke County Sheriff. A glossy photo captured the beloved candidate wearing his signature canine snarl, buttressed by a statue of Jesus and an American flag, his SIG Sauer M400 pointed at a handwritten note:

> Brother Ewell—
> A job awaits
> Easy $$$
> Call 704-GET-PAYD

"Prob'ly a scam," Ewell muttered, about to rip the leaflet in half when the stainless-steel band on his finger began sparkling like a spinner lure in a farm pond. This sometimes happened when the sunrays seeped through the branches of a nearby shade tree. But the sun wasn't shining, and the blackening sky spewed lightning bolts over tree tops on the distant horizon. Perplexed by the ring's flickering—with zero sunlight, no less—Ewell reckoned he might've grabbed the wrong joint and smoked a duster by mistake. Screambud never scrambled his brain unless it was dusted.

He reread the scrawled message.

No skin off his ass to make a phone call.

*****

Arnold DeWitt grimaced while ice cubes rattled in the cocktail shaker.

Like dice in a cup, he thought, assessing the risks he and his partner were about to take. Fools relied on luck, and Dwayne Mungo would rather roll the dice than focus on the boring details of their game plan. As usual, Arnold had to remind the swashbuckler to think like a high-stakes professional at a poker table, not some juvenile crapshooter in an alleyway. Any moron can kiss the dice and hope for the best. But a decent hold'em player sized up opponents and evaluated potential outs. They won big, even when they held lousy cards.

Only this wasn't a game.

Mungo gulped beer and gestured at the prepaid cell phone on the glass coffee table.

"He'll call, Arnie. You can bet on that."

DeWitt poured his concoction into a rocks glass. "What makes you so sure?"

"He's an unemployed, gun-totin' ex-con with a broken-down truck he can't afford to fix. He's running outta options."

DeWitt swigged rye and bitters. "How much we payin' him?"

"A grand plus a card for expenses. He'd better be done in a week. That's when his credit runs out."

"A one-week credit card?"

Mungo chuckled. "That's *his* spending window. We don't want him buying stuff once the real cardholder gets his first billing statement. I called the bank, so his spending spree shouldn't raise red flags."

DeWitt swirled melting rocks. Sure, it all sounded good. There was just one problem.

"Dwayne, his ugly mug is gonna be on every surveillance video in every flophouse and greasy spoon where that card gets used. He's gonna get caught. And he might talk."

Mungo shook his head, crushed the empty beer can. "He won't be nothin' but worm food by the time they're onto him."

*****

A skunky odor wafted through Ewell Underwood's mobile home.

DeWitt's nose crinkled. From his seat at the table, he glanced into the neighboring kitchen, zeroing in on an industrial trash liner, bulging with returnables, sandwiched between the fridge and the Formica counter.

Ewell glanced at the Visa card in his mighty calloused hands. "What kinda credit don't last more than a week?"

DeWitt forced a broad smile. "Good question, Mr. Underwood. As an independent contractor, your purchases must be applied before the end of the billing cycle. It's company policy."

Ewell studied the name on the card. "Who's Webster Burbank?"

"I'm surprised you have to ask. He's the founder of Burbank Security Consultants. A principal partner, Mr. Dwayne Mungo, highly recommended you. Mr. Mungo praised your knowledge of weapons and mental toughness. You're just the man we need."

DeWitt slid a manila envelope across the pockmarked table. "Here's half the money, a subway map and a roundtrip train ticket. The *Coastal Queen* departs for the Big Apple tomorrow at dawn."

Ewell gave him a slight, tight-lipped nod.

"You'll get the rest of your money one week from today," DeWitt continued. "At midnight, behind the old Elk Grove Baptist Church."

Their gazes locked. DeWitt looked away, his eyes resettling on a framed photo of a raven-haired man, shotgun in hand, squatting under a red maple with a beagle by his side.

"You a dog lover, Mr. Underwood?"

"Yup."

DeWitt rose from his chair and approached a window facing the front yard, pretending to study the landscape—a forest full of white oak and long-leaf pine, along with a gravel road that ran a good mile before the next home appeared. "You got nosy neighbors?"

Ewell shook his head.

From a briefcase, DeWitt produced a couple of 8-by-11 inch photographs. The first displayed a bald man, thirtyish and barechested, with caramel skin and handsome, chiseled features. Ropy muscles, like steel cables, coursed through his arms, shoulders and neck. A silver cross dangled from his left ear. A gold cross, tangled in a mat of chest hair, hung from a thick chain necklace.

"That's Reuben Hellywell, sex trafficker and drug dealer. At least that's what he does when he's not fightin' dogs."

The next picture showed Rueben laughing and pointing at an eviscerated pit bull.

DeWitt tapped the photo. "Mr. Burbank wants this no-count liquidated."

Ewell glared down at the snapshot, took a deep breath.

"If I wasn't broke, I'd kill that sumbitch for free."

"We know where he lives. He tweeted about a shindig in his neighborhood."

Ewell's features scrunched. "Tweeted?"

DeWitt nodded. "Mr. Hellywell bragged that a scene from the movie *Goodfellas* was filmed on his block."

He laid down another photo—a close-up of the Brooklyn street sign at the corner of West Ninth and Smith. "That's from the movie—near the end when De Niro points at a building and tells Ray Liotta's wife to go pick out a Dior dress. Reuben Hellywell lives on West Ninth Street somewhere between Smith and Court. There's a bar on the corner called The Blown Gasket. From there, he shouldn't be hard to find."

"I'll pop him," Ewell growled.

DeWitt grinned. "When you're done, we'll toast your success. Right next to Reverend Dunwoody's tombstone."

*****

Reuben Hellywell snickered.

He'd given those bumpkins an education.

He'd met DeWitt and Mungo under the clock at Grand Central Station, and they'd gotten well-oiled in a nearby bar. At midnight, they reconvened in Brooklyn, outside the Prospect Park bandshell where they made the exchange. The hillbillies gave Rueben one hundred and twenty grand; Reuben handed them five thousand oxycodone pills and fifteen thousand pastel valentine hearts—the edible ones with the cute phrases. Even the oxy was fake—counterfeit tablets from Sinaloa made with fentanyl. Several recent overdoses in the Carolinas had been linked to fentanyl.

He strolled down Clinton toward Ninth Street. If you went west a few blocks, you'd encounter a quaint community of breweries, wineries and chic restaurants. But Rueben went east, passing dollar stores, a dilapidated housing complex, and a vacant lot rioting with weeds. A blast of wind whirled dust, assorted trash and street grit under the Hamilton Avenue overpass where dealers used to push dope in plain sight. That was in the nineties when rents were cheap, and rooftop parties featured forties and blunts with a soundtrack by Tribe, Biggie and Nas.

At the corner of West Ninth and Court, he recalled the old timer who sold half pints behind bulletproof glass. In those days, he paid five hundred a month for his studio apartment in a three-floor walkup. But the lock on the outside door was broken and the vestibule light was busted, so every evening, he'd trip over junkies and baseheads on his way into the building—always on edge, always bracing for the prick of a dirty needle. He hadn't missed that at all, nor the empty crack vials and nebulas of dried blood on smudged walls.

A sudden gust whipped the rickety roof-access door—a personal problem, now that he owned the building. He'd gotten the place cheap after rats ran off the other tenants. But once he vanquished those rodent squatters, he still couldn't rent out the empty units. Wire mesh sealed the gaps between the baseboards and floors, spooking potential occupants. He'd filled the larger entry holes with broken glass and silicone, leaving behind further evidence of the scourge that had lurked behind those walls.

The view from the roof revealed a snarl of traffic slithering over the Brooklyn-Queens Expressway. On adjacent rooftops, trust-fund renters strummed guitars and guzzled White Claws. Their pilgrimage into the neighborhood began during the dot-com bubble. One of those brats even called the Health Department when something died within a shared wall—an issue any native Brooklynite would've shrugged off.

He glanced over at the hefty skylight beside him, its dome secured by two roofing nails. Down below, a rotting, sun-beaten deck separated his building's floor-through apartment from the weed-strewn courtyard.

His renovation effort would begin there.

After he repaired the skylight.

*****

Rural landscapes and images of small-town life flickered through the windows of the moving train like a feature film on fast forward. It would have a predictable ending—a bad dude gets what he deserves in Gotham's urban sprawl. If anything, this trip validated what Ewell and other Spoke County folk already knew—that real Americans lived in the backcountry, not the cities. Aside from stops in D.C. and the Rotten Apple, this train ride covered the vast rural acreage of the Piedmont, where both sides of Ewell's family scratched out a living, trying to provide better lives for their young'uns, only to have their savings whisked away by urban grifters with college degrees.

He sipped bourbon from a flask and reviewed DeWitt's photos, devoting his full attention to each one as his brain locked those images into his memory. Once the mental pictures stuck, he closed his eyes and sifted through each one again until the train's rhythmic clickety-clack lulled him to sleep.

He awoke to screeching wheels, grinding to a halt at Penn Station.

From his duffel, he retrieved Grandpa's heirloom—a vintage New York Yankees cap. Whenever Grandpa wore that thing, he caught all the bream and bagged all the quail. Ewell expected similar luck bagging this dog-killin' Brooklyn shitbird. Hopefully, the home-team swag would help him blend with the natives, too.

He swung his duffel around and shuffled along with the herd of passengers, scanning the crowd for suspicious faces, potential perverts and pickpockets, as he merged with other arrivals flooding the main area from adjoining railway tunnels. While the rucksack helped him forge a path through the mob, he prayed he'd wrapped his Glock in enough clothes to avoid discharging the weapon during his scramble to the nearest exit where another human swarm awaited. He continued southbound toward the Fourteenth Street subway station, his mind dialing back to the task that brought him to this hellhole.

It was a no-brainer, really. DeWitt offered him twice what he usually got for a hit plus roundtrip fare. But this wasn't the usual clip job. He wouldn't be popping a dude in a wooded area with a nearby lake for swamping the corpse. No sir, this job was way different. He'd have to ambush his mark on his way home or tailgate him into his building. He'd likely use the knife instead of the gun.

Underground, he encountered a subterranean stench of urine, creosote, and brake dust. A possum-sized rat traipsed between subway tracks sniffing garbage. Thumping bass beats wafted from the far end of the platform, where a skeletal figure with a weathered Bible rapped about the oncoming apocalypse. The mutant rodent seemed unfazed by the noise and throng. Nothing like the shy varmints who fed on his compost pile back home.

Inside a Brooklyn-bound train, ads hawked energy drinks, divorce lawyers and virility enhancers—the same products peddled by the hucksters who interrupt his favorite sports call-in show.

"All men got the same problems," he muttered to himself. "No matter which hog hole they come from."

*****

Hank Williams's lonesome warble, along with the familiar stench of stale beer and restroom funk, bore similarities to Purgatory, a Spoke County roadhouse where working men hammered cheap brew, grumbled about their wives and lied about the nameless faces they'd pounded in bare-knuckled brawls—a much rowdier bunch than this Blown Gasket horde of vacant stares. No food here either, just dollar draft and three-buck shots served by a stocky dude whose red mohawk and Van Dyke made him indistinguishable from the other impending disasters inhabiting this seedy dive.

"What'll you have?"

"Draft Bud," Ewell drawled, reaching for his bag to grab Papa's Bible and read a verse or two, a comforting habit since high school on nights before ball games. Now, he faced bigger challenges. But the memory of Mama's carping stopped him from setting the Good Book on a sticky bar that reeked of the Devil's Drink.

The bartender seemed friendly enough. He knew his patrons' names, though they didn't seem like generous tippers. He huffed and grunted as he served them with a disposition that might turn on a dime if a barfight erupted, demanding his intervention before everyone in the joint pulled their shivs, knuckledusters and other improvised weaponry.

"This used to be a great pub," he growled. "Cops and firemen used to drink here. Now the place is chock full of junkies and ex-cons. It's the first stop for every parasitic wastrel just outta prison or detox."

Ewell grinned. "Maybe you should charge more for beer."

"Boss won't let me. This cesspool makes too much money." He set down a frosty mug, brimming with foam. "I'm Rake," he said, extending a hand.

"Isaiah," Ewell replied with a firm grip.

"You're not from around here."

Ewell frowned. He hadn't even warmed the seat of his chair, and this punk already tagged him a redneck. He looked around. None of the no-counts hanging around this latrine would last a minute in Spoke County.

"Nope, I ain't from around here."

"So where you from?"

Ewell shrugged. "A right-to-work state where there ain't no jobs. I'm just a country handyman lookin' for work."

Rake smirked. "Don't say that too loud, brother. Brooklyn is Union Country. Non-union folks can't do maintenance here."

Over the sound system, Waylon and Bocephus reminisced about the Drifting Cowboy Band. "I didn't think city slickers liked country music."

Rake grinned. "We Brooklynites enjoy all music. We ain't prejudiced like some folks."

The entrance door slammed. Ewell glanced up to see a bald dude strolling in, wearing wrap-around sunglasses and a gold cross on a chain necklace. The newcomer cupped his ear with an amused expression. "What's this Hee-Haw horseshit?" he hollered, springing into the air, clicking the heels of his Caiman Hornback boots. "Yee-hah!"

Rake waved and made his way to the other end of the bar.

Ewell's gaze narrowed.

It was Reuben Hellywell, big as life, just like in the pictures. Hellywell sauntered to the bar, grinning at Rake. "Henny, neat."

Rake filled a rocks glass with a generous pour of cognac.

"Guess what?" Reuben asked. "I just bought out my landlord. Lotta work to do on my building. First priority is that skylight over my bathroom."

Rake chuckled. "You mean the one you crashed into during that rooftop football game? Tryin' to catch that wobbler I threw three buildings away?"

"Yep, just a couple roofing nails holding the dome on."

Ewell's brow wrinkled. *Top-floor apartment, broken skylight.*

He drained his mug, left a sawbuck on the bar.

Outside, enveloped by the damp chill, he donned a windbreaker and snatched a discarded tabloid from a steel-mesh trashcan. Front-page headlines pitched pieces about plastic-surgery mishaps, aging mafia dons and the city's rat problem. He delved into the rat story which pretty much confirmed his suspicions—that a pack of them sonsabitches could strip every ounce of flesh off his bones in minutes. They chewed through everything—concrete, brick and steel—with teeth that growed so damn fast they had to gnaw nonstop to keep their choppers filed down so they wouldn't slice up their brains. He considered the country mice eating his compost back home. They weren't a threat to anything but his tomatoes.

Wasn't long before Reuben Hellywell crossed the street and stopped mid-block to search for keys outside a run-down, three-story hovel of worn bricks and mortar. From the corner, the building's façade resembled the oblong face of a rotting corpse; ceiling lights burned within two vacant top-floor rooms—skeletal eye sockets hovering above a battered AC unit, flattened like a smashed nose. The ground floor's boarded-up windows were a pained grimace of clenched teeth. Ewell turned away and headed to Court Street glancing back at the flat roof of Reuben's building. A brick dormer sat on top like a pointy hat on a sun-beaten skull.

He hung a left on Garnet. Halfway down the block, a construction barricade ran all the way to the Smith Street corner. Nailed to the thick-green plywood was a sign:

> Work in Progress: Residential
> DANGER
> HARD HAT AREA

Trading the cap for his hard hat, he peered over the barrier at a concrete foundation surrounded by pallets of bricks. Nearby, someone had chained an A-frame ladder to a Bobcat. A leaning six-foot fence with vertical slats separated the site from the backside of Reuben's building which looked similar to the front except for a fixed wrought-iron ladder leading to the adjoining platforms of a fire escape. On the roof, the brick dormer appeared to contain a door. Once he freed the A-frame ladder, he could scale the fence and be on the roof in seconds. He'd enter the apartment through the skylight, maybe even the access door. A risky move, but safer than clipping the target in plain sight.

He made a mental list:
1) Dress like a lineman (or roofer)
2) Slip into the apartment while the mark is away
3) Use the Marauder on the victim; bring the Glock as a last resort
4) Find a cheap place to get some rest.

*****

Ever since he popped out his mama, Ewell Underwood took a full-night's sleep for granted. Even in the joint or during navy tours at sea, he'd gotten his rest. But plugged ears and a belly full of bourbon couldn't drown out the Brooklyn clamor of roaring trucks, blaring sirens and rumbling subway trains so close they shook the building. The moldy stench of motel carpet, the lumpy pillows, the brackish decaf coffee all extended the general misery of his insomnia. On the radio dial, he found a country station, and damned if it wasn't Brad Paisley and Jimmie Allen crooning about lost days and small-town comforts. Ewell never missed his single-wide trailer and compost heap more than he did now. When Hank Jr. roared about the resourcefulness of country folks, Ewell got a sudden hankering for fried catfish, Better Boy tomatoes and muscadine wine, but settled for lukewarm beer, saltine crackers and sardines.

An hour later, a hardware store on Court Street robbed him for rope, an adjustable wrench and a hacksaw. A Ninth Street diner cut further into his bankroll, charging as much for coffee as two boilermakers cost him back home. Seated at the window counter, he fixated on Rueben's front door as rain began to fall, hammering the street, sidewalk and parked cars. Wind whipped heavy drops against the glass, muddling his view, but he gave thanks to the Lord for the opportune weather. Bricklayers don't work in downpours.

He watched as Reuben Hellywell finally exited the building. The city slicker wore a grey trench coat and fedora, looking more like a G-Man than a gangster. In fact, Ewell wouldn't have recognized him if he hadn't been wearing them highfalutin gator boots.

*****

Except for the fresh mud on the vanity and bathroom floor, Reuben's single-room dwelling was spotless with spartan accommodations—a fridge, a stove, a chest of drawers, a desk, a full bookshelf, and a queen-size bed. Above the headboard hung a diploma from New York University. On the desk sat a photo of Reuben sharing a laugh with an elderly couple, all of them pointing at something outside the frame.

Ewell rinsed his muddy boots off in the tub, wiped down the vanity and bathroom floor, then stood on the desk chair to remove both bulbs from the light fixture. Now that he had seen this dump from all angles, he reckoned the neighboring brownstones were the only reason the building hadn't already collapsed. The chicken wire surrounding the room at the cove joint must be holding the floors and ceilings in place. And what about the silicone-filled holes in the baseboard and plaster? What the hell was that for? Had Reuben pumped silicone and joint compound into the walls to hold this sumbitch together?

Or was he staving off varmints? God only knew what horrors lurked within the guts of this building, and this country boy wasn't sticking around long enough to find out.

He grabbed a beer from the fridge, took a seat on the toilet.

During the wait, he stared at DeWitt's photo of Reuben and the gutted pit bull. He needed an answer to the question stuck in his head on an endless loop:

What kind of person murders dogs?

*****

The last man to point a gun at Joseph Reuben Hellywell, Jr. rested in the fetid swamp of the Gowanus Canal. The dead guy's name was

Russell. Reuben had once been his supplier for stolen laptops, audio speakers, amps, and electric guitars. But late one evening, Russell betrayed him at gunpoint and a fortunate distraction gave Reuben time to pull his piece and void their partnership forever. All of this occurred right outside Rueben's warehouse, on the picturesque moonlit bank of the Gowanus.

That was then. Now, he was the one staring down the barrel of a pistol with no clue who this troglodyte, missing-link-looking bastard was. Rueben had never been to the big house. But he figured this bruiser had; his mean mug had been punched too many times, scarred and pockmarked, featuring a frigid, double-barrel gaze as threatening as the nine millimeter in his liver-spotted hand. This dude was damaged.

So Reuben just stared back, hogtied, his head throbbing where this mutant freak had clobbered him, probably with the bloody adjustable wrench on the floor by the bathroom door.

After a couple minutes, the bruiser spoke:

"You're a sick, scum-sucking dog killer."

Reuben raised an eyebrow. "What did you say?"

Ewell held up DeWitt's picture of his prisoner and the disemboweled dog.

Reuben struggled to sit up. "Where'd you get that?"

"From somebody who wants you dead, dog killer."

"Now hold on a minute. You got played, man. They cribbed that pic off my Facebook page and Photoshopped the dead dog. That's the same picture on my desk. Just look at it."

Ewell tilted his head and peeked at the framed photo, then scrutinized Reuben's features. "How could somebody steal a picture that's still sittin' on your desk?"

"I just told you, that same pic is on my Facebook page. They lifted that photo, airbrushed my folks outta the frame and spliced in the dead dog."

"In English."

"They doctored the photo. Y'all ain't got Facebook and Photoshop in Hicksville or Podunk or wherever your wretched ass comes from?"

Ewell deadpanned. "I'm fixin' to pump a pound of lead into that empty noggin' of yours."

Rueben smiled. "Go ahead, make some noise. The Seventy-Sixth Precinct's less than a mile away. There'll be officers swarmin' into this apartment in five minutes." Rueben cocked his head. "How much they pay you to kill me?"

Ewell grinned. "A thousand bucks more than you're worth. Plus a credit card good for a week."

Reuben guffawed. "What kinda credit is that?"

"I wondered the same thing," Ewell grumbled.

"Hope you weren't stupid enough to use it."

"Nope. But now that I'm payin' my own way, this city of yours has bled me dry."

"That's too bad. But that was smart of you, not usin' that card. Now, bro, my back's startin' to ache. I gotta rest it against that chest behind me."

"Don't make a damn to me," Ewell growled. "Long as you get there yerself."

Reuben glanced down at his bound hands. He pressed them against the wood floor and pushed himself backwards, six inches at a time, till he reached the dresser.

"What you do when you're not breakin' into homes?"

"Handiwork, mostly. Thing is, most folks do their own repairs where I live. They won't spend money on maintenance unless a big storm hits. But that's when every dipshit with a ladder and a hammer starts a roofing company. A good handyman gets lost among all them jacklegs."

Reuben shrugged. "I could put you to work. I own this building. There's lots of stuff to do here."

"Why don't you hire one of your union buddies?"

"I can't afford union labor."

Ewell shook his head. "Naw, I can't work for you. I gotta finish this job."

"Who's payin' you, cornpone?"

"That ain't my name."

Reuben grinned. "Then introduce yourself."

"Nope. No names."

Reuben harrumphed, glanced up at the empty light sockets. He cocked his head and winked. "Those folks who's payin' you . . . how they gonna know you finished the job?"

"I'm gonna give them that cute little earring and necklace of yours," Ewell replied with a wink.

"Why don't you just take 'em right now and leave town *without killing me*? They'd never know."

"I gave 'em my word."

Reuben chuckled. "That's mighty white of you. I'd shake your hand, fine fellow, if I wasn't hog-tied."

"I'd have went up here and killed you for free if I had a pot to piss in."

"You said *'have went.'* That's bad English."

"How I talk is my business."

Reuben cracked a smile. "That's OK. Most of my relatives say 'have went' and 'had went'. They from the South, too. You Southrons never bothered to learn the King's English. My folks had to move up here to get away from you evil, hood-wearin' devils."

"Least we don't torture animals," Ewell grumbled.

"I don't torture or kill animals. I love animals. Especially dogs and cats. Now, dig this—I got money. So how about I give you a couple grand and my jewelry and you get the hell outta my building?"

"How 'bout I take your jewelry and money, then slit your throat?"

"You wouldn't know where to find the money, cornpone."

Ewell's face reddened. "That ain't my name, goddammit! Name's Ewell."

Reuben's eyebrows arched. " 'Yew-Wool' or 'You-Well'?"

Ewell frowned. "Now I gotta kill you."

"Now hold on, You-Well—"

"It's Ewell."

"Now hold on, Ewell. Ain't nobody gotta die. It's them hillbillies that hired you, ain't it?"

"Hillbillies?"

"Dimwit and Bunghole."

Ewell's eye twitched. "Dimwit and Bunghole." He sighed. "That's purty good. But if you ain't no dog killer, then what in the tarnation did you do to make 'em hire me?"

Reuben smirked. "We had a misunderstanding."

"That ain't good enough. I gotta know. They said you was a pimp and a drug dealer. I ain't got no use for pimps."

"I ain't no pimp. I got some dignity and self-respect. They lied to you."

"You could be lying to me, Rubes."

"My name's Rueben. Not Rube."

Ewell grinned. "I called you 'Rubes.' Rubes has an 's' at the end. It's plural. I learnt that in grade school."

Reuben glared for a moment. Then his features relaxed, and he cracked a smile.

"Ewell, you're one crafty dude—smarter than most folks I've met from Down South. But what makes you think Dimwit and Bunghole are gonna let you live after you hand over my personal effects? You're a loose end. You know too much. They gotta kill you."

Ewell stared down at the toes of his boots.

Reuben raised an eyebrow. "So, Ewell—where you deliverin' my shit?"

Ewell glanced up, face scrunched. "Your what?"

"My jewelry. Where you meetin' Dimwit and Bunghole to hand it over?"

Ewell considered the question. It was all out in the open now. It didn't make a damn, really. Not at this point. He could just as soon kill Reuben as not. But it no longer seemed worth the risk.

"At a cemetery," Ewell replied. "Saturday, at midnight, behind the old Elk Grove Baptist Church."

Reuben's eyes widened. "You're kiddin' me."

"I kid you not."

Reuben shook his head. "You're meetin' them in a graveyard, behind an abandoned church, at midnight?"

"I gave 'em my word."

Rueben whistled through his teeth. "Lemme go as your backup, just in case somethin' don't look right."

"That ain't gonna happen."

Reuben frowned. "They want you to snuff me. And then they're gonna put your light out."

"That's my problem."

"You gotta be crazy meetin' those clowns alone with no backup. At least change the meeting to a public place."

"I don't know how to reach 'em, Reuben. And they got the other half of my money. I gotta do this alone. I can't trust you right now."

*****

Elk Grove Baptist Church hadn't opened its doors since its charismatic pastor, Everette Dunwoody, hanged himself from a ceiling rafter more than a decade ago. He'd gotten caught carrying on with a married woman in the choir, and while the congregation sought another minister, Dunwoody's financial improprieties came to light, forcing the church into arrears and an eventual shutdown.

It wasn't easy to get there.

The blacktop ended in Hooks County where the winding descent down a gravel secondary road began—a road that hadn't been maintained since the church went belly up. Once you entered Elk Grove Holler, you drove on red dirt—unless it was raining—and then you forged on another couple miles, dodging deep ruts and straddling gullies if you were lucky enough to see them. Most of this section was either overgrown with wild grass or covered in fallen pine branches. By the time Ewell's four-by-four got him through that mess, he had second thoughts about collecting his money. What if the meeting really was a setup? Was it worth the risk of getting killed? For five hundred bucks? But then, only a punk would miss this meeting. Them lowlife sonsabitches owed him money.

The full moon illuminated the degradation of the lonesome country church whose steeple now leaned to one side. Some of its chestnut siding had begun to rot, too. Honeysuckle and wisteria vines slithered over much of the structure with each serpentine runner applying a separate stranglehold in a collective effort to choke out any spirit that remained there.

Ewell cut his lights, headed round back and parked near the rust-ridden gate of the cemetery. He removed his Glock from his shoulder holster. As fog coated the windows of the stifling cabin, he sipped remnants of lukewarm coffee from a travel mug.

Outside, the thick, humid air seemed refreshing. He leaned against the decrepit wrought-iron fence surrounding more than thirty well-worn tombstones, many of them hidden by tall weeds and wildflowers. An ancient live oak provided some cover when he took a dip of snuff to jump-start his sleep-addled brain. A gentle breeze pushed a blanket of fog over a seven-acre lake while crickets and bullfrogs crooned. Ragged shrubbery framed the entrance to the vestry. Yellow-green possum eyes stared from within the bushes.

In the distance, a pair of headlights wound through the tree-choked forest.

Ewell stepped out from behind the tree as a silver Lexus ES 350 approached the graveyard.

DeWitt hopped out with a bottle of Black Jack. "Good Evening, Mr. Underwood. I hope we're here to toast your success."

"That's why I'm here," Ewell drawled.

DeWitt set the bottle and two rocks glasses on Reverend Dunwoody's prominent tombstone.

He laughed. "Dunwoody, the philandering thief, bankrupts the church. And yet, they still found the money to bury his sorry ass in this graveyard. That's true forgiveness."

"That's what good Christians do," Ewell replied. "I sure wish this church was gettin' some use. Wouldn't take much to restore it."

DeWitt filled rocks glasses. "Show us what you got."

Ewell removed a satin bag from his front pocket and laid it on the tombstone. "Who's us?" he asked. "I thought you came alone."

DeWitt blinked. "I did. It's just you and me here. Us two." He dumped the bag's contents onto the tombstone. Moonlight flickered off the gold necklace and silver earring.

Ewell watched in amazement as bark suddenly peeled off the live oak. The sight was followed by a loud report. Ewell pulled his piece as additional shots rang out.

DeWitt clasped his chest and fell forward onto the ground.

Off in the distance, a slick, bullet-shaped head emerged from the shadows and fog. Ewell restrained a smile as Reuben approached him.

"DeWitt brought company. That shot that hit the tree was meant for you. I threw Bunghole off balance and finished him off. We should get the hell outta here. You touch anything?"

"Just your jewelry."

Rueben put on the necklace, inserted his earring. "You got something else that belongs to me."

"I still got your money. I wasn't sure you'd find this place."

"I got help from Google Maps. Now how about giving me a lift to my car. I parked down yonder," Reuben said, gesturing at a clearing alongside the road.

Ewell holstered his gun. "Will do." His eyes settled on Reuben's strained expression.

A blast of pain erupted in Ewell's head as Rueben's fist crashed into his jaw and cheekbone.

Reuben massaged sore knuckles, looked him in the eye. "That's for pointin' that gun at me."

Dazed from the blow, Ewell managed a nod.

"You're one tough cookie. That punch always brings a man down. But not you."

Ewell spat out the remains of his tobacco. "No hard feelings."

"You'd better pick up that chaw, man. Cops'll be scouring this place soon as these bodies are found."

He handed Ewell the satin bag for the spent tobacco and gazed up at the moon. "I don't think there's any way to make it look like these two jackasses shot one another."

"That would be difficult."

"We could stick 'em in that Lexus and swamp the car," Reuben said, tilting his head toward the lake. "At least they won't be out in the open. Might buy us some time."

"I don't know. I'd hate to do all that work to find the water ain't deep enough."

A sudden cool breeze cut through the heavy air. The pleasant, earthy scent of rain wafted by.

"You know what? I think you oughta come back to Brooklyn with me and hang at my crib till this shit blows over."

"Your crib?"

"My place, homie."

Ewell cocked his head. "You'd do that for me?"

Reuben grinned. "Like I gotta choice? I don't want you gettin' pinched and plea bargaining with the DA. And I was serious about all the work that needs to be done on my building. Just consider the loan an advance if you decide to take me up on the offer."

"I'll think about it," Ewell said, as they hopped into the cabin of his pickup.

"Well, you'd better think fast cuz my ass is headin' back tonight. And I'm ditchin' this pistol on the way."

Ewell dropped him off at a grey Honda Civic. "Flash your lights if I'm goin' too fast."

"10-4," Reuben replied.

Rain pounded the windshield. But at least the fog had lifted. Ewell checked the rearview now and then, his mind wandering over how much had changed in a week.

Reuben Hellywell could've killed him and returned to New York alone. Instead, he offered financial support and refuge when Ewell needed it most. With DeWitt and Mungo dead, every ex-con in the state would be hauled in for questioning. Rueben was right. He should hightail it to Brooklyn and lay low.

That was the best option.

His only option.

A Man of His Word
Kamal Mouhoune

I never thought it would end like this. Never. I just said yes to a job. A well paid job. Something quite rare in my field these days.

Three months ago, Boualem called me. He said he had a gig for me. Boualem is a black market currency trader, known in the area for all the wrong reasons. The curious kind, always trying to know more about street buyers and sellers. I needed some euros, quickly and in cash, almost six months ago, so I reluctantly went to his corner. Quite the smooth talker under his gorilla armor. I told him I was a professional translator and he seemed quite impressed by it. I was then data stored in some dark drawer of his twisted mind. Making a good impression on the wrong people is worse than making a bad one on the right ones.

He was not the finest gentleman in the city, but when a brute like him offers to pay you ten times the minimum wage for less than ten hours of work, you have to listen intently. My job was to be his interpreter and translator from basic English to an even more basic vernacular arabo-berberian slang, and vice versa for the other party. I didn't know who the other party was, and that's where I ended up with much more than I'd bargained for, money and trouble wise.

It was a hot and messy day when we met, two hours after his quick phone call. The money was motivating enough for me to confront the blazing sun and go meet him in a lousy cafe without air conditioning nor the minimum hygiene. Boualem came late with a guy looking at least twice as vicious and menacing as him. The two were dressed clean but nonsensically. Something in their physical attributes makes it difficult for any clothing style to shine on them. Boualem was a thirty something balding podgy gangster wearing his polo shirts too tight. He had large shoulders and thick forearms which somehow aesthetically compensated for his protruding belly and double chin. His sidekick had a similar body type but larger, sturdier and taller. The nameless bloke (Boualem didn't properly introduce him to me then) had a prognathic jaw and furnished menacing eyebrows. The muscular structure and strong bones gave an intimidating shape to the thick fat layer. Boualem ordered two coffees and two bottles of sparkling water then asked me what I wanted to drink. "*Walou*!" I declined politely. I was done with coffee, and the cup I ordered while waiting for them was not even empty yet.

"Cold coffee is bad for the stomach," he said. "For you, a Coke will do just fine," he insisted with a ferocious smile.

Quickly we started talking. Their demand was quite simple. A Chinese worker, living here in Algiers, was interested in buying some euros from them at a very low exchange rate. Boualem didn't care to explain how he could sell euros for such an interesting rate and I didn't ask anyway. The Chinwi, as he called him using our vernacular term for a Chinese guy, was buying euros for some shady business needs here in Algiers. He was operating for some other guys from the local Chinese community. They formed a kind of informal venture, selling counterfeit goods and different cheap gadgets. He was their minion and they were not much bigger. Just a bunch of hand workers and artisans trying to make a buck from the local bazaar economy without paying taxes. Boualem needed me to do some rudimentary translation from English to close the deal. The Chinese worker was previously buying euros at the regular black market rate from an informal currency exchange shop based in Bab Ezzouar, exactly Boushaki, the local Chinatown of the suburban East Algiers. That's where Boualem had spotted him multiple times before he decided to talk to him. Quickly he got frustrated by his drastically limited English, but somehow managed to make an offer, keep in contact with him and understand a few other things by sheer thug wisdom. Boualem had instincts and hunches trained by years of fishy operations in the financial black market. According to him, the Chinwi was going to keep the difference he'd gain for himself then give his business partners the rest of the euros as if he bought them at the usual rate from the Boushaki shop.

"A sneaky son of a bitch!" said Boualem. "You can't trust people who eat rats, bats and dogs!" His big silent partner slowly nodded in agreement.

"That's why I need you. Take his contact. I gave him a SIM card for the duration of our business operation. I need to understand everything this cat eater utters!"

He gave me the Chinwi's phone number and told me not to mention any name and keep words to the bare minimum. We talked about the money, settled the deal and decided we'd meet with the Chinwi after two or three days. Boualem would send the GPS location one hour before the meeting. We shook hands then I went home happy about the unexpected windfall.

During the following day, I contacted the Chinese guy. His name was Lei and his English seemed decent. The name was so stereotypically Chinese I doubted his veracity and thought it was just a fake name he was using to operate with us. I always kept referring to him as the Chinese guy, or the Chinwi with Boualem, who didn't care about anything not currency exchange related. It kept things to an impersonal, strictly transactional level, which was appreciated by everyone including me. Lei seemed laidback but somehow curious and maybe slightly anxious. He was bombarding me with questions "just between us" that I ignored because I didn't know how to answer them. It was obvious for me that it was an important transaction for him, and that a lot was at stake. I translated the messages he was sending me for Boualem, who then would text me his responses, which I'd translate and send to Lei. I tried as much as possible to be the transparent link between the two, but despite my efforts and the apparent simplicity of the phrases, it sometimes felt like I was the fragile bridge between two completely different worlds. During their exchanges I discovered in disbelief the amount of money that was to be converted in euros and understood why Boualem was paying me so well and why Lei was so excited about the deal. I also had some second thoughts. But who cares? Certainly not me. I'm just a translator, if anything was to go wrong between them.

*****

It was a hot and humid Tuesday morning. I received the GPS location followed by a winking emoticon. I forwarded it to Lei. The scorching sun was there for the entire week, so I was happy when I read that the meeting was scheduled at 7 p.m. I took a refreshing bath at 6:00 then drove half an hour with my crumbling Maruti 800 through some bad roads, following the direction given to me by the cold voice of Lady Android. It ended on a vacant lot adjoining what looked like an abandoned industrial shed.

I called Boualem. He appeared from a bushy path, coming from a back entry. He painfully opened the clunky rusty gate and told me to park the car inside. He was scrutinizing the place around while miming wheel directions to help me get inside. Once the car parked in the shed I helped him with the rusty gate. The interior was damp, dark and smelly. Furnished with a filthy plastic table put against the wall and crooked chairs scattered all around.

"Premium comfort!" Boualem said with his carnivorous smile.

The big unnamed bloke was sitting on a chair smoking a cigarette. Mouth shut as always.

"I have the money in cash, hand and machine counted. It shouldn't take more than ten minutes with the Chinwi. You didn't tell anyone that you were coming here, did you?"

"You told me from the start to keep silent about our business, Boualem. I'm a man of my word. You should know this."

"Man! I know you are. There's no need to be so bold about it. You think I can't recognize a man's value? I was just asking the question like… you know the word… when we already know something but just ask about it… to… you know!"

"Rhetorical. A rhetorical question."

"Yes… that's the word! That's what it is… I shouldn't even have to explain it to you, smartass! Or should I? Sit down. As I told you before, there's nothing to eat or drink here."

I sat with them in complete silence for almost half an hour. Me and Boualem eyes down on our smartphones while the silent bloke was smoking cigarette after cigarette staring into the void. I was somehow keeping an eye on the place while playing Tetris on my Game Boy emulator. There were remnants of some car mechanics tools, big cardboard boxes and plastic bags filled with junk everywhere on the greasy floor.

The big bloke suddenly stood up grunting, slowly moving his huge body to a dark corner. He then disappeared behind a stained partition wall made of bare concrete blocks. The grainy sound of him taking a piss was reverberating through the empty shed.

"I strongly advise you to retain your natural urges. The toilets are tough on the eyes and the stomach," Boualem said to me while scrolling through his social media.

It was almost completely dark outside when Boualem switched on a dim flashlight and hung it on the wall.

"Where's the Chinwi?" he asked. "No new messages?"

"He's coming. Be patient!"

*****

At 8:10 we hear a car parking behind the gate, engine headlights shredding the dark interior through stained windows.

We open the gate. The Chinwi is there behind the wheel of a pick-up truck branded with the logo of a Chinese construction company. I tell him to park his pick-up inside, next to our cars. It's a bit tight but the Chinwi smoothly slides the vehicle in. While the nameless bloke is outside scanning the area, the Chinwi hops out of the pick-up truck and loudly greets us in broken Arabic.

"Assalam alaikoum. I am Lei!"

He's of short stature and weak frame, wearing muddy shoes, worn out jeans and a sweaty shirt. Nothing remarkable about him, except a thin tattoo on his skinny right forearm.

He looks at me and asks, "Are you the translator?" in a weird Asian accent.

"Yes I am," I answer, strangely satisfied.

He looks around quite suspiciously and asks me, "Who is the weird big guy?"

Boualem instantly inquires, "What did he say?"

"He's asking about your friend…"

"It's none of his business. The less this bat eater knows, the better for us."

"I also don't know much about him," I responded.

"I appreciate that you never asked. Let's keep it that way. Tell the Chinwi to mind his own business and to show us the money. We have work to do."

I translate what Boualem says in gentler, friendlier words. The Chinese guy reacts well and seems completely relaxed and chill. He opens the passenger door and fetches a big bag from under the seat. The fact that he seems so relaxed and assured, bringing that much money in a bag to a guy he barely knows, suddenly stresses me out.

Unnamed big bloke comes from the back entrance of the shed.

Boualem orders him to bring the money and the bill counter from a cardboard box.

"Tell the Chinwi to empty the bag of money on the table," Boualem almost shouts at me.

I don't like the way he talks to me since Lei is here. He seems rude and sultry all of a sudden.

The Chinwi demands to count his euros too.

"I will count my dinars first and only then I'll give him his euros," utters Boualem condescendingly, while inspecting the battery operating currency counter.

I translate to the Chinwi. Here again, gently. This time his patience begins to show its limits. He yells at us vehemently in Chinese. I keep my composure, repeating that I don't understand a single word he says, but his face is still angry.

"Tell him to behave himself because I can end this business anytime I want..." Boualem is shouting in Arabic at the Chinwi who in response shouts louder in Chinese. Tedious. Unnamed bloke is standing next to Boualem, frowning. Boualem tells him to stay cool. Lei seems to recover his calm gradually. After some soothing words from Boualem, that I'm handing honey coated to the Asian, everything is settled and the four of us are finally around the money garnished table. Boualem unties the bundles of two thousands dinars bills while unnamed bloke feeds the money counter with them. Meanwhile I'm having a polite chit-chat with Lei who really begins to appreciate my presence. I sometimes struggle with his accent as he certainly does with mine, but everything's flowing otherwise. He explains to me how I could get some good deals on electronic devices he brings from China. His voice is so loud I barely hear the noise of rotating paper bills and the words Boualem and his acolyte are exchanging. Suddenly the noise of the bill counter stops and I can clearly feel a tension.

"Counterfeit money!" Boualem exclaims in a gloomy tone.

"Really? The bills are..." I inquire.

"Fake!" Says Boualem, staring angrily at the dirty wall in front of him.

"What is happening?" Lei asks me with a stare of incomprehension.

"Did you recount?" I ask Boualem.

"Of course we did. Two times while you were chatting with your new friend. The bill counter is new and professionally calibrated to spot fake dinars. This bat eater is a disgusting swindler."

"Slow down Boualem. I'm sure there's an explanation."

Unnamed bloke is looking at me hostilely.

"What's happening? Please explain." The Chinwi is now becoming anxious.

"They say that there are fake bills in the bundles you brought."

"Fake bills? The money is coming straight from banking agencies. I'm not gonna say how but all the money is coming from regular multiple bank accounts. Can't be fake!"

When I translate these words to Boualem and his acolyte they remain silent for long seconds. Unnamed bloke takes a puff of cigarette. Boualem then says to me straight in the eyes, "Are you with us or with the rat eater?"

"What the hell are you talking about?"

"This seemingly harmless son of a bitch is cheating his own people and you think that he's gonna play straight with us?" Says Boualem, angry.

Unnamed bloke is now standing, towering the livid Asian with a menacing stare.

"What's happening?" Lei keeps asking me.

"There's apparently a problem with the money," I respond hesitantly. My voice is not reassuring at all.

"How much money is fake?" he asks.

I translate.

"Almost half the bundles are fake," says Boualem.

I translate.

"Half? No way. Impossible! I want my money back!" screams the Chinese guy, standing and pushing away the rotten chair.

Unnamed bloke storms at him, hitting me aside with his massive left shoulder. I fall on the floor and in a snap Lei is immobilized with a rear arm-lock.

Everything happened so quickly.

The Chinwi, shocked, is at the mercy of the giant bloke.

I look at Boualem with an incredulous stare. He gives me his hand so I can get on my feet.

"Stay calm. Don't panic. Everything's under control," he told me when I stood up, still firmly grabbing my hand.

The Chinwi is looking at me with begging eyes.

"You're not the one who can break his arm. Why is he looking at you like this," says Boualem, grinning.

"He's not looking for my pity. He's looking for my translation."

"Tell him in good English to go to hell!" Boualem replies with a cold tone.

Unnamed bloke quickly transitions to a choke-hold position. The big apathetic lad turns out to be a redoubtable killer. He pressures the thin neck of the Asian guy with his big arms. He keeps squeezing and pressuring the neck. Boualem is pushing me backward with his beefy body and his hand still firmly grabbing mine, carefully but forcefully, like we'd do to a child who should not see such nasty things. Lei tries to escape the perfectly executed strangulation but it looks so vain and useless, his protruding eyeballs almost popping out of the reddish bloated face. Suddenly Lei is not moving anymore. His right arm falls off limply and his body stiffens. Nameless bloke then violently smashes his head against the wall a couple of times. The head percussion produces an explosive, muted sound. He sure will never get up again.

My legs become weak. I'm overwhelmed and dizzy.

Unnamed bloke calmly puts the lifeless body on a chair and tries to maintain it perfectly still. Bloody head leaning to the left side, drool foam dripping from his mouth, bulging eyes still expressing a static shock, Lei is different dead. Like a slaughtered sheep version of him. I run to the smelly dark corner of the shed, vomit my meager lunch and expel more than I thought I can, helped by the pestilent odor emanating from the toilet.

I didn't believe what I saw. I couldn't process such horrors.

Everything happened so quickly.

I'm sitting on the dirty ground, my back on the toilet separation wall, next to my puddle of fresh vomit, mind outside of body.

Boualem and the big silent killer are now counting the money under the dim flashlight, next to the chair where the dead Chinese worker is sitting.

Boualem puts some bundles of money in a black plastic garbage bag. I don't know how many bundles but it seems like quite a lot. He walks slowly towards me holding the bag; waiting for me to take it from his hand.

"Congratulations! You are a rich son of a bitch! There's much more than what was agreed upon."

I contemplate the bag full of money but can't grab it. Boualem drops it off on the ground near me.

"It's legit money. If I were you I'd just go home now. Take a bath, relax, watch some movies. Your job is done. We'll clean up the place and no traces will be left. No one will catch us. No one can. Of course that is if you keep being a man of your word. Do you remember our little silent business oath? It'd be stupid to take it lightly. You could regret it."

I blankly stare at him.

"Just go home and forget about what you saw. You can say that you are a lucky guy. We did the dirty job and you get a nice part of the cake. You are rich thanks to us. Not as rich as me and my friend though." He smirks while pointing out all the money bundles on the table. The giant killer is throwing all of them into several bags.

"Stand up now! It's over." He gives me his hand for the second time this evening.

I stare at his clean chubby hand.

"Come on!" He is friendly, elated, relieved that everything went as planned.

I stand on my feet by myself. He doesn't seem to take offense.

I take the money bag.

"Help me open the gate. Quickly. I think I'm about to puke again."

*****

Once in my studio flat I didn't sleep. The humidity was eating the room. The old fan was keeping the beat of my rumbling heart steady. All night I couldn't close my eyes for more than thirty seconds without visions of Lei strangled. I gave up on sleeping and kept staring at the ceiling until it was sunny outside. Sunny but still quiet. I could hear the first neighbors leaving the building. Noises of children going to school for the last week before the summer holidays.

The money was still in the garbage bag. How much money? I didn't know exactly. Couldn't count. Didn't ask. A lot more than what I expected as Boualem told me. I'd say something between four to five million dinars. A little fortune for me. Not one bill was fake. They killed him like a cockroach. He was an easy target. It was all planned from the start and I was just a pawn in their game. Framed. What could I do now that wouldn't send me to prison or make me an easy target for Boualem and his thugs? Keep my mouth shut for the rest of my life.

A poor expatriate Chinese laborer with no family or real friends here. A little swindler probably but not much else. Boualem masterfully planned everything from the start. They only exchanged messages via outdated dumb phones using second hand chips from the black market. They sure had already started the dismantling of the company's pick-up truck. Extra money in spare parts. That's how they do. They count coldly. They count as they kill. That's how successful people do. They count, they kill. That was a glorious night for them.

I fell asleep for maybe an hour. I don't know how it occurred but I lost consciousness at a moment or another between 10 and 11 a.m. It was noon and I was desperately awake facing my new reality drenched in sweat: I took part in a heinous crime. That's the reality I would wake up to every morning for the rest of my life. And it terrified me. My hands and feet were shaking. I furiously ejected myself from the soaked sheets. For an hour, I circumambulated the flat like a zombie. I got hold of some lucidity and managed to wash my face. I wore a t-shirt. I got out.

The streets were immersed in a shattering heat. People were hiding in the shades. I was meandering like an unhinged madman. I couldn't stay still even without eating for twenty-four hours, even with so little sleep, even under a killing sun. My mind was running wild. Images of the contorted swelling face of Lei were flashing through my eyes. Scenes of cops, prison, humiliation, family shame kept playing somewhere in my sick mind. Crazy scenarios of my own demise. It was a fire of anguish consuming me. With shaky hands I grabbed my phone and called Boualem. He was sleeping. His voice was more cavernous and bestial than usual.

"Why are you so fragile? Why all the drama? Stop acting like a wuss! Don't buy into all the crap you see and read like it was reality. No one's gonna catch us. Nothing will happen. Right now the corpse of the Chinwi is dissolving in a bathtub filled with acid. There will be nothing left of him except a chemical soup of bones and flesh that will be thrown into some open dump. Nobody will grieve for this Asian grifter. He won't be regretted by anyone. Except maybe his scattered little family in China. His so-called business partners will only mourn their money. They're paying for their stupidity. Trusting a crook is just plain stupid and they've been indirectly punished for that. We just protected our interests. We couldn't let him get away with it and talk shit about us. About Boualem. Calm down, brother. Be wise. They will report his disappearance. They'll think he stole the money and the pick-up truck and drove away somewhere far to enjoy the fruit of his theft. Believe me no one cares about him, no one respects him. I have all the necessary information about him. I know what I'm talking about. I have to sleep. Forget about what happened. Forget about me. What is done is done. Enjoy your money. And have some sleep." He ended the phone call.

I went home and slept. I slept for hours. For days. I desensitized myself with sleeping. I went numb dozing. And it felt good. It didn't redeem the pain though. Nothing could. It just felt right to wallow in an emotionless scruffy lifestyle for days. Eating scarcely, listening to long videos of self-improvement gurus and conspiracy theories on YouTube, while waiting for the next phase of sleep to come. Laying on the couch, watching the ceiling. I let the words of Boualem infuse my mind with their thug wisdom. Boualem, a psychopathic thief, the ultimate self-development mastermind. What is done is done. The Chinwi is dead. I can't do anything about it. What I can do now that I have some money is buy a nice car, a new hi-fi system, new fashion clothes, eat at fine restaurants and pay my rent for two years. Look after myself. Take care of myself and those I love. Buy things. Enjoy life. Yes.

*****

Life was somehow set on track after two or three weeks. I was sleeping less and better. I was able to enjoy some moments in a day. A nice cup of coffee in the morning, a walk by the seashore, nice music playing through my new audiophile speakers. I hadn't heard from Boualem but was constantly thinking about him. I was starting to believe that I could somehow have a normal life. I would never forget what happened in the shed that's for sure, but I could at least keep it encased in a dark corner of my brain maybe with nightmares about it some nights. That's bearable.

I sent some nice and expensive presents to my family. My mother, father and older sister, left the east of Algiers and relocated in the countryside a decade ago. It felt great to treat them. Fancy Italian shoes, high-end perfumes, fine garments in noble fabrics. They all called me to inquire about my sudden fortune. How did this happen? I invented some incredible contract I signed with a big multinational company here in Algiers. They were all so happy for me.

I pampered myself too. New wardrobe, new TV and other high-tech gear. I thought about buying a nice car but had fears that it was too showy. It could attract curious eyes. And I wasn't that rich after all. I contemplated some nice vintage eighties and nineties Mercedes and BMWs, and just the idea that I had enough money to buy one was thrilling for me. Those were some of my highlights in a day still mostly made of depressing ideas and gloomy thoughts.

*****

Once a fantasy, always a fantasy. Rym. I always enjoyed her monosyllable, evocative name. A brief emission of sound that conjured up her souvenir and fitted well with her fleeting appearance and slender silhouette. We met at a grocery shop and she recognized me. I didn't even remember the last time I saw her but it sure was around my last year at the University. She never cared for me though. She was the popular sought-after feminine dream girl. She complimented me on my look while filling her basket with milk, biscuits and chocolate. My nice new outfits pleased her and it was such a boost for my dismantled ego. She was sloppily dressed and looked tired, but strangely still graceful and ethereal; with strong remnants of the Queen of the Campus she not so long ago was. I decided on a whim to take a chance and invite her for coffee in a nice place. She smirked and uttered an unconvincing "why not!". She wasn't wearing any engagement ring on her finger but I just realized it once I did the move. Something in her just screamed "still single".

"Name the place if you want but time is right now!" I pompously said.

"Wherever you choose, as long as I can be home in an hour or two!" she replied defiantly.

Five minutes later, I was opening the trunk of my Maruti while painfully holding our groceries. I nicely huddled the shopping bags together to make sure everything held well. I closed the trunk then saw a disgusted silent face on Rym. The crumbling Maruti came as a shock to her apparently. She sure had thought I had a nicer car judging by my nice outfits. Sorry to disappoint.

Once inside the car I realized how greasy and dusty everything was. I was seeing it through her revulsed eyes. The steering wheel, the ugly dashboard, the seats. The cheap plastic finish was layered with a surplus of dirt. I also realized how much I wasn't paying any attention to daily life routines since that terrible day. I was barely maintaining personal hygiene and spending money on futilities to alleviate the pain. Inviting the Fantasy on a whim was a terrible idea. To put another nail on the coffin, she fetched a tissue from her handbag and disposed of it on the seat, as if to not stain her rather bulbous buttocks. Supreme humiliation. She remained silent and impassive, waiting for me to start the car.

A Man of his Word

I drove ten minutes straight to a nice coffee shop. Ten minutes that she spent staring blankly at the scrolling urban settings, barely replying to my desperate attempts to reestablish momentum.

We sat at a corner table next to the one-way vision window. We ordered a coffee for me and a cappuccino and cheesecake for her. Only when she faced me did I realize how dead her eyes were, how devoid of any candour. Did I see her in some kind of blinding halo in the grocery store? Probably. She then began to ask me multiple questions trying to coldly assess my situation. I answered in the straightest way possible, leaving very few doubts about how unexciting and few and far between my interpretation and translation gigs were. She seemed completely disoriented by the signals she received from me. One minute I was the nice dork from University that was exhibiting some exterior signs of success and high standing (cashmere blazer, immaculate quality cotton shirt, oozing high end designer brand cologne), minutes later I was the eternal loser nervously driving his ugly oily dumpster car.

"So you're still in the translation field. Interesting. I'm sure you're doing better than what you seem to suggest anyway." she told me in an uneasy tone. "I had to give up on it. I mean translation business and this kind of tedious, didactic jobs. I also have a marketing business degree from a renowned private school. I studied there after my English license. I work at Cemortal Industry now as first assistant to the Head of Communication and Public Affairs. All those years studying English really paid off well in the end. Everyone is still so attached and almost neurotic about French in the Company. I'm gonna change that. I naturally found my place there as the only copywriter in English." She ferociously smiled. "Believe me they're paying me much more than the fair price for every bit of it!"

"Great!"

She never was short of words about how important and essential she was to the Company. She complained about how difficult it was for her to find a husband, and about the laziness and lack of ambition most men she encountered suffered from. She also talked about the pressure to marry and settle down and her lack of willingness to compromise and comply. She talked for twenty minutes straight. She complimented my choice of the coffee shop. The cheesecake she ordered was excellent according to her. She then was back at me trying to decipher my situation, asking questions, trying to corner me. Where I was living, was I renting or paying a bank loan to a nice apartment, was I in contact with diplomats or foreign embassies, how can I pay for such a nice tailored blazer in the end. I felt that her questions were filled with frustration.

"Can you be more specific about who you work for in general? Or are your clients so important that you have to keep it confidential!" She smirked again, but now it was getting on my nerves somehow.

"Oh yes absolutely! I work for dangerous criminals my dear. So I have to keep it confidential for obvious reasons"

"Oh please!" She pouted with those eyes devoid of empathy.

"I'm dead serious! Well maybe dead's not the word. Cause I'm still alive. Alive and well. But others are not. You see, those people I work for, they strangle you with their bare hands. They dismember you and get rid of your limbs in garbage bags. They take your money, they choke you to death and then they bury your butchered corpse somewhere in an open dump. For business purposes of course. It's all about business."

She looked disgusted again. Crumbling Indian Car level of disgust.

"I really thought we could have a good conversation. I sometimes see old friends from the University and that's so heartwarming and inspiring when they do great things, become successful or attain a certain level of achievement. But sometimes they remain as they always were: dorks, creeps, strange asocial kids, eternal brats thinking they're so funny. You know where you belong, isn't it?"

She was talking to me while typing frantically on her smartphone.

"Please don't bother yourself, I'm hailing a ride by app to get back home. You see, I don't need jerks like you."

She stormed off the table, leaving me staring at my half-empty coffee cup. She appeared 20 seconds later on the other side of the one-way vision window, staring at a hypothetical me, miming precise gestures, mad that I could see her while she couldn't. She needed her groceries, neatly stacked in my dirty car, back. At that moment she somehow recovered that charm she had in my memory. I insisted on driving her home, or close to home as her father was scrutinizing her moves, but she vehemently refused because my mental health was questionable for her.

Once back home, I just decided to laugh about the improvised date. I stored my groceries, cooked some noodles for dinner and poured myself a glass of local soda. I started to download dozens of shitty series and eighties horror movies. Good for mental health improvement. I checked my phone later that evening and realized I missed a message. It was my dad's. My dad, who never complimented me on anything, sent me a text that shook me.

"I don't care about the leather shoes (they're great by the way), I'm just happy you landed that contract. I didn't know you could make such money with your job as a translator. I'm proud that you are doing so well."

That brought tears to my eyes. Tears of sadness and bitterness. I really hated myself at that moment. Couldn't send any substantial response to his message. I just sent "Thanks" three hours later. That night was harsh.

*****

It was one of those nights again: hot, humid, tedious and full of harassing, self-loathing thoughts.

Lei kept coming back to haunt my solitary nocturnal ramblings. The noisy fan was blowing hard on my sticky body, stripping me from excess sweat and any hope of sleep. Two or three relaxing playlists had been played entirely and I was still awake. It was almost 3:00 in the morning and my heart was pounding heavily. I couldn't get rid of this strange sensation I had in the late evening. An urge to scratch off and tear up my skin to let something pour out. I never felt like this before and I didn't know how to reduce this bizarre itch. I left my bed and stood at the opened window, contemplating the empty neighborhood. Five minutes later I was out in the street, wandering alone through dark alleys.

I walked to a small public park at the center of several blocks in the area. Abandoned, barely maintained, the place served as the perfect lair for youth gangs, outdoor drunkards and zetla smokers. It was around 3:20 a.m. and the park was quiet and deserted as far as I could see. I sat on the last remaining wooden slat of a bench and got quickly absorbed in my toxic thoughts. In the darkness of the poorly maintained park, sitting on a vandalized bench, I strangely just wanted to stay there for the rest of the night. Anxiety is more palatable in the open air, when a pleasant slight chill begins to set in. But minutes in, something was wrong. I felt stared at. I thought I saw a shadow moving behind the trees. A distant moving shadow, without definite contours. It suddenly emerged from the dark vegetation and its contours became clearer. It was what we can call a man. He was walking toward me at a steady, slow pace. He seemed puny, slimy, sick. The man, however, as he was approaching me under the scarce moonlight, took on the frightening and familiar appearance of someone I knew. Someone who looked like me, a disturbing replica of my own deformities and small physical defects; an enormous belly for a fragile complexion, a rough skin, sickly pale, streaked with reddish veins; messy greasy hair, thick dandruff invading ears and shoulders; small stern eyes, rendered mute by sleepless nights. I shuddered as the weird fellow took place beside me on the bench. I could clearly see all the little horrible details of his monstrous physique. I stood up, moved a few feet away from the frightening figure, then faced him obnoxiously.

"Who are you?" I whispered.

"Who am I? I am a nightmare and a conscience. A foreknowledge of evil. Guilt, weakness, disease, shame, fear. I am the mirror devoid of all complacency that you never had the courage to take a look at. Look at yourself! What do you see except your little exaggerated physical flaws, except this disjointed carcass containing so much rage and bitterness, disappointment and ill-being. What do you see there? Look at yourself with your little miseries, your big mistakes, your unforgivable passivity, your cowardice, your compromises. Look at the scars, the bedsores, the pus that you wanted to expel from your intoxicated body!"

He then pressed his finger on a pustule on his greasy forehead. Large quantity of thick pus came out, slowly dripping down his face. I looked away disgusted.

"Why are you looking away? There's no one but you here. I know how painful it is for you. There's nothing to look at that justifies a tiny bit of self-esteem, some respect for yourself."

That's what was torturing me during the night. How didn't I figure it out? The envy of guilt vomiting, guilt expelling. The metaphysical urge to vomit, to empty myself of the toxicity of my new life. To internally cleanse. For some ephemeral relief. Like in the shed just after the killing of Lei.

I ran away, my hand on my mouth. "I am your dark soul! You recognized me!" he shouted at me from the bench. "I know you recognized me!"

*****

More than a month later it was like nothing had ever happened. It seemed like nobody here had heard about a missing Chinese worker. I was still living with it inside my head but I could at least sleep and have my daily routine and regular business done. I cleaned my Maruti 800 and put it for sale on ouedkniss.com. Lei was a ghost dwelling in my head and I got used to it: his voice, his face as he was choked to death, his eyes while life was drained out of him were a part of my daily imaginarium. Still having nightmares and intrusive visual memories of the killing, sometimes during the day and almost every night. Panic attacks were looming just by seeing a random Chinese guy walking in the streets of Algiers.

One morning I perused the web searching for anything related to Lei in the news. Nothing. I spent hours on the most known and less known press titles, their sites and social media pages. In Arabic and in French. Nothing. Maybe Boualem was right, no one really cared for that guy. They all think he ran away with the money and the pick-up truck. He was an incarnated insignificance. A nobody coming from a distant fantasized land, trying to earn a living by his hands in an equally distant and ignored land. I remembered the first wave of Chinese construction workers here in the east suburbs of Algiers in the early nineties. The crazy stories about them chasing dogs and cats to eat them, some mothers telling their infants to never talk to them, never accept anything from them. I remembered Walid, a friend of mine who was selling cigarettes and chewing-gums in the streets to help his poor family. He always priced cigarettes way higher for the Chinese workers. When they were drunk and in packs he was exulting because he thought he could basically do whatever he wanted with the prices. Classic scheme of poor people from around the world tricking each other for miserable gains. Unfortunately for him, they discovered the swindle and not one Chinese worker bought anything from him anymore. They superbly ignored him. To an extent, they did the same with the larger population as well. They began to develop their own businesses with their own products and small shops. They were a visible minority, mostly respected for their work ethics. You could see them frequently in the streets, but there was a wall of glass between us and them. Some of them, a minority in the minority, converted to Islam and married Algerian women. Some others knew how to navigate the intricate mindset of Algerians, developing fruitful business partnerships. Maybe that's what Lei intended to do in his own twisted way.

At the end of that beautiful summer afternoon, a strange envy took hold of me while I was strolling by the seaside. It was the right thing to do for me at that moment. I got in my car then drove half an hour to a worksite where I suspected Lei had been employed. I parked my car near the exit. The huge information panel stated that it was a building intended for a subsidiary of the national oil company. The construction company logo, that was all over Lei's pickup, was printed on a big backboard over the portal. The Chinese workers were leaving the worksite in groups after a long day of hard labor. They were solidly put together and well organized, heading toward the dorm facilities. I remembered when I was searching the web for Lei, stumbling upon the different meanings of the name. It is mostly a family surname apparently and also a first name. How many Lei were there among those laborers? And was Lei really Lei? Not sure. I'd have loved to talk to them and ask them questions.

"Do you know Lei?"

"Which Lei are you talking about?"

"Lei the worker. Lei the swindler. Lei the failed businessman. Lei the man who disappeared more than a month ago. Lei, whose name is probably not Lei."

I just laughed at myself imagining the dialogue. They would have laughed at me too, or most likely it would have creeped them out.

They were crossing the street in groups, a sense of solidarity and fellowship emanating from the swarm. They were laughing and smiling and joking about each other. They seemed to really enjoy themselves in their communist communion. So seemingly grounded and yet so detached from reality. The reality of their comrade killed by ravenous thugs not so far from here, not so long ago. Boualem was right, nobody liked the guy. They just really didn't care that Lei was dead. And neither should I, an internal voice kept telling me.

*****

It was 9:30 in the morning. I was slowly walking to the cafe where I usually take my breakfast, when I heard the familiar and unsettling voice of Boualem behind my back.

"Get in the car."

He was in a beautiful and well restored 1992 Benz. Like the ones I was drooling over. We had some tastes in common and that didn't surprise me at all. He seemed disturbed or annoyed by something. Not a good sign.

"We go to the cafe? My stomach is empty."

"Order a take away. I don't want to talk there," he replied dryly.

Ten minutes later we were parked in the shade of an abandoned building. Boualem knew all the shady abandoned spots of the city. I was sipping my coffee, hot croissants still packed and oozing a delicious aroma. Exquisite smell, heavy atmosphere. I noticed travel bags under the backseat. For long minutes he didn't utter a word, nor did I.

"You're a man of your word, aren't you?" he finally asked with a monotonous tone.

"You know the answer, Boualem."

"I was driving to the shed yesterday evening. When I got near the lot bordering the place, I spotted a car with tinted windows that aroused my suspicions. Usually some cars park in the area in the morning. Mostly couples looking for a calm place. I don't remember seeing any cars there after 4:00 p.m. the last two years. I took the road back home. I kept calling Big Fa all night but he didn't answer…"

"Wait! Who's Big Fa?"

"Farid! The guy who was with us that night! Seems obvious!"

"Ah! The cold killer. I finally know his name! Great!"

"Couldn't close my eyes all night. I went back early this morning. Another car parked at the same spot. They're watching the shed. Farid is still missing. He didn't pick up his phone and he didn't call back. He never did that before. I stopped calling and turned off my phone anyway."

"You're so fragile! Nothing will happen! You remember when you said this to me?" I asked with a nervous smile.

"I'm not joking! I smell shit!"

For the first time ever, I detected something resembling fear in the voice of Boualem. It violently triggered my internal repressed anxiety.

"You think they're cops, right? *Chkoupi*!"

"Yes. Of course they're cops!" He swallowed his saliva. "I tell you I smell shit. I came to see you... To see you straight in the eyes. Maybe you have something to do with it…"

"I've done nothing wrong Boualem! I never talked to anyone about what you and Big Fa did."

"What me and Farid did? Me and Big Fa? Are you serious? You're that stupid? You're with us in it! You're in deep shit! What we did! You dumb nerd!"

He was laughing like a mad hyena.

"What are those for?" I asked, looking at the travel bags in the back.

"I'm going to disappear for a while. I suggest you do the same."

I was shuddering.

"Take me home. I'm going to pack up."

"No. I'm leaving you here. Twenty minutes' walk and you're home. I'm gonna take a detour that leads directly to the highway. I'm really going to disappear. The soil will swallow me," he said, contemplating the visible lines of the highway, far beyond the old roofs of the rotten city.

I got out and loudly clapped the door. He looked at me behind the rolled down passenger window. "It was a pleasure working with you. And thanks for the croissants. They smell terrific!"

He drove off in a cloud of dust, leaving me standing there like an idiot, baffled by that sudden turn of events.

*****

A Man of his Word

The neighborhood seemed quiet as usual. The entrance to the building was as spooky as ever, even in the daylight. Nobody was there except a very old neighbor staring at the dry soil of our lifeless garden area. I took a deep breath and ran to the entrance. I climbed the stairs two steps at once. I got inside my studio apartment, closed the door and immediately began to put some clean clothes in my old travel bag. Not even five minutes later I heard someone knocking on the door. I froze. I heard multiple voices behind the closed door. They kept knocking on. I felt the percussion of the heavy hand on the wooden door bumping into my guts, flowing through my limbs.

"Police! Open the door!"

The world was falling apart on me. Everything was crumbling in ruins just there before my eyes. The humiliation. The fear. The resentment. And a lot of self-loathing. In the blink of an eye, I drank this cocktail of emotions to the dregs. It felt so dense and quick. They kept knocking on the door, harder and harder.

"Police! We're going to use legal force! Open the door!"

A sense of resignation suddenly took hold of me. It was the end. My end. What is done is done, as Boualem told me. Better accept it. There was nothing I could do at that moment. As there was absolutely nothing to do when Farid was choking Lei to death. I opened the door and surrendered to the police. Surrendered to my fate. Thug wisdom at its best.

They spread around through the door into the small studio flat like a bunch of rabid dogs. There were only three cops, but in my mind it was like an army assaulting me. They handcuffed me quickly. It didn't take them long before they found the cash bag. They were talking to me but I completely shut down. I reverted inward, hid into my head. I was just seeing angry cops yelling at me. And one of them, it seemed, was asking me questions. But I couldn't answer. I couldn't open my mouth. I was then dragged around the block like a dangerous criminal, under the incredulous eyes of the neighbors gathering at the entrance of the building.

*****

Fifteen minutes later I was at the police station. The interrogation room was sinister and humid. The paint was peeling off the walls, the corners were dusty and the chairs clunky. Barely better than the shed's decoration.

I was paying attention to the filthy little details just to avoid the vindictive stare of the detective who was thoroughly interrogating me.

"This is how it happened…" he told me with his raspy voice, "you baited the Chinese guy. You were his main contact as you're the one speaking English. We know he could speak some decent English. You talked to him about some enticing exchange rate from national money to euros. He wanted to benefit from it. He collected a big sum of money in national currency from members of the Chinese community here in Algiers. Legal and illegal money alike, from honest workers and dubious businessmen. You told him to go to the abandoned industrial shed where he would meet you with the money. But you didn't tell him that Big Farid was there waiting for him. Two options here: Farid told us that you contacted him just for body guarding purposes. He said that when you ordered him to kill the Chinwi, he refused. Left with no other choice, you just did the dirty deed yourself. You shared the money with Big Fa to buy his silence. He also dismantled the pick-up truck to sell it in spare parts."

He marked a pause, looking deep into my eyes.

"Second and more plausible option in my opinion: Farid did the dirty deed. His job was to kill the Chinwi and he did it like he ate a piece of cake. We believe he took a big chunk of the money too. You split it in two parts. Who took the biggest part? I don't know. We found your part. We haven't found Big Fa's part yet. Knowing the big thug a little bit, I'm inclined to think, as I already told you, that the second option is the right option; and looking at you now I'm sure you're the mastermind behind all this criminal grift. But if Big Fa wanted you to follow some of his uncanny rules, I'm sure your, let's say modest physique, wouldn't allow you to say no. Any thoughts?"

Nothing. I didn't respond. I kept staring blankly at him. He leaned over me.

"Whatever the truth about the Chinese guy's disappearance is, it's just a combination of situations involving both of you and Big Fa. We have a bag full of the cash you were storing in your shitty apartment. Hopefully the bills are covered with the Chinese guy's fingerprints. We have the spare parts of the company's pick-up truck Lei used to drive. With the fingerprints of Big Fa all over them needless to say."

That was how it all collapsed. The pick-up truck! The police electronic brigade spotted in ouedkniss.com a web sale announcement of several mechanical and electrical parts dismantled from the pick-up truck. It was Big Fa's brilliant idea to sell them using the most popular online marketplace in the country. They bought all the lot and identified every part as coming from the Chinese company's vehicle. Farid was after that an easy catch. His fingerprints were all over and he was in the police suspects database for years for different crimes and thefts. A GPS module that was used to track the employee's movements was found among the lot. It led the cops to the shed. Big Farid sent them to my shitty apartment. From what I understood he didn't tell them anything about Boualem. That's what I'd call trustworthiness. Boualem thought our demise would come from disloyalty. It finally came from stupidity. The stupidity of Big Fa, and mine to an extent. Stupid enough to accept the idea that an association with such gangsters would have no consequences on me other than a broken mental sanity. For the police, I was in this together with Farid. And just the two of us, apparently. Boualem succeeded in his narrow escape, but I guess that he was still wary of our potential disloyalty. He didn't obviously hold Big Fa's intelligence in high regard, but I thought he'd do a better job at managing the unfortunate moves of his big dumb partner.

"What do you think about my story?" the cop asked me.

"I think you did well with what you got. It wasn't that hard for you to put it all together. The result is decent. Nothing more. The plot could be much better. And I want a lawyer."

"I think that my plot is great. I think you're a wolf in sheep's clothing. What I can tell you for sure, is that you're going to be held in custody, waiting for the forensics results. You stirred some shit with your story, between the local authorities and the Chinese diplomacy here in Algiers. The company this Chinese guy was working for is an important contractor for the government. I can also tell you another thing. I can see right through your eyes. And your eyes are telling me that you have a lot to do with this Chinese guy vanishing into thin air."

*****

Being in the cell is a form of relief. At least I don't have to endure the creepy cop stare. I am left alone contemplating my own demise like it's some kind of modern tragedy. Until Boualem shows up to disrupt my train of thought with his thug wisdom. Yes, he was right, I'm too much into drama. Books and movies. A modern tragedy! Too embellishing for such a vile crooked up story. It's just a miserable swindle that turned bad. Maybe life is just a series of random traps. You smartly escape some, fall stupidly into others. I can't rationalize it any other way. What should I have done differently? What was right to do? To call the cops probably. And give the little fortune back to its owners. Continue my miserable lifestyle made of small translation gigs and scrambled eggs as a daily diet. And live under the threat of a revengeful stab from Boualem and Big Fa's assassins.

While I'm here waiting for a lawyer, and the cops are setting a case for me and Big Fa, I can't help but think about Boualem. Do they have a clue about him? Do they know about any of his connections to the case? Their storyline involving just me and Big Fa, contrary to what I said to the detective, is pretty much solid. Where is Boualem now? Probably driving his Benz straight to some dusty hole in the Sahara. A place where he already planned to hide if anything was to go wrong. Or maybe he's cruising along the narrow Mediterranean coastal roads, seeking refuge in cheap hotels. I can picture him living for years with a false identity, hiding in some lost village in the mountains, slowly spending his money like a retired old man. Living a low-key, simple, bucolic life. He would sometimes laugh at me and Big Fa, thinking he outsmarted us. Never anxious about being caught, counting on our ability to remain silent for the long years we'll spend in jail. You can sleep tight, Boualem. I'm a man of my word.

Blueberry Fields
Rand Gaynor

In the middle of a gravel road, in the headlights of their parked car, Seh Goodnight and his friend Eward get into their gear. Eward puts on his leather chaps and jock strap that, honestly, is a bit too small for him, but he doesn't seem to mind. Seh gets into the skin tight body suit that he had soaked in various olive and brown and khaki dyes and slashed with scissors here and there. Muddy makeup on any exposed skin finishes the look, that he has just crawled out of a swamp. Eward, chest and shoulder harness in place, swirls on a leather batwing-like cape and smears some of Seh's muddy makeup on his chest and handsome face. Both of them have fangs made by a denturist friend, that are very convincing.

As Larry had directed, just past some abandoned railway tracks that cross expansive blueberry fields, his house appears, a jet black silhouette in the late-summer twilight, orange lights in all its windows creating eyes and teeth of a deranged jack-o'-lantern, fitting for Larry's annual costume party although Halloween is still two months away. His house is a collection of small buildings of unknown origin, of various materials and dimensions, all cobbled together around a central room, a rambling place with steps up and down between rooms, its windows random heights and widths. Locals often report odd occurrences around the place, like whole areas of ripe blueberries suddenly disappearing. It had been abandoned more than twenty years ago when its owner was found dead inside. Police say it was from a blunt force injury to the head.

Seh and Eward ignore a barking dog and approach what they believe to be the main entrance to the house. A faded Boy Scout hat hangs in a window next to the porch door, a yellowed, hand-written note pinned to its rim: 'Please be quiet. The Mounties are asleep."

"Looks like Larry left the existing security system in place," Eward says.

"Well it probably worked," Seh says. "I doubt anyone has tried to rob this place!"

They knock on the door, then step inside where a costume party is trying to get started.

"Welcome to my humble abode!" Larry, a bearded Snow White, exclaims.

Seven pairs of little dwarf legs and feet hang out from under her skirt—Larry always wins the costume contest. Seh glances around the room, infused with the earthy scent of its old wood floor and of new wood burning in the stove. An overstuffed fat man smoking a fake pipe, a mummy wrapped in many metres of three-inch cotton strips, and a teenaged werewolf in a fluffy monogrammed sweater and poodle skirt, carrying a box of 45s, sit quietly.

"You can put your stuff in Arthur's room down there, off the porch," Larry tells them.

They have brought backpacks, planning to stay for the weekend, and are carrying their coats and sneakers, neither necessary for the Lord of the Underworld or his swampy sidekick.

"This is kind of creepy," Seh whispers, "we don't really know these people."

"Well," Eward assures him, "I'm the Lord of the Underworld and you are my extremely vicious minion, so between us we'll probably be okay."

*****

The evening conversation revolves around the blueberry heist of a few nights ago.

"It is still under investigation," Larry says. "No one can figure out how entire fields of blueberries could be picked clean overnight. The berries haven't appeared at any of the local fruit stands, none are available as contracted to the large food processors. Whoever did this was experienced and well organized. My income for this year has been devastated."

*****

More guests begin arriving: one dressed as a romantic dining table set for two, with a French lace tablecloth, a baguette, a small jar of blueberry jam and a live woman's head on a platter in the centre. There is a convincing old zombie carrying a blueberry rake with actual blueberry juice on it—a nod to the house's previous occupant—and a hobo in an old, long underwear onesie, with a red nose and dopey hat, worried about her wife, Susie, who is supposed to be here, but isn't. Adam, a stark naked man holding an apple, enthusiastically chats up the provocatively-costumed Eward. Eve is nowhere to be seen.

Seh explores Larry's ramshackle house made even more surreal by costumed party guests, like the pair of vampires huddled in a dark corner. He stumbles upon Eve in a hall closet, crouched in a fetal position, naked, crying, hugging a two-metre, multicoloured, toy snake.

"Are you okay?" he asks.

"No," she says. "My husband is drooling over that creature with its balls hanging out of its jockstrap."

"Oh," Seh says, "Lord of the Underworld."

He pauses a moment, unsure about what to say.

"Are you going to join the party?" is all he could come up with.

She reaches for the closet door, pulls it shut. Returning to the kitchen, Seh sees that Adam isn't all that concerned about Eve.

Three guys with guitars show up dressed as a rock band and are pretty good, especially on "Hotel California." The old zombie accompanies them on piano, from a couple of rooms away. A burlap sack full of potatoes on the floor behind the stove begins to move, then stands up. To the hobo's relief it is Susie, who has been sleeping there where it is warm. Naked Adam and Eve leave early, with Eve stomping out of the house dragging her two-metre, multicoloured toy snake, convinced the Lord of the Underworld had eaten Adam's apple. Larry's party continues long into the night; a few partygoers plan to crash here.

*****

As Seh and Eward get into their rickety twin beds, ten feet apart in this large room, Seh hears the piano, someone faintly banging out "There's no business like show business!"

When his bed begins to vibrate gently, Seh figures there's a train going by, close enough to be felt but too far away to be heard. The coarse wool blanket starts to feel itchy, he can feel it right through the thin flannel sheet. And then, what feels like an index and middle finger walks up his lower leg, walks slowly along his thigh up to his hip and slips under the blanket.

As the itchy sensation subsides, Seh drifts off into dreamland. A long, black hearse stops right in front of him. The passenger door opens automatically, silently. He gets in. The driver steps on the clutch, shifts a few gears causing the hearse to levitate, and then fly in slow motion above the house and fields, then higher than any airplane Seh has ever been in and even higher into the infinite outer space. Seh realizes that hearses don't fly. This has to be a dream. He has had dreams before in which he was aware that he was dreaming and sometimes could actively participate in them, interacting with the many odd characters he met there. This time he would just relax and watch the dream unfold, a silent observer inside a 3D movie.

The hearse lands in a decaying old town, a maze of crumbling stone buildings. In its dark alleyways, crowds of people huddle silently in corners, not speaking, not moving, many seeming afraid, some shuffling, some cowering behind others who seem unconcerned. Many of them cling to precious objects, like photographs and stuffed toys and wads of dollar bills. An old man clutching a bunch of magazines and a blueberry rake walks up to Seh, and smiles. Seh recognizes him—the old zombie from the party.

"You think this is a dream?" he asks.

"Well, yeah," Seh replies. It's obvious.

"If this is a dream, then you could put your hand right through that stone wall, couldn't you?"

"Well, yes, I could," Seh thinks.

"So," the old man says, reading Seh's mind, "go ahead."

Seh punches the very solid wall, feels the pain all the way up to his shoulder. He is jolted awake. Eward stands by the window, looking out over the fields.

"Morning," he says.

"Morning," Seh mumbles.

"How'd you sleep?" Eward asks.

"Okay….well, I was kept awake for a bit by an itchy blanket."

"My bed seemed to shake," Eward says, "it was kind of strange."

"I felt that, too," Seh says. "Must have been a train going by."

"Those tracks have been abandoned for years," Eward points out.

*****

Larry and the others are in the dining room enjoying a continental breakfast of fresh croissants and other pastries with apricot and cassis jams, orange juice and very strong coffee, when Seh and Eward join them. The entertainment centers around some old magazines Larry found when cleaning out the house. Seh recognizes these magazines, the same ones carried by the old man in his dream.

"Where did you find these?"

"In Arthur's room," Larry says, "when a couple of friends were helping me clean the place out. Arthur was the old man that lived here. He sold blueberries on the side of the road; the train would even stop so passengers could get off and pick their own. The first time we went into his bedroom I swear there was something in there, something passed right through us. I've never noticed anything weird in there since, except that the dogs won't go there, sometimes they just look in the door and growl."

Everyone freaks when Susie comes crashing through the ceiling and lands on the dining room table. Larry had asked everyone (except Susie, it seems) to not go in the room above the dining room, as there was no floor, just joists and the drywall of the ceiling below. She is okay, but has created quite a mess with all the pastries and strong coffee and broken dishes all over the place. Thankfully, she didn't land on the woodstove.

*****

The wool blanket doesn't feel itchy on the second night, no trains pass by, no ghostly fingers fondle. As Seh drifts off to sleep, Arthur's bedroom shifts into that dark, crumbling town. The old man is still standing there holding his things.

"Arthur?" Seh suspects.

"Yes," Arthur confirms.

"What are you doing here?" Seh asks.

"Waiting."

"Waiting for...?"

"You," Arthur says. "This morning, I got my new magazine out of the mailbox and went in the house to look at it. See," he says, holding a copy of an old magazine. "You are on the cover."

Seh is stunned to see himself on the magazine cover, dated 1962, years before he was born.

"After I finished looking at it, I put it in the box with the others," Arthur says, "and when I stood up I lost my balance and fell over, banged my head on the corner of a table and knocked myself out. When I woke up, I was here."

Arthur is stuck in this place, waiting, waiting interminably with thousands of grey, expressionless others, just waiting.

"There's not much to do around here," he says, "not even a movie theatre. I haven't seen a good musical in ages. But I do get back home sometimes. I went to a party there last night, played my piano for a while."

"Went out to the fields last week and harvested the berries," Arthur continues. "Well, a few of my friends helped, pickers from the train. Cleared the entire field. Made quite a bit of money so I now can get that upstairs floor finished."

"But you don't have to do that," Seh says. "You don't have to stay here."

"Don't be foolish," Arthur scowls.

"Put down those magazines and that rake and I'll show you."

Seh knows that since this is a dream, he is able to do anything he wants. He slowly levitates.

"Come up here," he says, inviting Arthur to join him a few feet off the ground.

Arthur manages to rise up a bit, but quickly drops back down. He tries again. And again.

"Maybe get rid of that heavy wool trench coat," Seh suggests.

Arthur drops his coat, stands there in his white t-shirt and boxers. A gentle breeze blows toward them, a breeze that strengthens into a wind, hurricane force.

"Lean into it," Seh calls to Arthur who has already been picked up like a kite and is hovering above the dark and crumbling old town.

"It's a lot brighter up here," he calls out to Seh, "It's beautiful here, I think I'll keep going, see what else is up here. But you really didn't have to go to all this effort to get rid of me. I would have gone long ago if someone had just smudged my house with white sage. I can't stand the smell of it."

*****

The next morning, Eward and Seh decide to get on the road early. Through the light mist gently moving across the fields, they see blueberries, oceans of fully ripe, juicy blueberries, ready for Larry's harvest.

Broken Clocks
Rob Loughran

"They found the body," said Peggy.

"What body?" said John.

"Michael's."

"I need a drink."

"We both need a drink."

"All three of us," said Krista from the phone, "need three drinks."

"I have Krista on Face Time," said Peggy.

"How are you dear Krista?" said John. He picked up the phone and smiled at Krista's tiny image. "You've lost weight."

"You can't see my ass," said Krista.

"Yeah, how is Christopher?"

"You are so clever."

"Sarcasm?"

"You bet."

Peggy walked to the bar and mixed two dirty vodka martinis. "Extra salad in mine," said John. Peggy added another olive.

"That sounds good," said Krista from the phone. "Give me a minute and we will further discuss this Michael matter."

Peggy and John sipped their martinis until Krista returned and John said, "What the hell, exactly, is going on here?"

Krista said from the phone, "I was surfing online when I saw a blurb about a discovered body, a skeleton, actually, in an old mine shaft in Coloma. I clicked on the link and read the blurb. The body is as yet unidentified but has been determined to be a male. Further, to be a male in his early thirties that has been interred since the nineteen eighties. And his skull had been bashed in."

"Who found the body?" said John.

"A LGBQT youth group on a spelunking adventure," said Krista. "There was no jewelry or any other clues as to the body's identity."

"We should have," said Peggy, "just poured him another double shot of Wild Turkey and let him play Russian roulette. It would've saved a whole lot of drama and heavy lifting if he'd had the common decency to kill himself."

"Perhaps so," said Krista.

"Is there any way," said John, "if they identify the body, "that they can connect us to Michael? DNA?"

"They could test for DNA but Michael wouldn't have a matching sample in the system." said Peggy, "Even if they do identify the body as Michael Lazarus we will be above suspicion because we reported him missing when we returned to civilization."

"Precisely." John finished his olives and set the glass aside.

"And there was rumor and speculation that he was facing an audit, fines, and jail time," said Peggy. "I discovered that we had two sets of books for the restaurant. People will just assume he took off, changed his name and continued his scams. If they do identify Michael's body they'll assume it was an accident. We'll be fine."

"That's easy for you to say, Peggy," said Krista. "But as you recall John and I were the ones who killed him."

The trio was suddenly silent, lost in their thoughts.

KRISTA

That's all I need, thought Krista, is a murder investigation besmirching my character and reputation as I try to sell my business and retire. Should I initiate some sort of discrete inquiry into the body's identity? To find out whether this skeleton really was Michael Lazarus?

No.

He needs to remain unidentified, anonymous, and abandoned. Even if somebody bothers to go back thirty-seven years and figure out who he is I think we will be fine. Didn't we report Michael missing to the El

Dorado County Sheriff—with appropriate confusion and sorrow on our faces and in our voices—as soon as we returned to paved roads? He would be just another missing person mystery solved and we should be in the clear. Besides, it was his idea to take this wayward wilderness bonding adventure.

The bastard brought it on himself.

Krista laughed. That's a rationalization but if anyone needed killing it was Michael Lazarus.

That sexist pig.

What was that mantra Michael had? *The Cattle Company doesn't tolerate sexual harassment; we rate it on a scale of one to ten.* How many seventeen-year-old hostesses had Michael grabbed, groped, fondled and exploited? How many had he shamed and embarrassed? How many had he inseminated? How many abortions had he paid for with cash skimmed from The Cattle Company?

Michael had two sets of books and screwed over investors, customers, and employees. But it wasn't, Krista thought, the money that motivated Michael. It was the endless supply of high school and college aged females. He was a pervert. An insatiable shameless alcoholic satyr.

Michael Lazarus, goat boy. The only sexual act that he hadn't performed on that couch in the upstairs office was necrophilia and that is only because he lacked a sufficiently fresh and pliable body.

The thing that amazed Krista was the same thing that disappointed Krista: that her fellow females were so lacking in self-esteem that they would submit to his sexual advances in order to get a minimum wage hostess or waitress job. Krista could see sleeping or sucking her way to the lead in a movie, basically her first two marriages were economic adventures where she traded her dignity, self-respect, privacy, and standards for financial security. But to trade a blowjob for a part-time restaurant job astounded her.

Then she remembered, suddenly and specifically, Florence Nestor.

Flo was a sweet, bright, chubby little round-faced cherub who, for all practical purposes, was repeatedly raped in that upstairs office. On that noisy, sticky, cold Naugahyde couch. What kind of insecurities do you need to nurture in order to fall in love with a man who abused you sexually, professionally, and emotionally. Krista smiled thinking that's the standard male rationalization: the blame always resides somewhere within the female. A fault in her character or upbringing that paints a bullseye on the victim and absolves or at least explains the predator's actions. But somehow the upbeat born again Christian Flo saw no abandonment of her Christian principles in her submissive capitulation to Michael's advances. Krista recalled—despite the nearly forty years that had passed—when Flo spoke of Michael's potential as a man, as a father, as a husband. And how, if Flo had enough faith and provided enough support, she could turn him into a decent Christian family man.

That was the day before Roberto Castaneda's birthday party where Michael provided the entertainment: a videotape of Flo naked on that Naugahyde couch.

Krista would never forget how Flo sat at the party, watching the video, paralyzed by shame with a piece of untouched birthday cake on a paper plate in her lap; paper napkin tucked demurely into her budding cleavage. She refused to move. She refused to cry. After four minutes, with every eye on her, she untucked her paper napkin and set it neatly with the cake. Flo drove home to her parents' clean and quiet and stately home, pulled into the garage lowered the door and left her Honda Civic running. She inhaled the brown wind of doom while softly singing a song of praise to her Lord and Savior.

Michael addressed the congregation at the funeral and delivered a moving and seemingly heartfelt tribute brimming with biblical references and scriptural anecdotes. It was after the service, Krista recalled, that Michael presented herself, Peggy, and John with his idea for a management teambuilding wilderness adventure in Gold Country. The four of them would spend a week in El Dorado County's wilderness living off the land. Bonding. Reinventing. Growing.

So the four of them packed up meager bags filled with the bare minimum they would need to survive and hopped into a rented Lincoln town car and drove up US 80 to Coloma. A luxurious and ironic vehicle to ferry them to their Spartan wilderness adventure.

Krista, whose idea roughing it was no room service, amazed herself on two counts during her minimalist adventure. She was amazed to discover that she enjoyed the outdoors. She had never slept in a tent or sleeping bag. She had never experienced that deep restorative sleep that snoozing beneath the stars engenders. She also amazed herself at the ease with which she and John murdered Michael. Peggy, that bitchy and holier-than-thou vegetarian, had refused to accompany them fishing and remained at the campsite. John, Michael, herself and a bottle of Wild Turkey had gone fishing in the clear cold South Fork of the American River. Bait had been lowered into the water. Their voices and interpersonal rancor rose as the level of the bourbon fell. Michael cajoled and mocked and challenged until John, with a fated and casual brutality stabbed Michael in the throat with a fishing knife. After John had stabbed him she held Michael's head beneath the swift and clear river water until bubbles streamed out of his nose and mouth.

Krista, all these decades later, remembered clearly the brilliance of the multicolored stones that sparkled beneath the crystal water as she held the fading but still struggling Michael beneath the water. She had kept Michael submerged until his lips were blue and rubbery. Then they left him there, face down, torso in the water, legs on the riverbank. Feeling not that she had snuffed out a life but that she had somehow made amends for Florence Nestor's demise and in a small way, subtly, somehow improved the world.

JOHN

Michael used to call it, thought John, taking out the trash. I remember the first time he invited me to "take out the trash." We were closing up the bar on a Tuesday. It wasn't 2 o'clock, we were closing on a soft night around 12:30 and he said to me, as we're leaving the restaurant, "Do you want to take out the trash?"

I answered, "Already have."

"That's not what I mean." We hopped in his orange 280 Z and drove down Petaluma Boulevard to the river. He parked at the boat ramp on the Petaluma River and turned the car off. I didn't say anything and we sat there in silence until he, from the driver's seat, reached across and let the glovebox fall open. He fumbled in the glovebox until he extracted a pint of Rumplemintz. He opened the bottle, took a pull, and passed it to me. The sickening, boozy smell of peppermint almost turned my stomach and I pushed his hand away. "We could have," I said, "stayed in the bar and drank."

"That is not," said Michael, "the point of this adventure."

I was afraid to reply. It would only encourage his perverse compulsion to control and manipulate every situation so I sat there, quiet, as he sip-sip-sipped at the cloying peppermint liquor. After about twenty minutes of silence he capped the bottle and returned it to the glovebox. He said, "Go time." He opened his door and I noticed for the first time that the interior light didn't come on, then I realized that the light to the glovebox had also been disconnected. We exited the car and over the roof I could see that he put his right index finger perpendicular to his lips like a kindergarten teacher shushing the class. He closed the door silently and made an elaborate show of pulling on a pair of motocross gloves. He began walking towards the river. I left my door open and followed.

"Time to," said Michael, "take out the trash." He walked to the river. A buttery cue ball of an autumn moon lit the way as we strode past the boat ramp and down the embankment. Scattered at my feet as we approached the grassy patch alongside the river I noticed hillocks and lumps on the ground. Michael walked up to one of these lumps, nodded at me and again held a gloved finger to his lips. Then he lifted his left foot. He looked like an aerobics instructor leading a class in the midnight moonlight as he brought left foot down then right and left again on the lump nearest him. That's when I realized the huddled form was a person, homeless and comatose from drugs and drink. Michael continued his assault by dropping his right knee into the center of the groaning mass and incorporated his gloved fists into the attack. Thud after muffled thud sounded. The sound became wetter and his breathing deepened. Michael motioned me to join in on the fun. I turned and walked back to his car. The sick bastard stayed out there for ten more minutes. The moonlight was bright enough to illuminate his gleeful brutality as he moved to another huddled form. This one protested: "No no no no no," as Michael added elbows to his fists and feet. After he returned to the car he quietly closed the driver-side door and daintily, like a delicate debutante at her sweet sixteen, removed the gloves finger by finger. They glistened in the darkness and I couldn't tell if it was the leather's natural sheen or some poor homeless bastard's blood. "I hate to admit it," said Michael, "but when I do that I almost get a stiffy. You?"

"Not so much," I said.

All feeling for that sick sonofabitch drained from me. It was as if a physical manifestation of the essence of evil had touched and soiled me. And yet I bore no malice toward him. The only thing I wanted, needed, was to distance myself from him. To run away from the chill he gave my soul every time he walked into the room.

But I couldn't.

I was like a spouse or child an abusive relationship.

I depended upon Michael for my livelihood and future. Where else would an almost thirty-something with a master's degree in philosophy get a six-figure a year job? He reeled me in with that salary that benefits package and that 401(k). And I've come to realize it wasn't me that he wanted. He didn't have any specific type, gender, color, or age, in mind when he hired me. He just wanted and needed someone to manipulate. Not someone who was weak and would bend instantly to his every whim. But someone like myself who would stand up to him—this case of the boat ramp beatings notwithstanding—to fight him and oppose him. He wanted an adversary. But more importantly he wanted to dominate and ultimately humiliate that adversary.

He wanted to know what line I wouldn't cross and he found it at the boat ramp that night. We had been out before and I always eventually acceded and buckled under as he paid for our debauch: drugs, booze, and whores. That style of depravity and abuse, apparently, was fine with me and I could only draw the line when it came to whupping up on helpless drunken dregs down by the Petaluma River.

I wanted to flee from Michael but I couldn't leave the money or my future behind. I never planned or even wished him any harm, I just wanted to distance myself from him, so it was as surprising to me as it was to him when on the third night of our El Dorado County adventure I plunged a knife into his throat and twisted.

PEGGY

Upon meeting him, thought Peggy, I realized immediately that Michael was a charismatic cretin. He was a vain and venal, emotionally arrested, entitled little twit with sadistic, abusive, manipulative and alcoholic tendencies.

Whether the drinking led to the sadism or the guilt of sadism led to the drinking Peggy never ferreted out but she knew that the two traits were inextricably linked. But Michael's twin traits, as dangerous as they were, made him frightfully predictable in both the business and personal spheres. With the charm and guile of a sociopath he began all his relationships with an effervescent and magnanimous charm.

Until he found a weakness.

Then he wouldn't immediately exploit your weakness to his advantage. He would foster and cultivate the weakness until he could utilize it in a way that would be advantageous for him and demeaning to you. I remember the first time he ran his game on me. I had been working at The Cattle Company for a little over a year when Michael placed me in an exquisitely orchestrated situation where I could achieve my professional and financial goals and all I had to do was to help Michael set up a nonprofit organization to help abused women. We filed all the necessary paperwork with the IRS and the state of California complying with all the necessary stipulations. We waded through the legal minutiae and were granted nonprofit status. I knew that Michael was setting up a piggy bank for himself when he offered me a portion of the profits that were flowing in to this "nonprofit." But the price I had to pay, the way Michael ran his game on me, was he wouldn't take one nickel for himself until he had finessed me into stealing the first little bit of money myself. The possibility of profit, skimming from this fund, would be small and steady but over the years substantial. But the money really didn't matter to Michael except as a way of keeping score. He didn't need the money; he probably didn't want the money.

His goal was to get me to abandon my principles and enjoy some forbidden fruit.

Michael's fruit was the leverage.

If I had dipped into the nonprofit for either a fortune or a farthing Michael would have used that illegality to manipulate, humiliate, or destroy me. But the bastard did not fool me for one second. He just reminded me of my parents who spent every waking moment running games on each other, attempting to advance their standing in the relationship by debasing, humiliating, and destroying the partner they had once vowed to love, honor, cherish, and obey.

Given my upbringing it was easy enough to tread lightly through the emotional and psychological minefield—continually shifting—that Michael had implemented for his managers and employees to negotiate.

But even a broken clock is correct twice a day.

What do I mean by that?

I mean that when I had my procedure to remove an ovarian cyst and they discovered I actually had ovarian cancer and would need surgery and an extended round of chemotherapy Michael dropped a real bombshell on me one night when we were closing the bar. "Peggy," Michael said to me, "sit down."

I sat.

"How long will you be out of work with this cancer treatment?"

"With recovery time they said about three months. If everything goes well."

Michael sat silent for a full minute before he said, "Don't apply for workman's comp."

"Why?"

"Just don't."

I remember studying Michael, gazing into those beguiling gray-green eyes, and wondering what he was up to. "Why not?" I said.

"Just don't," said Michael. "Okay?"

To this day I don't know if it was curiosity or self-loathing that compelled me to agree to his plan: I did not apply for workman's comp and I never would have imagined Michael's response to my sickness would have, or even could have, taken the form it did.

As I was convalescing immediately after my operation, while waiting to begin chemotherapy, I received a certified letter. I didn't recognize the return address. I have an odd curious habit of opening mail over the kitchen sink. I don't know why. No one in my family ever did so it was not one of those nonsensical family traditions; it was just something I did. And I will never forget opening this registered letter over the sink and watching six wrinkled and well used hundred dollar bills tumble out of the envelope and into the stark white porcelain of the sink. There was no note of any kind. I received one of these Care Packages every Tuesday for every week of my treatment and recovery. Despite the lack of any hints or intimations of identity I knew the money was from Michael Lazarus. All the bills were soft and worn and wrinkled: cash he had skimmed from The Cattle Company.

How do I know this?

I just knew.

If I thanked him for this stipend it would have been taken by him as an implicit approval of the way he ran the restaurant. The way he skimmed and scammed. The way he treated vendors, customers, and employees as chess pieces to be manipulated and sacrificed.

If I did not thank Michael for the money he would've seen our silent collusion, again, as an implicit approval of his moral and financial shenanigans.

Or was Michael being, for once, magnanimous and I was misinterpreting his motivation?

I just don't know.

But I do know that when I discovered Michael on his knees in the river's shallows, bleeding from the throat, coughing up water, and struggling to make it back to shore it was surprisingly easy, perhaps almost fitting, that I helped him—as he had helped me—out of the shallow water and into a seated position on a fallen tree. Then I picked up a flat heavy stone and hit him from behind.

My secret but not my shame. I saw my action as perfectly appropriate.

As an expiation.

A catharsis.

Michael was a demon seed and needed to be destroyed. So I destroyed him. John and Krista initiated the act by virtue of their stabbing and attempted drowning of Michael. And until today we three had never spoken of Michael's murder.

At dusk Krista and John returned to camp with fishing poles and an empty Wild Turkey bottle. They told me what they had done and where the body lay. We walked to the river and they expressed wonder that Michael could have risen from the river, from the dead, struggle ashore and apparently fall, striking the back of his head on a nearby stone. I helped them lug the dead body to an ancient mineshaft but they never knew nor will they ever know that I had struck the fatal blow. They merely thought I was an accessory, as they say, after the fact. But my capitulation, my silence, was setting myself up with potential leverage over the woman who remains my best friend and the man who would become my husband.

Just in case.

"So we agree," said John "that the best solution is silence?"

Krista said from the phone, "I don't see how anyone could connect this newly found bundle of bones to us."

"And we told the sheriff," said Peggy, "that Michael was Jim-Morrison-drunk and weaved off into the Ponderosa pines."

"We say nothing; we do nothing," said John.

"I thought getting away with murder," said Krista, "would be more exhilarating, but I'm just exhausted."

Peggy smiled but remained silent. She realized that she had known Michael Lazarus, his needs and desires, better than anybody she had known or would ever know. That he was a monster and the control and smug superiority she felt right now was what he had craved and never experienced. She was ashamed, elated, and oddly relieved knowing that Michael would have been proud.

My Own Private Roach Motel
Edward St. Boniface

Timeline: September-October, 1977.

I groove on the parasitical lifestyle and see myself as a symbiotic organism; but I hate what occasionally attaches itself to me in the vector transmission thang.

Hubbard St. John, popular newly-appointed joint chairman and managing director and corporate evangelist of the Nu-Community Foundation, 1973. He is making his inaugural address to an extraordinary general meeting of foundation supporters, contributors and stakeholders at its New York headquarters on investiture to office. Preliminaries are followed with a lengthy and innovative presentation of his imaginative plans towards modernising organisational policy for this noted social initiative and medical charity. Event concludes to rapturous laughter and applause and unanimous approval given by all voters present and observing via audio-visual link. Taken from the 1974 company statement.

*****

Transcript-excerpt from *Black Hand Incorporated* operational archives, operational file HStJ-77 (interrogations subfolder, see scale of pharmacological charges to client). Original spoken recording and subsequent audio dialogues captured using replica micro-miniaturised tape recording device once the property of the Central Intelligence Agency. Location is converted sub-basement store-room in *The Manhattan Project Pico-Panopticon Repertory and Adult Cinema (18+ only)*, Steeg Van Verderven Way off 42nd Street nr Times Square, New

York City, 11:46-11:50, 03.11.1977. All company officers present (Part One of dialogue).

> HUBBARD ST. JOHN (*hoarsely*): "…all heard him. I mean; *'Nabbit!* First he confesses to everything, including a lot of stuff I didn't even suspect, and then *he* calls *me* 'truculent'. This no-comps creep makes Henry Kissinger look like Bullwinkle. (*Interrogation subject name classified*), you are condemned like a Hell's Kitchen condo. I'm gonna send you down to join Ho Chi Minh, bad Weatherman Ted Gold and that lisping loincloth lizard Gandhi in commie hell!"

(*Sound of gunshot, long silence.*)

> COMPANY PRESIDENT GARY BANOMENA: "That's your projectionist, Hubbard."

*****

Excerpted from the October 1977 monthly published illustrated programme (free of charge at cinema, 25¢ local newsstands, $15.00 annual mailing subscription and cinema discount card weekdays before 5pm), *The Manhattan Project Pico-Panopticon Repertory and Adult Cinema (18+ only)*:

'*Hell's Porch* might not seem the ideal setting for your usual cultivated culture-vulture to hang out. Uptown dowdy dowagers and slick silver-haired patricians are seldom to be seen here, unless slumming the urban Sodom and Gomorrah in heavy rain-coated disguise. However, a combination of generous zoning laws, municipal incentives for liberal social and civilly regenerative projects and continuing sponsorship from *Polychrome Pesticides* makes it innocently possible!

Collectively allowing us to offer a uniquely eclectic programme at our small but punching-above-its-weight big screen bijou. Classic

American and interesting global cinema gems from all the nations. Features and documentaries and oddball experimental oddities otherwise difficult to screen even for the diehard-fanatical cineaste.

A fifteen-minute informational motion picture on *Polychrome Pesticides'* wide variety of products and good domestic hygiene practice plays between all feature presentations. In it you will discover the fascinating and grisly history of modern pest control technology. The award winning featurette is in part hosted and narrated by famous counter-cultural author and former exterminator William Burroughs.

There's also an early morning, every-morning *risqué* schedule of the best contemporary quality erotica and adult-themed Arthouse productions available in the Big Sinful Apple. Perfect for all you late-night habitués and extremely early risers. Themed shows and coffee begin at 6am.

Times Square and its immediate environs have the unflattering and undeserved nickname of Hell's Porch, a riff on the more famous nearby Hell's Kitchen district, or 'Clinton' as more sedately known to city authorities. An unjust moniker of long standing. *Hell's Porch* is also the 1965 title of an outstanding early neo-noir thriller with the young Sean Beatty in one of his first starring roles.

Filmed almost entirely in the vicinity of the Square and Sixth and Seventh Avenues, it is simultaneously an excellent crime mystery and surprisingly raw street-level documentary of a fast-changing scene in the district at the time. A newly-minted idealistic police college graduate finds himself in a dangerous deep cover operation at the dark heart of Manhattan's most notorious branch of Babylon. Only to discover both local mobsters and his own colleagues involved in illicit 'snuff' movie productions are setting him up for a string of XXX-rated actor and actress murders.

Heavily influenced by the French New Wave style and American independent directors such as John Cassavetes, the film is a landmark in gritty and intelligent social commentary worked with surprising fluency into a genre crime picture. Notably all its daytime scenes are photographed in dreary stark slow-moving monochrome while the night-time is exaggerated hyper-realistic Technicolor, accelerated action and heightened jagged jump-cuts and wide-angle lens shots. It's playing here all month in a double bill with Beatty's equally superb Greenwich Village-set 1970 urban spy mystery *Empire Ward*.

Advance-book today!

Please note the cinema is available for private group bookings. Daily schedules may occasionally be superseded on short notice. All enquiries and refund requests to the Box Office number listed on the programme, premium rates apply.'

*****

Times Square, Seventh Avenue and 42nd Street were not parts of Manhattan that I and the other guys would normally visit. Apart from a couple of good places like *The Little Rialto Repertory Cinema* and *The Green Aphid Jazz Club*, it was foreign country. We made a point of knowing the streets of downtown and uptown comprehensively.

Midtown areas like that weren't part of our usual urban geography however, apart from Greenwich Village. Surveillance and executive reassignment operations would seldom be that out in the open. Central sectors of the city were far too well-policed.

So the invitation from an interested corporate contact to night-meet me at what sounded a desperately cheapskate porno cinema at the very heart of the worst vice quarter in America seemed ludicrous. Either it was an obvious trap or the clumsiest kind of *faux*-secrecy attempt. To my surprise though, Survind my deputy and chief of company security made a comprehensive series of calls and enquiries and eventually pronounced the quixotic come-hither a bona fide one.

So, trusting his judgement, I went unarmed. Travelled on foot from the Port Authority bus terminal instead of the much nearer 42nd street subway station. Getting the increasingly carnal vibe of the street as I went, until I was engulfed in the tawdry clangour and frighteningly blatant sordid commerce of the Square.

Dismal did not begin to encompass it. Neon and electric signs cast down coldly severe illumination. Jittery and buzzing abrasively and flickering with dangerously disorienting unpredictability. Stale air poured out of open stores and cafeterias and other highly dubious emporiums.

Even the impressive Times Tower motograph 'ribbon of light' perpetually scrolling news bulletin and its rapidly moving lightbulb letter displays looked impersonal and cheerless. In documentaries and feature films it was always impressive. Seemingly radiant with a special warm clarity.

Too-bright livid glariness it forces into my eyes makes everything around me seem wan and etiolated. All the faces drifting by look too young or too old or frozen in a rictus of terror and malevolence. 'Hell's Porch', which I've heard the Square called, seems a forbiddingly apt label to hang on this garish human abyss.

Despite being late in the year it's not especially cold. So instead of the usual trenchcoat I'd wear to a clandestine meeting like this I'm just wearing a lightweight charcoal anonymous suit and turtleneck sweater. Wide-brimmed black hat I can easily tilt to conceal my face, effect enhanced by oversized mirrored spectacles.

Realised leaving the trenchcoat behind was a mistake when I see the typical loitering-with-intent population. Practically every man here visibly over the age of twenty-five is in a trenchcoat and hat and sunglasses with an 'I'm Just Passing Through, Don't Pay Attention To Me' half-panicky demeanour. It's like a military-issue uniform.

I stick out like a crow dyed fluorescent orange.

Worse, despite the late hour when the usual depravity business should be at its crowded raucous height, the Square and surrounding streets are almost quiet. Apart from a mass of pocked-looking yellow taxis pulling in and out around all-night cafeterias and the occasional passing bus, there's nearly no traffic. Uncomfortable numbers of police cruisers are also parked hard by the snack bars, and a few lounging officers sip steaming coffee from paper cups as they linger outside.

Some of them jeer as I pass. In response I ironically raise my hat without looking back, which raises some snide laughter. It's almost invariably better to react wryly than furtively attract suspicion.

Cops will habitually exercise the practiced brutality and impunity of the job if you give them a reason. Make them hee-haw and snicker at your expense and you're pretty much safe. Tense at the best of times in any locality, in New York the street police are on a perpetual hair-trigger.

So every single hackle in me is poised and alert. Fundamentally this is enemy territory. I'm way too deep into it.

Steeg Van Verderven Way is almost just around the corner off 42nd Street, far too close for comfort. If I have to beat a hasty retreat it'll be almost impossible not to be noticed running. Narrow and ominously dark, there is a single blazing sign far, far down its length at an improbable distance with no other lighting.

Intimidating somehow, and as I draw closer I see the unusually large sign is in the form of a bloated and beady eye. Bakelite letters in black spell part of the given name of the cinema: 'PANOPTICON' in a hemisphere with steel lightning bolts punctuating it. At whatever angle you look the eye's baleful unwinking gaze seems to follow you and the effect is unaccountably dismaying.

By the time I get under it and to the almost invisible heavy black-painted old style wooden door I feel distinctly shaky and off-balance. Realise the effect is very intentional and well-calculated. Irritated, I'm prepared to shoulder open the ominous portal rather than knock, but again to my surprise its open.

Instinctively I check my watch: its eight minutes past ten. I'm a little early. So much the better.

Faint brokenly bleeding scribble of light at its hinged edge swings open to an almost blinding coruscation. Walk into a cramped but stylishly lit and fastidiously clean glittering Art Deco lobby. Clearly restored quite recently, there's nothing seedy and down-at-heel in the place as I was naturally expecting.

Wide staircase goes down into unknown depths, not the elevated auditorium entrance I was also expecting. Ceiling is parqueted with electricity and abstracted cinematic motifs. Even a clear silhouette of the director DW Griffith in his characteristic suit and hat, carrying something that when I look closer is an alarmingly over-scaled megaphone.

Gleaming stainless steel bar has been converted into a luxury coffee and concession stand. Huge chromium percolating urn set onto the counter looks like something out of *Metropolis*. Filling most of the back wall is a solar-system mural lacking Pluto.

Indisputably dating the interior fixtures and decorations authentically before 1930. An object at the far elliptical frontier is marked 'Planet X'. Lavish quality craftsmanship from the very height of the era before the Great Depression.

A very well-dressed man sitting in an elegant patron's fan couch below the mural is waiting for me. Unhurriedly half-turning an oddly masklike grimacing face in my direction, he gives me a crooked smile, taps his watch and half-raises a cigarette without rising. It's about the most confidently sardonic and subtly disrespectful gesture I've ever seen.

Hubbard St. John.

*****

(*Dialogue captured by company recording device, location* The Manhattan Project Pico-Panopticon Repertory and Adult Cinema (18+ only) *cinema auditorium, 14:09-15:53, 19.10.1977, all company officers present. A screening is in progress as indicated.*)

GARY BANOMENA, COMPANY PRESIDENT: "Hubbard, where the hell did you get row seats this small? And do we have to watch that goddam exterminator's horror movie? It's ghoulish."

HUBBARD ST. JOHN: "Award-winning ghoulery, Gary. Swiped the seats out of this shut-up-for-the-winter kiddie museum pantomime theatre down in Poughkeepsie last year. Don't want the marks getting too comfortable and dozing off. Ever seen *Phase IV*?"

GB: "I have. Directed by Saul Bass. Genuinely visionary and intelligent science fiction beyond the grotesque."

HStJ: "Amazed me too. Goes so far Out There you can't come back for awhile if you're in the right mood. Don't watch it when you've got unhappy pills in you."

GB: "*Phase IV*'s clever twist right at the end frightened me even more than *A Boy And His Dog* for the post-apocalypse future and *THX-1138* for the dehumanised dystopian one. That same director's latest offering this year is even grimmer."

HStJ: "Came right outta nowhere, that one. All the hype for this summer was around *Damnation Alley*. All the sets and monsters looked like latex and chipboard and polystyrene, 'tho. Roger Zelazny must wanna hire you guys to reassign the producers."
(*Chuckles from company officers.*)

GB: "I'd do it for free. That was ninety-one minutes of my life I'll never get back. I'd take just that long on the whole production team."

HStJ: "Speaking of which, this director's moving into low budget horror-mutilation features out of documentaries now. On the side I help distribute him and a few other up-and-comers. I think he uses actual out-takes from his day job stuff. You should see some of his medical operation training flicks. There's one on tracheal resections that made me gag, and I've done industrial vise-clamp jobs on rivals myself."

GB: "What the hell kind of award did this pitiless infomercial win?"

HStJ: "Second place in the Agro-business category after *Innovative High-Volume Apiculture in the Midwestern and Southern States*."

WARKENTIN WESTGATE: "Who in the hooting heck puts on a show for stuff like this?"

HStJ: "*Industrial and Commercial and Public Information Films Awards* grubstaked on the public dollar. Hosted jointly by the US Departments of Agriculture, Commerce, Education, Labour, Medicine, Health and Human Services and the Environmental Protection Agency.

Quite a seriously big event, actually. Held at the Cosmo-Drome early every year over on Coney Island. That big arts centre and stadium? The three military branches do a parallel show. Runs for a whole week."

GB: "I think we got tickets to that as equity investors. I decided against it at the time. Trucker, make a note: we definitely go next year. Sounds like the perfect networking opportunity."

SURVIND ('TRUCKER') JUGGERGHAZI: "Filed, Gary. Is there a rating system for these films, Hubbard?"

HStJ: "Negatory. You can basically show anything in 'em 'cos they're classified Special Interest or Ed-biz. Most sex-ed films are more hardcore than *Deep Throat* these days and they show 'em in schools. Lunacy of the age, eh? Hey, check out this next part. 'Bout one zillion hungry greenflies swarm and carpetbag this huge tarantula. Munch him down to throbbing grist in under a minute while he does the jackhammer jitterbug."

(*Groans and negative comments from audience, spoken narration audibly moves on to a new episode.*)

GB: "There is no vocabulary for this. Basically it's diabolical. Are those cockroaches stuck in the adhesive box interior eating each other before they die? Camerawork there is the product of a psychotic fiend."

HStJ: "Told me he fed his pet scorpion live mice for fun when he was a kid. *Polychrome Pesticides* pay my bills for the joint as a charitable write-off. So unfortunately by contractual obligation I have to keep their bad-trip-to-bug-hell promo running whenever there isn't a feature on the screen. Even when it's just us here."

S('T')J: "Is that the voice of William Burroughs narrating in blank verse over the immobilised caterpillar host full of hatching wasp larvae?"

(*More groans, shocked noises from audience.*)

HStJ: "Yep. Beatnik's me why. Strange Billy worked as an exterminator back in the day according to his badly-written screwball books, but did more snorting the powder than using it on jobs. Comes out in that rackety voice like a junkie actor I know. Use him for my crank calls to the powerful and *whoo*, does it psych their tiny minds out. I got to Tricky Dick during the last days of Watergate and I was thinking of trying NORAD."

S('T')J: "Burroughs sounds much the same as when I met him briefly at Andy Warhol's 'Factory' workshop ten years ago. He stole my cigarettes, as I recall."

HStJ: "Happened to me too; degenerate must have six arms or tentacles or sumpin'. Beware of your precious ectoplasm with that jaded prodigy, my friend. His grating voice is what makes this flick a real Tenniel job. Weirdo arthouse movie and infotainment spiel and mentally snafued all the way. It's been banned in some states when they tried to use it as a supporting feature."

WW: "My youngest boy came home crying one day, he was in second grade and they showed this biology film in class about insect predators. I asked to see it and I barely slept for a week. My better half wrote to the school board along with all the other parents but they still kept it on the curriculum."

HStJ: "Yep, the nature zoids are turning our kids into brain-sprained praying mantises. I've had people finally crack up and run out when it gets to the extreme close-up ladybug gassing part in a minute. Pandemonium music on the soundtrack short-circuits my tiny consciousness. Some greasy Greek freak called Vangelis wrote it. He also did that crazy space concept album *Albedo 0.39*."

GB: "Better than *Oxygene* by Jean Michel Jarre, apart from track five."

HStJ: "You're my kinda space monster, Gary."
(*Noticeably abrasive electronic music on feature soundtrack in background begins, waxes steadily in volume.*)

DAG ULKÖLN: "*Ugh*. I hate insects and pests that infest, but not that much."

WW: "Gratuitous cruelty is what I see. Even to creepy-crawlies. Kill 'em yeah, but don't gloat over it."

HStJ: "Burroughs actually appears at the end. He's wearing Slinky's as antennae. Babbles to camera that it's all a profound metaphor of the life force. Lots of other thangs equally flaked-out and badly versified. According to him we start as bacteria and spend untold millions of years down there in the microscopic and arthropod world. Carry it like a loadstone up the evolutionary chain to now as *Homo Saps*."

S('T')J: "Esoteric mythology makes some similar suggestions about karmic growth towards metamorphosis of being from lower mortal states to higher transcendence."

GB: "Kafka got it 'zackly right at the start, Trucker. Existence is a Bugaboo in every sense of the word."
(*General laughter.*)

HStJ: "So enthrall me about the interrogations I mentioned before. Do you guys cut 'em up excruciating and slow and surgically on the operating table like a pyscho former CIA sawbones I know, employ actually, or that thing with the steel ship's rivets and rubber bands? Even I winced when I heard about that one."

S('T')J: "As Gary explained Hubbard, we do not as a rule practice that kind of harshness for or to our clients. We have done so, but only in *extremis* where there was no other choice and time was pressing. We are assassins to order yes, but not torturers."

HStJ: "What I need is a lot of accurate information spilling reliably out of my selected targets in a very short time before demise. Third degree martyrdom using machine shop tools and facilities is usually the quickest way."

GB: "Trucker here is an expert in assisted chemical confession."

HStJ: "Drugs like the Agency and assorted scary spook outfits use?"

S('T')J: "Including them, certainly. Hypnotic and mesmeric treatments require a wide variety of methods to be most successful. Patience and attention to detail are essential in plumbing a subject's subconscious for the purpose. Gary is over-generous to me. We have all become adept at extracting detailed intelligence using these techniques with subtlety. Persuasion is far more productive in general than painful coercion."

HStJ: "I can get you all the Rangoon Swoon you need. Boy, does that stuff work miracles. Got a direct connect with the local hooded-eyed hoodlum pipeline to Old Siam and Khmer. Comes in straight via diplomatic bags for premium primo customers only. That's my kinda bag; man."

S('T')J (*pause*): "That could assuredly help. It is delicate and takes care to administer. Very reliable when used shrewdly. In most cases *Papaver somniferum Omni* will unlock the most resistant and stubborn minds."

HStJ: "Tell me 'bout it. I brainsicked up all my worst *lassiez-faire* capitalist enterprises under said influence. To my brainiac major domo. A minor condition prior to him approving my current role at the foundation. Cain't use him for this though, so I need experts like you. According to him, my madcap adventures add up to about seven centuries of federal time. Mebbe a century and a half off for good behaviour."

DU: "What we up to, Trucker?"

S('T')J: "Nineteen centuries. No remission."

WW: "Think the *Boekheed-Carmichael Aerospace* job last month might add to that, Trucker. Remember? The full baker's dozen score in the boardroom bombing."

S('T')J: "Ah; yes."

(*Low prolonged humorous whistle from Hubbard St. John.*)

HStJ: "Groovily grody, dad."

GB: "My deputy keeps a meticulous tally of all Title 18 federal offenses undertaken by our company in its client operations."

HStJ: "Who for, Griffin Boogie-On Bell?"

S('T')J: "A rejuvenated *RKO Radio Pictures*, given the low state of public movie taste at the moment. Fortunately both the current attorney general and director of the FBI Clarence Kelley are on record disbelieving our existence."

HStJ: "Snoop hound-dawg Tumesne covers an outfit like yours in that *Necrobiz* trilogy of his. He's gotten way too close to my anti-establishment establishment too. Did a bunch of speculative articles a few years ago that almost nailed us. Helped write that TV movie *The Periphery* with Lorenzo Semple back in '70. Deliberately trying to expose you."

GB: "I liked Frank Gorshin as the sinister boss and Angie Dickinson as his revenge-mad poisoner wife who finishes them both. Unfortunately we don't have any cute killers like Barbara Luna and Grace Lee Whitney on our books."

HStJ: "Naw; jest that dyke Solanas drilling Warhol. He owed me money, too. Did that one put you guys on the go-to map. I love *The Periphery*. Got me a 16 millimetre print here if you ever wanna see it again. It's a cult hit now, y'know. Every time I advertise I have to screen it twice 'cos I'll get three full houses."

GB (*pause*): "That might be a potential revenue stream when we retire: hyper-overwrought conspiracy movies. Transnational big-biz instead of Bolshevik no-goodnik plotting. So I'm writing a screenplay on the side. Dramatizing our pioneering role in legitimately establishing bespoke executive reassignment for corporate America."

HStJ: "What a screecher creature feature that'll be. You'll make the radically revolting roach motels on the screen up there look like *Peyton Place*."
(*Uproarious laughter.*)

GB: "All right, let's start planning how we'll add to that Title 18 tally for you, Hubbard…"

*****

Ten years as professional corporate executioners had seen us undertake a surprising number of unusual assignments. We'd done several premature burials and live brick-entombments for example, usually minus the genuine cask of Amontillado. Even a couple of re-enactments of the Pit and the Pendulum.

One of *Hop Frog*, which proved surprisingly technically difficult. I had to draw the line at one request for *The Murders In The Rue Morgue* because Warkentin and Dag refused to dress up as Kong on mobility grounds. Edgar Allan Poe was surprisingly popular.

Torture was a too-frequent specification in our early days, and inherently risky. So we had to draft special health and safety guidelines. Included in stipulations only if implicit to the induced cause of death.

I agreed to Hubbard St. John's programme of interrogations and contract capital punishment only because he finally accepted that. We talked for over an hour so that I could be sure he was serious. Instinctively though, I recognised someone as disciplined and methodical as I had forced myself to become.

Degree of his obsessively thorough advance preparation surprised even me, though. Expensively refurbished a long-derelict tiny cinema site he discovered, using the help of a sponsor he secretly canvassed out of his numerous charitable contacts for the purpose. Organised and supervised and administrated it entirely himself.

Actual reason for all this startling effort and planning and contrivance and conspiracy was even more astonishing.

*****

(*Dialogue captured by company recording device, location* The Manhattan Project Pico-Panopticon Repertory and Adult Cinema (18+ only) *cinema lobby, 22:09-23:53, 18.10.1977, company president and host present as indicated.*)

HUBBARD ST. JOHN: "I am Chairman Meow-Meow. This is my Little Polychrome Book. Please read from it every day."

COMPANY PRESIDENT GARY BANOMENA: "Pray elucidate, Chairman Meow."

*****

Hubbard St. John offhandedly passes me what looks like a child's school homework ring-binder as I join him on the velvet-upholstered fan-couch. Binder has a visually smarting and eye-twisting cover of garish metallic rainbow colours in a cleverly ascending spectrum from ultraviolet to infrared. Within are an extensive series of personnel dossiers grouped neatly in transparent plastic document holders.

*****

(*Resuming prior lobby dialogue as indicated.*)

    HStJ: "I plan a great leap forward on behalf of the Nu-Community charitable foundation. I will be its great helmsman. You will be the agency of a Great Brownian Cultural Revolution within our councils."
    GB: "And how does that translate to sane English?"
    HStJ: "I have a grand guignol problem in my senior management."
    GB: "Do tell; Comrade Obscurantist."
    HStJ: "Nice riposte. In that Capraesque spirit, the 'Brownian' thing earlier was referencing a former alias of mine. Okay, straight to the brass nine inch crucifixion nails. My upper echelons in the company are full of Grand Guignol gonzoes. I want you and your crew to 'fess 'em up then neato-nullify 'em."

*****

While I leaf through his unlikely book of death warrants, Hubbard St. John rises unhurriedly, goes to the stainless steel standing bar and makes us a couple of excellent cappuccinos. I note he's using a trademarked professional coffeehouse vendor machine behind the gleaming counter. Despite myself I'm impressed by the professionalism of the façade I'm being presented.
    Casual mention of the director Frank Russell Capra and by implication his classic comedies with their distinctive fast and smart repartee dialogue startled me. I had to force myself not to show it. Only a few months before I had been trying the metropolitan dating game and met a woman who compared me to that as well.
    She was a commercials and documentaries director making her way

into features. Devastatingly smart and interesting. Utterly beyond my reach.

Only last week I'd seen a tabloid photo of her. She was on the arm of respected and celebrated actor Sean Beatty at a premiere of his latest film, a daring downbeat social exposé picture about the violent rise and fall of a street level drug dealer in an unnamed broken-down city. I think it was called *Short Order Cooke* after the doomed main character.

Veranilda Gissing, that was her name, was slightly in the background but her profile was unmistakable. She had liked me a bit, but the week after a halting stop-and-start first date she got the call to Hollywood and I never saw her again. I'd done my best nice-guy performance and it had availed me nothing.

Sassy comedy is probably not my forte.

*****

GB: "Nice cappuccino. Caffeine rush is sharpening all four of my square corners, Hubbard. Presumably the usual option of a generous executive compensation retirement package for these individuals is not applicable."

HStJ: "Nada to the Nth degree, dad. These are heads of department. Senior executives for decades before me. They know too much and all have their own agendas. Private fortunes of money siphoned from the company have been cleverly ensconced beyond my reach. They know I know they know. I can't get rid of them conventionally."

GB: "Assassination on this scale seems like an overreaction. As a rule I counsel trying all possible alternatives of negotiation and compromise before hiring us. Maybe you should try a leisure retreat or an encounter group scenario to lighten the mood at the office."

HStJ: "Retirement in this outfit effectively means becoming a made-to-measure corpse. Part of how we stage the necessary accidents. Quite literally it's them or me. And the certifiable psycho head of the Surgical Department loves me the way the Coyote loves the Roadrunner as a floating full-garnish dinner plate. So cut the cute comedy and cue cut-throats for hire on stages left and right and centre, up from the trap room and straight down from the fly system. Got the photo?"

*****

Nu-Community had various rumours quietly swirling around its actual purpose and enterprise objectives and surprisingly wide operational reach. Some of it fit with Hubbard St. John's over-elaborate and distinctly paranoid pitch to me, some didn't. Clearly I wasn't being told the full story.

Exactly like most of our clients, really. Survind had already verified he could pay us. Non-refundable consultancy and advance planning cash fee I always insisted on had been duly delivered to our usual bonded bank safe deposit box for the purpose.

Unnecessarily exorbitant, that fee was never less than twenty-five percent of what we ultimately intended to charge. It had the effect of reliably separating who was serious and who wasn't. Hubbard St. John had paid it without query.

Naturally I was suspicious.

*****

GB: "Naturally I'm suspicious, Hubbard. You must be planning a pretty radical change of direction to be this sure of retaliation."

HStJ: "You could say that. So far Nu-Community has grown by thinking small and careful with miniaturised communities of what we call 'Converted' individuals. That's people who've changed their identities and appearances and whole direction of life with our assistance. The charity and medical innovations stuff are a front integrated into the main business."

GB: "Vague rumours say you resettle them in these mini-outposts just a few at a time and work them into the local urban community life thereabouts."

HStJ: "Yeah. We stage their deaths, actuary the insurance and legacy pay-outs, rehabilitate them and integrate groups into various localities across the country. As a business model it's worth awesome dividends."

GB: "Tricky to manage, but I can't see a viable growth limit to an idea like that."

HStJ: "Neither could I when I joined, but I was wrong. My aforementioned major domo told me there's a natural saturation point. Kind of a bombshell to land on you while you're learning the top job on the old set of rules."

GB: "Ecologist on the payroll?"

HStJ: "Head of the psychological conditioning and rehabilitation department, so he should know. Now that the dangerous thousand year-old *Crockosaurus Rex* who founded it all has gone to the great fossil field in the sky, my nominal assistant is the one who really runs things around there. Repeating the same micro-colonial model isn't working anymore, according to his very reliable calculations. Numbers are getting too great."

GB: "So you need to think bigger."

HStJ: "We need to found an eco-city."

*****

Impressed despite myself, that still wasn't the real point. We had no inherent stake in whatever company vision Hubbard St. John wanted to sell to his donors and patrons. Deviously, he knows that.

So far he's self-evidently given me only half his sales line. He needs to rope me into his plans, because he knows I could turn him down, and that means something more circuitous. My hackles are still fully up from the walk here and his crafty mien gives me no reason to quiesce them. Now I'm waiting for his real serpentine incentive, knowing I'm not going to like it.

*****

HStJ: "You'll love this next part. I can collectively offer all of you the rest of your lives in it as part of the fee and take you away from all this."

GB (*long pause*): "Tall order."

*****

Dread almost infinitely worse than my fear of momentary police attention or the natural chaotic dangers of Times Square itself fastens into me at that. Most physical or other inherent hazards in our line of work at *Black Hand Incorporated* were easily dealt with. Careful avoidance of danger by operational planning and keeping out of the gaze of law enforcement professionals was the natural solution to most of our dilemmas.

All of that held us together in a mutual security. That was unspoken. Real danger came only from what could instil mutual fear and doubt and potentially divide us.

This was it. He knows I have to put his temptation cleverly disguised as a business proposal to the other guys, that it's not up to me in the end. A viable and short and perfectly camouflaged way out of the hellish risks and murder and mayhem on which we've built our considerable fortunes.

*****

GB: "I'll think about it."

HStJ: "At your *en masse* leisure, my rapier-witted and viper-deadly wiseacre. I'm free to meet you all here at lunchtime tomorrow."

*****

And that was that. We stand up from the couch and Hubbard half-raises that cigarette again, last of a full pack he's energetically smoked in the time we've talked. Just doesn't quite entirely give the impression of imperiously dismissing me like a lower ranking lackey on my way out to do his bidding.

When I get back to Times Square it's deserted and empty and haunted. Night is suddenly cold the way it should be in an Atlantic-facing late October. I shiver and can't find a taxi anywhere and am finally forced to resort to the bleakly illustrated and drab and dingily dangerous subway.

*****

Transcript-excerpt from *Black Hand Incorporated* operational archives, operational file HStJ-77 (miscellaneous contractual details and staff discussion notes subfolder). Location is original company headquarters (in temporary operational use), Blackwells Island, New York City, 09:17-10:33, 19.10.1977. Recording made with usual portable device by company president in his personal office. All company officers present.

SURVIND ('TRUCKER') JUGGERGHAZI: "Remarkably attractive offer."
DAG ULKÖLN: "I don't like my face anyway."
WARKENTIN WESTGATE: "Family might take some convincing, but reckon I could just about swing it."
(*Long pause*)

S('T')J: "…Gary?"
GARY BANOMENA: "I wonder if they use the same kind of plastic for their surgery as LEGO."

*****

So we naturally went to the meeting Hubbard had decreed that afternoon. Retirement was something each of the other guys had hinted at to me over the last year or so. It was my worst imaginable combination of circumstances, or so I thought.

Millions in cash and investment equities meant we technically had the bow-out option. But I lived in terror of Michael Tumesne our nemesis crusading journalist. The man was terrifyingly smart and he was getting closer to us all the time.

Necrobiz trilogy and the television movie *The Periphery* Hubbard had given me the unwelcome news about were only the start. Instinctively I knew that. What we did was becoming a popular culture trope.

We had too many victims and vengeful clients. It kept adding up, and I just knew something somewhere would rise from its premature grave to haunt us. In the case of the billion-dollar indebted chairman of *Crassus Construction* this had literally happened; one of our rare screw-ups.

That was only six months ago and we were still picking up the pieces reputationally. Hubbard's offer could only reinforce the concept. I had no idea how to side-track it.

Purging his foundation of dissident and corrupt long-standing senior managers was straightforward. He would invite targets informally to a private cinema screening. We would be waiting posing as staff to grab and take them down to a converted sub-basement room for the grillings and the hapless subject's subsequent lethal injection.

Anyone who was suspicious and refused, we were tasked with abducting. We delivered them, generally drugged and easily manhandled, to the cinema service entrance. This was conveniently just up the alleyway from the main door in a secluded alcove and doubled as the fire exit with a big metal door.

Since the alley was unusually narrow we had to get a much smaller truck than usual to transport and deliver our quarries. Hubbard had anticipated this too. He supplied us with a small luxury butcher's van that could fit and reverse in snugly.

Cramped and overcrowded, barely fitting two of us even lacking an additional body. With the rest of us following in separate cars as front and rear lookouts, it nevertheless proceeded smooth as clockwork. Dressed in butcher's smocks and sanitary hats and masks, not even looked at once on the street, we did all our grabs with chloroform and concealed syringes in broad daylight.

All resulting bodies eventually went down into the clay beneath an adjoining deeper derelict sub-basement later cemented over by us as well. Hubbard St. John said he wanted all his late colleagues in one grave like *The Tell-Tale Heart*. Actually I think he was referring more to Frank Capra's macabre comedy masterpiece *Arsenic And Old Lace*.

Neither allusion was comfortable.

*****

Transcript-excerpt from *Black Hand Incorporated* operational archives, operational file HStJ-77 (interrogations subfolder, see scale of pharmacological charges to client). Original spoken recording and subsequent audio dialogues captured using replica micro-miniaturised tape recording device once the property of the Central Intelligence Agency. Location is converted sub-basement store-room in *The*

Manhattan Project Pico-Panopticon Repertory and Adult Cinema (18+ only), Steeg Van Verderven Way off 42nd Street nr Times Square, New York City, 23:36-03:49, 22-23.10.1977. All company officers present.

HUBBARD ST. JOHN (*hoarsely*): "Where the hell are my ten million cartwheels'-worth of treasury certificates (*interrogation and executive reassignment subject name classified*), you moustachioed moronic mutant?! Those crappy carbon copies stuffing your safe ain't even worth their weight in Monopoly money!!"
(*Supporting note: subject is incumbent* NuCF *head of documents division.*)

S('T')J: "Hubbard, I've indicated before that shouting and aggression substantially diminish the receptive effect of a deep hypnotic state. Let me ask the appropriate questions. I have regressed the subject to childhood on a solitary safari trip he often fantasised. Please do not break his concentration."

HStJ (*audibly stressed*): "Find out where he's stashed the company's fake credit testimonials and gilt securities and currency reserves. And the banknote printing templates with full watermark sets. One hundred million clams are at stake."

S('T')J (*long pause*): "Now then (*interrogation and executive reassignment subject name classified*), are you enjoying your time in the Veldt?"

INTERROGATION SUBJECT: "…Who or what was that horrible electric blue rhinoceros with the fly-eyes that just crashed through here?"

S('T')J (*gently*): "He is gone now."

IS: "Ugly didn't begin to describe him. Ever seen anything that ugly? I mean, his face was like the wrong end of a baboon in heat or something…"

S('T')J (*swiftly*): "You were telling me about where you buried all those nice pictures and greeting cards, remember? Mother's day is coming up and I'm sure she'd love to have one from you."

IS: "Are you there, Mum?"

S('T')J (*softly*): "It's nice to hear from you, son."

IS: "…Dad?"

GB: "She's waiting, boy."

IS: "…What in the world are you both doing in the middle of Rhodesia?"

GB: "This is gonna be a long night; Trucker."

*****

Forgery department at the Nu-Community Foundation would make collective jaws of the CIA and secret spooky services across the spook world drop right to the floor, as Hubbard St. John colourfully put it to us. Management recruited America's best straight out of the prison system, where they had extensive contacts. Company teams were quietly regarded as some of the best in the business.

All kinds of things had to be provided for clients. University and other higher study diplomas and qualifications. References and certifications. Diplomas and other authorised credentials of every description.

Across the widest spectrum of arts and commerce and science and academia and many, many more orphic disciplines. Manufacturing credible new identities had to be expertly and comfortably obscure. Requiring a collective counterfeiting expertise of the very finest professionalism.

Ditto NuCF surgical and rehabilitation and other medical departments. Most personnel were culled from former military backgrounds or other highly confidential sectors. All of them had succeeded and prospered in harder-than-usual schools long before they came to Nu-Community.

Top plastic and reconstructive specialist surgeons were even flown in sometimes from California where most of the finest roosted. Apparently the New York headquarters building had a secret private hospital better than Cornell and Johns Hopkins medical centres combined. No rehabilitative resource was spared.

Psychological conditioning, analysis and remedial treatment was headed by a man whose articles I read fairly regularly in *The International Journal of Psychiatry*. That really did stun me. Major Domo that Hubbard mentioned almost negligently was one of the most respected social scientists in America.

Expert Special Operations Branch, which Hubbard himself had once belonged to under the prior alias of 'Brown', did the kind of dirty work we were doing now. Some time ago he had gone in for face-changing surgery and rehabilitation himself as part of assuming control of Nu-Community. Hence his odd new name and slight immobility of features I had noticed on first meeting him.

Of course he couldn't use company personnel for a violent internal *coup-d'état* like this. Naturally I was worried they could get onto us and retaliate. For all our experience of the clandestine world we'd barely heard of them.

*****

HStJ: "Nah, Gary; Nixon would have better luck tricking with Grace Jones and Hanoi Jane at Studio 54. I get all the S.O.B.'s working out of town missions on the dates of disappearances and abductions so they can't mobilise at headquarters. False trails in every direction to keep 'em running in circles. This all has to happen in the absolute silence of the top-class trippiest tomb. Slightest rumour I was orchestrating everything would get us all a date with Doctor XXX in the old surgical abattoir where we make the stand-in stiffs. Former CIA quack and make-'em-howler. You should hear some of his charming stories from Honduras and the Kingdoms of Cambodia and Iran. Him and his trusty cranial drill. Prob'ly slightly less painful than facing a Midwestern yokels-on-safari audience doing stand-up. I tried that once, y'know. Warmed up for Sammy Davis Junior no less, at *The Necropolis Hotel Lounge of Death* in Vegas a few years ago. My first and last gig. Told an off-beam joke about Mary Poppins and then some *federale fascistas* showed up and boobed me offstage. Total wash-out professionally but

Sammy saved the day as usual, like he told me later. Wish I could get him for this gig; he'd crack these corporate creeps right down the middle as a professional interrogator…"

*****

Transcript-excerpt from *Black Hand Incorporated* operational archives, operational file HStJ-77 (interrogations subfolder, see scale of pharmacological charges to client), continued, all company officers present. 13:19-20:55, 28.10.1977 (several sessions).

(*Subject of interrogation energetically sings* You've Got That Thing *by Cole Porter in a child's voice.*)

HStJ (*audibly highly-strung*): "This is *not* what I meant when I said 'Take him back to the beginning', Mr J."

S('T')J: "He appears to have regressed to his childhood without my prompting. It happens sometimes with *Papaver somniferum Omni*. I will have to slowly and patiently coax him towards his adult life and employment with your organisation, leading up to his more devious recent activities."

HStJ: "(*Interrogation and executive reassignment subject name classified*), soon to be my very former Treasurer and Chief Actuary, is also sitting on a pile of company money. Maybe as much as a billion dollars-worth. Diverted property and assets. Hidden contingency funds. Blind-brokered equity holdings. Complicated investments hidden in covenants and trusts we've got no reliable records for. There's a helluva lot and I want accurate information for all of it while we've still got him in the land of the living dead."

S('T')J: "Then undoubtedly this will take considerable time and patience."

HStJ: "I'll get us some pizzas for the duration."

S('T')J: "I'm a Vegan, Hubbard."

HStJ (*infinitesimal pause*): "Fine. Zucchini and lima beans on yours. Meathead Specials for the rest."

(*Sounds of HStJ departing rapidly, quick footsteps on wooden stairs, muffled crash-slamming of fire exit door upstairs.*)

GB: "Money is definitely not a gas, guys."
(*General wry laughter as subject of interrogation segues into* Bidin' My Time *by George Gershwin in an adolescent-sounding voice.*)

*****

Transpired eventually that at least half of Nu-Community Foundation's heads of department were running some kind of scam. Considerable company resources under the control of too few officers meant incredible frauds were perpetrated. Necessary secrecy led to some quite extraordinary lapses of supervision.

Property management division had millions of dollars-worth of houses and even a full apartment building off the company's official books. Rents were going straight into a network of dummy accounts. That unit actually had its own office.

Private bank operated for clients had a small secret branch with safe deposit boxes and a vault no less, completely unknown to the Accounts department and profiting only the branch manager. Supplies and Procurement had a discount resale and auctioning subsection equally unknown. Even the company's small Intelligence bureau was doing private commercial and industrial espionage jobs on company time as a side-line.

Corporate kleptocracy is what it looked like once we got fully into the inquisitions. Founder of the company had originally relied on trust and his own very remarkable memory and good judgement for the many shadow dealings the business required. But too many officers had been in those jobs for too long.

Old man who founded everything so many years before had become too reliant on their integrity. Too many of them repaid him by creating whole companies of their own within the bigger company. Full extent of Nu-Community's holdings was indeed awesome.

Some of the profiteering matched it. Magnitude and cleverness of some of the graft was astonishing. And fiscally clever in ways I'd never even imagined, so I made sure me and Survind took extensive private notes for our own purposes.

I'd also had to literally restrain myself from doing an open-mouthed double take when Hubbard St. John mentioned his debacle at *The Necropolis Hotel Lounge of Death*. Because I myself had been at that same bizarre performance. Treating myself after the rather difficult intelligence gathering surveillance of a target at the same hotel.

Conveniently booked next door to the chairman of the board at *PanGlobal Practical Polymers*. He was doing a corrupt deal with even more corrupt regulators at the Environmental Protection Agency. Waivers on safe-disposal requirements for his factory's most toxic product residues.

Effectively he was buying licenses to dump hideously poisonous and carcinogenic chemical waste untreated or neutralised directly into local rivers and lakes. Along with government-sponsored injunctions forbidding future prosecution for same. A couple of senators with recognisable voices even showed up for the legislative side of the long discussions.

Fortunately I got it all on tape with the connivance of obliging hotel staff including some of the management. Survind had carefully and lavishly bribed a ring of them on a previous visit without specifying dates or the job type. When I showed up I simply gave a pre-arranged code phrase and paid them all the same again.

This was even more devious than that. And even more than a billion dollars in bribes and graft were involved. I could not believe what I was hearing.

*****

INTERROGATION SUBJECT (*desperately*): "…You believe me, don't you?"

HStJ (*long pause*): "Of course I believe you, (*interrogation and executive reassignment subject name classified*). And I also believe that Howard the Duck actually won the presidential election last year. He just dresses up as Jim 'Peanut-Man' Carter and puts on that clodhopping okie-hillbilly accent when he has to go on camera to drawl to the nation. Mr J, a double-dose of sodium pentothal, if you please…"

*****

Edgier and zanier veering into outright mental atomisation was how Hubbard St. John became over the fortnight or so our entire joint operation took. Uptown headquarters of Nu-Community was apparently buzzing with carefully contradictory rumours planted by him. Rival organisations, corporations and opportunistic freelancers were all mysteriously involved in the disappearances.

Terror of discovery weighed down on him like an anvil, of course. Nu-Community Foundation was merciless to its malefactors. It had an entire infrastructure using secret internal executions for company profit.

At the same time he was heavily involved in byzantine negotiations with the federal government. Numerous other forward-thinking charities and philanthropic organisations. Gathering permissions and part-funding and environmental tax incentives for the experimental full eco-city project he'd extolled to me.

Hubbard told me he was even getting material support and expertise from the Cosmo Salamander Foundation. They had one of the world's few successfully functioning 'ecovillages' on their nearby island headquarters a few miles off Montauk Point. We'd been there once.

All of which led naturally into conversations about the one thing I didn't want. Inevitably creeping into our meetings. Inflecting itself into the razor-sharp tensions of long and gruelling inquisitorial sessions.

New lives. 'Converted' lives as Hubbard dubbed them. Far away and safe from the savagely rapacious world of our workaday executive reassignment milieu.

Needless to say he had an even more annoyingly succinct way of putting it.

*****

HStJ: "…when this is all over I am *so* gonna lift you rat-finks outta the rat-race into a better class of sewer..."

*****

Nightmare scenario came, as they usually do, at the point of vulnerability I was least expecting. Hubbard offhandedly revealed he had started seeing an analyst. Jokily I said he should ask whether his counsellor was a Freudian or a Jungian, because you'd get a completely different diagnosis each way.

My employer gave me a peculiar and searching look. Said his analyst told him an irregular patient had once asked him that very question. Suddenly and coldly I realised the counsellor was one Doctor Raymond Opichinski, who I myself had been confidentially seeing without the knowledge of the other guys for several years.

Last secret in the world I could afford to be known, especially to a professionally treacherous man like Hubbard St. John. If my colleagues even suspected I was doing this, it meant an automatic death sentence. Despite our close friendship and shared dangers down the years, that was one rigid company rule with no right of appeal.

After all, I'd written it myself.

Luckily Hubbard and I were almost alone, preparing to finish off one of his senior colonial administrators. This had been one of the most severe of the increasingly fraught and angry cross-examinations and the subject hadn't helped either of our tempers. The man was a braggart and pathological narcissist.

All through the sessions he boasted he'd 'conquered' about half the female Converted clients in his respectably-sized colony. It was somewhere called Hadesbridge County. He'd also managed to get millions of their insurance settlement dollars signed over to himself in return for what sounded to me like a deranged breakfast-afterwards fixation.

My current employer told me with his usual grating and genial condescension that the man was actually calling himself a 'serial lover', not what I'd naturally thought. It just reminded me of my depressingly failed rudimentary foray into the metropolitan dating scene a few months before. Suddenly I saw all their mingled sympathetic and amused and in one case badly-shaved faces at once and lost control.

Hurriedly I gave the victim an overdose of our executioner's compound, which induced conveniently messy convulsions. We had to call back in the others to clean up and got the body down into the makeshift cemetery next door. I'd be glad to leave this particular job far behind.

But of course I knew Hubbard St. John wouldn't forget.

*****

Transcript-excerpt from *Black Hand Incorporated* operational archives, operational file HStJ-77 (client relations and task implementation discussions subfolder), all company officers present. Location, lobby of *The Manhattan Project Pico-Panopticon Repertory and Adult Cinema (18+ only)* 04:10 – 04:49, 31.10.1977.

HStJ: "Status report, gents. The *Federale Fascistas* ain't gonna give me the money or the tax breaks for my full-on eco-city mega project. Managed to build a consortium of the environmentally progressive and embarrassedly filthy rich, 'tho. We are getting some decent tax-free funding funnelled through said vested interest vehicle. Plans have therefore changed to reflect that. Instead we'll be founding smaller dispersed eco-villages. All of them will be adjuncts to existing urban satellites. We work outwards from there and expand on the colonial model we've already successfully followed for decades. Big tax deductions are available for at-the-start investors. If you want to go in for the treatment at some near future date, now's the time to pick your new boffo 'burb."

*****

Hubbard hands us expensive-looking and exuberantly illustrated catalogues. They're double a normal periodical thickness, bigger print format than LIFE magazine. Tells us these were used in all his most successful pitches.

They're full of wildly over-enthusiastic hyperbolic write-ups.

Articles and endorsements by prominent respected journalists and world class scientists and activist celebrities crowd the beautifully designed pages. Bold new futuristically innovative ecologically integrated 'bionomic boroughs' for any who care to try living there.

All the brave new green-world projects to be sponsored by Nu-Community Foundation and its partners. Relentlessly huckstering the environmentally friendly micro-urban better tomorrow. Even grander plans for the future of this Future envisioned by all the most zealously prophetic sustainability-conscious architects of the age.

*****

WW: "What's this 'BOL' thing in the Special Interests section, Mr St. John?"

HStJ: "Bug Out Location, Warkentin. It's a survivalist isolation underground bunker community thang. Kind of a niche market in the eco-habitation biz. Growing in popularity, too."

WW: "I think my boys would like this. They're both expert marksmen now, and one's recently discovered surveillance society culture. He builds microminiaturised tape recorders better than I can, and he's only ten years old."

HStJ: "When he gets a bit older, put him down for some *'Prepper For The Liberal Apocalypse'* classes listed on the following page. Training movies are presented by Ragnar Benson and Howard Ruff and Nancy Tappan; they're a scream."

DU: "This ecovillage project at Hadesbridge County with the big female contingent looks pretty good. What in the ballah-wallah bing-bang does *Ecofeminism* mean?"

HStJ: "Legal nude beaches and bacchanalian free love hippie parties. Watch out for the thin lizzie covens, 'tho. Overdone black eyeliner jobs give those ones away every time. Most of 'em look like angry pandas."

S('T')J: "*Hmp*. This Herbarium Institute mentioned for the same location interests me, Hubbard. I cultivate many rare horticultural specimens. This might be worth specialist investment as a possible retirement option."

HStJ: "The brave new I Eats Me Spinach And Greens greened-up greenalicious world to come is still gonna need a regular quality poison supply; Mr J. Word on the grapevine is you da man; man."

*****

While the others talk, I leaf through my brochure. Eventually I have to stifle laughter. It reads exactly like science fiction.

*****

HStJ: "It's all sci-fi, of course. Got most of it from Edward Bellamy's *Looking Backward* and Frederick Spencer Oliver's *Dweller On Two Planets* and Aldous Huxley's *Island*. Rest I cribbed from Ernest Callenbach and Barry Commoner and Murray Bookchin and a bunch of those other tree-hugging Trotskyites. Luckily the best stuff is basically all in the public domain. I even snuck in some presciently hyper-radical eco-freak stuff from Ed Cayce. That 'Snoozing Prophet' guy. He's not the only wild and crazy cosmic beatnik in there by about twelve parsecs either. Dig on this one. Ever read Charles Webster Leadbeater? Theosophist and clairvoyant and diehard veggie. Got him in the Sustainable Diet section. He's even better than Ignatius Donnelly gibbering all that Lemuria and Atlantis stuff in *The Antediluvian World*. Leadbeater said bees came from Venus. I can buy into that one, it's just far out enough. When I'm being a goon on the Swoon, anyway, like now if there is any such concept. Polluting the astral plane on my bad karma travels, it all seems to make a Fluxus-upped kind of sense to my hive mind. That's why I flavour all the coffee here with organic honey, to get that interplanetary vibe. I flavoured the coffee of the federal government and charitable committee conference that finally approved my scaled down eco-village funding with Rohypnol and jest a leetle more Swoon on top. Guess I'm jest crazy; man. We can all calm down from the stark staring fly-eye insanity when we're comfortably retired in the spaced-out colonies in the brochures. Do I sound like I'm rackety-wackety babbling here? Mebbe I'm psychically atomising. Feels like I'm in the basement of the continuum. Along with 'bout a trillion empty pickle jars and innumerable other obnoxious pickled Me's infesting the infinite dimensions…"

*****

As Hubbard described in his self-referential way, he was taking *Papaver somniferum Omni* regularly by this time. Incredibly, he seemed to have developed a kind of resistance to it. Trucker told me he personally saw Hubbard St. John take enough to put a man into a catatonic visionary trance for a whole week, if not actually fatal.

At this point Operation HStJ-77 reached an unexpected apotheosis.

*****

(*Independent recording, 11:39-11:42, 03.11.1977. Sounds of energetic activity.*)

CINEMA PROJECTIONIST: "Uh, Mr St. John, why are you strapping me into this chair here? I've got to change the movie reels over for the second adult screening session. We're starting off with *Lolita II* and it's a tricky print..."

HStJ (*whistling unknown tune*): "…Your credit is nil; you'll never make a mil…."

CP: "That's a bit truculent, isn't it?"

(*Sounds and voices of all four company officers entering sub-basement interrogation room, murmurs of surprise.*)

*****

Maybe an epiphany; depending on whether you were a Freudian or a Jungian.

*****

Transcript-excerpt from *Black Hand Incorporated* operational archives, operational file HStJ-77 (interrogations subfolder, see scale of pharmacological charges to client). 11:51-11:59, 03.11.1977. Location is converted sub-basement store-room as per prior interrogations. All company officers present (Part Two of dialogue, slight gap between recordings).

S('T')J: "Fortunately this revolver of yours is empty. I took the precaution of removing its bullets last night while the rest of you were working down in the other sub-basement interment area. Our man is not deceased but merely fainted. Do I hear a whirring sound nearby?..."

HStJ: "So let's finish him off, get the last body stowed and pour the concrete over the meat down there. I got the mixer going. He's a witness I can't allow to live."

S('T')J: "No, Mr St. John. This operation is over. Our final inquisition was last night by your own description. The foundation's human resources manager, I believe. Killing innocent bystanders happens during operations, but it is not our company's policy as I have previously explained to you."

HStJ: "Are you kidding? Let him *go*?! He knows everything!"

S('T')J: "Hardly. Your employee has seen little or nothing. We have done everything between his regular shifts. Plus he is technically an accessory to multiple murder and illegal inhumation by default. He will hardly risk a Title 18 set of federal charges against himself."

(*Murmurs of agreement from company officers.*)

GB: "Sections 3 and 16, to be specific. Multiple Chapters 51 and 55 ditto. Your whole Nu-Community is one big Chapters 77 and 95. For him it would come to about five hundred years minimum with mail fraud taken into consideration on the illustrated programme subscriptions."

HStJ (*very long strained pause*): "I'd have to take legal advice, but my main company attorney is down there in the other sub-basement with the rest of them. Fine. We'll leave it at that. Get rid of the creep with my very grudging not-blessing."

*****

Dag and Warkentin hauled the poor confused projector-jockey up the stairs while I followed. Survind watched over our highly dissatisfied now-former employer with his own newly-reloaded revolver. Operation was indeed over.

The guys disappeared back downstairs to finish the work of pouring and levelling a new solid cement floor in the sub-basement. Entombing our crimes down there, hopefully forever. Hubbard St. John could hardly complain at the generally successful outcome, his corporate *coup* had been completely successful and his own role undetected.

At the back entrance I told the still-groggy projectionist it would be highly advisable to forget everything that had happened. Our joint former employer would probably not move against him if he simply resumed a freelance life around a network of other repertory cinemas where he was known, and remained silent. Just regard it all as a bad out-take and leave it on the cutting room floor; hey?

Gave him all the money I had on me, threw in my winter overcoat. Sent him on his bewildered and over-talkative way into the frigid and bleak November afternoon. Like him, I'd had my fill of Hubbard St. John by that time.

*****

S('T')J: "I think we've all had our full measure of Hubbard St. John, Gary. Carelessly I let myself get carried away by his rather strange charm and quixotic ambition. But he is duplicitous and cruel and would clearly double-cross us all on a whim if we were in his power. So we've collectively decided not to pursue that dubious retirement option, at least while he's still in authority there."

*****

Leaving me with an intact team unit, but a sense of badly broken continuity. My secret confessions to a psychiatric analyst were fatal for me. But so was the underfloor of that crowded and thoroughly air-conditioned new solidly cemented sub-basement repertory and classic and adult film reel storage vault for Hubbard St. John.

Knowing each other's worst guilty secret was no kind of security, but one I could do nothing about. Each side could devastatingly retaliate against the other, and so like international nuclear politics of the moment it meant Mutually Assured Destruction. Like most intolerable close things and proximate insufferable people, you simply had to suffer them.

Deafening silence made none of it go away.

*****

Excerpted from the December-January 1977/8 bumper holiday edition published illustrated programme (free of charge at cinema, 35¢ local newsstands, $17.50 annual mailing subscription and cinema discount card weekdays before 5pm), *The Manhattan Project Pico-Panopticon Repertory and Adult Cinema (18+ only)*:

'Merry Yuletide and Happy Hanukkah and all those other cheerful into-the-netherworld celebrations, hardcore cinephiliac-maniacs! This special year-end edition goes straight to the thirty-first of ye olde month of Janus. On the following page, it includes several special coupons for selected free screenings and concessionary stand discounts over the course of the joint holiday period into the New Year.

This is by way of apology for our unfortunate hiatus in late October into early November, occasioned by essential maintenance and rebuilding work to provide you with an even better cinema experience. We now have a slightly larger auditorium and more spacious seating plan, a fully licensed lobby bar and best of all, a proper film library of much-loved classics to complement our ever-evolving avant garde travelling programme.

Combinations of unavoidable pressures led to repeated unexpected closures causing a late mailing for November, so all new subscriptions made before the end of this year will be at a special half price rate to compensate our loyal aficionados. Thank you for bearing with us!

Through December and into January we have our usual offerings of much-loved movie *magnum opuses* and assorted global cinema new releases. Running parallel: a very special season of recent and classic motion pictures tackling that most controversial of subjects, multiple murder. Finest of past and present and a very special exclusive preview!

Join us for such macabre classics as Fritz Lang's awe-inspiring *M* (1931), Frank Capra's hilarious *Arsenic and Old Lace*, (1943), Charles Laughton's surreal *Night Of The Hunter* (1955), Powell and Pressburger's career-busting *Peeping Tom* (1959), Alfred Hitchcock's immortal *Psycho* (1960), Richard Brook's landmark *In Cold Blood* (1967), Hitch again with the frenzied *Frenzy* (1971), Richard Fleischer's shocking *10 Rillington Place* (1971), Terence Malick's uncomfortably epic *Badlands* (1973), Tobe Hooper's almost unendurable *The Texas Chainsaw Massacre* (1973), Bob Clark's pioneering grisly *Black Christmas* (1974), the premiere of Nu-Grue director Wes Craven's freakish *The Hills Have Eyes* (this year) and a special rough-cut screening of next year's forthcoming new slasher-flick *Halloween* by our favourite director John Carpenter starring gorgeous young newcomer Jamie Lee Curtis and solid creepy standby Don Pleasance. You can see this one at the *Pico-Panopticon* alone. These and many more to offset the more saccharine goodwill of the season. Our graveyard shift is always open for you; so to speak!

Early riser 18+ adult programming continues (with gallons of coffee!) as before, all weekdays from 06:00, and some nifty new federal sponsorship also allows us to regale you with an exciting series of surprisingly diverse supporting features from the national annual *Industrial and Commercial and Public Information Films Awards* several years running, which play variously between all feature presentations. We look forward to welcoming you back and years of great cinema-going to come.'

The Usual Unusual Suspects

Anthony Kane Evans has had around sixty-five short stories published in various UK, French, US, Canadian, Nigerian, Singaporean, and Australian literary journals, e-zines, and anthologies. Journals include *London Magazine* (UK), *Orbis Quarterly International Literary Journal* (UK), *Mystery Magazine* (Canada), *Mystery Tribune* (USA), *Going Down Swinging* (Australia), and *The Antigonish Review* (Canada). E-zines include *Litro Magazine, New Pop Lit, Brilliant Flash Fiction* and *Short Édition*.

Though born in Manchester, UK, he is currently to be found in Copenhagen, Denmark, where he has made several documentary films for the Danish Broadcasting Corporation.

Carlos Ramet has written extensively on popular fiction and film, especially on the mystery and thriller genres, and teaches creative writing at Saginaw Valley State University in Michigan. His short stories have appeared in *The Critic, Inlandia,* and *Red Earth Review,* among other publications. He is the author of two books of literary interpretation and criticism, both on the popular novelist Ken Follett, and the recently published novel *The Quiet Limit of the World* (2024, Running Wild Press/RIZE).

Tristan J. Deehan is a USA-based writer of Jamaican and Irish descent. *Belfast by Train*, a short story he completed back in early 2023, marks his debut appearance as a Crimeucopian. He is currently working on a novel and screenplay tentatively titled *All Messed Up Inside* and *Patricide*, respectively. Although the mechanics of writing have been a nearly lifelong interest of his, it was not until somewhat recently that he decided to try his hand at writing in an artistic context.

Christopher Deliso is an American writer who began his ongoing *Detective Grigoris* international-intrigue and mystery series in 2021, drawing on over two decades of professional experience in field reporting, analysis and travel writing for major global newspapers, magazines, websites and other media, like *The Economist Intelligence Unit, Jane's, Lonely Planet* and monographs on history, culture, and current events of Southeast Europe for *Greenwood and Bloomsbury Academic*. With an academic background in Byzantine History (MPhil 1999, University of Oxford), and long-time study of literature and philosophy, he has published short stories, reviews and analytic pieces widely as well. For more information, visit the official author website https://www.chrisdeliso.com

Tucker Struyk is a writer and podcaster for *Hookswitch Hotline*, and holds both a Bachelor of Arts degree and a Bachelor of Fine Arts degree from the University of Nebraska at Omaha. Widely published in such diverse places as *Cosmic Horror Monthly, A Coup of Owls, Eerie River Publishing*, and several other publications, his piece *Our Father's Judgment* was published in the spring 2021 issue of *13th Floor Magazine*, where it was rewarded with an Editor's Choice Award. His piece, *Getaway*, was given an honorable mention in the Fall/Winter 2022-23 issue of *Allegory*.

Ed Teja is a lifelong storyteller, as well as a martial artist, former Caribbean boat bum, blues musician, and magazine editor. His stories blend and crisscross crime and speculative fiction and the strange situations and people often come from his somewhat surreal life. Ed's *Crimeucopia* debut is in *Crank It Up!*
For more information and news, go to www.edteja.com

Gene Kendall has lived in many places, but is usually surrounded by more deer than people. His work explores drama, music, and pop culture with wit and no small amount of sympathy for the losers and also-rans. He's drawn to protagonists that say the wrong thing, actively resist their character arc, and possibly save the day by accident. His work has appeared at the *Saturday Evening Post's New Fiction Friday* series, *CBR.com*, *Gentlemen of Leisure*, and *Not Blog X*.

Hal Dygert practiced environmental law before taking on supervisory responsibilities within the Washinton State Office of the Attorney General. He devotes his free time to writing crime fiction and fishing, especially for bass, and is current President of the Olympia, Washington-based Puget Sound Writers Guild. In continuous existence for more than 30 years, the PSWG provides instruction to novice writers, supports a weekly critique group, and sponsors craft seminars led by, among others, Hallie Ephron, Robert Dugoni and Allen Eskens, Edgar nominees one and all. Mr. Dygert's taste in literature embraces the hard-boiled crime classics, contemporary neo-noir, especially that set in the classic era, as well as literary fiction. Mr. Dygert is an avid fan of the noir films shown by Eddie Muller, The Czar of Noir, on his Noir Alley series for Turner Classic Movies.
His debut story 'Something to Tell' appeared in *Crimeucopia, Through the Past Darkly*. For samples of Mr. Dygert's writing (novel excerpts, song lyrics, reviews and blog posts) please visit his website at https://haldygert.com/

Ian Blackwell lives near Glasgow, Scotland. A stray cat chose him as his human and has ruled the house ever since. Ian inherited a sheep's skull called Bernard, who has the final say on all the most important matters. Visit his website: www.ianblackwell.com — or follow him on X (formerly Twitter): www.twitter.com/ianblackwell27

L.C. Adams has now retired from full time working life. She writes as often as she can, walks to explore her beautiful surroundings, and loves to capture her experiences on camera. She also plays the ukulele! She has had recent material published in *Cafe Lit*. She is currently writing a psychological thriller.

Patrick Ambrose lives in North Carolina with his partner Kim and their three cats, Ashton, Shelton and Monster. His work has appeared in

Mysterical-E, Timber Creek Review, The Morning News, Creative Loafing, and other print and online publications. His debut *Crimeucopia* appearance is in *Totally Psycho Logical.*

Kamal Mouhoune was born in Algiers in 1979 and works in the fields of advertising and lately animated films production.

He wrote in French some bad poetry in his youth and some unfruitful noir novel attempts in his adult years. He made his *Crimeucopia* debut appearance with *Who's Moz* — his first short story written in English — in *Totally Psycho Logical.*

Unless the ghosts of Shakespeare, Agatha Christie and John le Carré decide to gang up to prevent it, he firmly intends to commit his future literary misdeeds in English as well.

Rand Gaynor's "careen" took him to the University of New Brunswick where he was awarded a specially-created scholarship for his creative writing. After also graduating from the Nova Scotia College of Art and Design, he wrote and illustrated the children's book, *Henrietta's Book of Days,* published in 2015, and a short story collection *New Old Stories,* in 2019. Recently retired from a decades-long career in publications design, Rand has recently completed his first novella, *Escape from Dog's Breath,* and is presently working on his first crime/mystery.

Rob Loughran began his life as a small child. He lives in Sonoma County, CA and has eight grown children and a battalion of grandchildren. He has five novels in print and also enjoys a career as a failed screenwriter. He enjoys activities that don't require a cellphone or computer.

Edward St. Boniface lives and works in London UK and writes across various genres including crime, Science Fiction & Fantasy and contemporary literary fiction. He's always interested in exploring an unusual angle to a story, and is keen to build up a readership. He believes literature, like all the arts, should start from being Fun; and hopes you enjoyed his story.

Ed has had two crime short stories in his '*Black Hand Incorporated*' series published on the Mystery Tribune website including the dark humorous piece FACTORY SETTINGS where Gary and his resolutely Square colleagues mix it with the eccentric cool characters populating Andy Warhol's famous workshop. You can read it here, with an additional site page link to another published story POLITICAL MAGNICIDE: https://mysterytribune.com/factory-settings-neo-noir-short-fiction-by-edward-st-boniface/

He also has another '*Simon Magus Iscariot*' story, IMPERATRIX ABYSSA on the Eternal Haunted Summer website: https://eternalhauntedsummer.com/issues/winter-solstice2023/imperiatrix-abyssa-or-queen-of-the-damned-from-themisadventures-of-simon-magus-iscariot/ — and hopes you will read his madness-inflected forays into those worlds respectively! For Ed's works otherwise available on the Amazon website, go to: https://www.amazon.co.uk/Edward-St.-Boniface/e/B00JBCZMDS

His most recent Crimeucopia appearance is in *Through The Past Darkly*, with the Simon Magus Iscariot story *JUDAS*.

I Remember the Dame Well...

Mainly as she had a laugh that reminded me of two cheese graters energetically fornicating in an iron bathtub. I looked out the open window at the Johnson Memorial, standing upright and resolute in the persistent rain. The clock on it said it was 3:15 in the a.m. and I figured, what-the-Hell, it was time to review the 14 case files scattered across my desk.

I glanced back out across the skyline and wondered: *Why is it* always *raining in Noir City?* I got up and moved over to the chess board. I hadn't see the cat in several hours, so I rearranged the pieces a little to give myself a bit of an advantage...

As with all of these anthologies, we hope you'll detect something that you immediately like, as well as something that takes you out of your investigative comfort zone — and puts you into a completely new one.

Because, in the spirit of our Murderous Ink Press motto:

You never know what you like until you discover it.

Paperback ISBN: 9781909498624 eBook ISBN: 9781909498631

It Was In The Year Of....

Historical/Period Crime short fiction ranging from Comfy Cosy, Period P.I.s, Narrative Crimes, Old fashioned NOIR, and a wealth of Crime sub-genres in between.

21 authors — Gary Thomson, Edward St. Boniface, Terry Wijesuriya, Frances Stratford, Dennis E. Delaney, Joan Leotta, Hope Hodgkins, Karen Odden, J. F. Benedetto, S. B. Watson, Hal Dygert, Merrilee Robson, John G. Bluck, David Hagerty, Avi Sirlin, Karl El-Koura, Penny Hurrell, Kai Lovelace, Maddi Davidson, J. Aquino and Kirk Landers — take you from 420 BC through to AD 1969, and give you a criminal history, laid out in a case by case Crimeucopia Crimeline.

Paperback 9781909498587 eBook 9781909498594

CRIMEUCOPIA

Let Me Tell You About...

If Looks Could Kill, She Would Have Been An Uzi...

...Or more likely a shotgun. I mean, Lawd knows what those two ever saw in each other in the first place, and that's a fact. Don't believe me? Well, let me tell you about the time when.... But that's how it usually starts, doesn't it? Someone says something, which reminds someone else about.... And so the anecdotal avalanche begins.

This time there's 19 storytellers: **Vinnie Hansen, V.S. Kemanis, David Krugler, Robert Jeschonek, Beverle Graves Myers, Kirk Landers, James Lee Proctor, Victor Kreuiter, K. Arlington Andrews, Michael Bracken, Kevin R. Tipple, William Flores, Robert Sumner, Jim Guigli, James Roth, Michael Zimecki, Sebastian Corbascio, Martin Zeigler, and John Bertram Fawet III**

All gathered around the front counter of the Crimeucopia *Shots to Hell* Bar & Grill — and more than willing to tell you about how it is, or was, or even will be....

So, over the background sounds from an old jukebox loaded with worn out 45s (vinyl rather than the likes of a Px4 Storm), settle back and take in their individual stories – and we guarantee there's going to be Crimesapleanty indeed...

Paperback Edition ISBN: 9781909498600 — eBook Edition ISBN: 9781909498617
Amazon Paperback Edition ISBN: 9798337923338

Totally — **adverb:** completely; absolutely. Used to emphasize a clause or statement. "He/She is totally bat-shit crazy!"
Psycho — **noun:** an unstable and aggressive person. "Don't you know? My ex is a total psycho!" — **adjective:** exhibiting unstable and aggressive behaviour "There's some kind of psycho nut job on the loose out there!"
Logical — **adjective:** characterised by or capable of clear, sound reasoning. "His/Her logical mind? Are you nuts or something?"
But are all psychos 'nut jobs'?
Laurie Stevens, Jesse Aaron, Patrick Ambrose, Stephen D. Rogers, Wendy Harrison, Jan Glaz, Brandon Doughty, Elena Schacherl, Joyce Bingham, Jeff Somers, Glenn Francis Faelnar, Douglas Soesbe, C.G. Merchant, Daniel C. Bartlett, Richard J. O'Brien, David Bradley, and Kamal M present 17 cases for the defence.
Paperback 9781909498563 eBook 9781909498570

Printed in Great Britain
by Amazon